D0904976

Saul's Book

Saul's Book

A NOVEL

by Paul T. Rogers

THE PUSHCART PRESS

6/1983
Am. Lit.

PUBLISHER'S NOTE

This novel is a work of fiction. Names, characters, places, and incidents are either the product of the author's imagination or are used fictitiously, and any resemblance to actual persons, living or dead, events, or locales is entirely coincidental.

Winner of the first annual Editors' Book Award

Sponsoring editors for the Editors' Book Award are Simon Michael Bessie, James Charlton, Peter Davison, Jonathan Galassi, David Godine, Daniel Halpern, James Laughlin, Seymour Lawrence, Starling Lawrence, Robie Macauley, Joyce Carol Oates, Nan A. Talese, Faith Sale, Ted Solotaroff, Pat Strachan, Thomas Wallace. Nominating editor for this novel: Jonathan Galassi.

ISBN 0-916366-16-2
LC 82-81638

© 1983 by Paul T. Rogers

Manufactured in the United States of America by RAY FREIMAN AND COMPANY

PUBLISHED BY PUSHCART PRESS
P.O. BOX 380, WAINSCOTT, N.Y. 11975

For Chris,
with my love and devotion,
now and forever

Now Stephen, full of grace and power,
was working great wonders and signs among the people
. . . . . . but they cried out with a loud voice and stopped
their ears and rushed upon him all together.
And they cast him out of the city and stoned him.
And the witnesses laid down their garments at the feet
of a young man named Saul.
And while they were stoning Stephen he prayed and said,
   ". . . Lord, do not lay this sin against them."
And with these words he fell asleep.
And Saul approved of his death.

(*Acts*, 6:8-7:60)

Saul's Book

1

SUMMER

*They asserted that they had found the country where virgins
become pregnant through drinking water and when they give
birth the children of the male sex are dogheads. Dogheads are
creatures who have their heads on their breasts. . .*

—Adam of Bremen

IN THE BEGINNING I suppose there was a God, but he must be too
bored by now to care about anyone or anything and certainly too
preoccupied to take any note of the chipped plaster saints, the
multicolored candles, the fragrance of incense, the dishes of
mangoes and bananas and pennies, the gilt prayer cards: in
short, all the elaborate equipment of Santeria which my mother
assembled.

But to me that collection of sanctified junk from botánicas and
mean storefront churches called forth the most primal emotions:
awe, fear, the certainty of my own insignificance and an overpowering nostalgia for—what? Paradise lost? A nostalgia I still associate
with the scent of decaying flowers.

Though I have long ago decided that God is worthless or
worse, I retain a healthy mistrust—or it is respect—for the spiteful
potency of the implements of his service. The spite on which I now
thrive is but a reflection of my faith, a faith that reflects my infant
terrors, which centered not on God, but on my mother. It was not
her aloofness, or scorn, or even her madness that bothered me.
No, it was the certainty that I deserved them.

It is still impossible for me to distinguish her image from those to which she addressed her bitter demands. I have always seen her through a glass darkly. I could never predict when I was to be humored or humiliated, petted or pampered, cursed or caressed, since her moods all welled from the same bottomless pool of overwhelming self-indulgence.

If it is true that children are merciless and therefore akin to the beasts, then my mother was a child—innocent and blameless. My sister resents her; my brother hates her. But they are only partially Puerto Rican and more impatient than I. Besides, I was the oldest and beaten the least. For me, she reserved not the belt, but the full fury of her scorn. To the little ones she was basically indifferent and I think secretly delighted that they were ordained to misinterpret her intentions, or her rages. But my rages and swift changes of mood were so like her own that they threatened her not at all, so it was possible for her to truly hate me. My mother was too ordinary to suffer, too bitter for charity, and too vengeful to open herself to divinity. I think I share these qualities with her. Self-awareness was never one of her strong points, nor one of mine either.

My mother. Me. If I try to justify my beginnings by beginning with justifications I become hopelessly entangled with her and, thus, with Time. Time, Saul once told me, is a wishful fancy that arises from the need to impose order on what is given to us. I imagine he meant chaos, but I'm sure I didn't ask him. At the time I was about sixteen, twisting painfully in a hospital bed, kicking a drug habit, while simultaneously bleeding internally from a near-fatal stab wound. Besides I wouldn't have questioned his "philosophy" in those days. I still took him seriously, just as I still took wisdom seriously.

Since I was a barely literate dropout I knew only the ways of the City, which for me was the world, and in that world wisdom must be taken very seriously. It's a matter of survival. It was only later in prison that I discovered words and books and what I thought to be knowledge, and somewhere in that quest for knowledge, wisdom went by the boards. The years of lonely cell study were spent in vain. What I learned was to reject a God who, by definition, must remain outside of time and therefore outside of man. And yet I still accept the notion of divinity itself, without which life, my life, would become an insupportable practical joke.

I invent an image of Saul shaking his head in disagreement when I say that the whole world seems to be a colossal blunder, because Time provides no guarantees. But Saul is dead and my catalogue of his wisdom and folly is complete. It must stand without correction or improvement. There will be no more arguments, no more disputes, for Saul is dead.

Saul. Oh, Saul. I am surprised by my tears just as I was angered by my son's tears when he was small. I feared somehow that I would be contaminated by them. Salvador is now fourteen. When I was his age I was as free with my tears as I was with my laughter. I enjoyed suffering because I was totally unaware that I suffered. As for my feelings, I kept them mostly to myself. I was free with my feelings only with Saul and now, I realize, he had little interest in them. Because he was concerned for me, his concern was that I learn how to dissemble. What Saul wished for me I wished for my mother and now wish for Sal, but we don't talk about such matters when I see him, which is seldom. When I do I am pleased that he withholds his sorrows from me and seems to have become selfsufficient enough to savor them in solitude. His pain is no concern of mine. He is a stranger. Sometimes I feel I should tell him that we should see more of each other. But then, why should I tell him an obvious lie? I prefer politeness to intimacy at this stage of the game.

His mother who, fortunately for all concerned, I never bothered to marry, says that he lies and steals. I suspect he may be using drugs. Well, if he does, so did his father and his father managed to survive. He appears to be intelligent, but he is indifferent to school. I don't know whether he is overworldly or just bored, stoned, spaced out. Whatever—he is definitely not sentimental, and that makes me wary of him. I have no idea who he is. Is there a core in him, a changeless core incapable of being altered or influenced by the outside, by the world, by God? Is there an impenetrable center in this "I" called Steven? Is there one in Sal? Was there one in that "he" that was Saul? Or are we all, the living and the dead, merely unwilling stooges in a conjurer's trick? Will there ever come a time when I can say that I am actually present, when I can be sure that I am not just an image projected from some little black box?

13

Most teenagers carry boxes. Sal does. A box is an elaborate radio so heavy that it is a burden, a burden that is both a luxury and a necessity. It is the instrument through which an adolescent assures himself that there is a present and that he can be connected to this present because he can plug into it. Sal apparently needs his box far more than I did at his age, for I used to lose my boxes with a regularity that should have made me pause to consider whether I was already committed to going through life unplugged. According to his mother, Sal sleeps with his box cradled in his arms. I assume that he would no more permit himself to be parted from it than he would permit himself to be raped. This last thought puzzles me, since obviously it is impossible to consent to an act that requires the withholding of consent. What is it that I want Sal to consent to? I think I should avoid that question.

Boxes and presence, rape and consent. What do I seek—some point of correspondence with my son? I have never told him much about myself. I have never told him that at his age I already felt like an outcast abandoned into life. I have never told him that all of the knowledge a man can acquire will never prevent him from believing that he is an outcast, if that is his core—to be an outcast. If there is a core.

Sal will learn who he is by himself or he will not learn. I take no responsibility for revealing the world to him. To do so would require an act of love, and I learned early on from Saul that an act of love ordains an act of betrayal. And so I keep my distance from my son. I can think of nothing helpful to say, so I choose silence to mask my own confusion and cowardice. Only Saul had a way with the boy, but that was long ago and, as I think I have said, Saul is dead. Now at last I can leave love to the past where it belongs, safe from God's malice.

At birth Salvador was bound to suffer for the sins of others. Maybe he is aware that I can never truly be a father to him because I can condemn him for nothing. I leave that sort of thing to God. Yes, I know that in the beginning someplace there was a God mixed up in it all, but for a long time he has left me alone and I find that he, like my son, is infinitely better off without me. I have my own burdens to bear.

I suppose now that Saul is dead and I need no longer puzzle

over intentions, his or mine, I should feel that a burden has been lifted from me. The bonds joining me to childhood have been irrevocably severed, but the core is no closer than it ever was. There is neither mourning nor relief. Not even grief. What Saul has left me with is the rage and awful aloneness of a small boy who waits in vain for his mother's return.

From the time I was twelve I existed only in relation to Saul, so I have nothing that is my own. I lived my life through him—in him and in spite of him. I found no pleasure in living for myself. I despaired, I loved, and I survived. But who is to say whether survival is a virtue or a vice? Who is to say that he did not force me to survive merely because it amused him to do so? Yet even he could not convince me to accept a world that guarantees nothing, not even the sanctity of the past. My past is protected only as long as I remain alive, and when I am dead my past will die too, unless it is wrenched from me by one who is to come as I now wrench Saul from both his past and mine.

Saul was not a brave man. He was frightened to death of dying, a hypochondriac who hugely enjoyed his undiagnosable chest pains, his stomach cramps, his blurred vision, and his shortness of breath. Our medicine chest was crammed with unmarked pill bottles whose contents had been prescribed for forgotten symptoms. But he was that odd sort of hypochondriac who shunned doctors. I was the one who had to wheedle, plead, and half drag him to some Medicaid clinic from which he would emerge triumphant, like a condemned man who, already shriven and shorn, learns of his temporary reprieve.

What complicated matters was that his fears had a strong basis in fact. His liver was a disaster area, his pancreas a mess. He tolerated no discussion from anyone, though, on the subject of those particular organs, since Saul was a drinker of heroic proportions. His stays in prison offered no respite for his long-suffering innards. He was perfectly satisfied with hooch, a potent and sometimes poisonous concoction of yeast, sugar, and whatever fruit juice was available.

"Sinbad, my boy," he advised, "when it's your turn to reside in that stately castle on the Hudson you will discover to your pleasure that well-prepared hooch is a decent beverage that maketh glad the heart . . . superior in fact to your average table Rhine wine." Once at liberty Saul was never one to let work, crime, or even sex interfere with his drinking. If there wasn't enough money for booze he cheerfully tossed off quarts of the cheapest port with the ceremony due to a major LaFitte.

If he arose when the bars were not yet open he grudgingly guzzled beer, which he abominated. If even beer was not at hand, say early on a Sunday morning, he could sniff out certain seedy bodegas on even seedier avenues where rum was sold by the shot under the counter. Ordinarily, if the bars were open money was no object, for credit was liberally extended to him. Saul made it as much a point of honor to honor all obligations incurred by drink as he made it a point of principle never to honor any other lawful debt.

Saul was considered a regular in dozens of bars. When down on his luck he would appear in any one of them to replay his burlesque Falstaff routine to an appreciative audience of old drinking buddies with whom he would then "engage in the game." The game involved three piles of pennies from which two contestants picked in turn. Whoever picked the last penny had to stand for the drinks. He never lost. Never once in all the time I knew him. I begged him, I implored him, to show me the trick.

"Sinbad, my boy, I assure you there is no trick. None at all. Skill, mathematics, concentration. That's the secret of success . . . mmmph . . . certainly not tricks. Have you no shame? Would you imagine that I could chump off my friends? Tricks, indeed!"

I believed him. But in the end I finally tricked him into showing me how he won and, indeed, it was a trick after all.

There were no tricks needed, though, when his fortunes flourished. He drank at least two quarts a day of scotch, or vodka, or rum, or sour mash, or forsaking all others whatever the elixir he currently cherished. He was a fickle lover, even in drink. Where for months nothing but stingers would suffice to quench his monstrous thirst, he would, without warning, spurn my free-will offering of a bottle of reasonably priced brandy—the fruit of my own ill-gotten gains—and plead dyspepsia, insisting that nothing, but nothing would do but a "very dry Gibson, hold the onion and float a scant teaspoon of Pernod on the top, there's a good lad."

His tastes, to say the least, were catholic: Bloody Marys, Strega, Southern Comfort, Passion Fruit, Galliano, Gorilla Anis ("Not anisette, you oaf, an-ee. Gorilla An-ee. What kind of Spic are you anyway, ignorant of your regional drink?")—all were fuel for the bottomless pit.

Saul was not only a serious drinker, but took his drinking seriously, prided in his capacity, and rarely seemed drunk. On those other occasions when he overindulged, when he misjudged his own mortality ("We all have limits we may not transgress, my boy. Man *is* a finite creature."), he was pugnacious and indiscriminately lecherous. But seldom did those who knew him take offense, although many ran to hide their own liquor upon his arrival in their homes.

He began the day with a morning "wake up" (four fingers straight), according it the devotion an acolyte gives to his matins. Given a chance he would religiously continue to consume alcohol until he retired or until he was retired by an excess of zeal, and lay stricken like a snoring beached whale upon his outsized bed.

But there were bad times, hard times, when he reached bottom, when there was no booze, no wine, no ale, no beer, no friend, no credit, no game, not even carfare—when, in short, he had nothing at all to drink. Then he became impossible. He raged, he sulked, he paced while reviewing and rejecting possibilities. He flapped, he gesticulated, he sweated, he slumped miserably in a chair. He tried in vain to sleep away the day and groused some more when he found sleep inseparable from drink. He cursed the world at large. He cursed all those who conspired to deprive him of the necessities of life. He cursed me in particular for being thoughtless enough to be as flat broke as he was. He accused me of deliberately keeping away when he was going through one of his "temporary setbacks." And despite my avowals of innocence he was, of course, right. I simply could not stand being in the company of a boozeless Saul.

Everyone thought that cirrhosis would kill him, and I am sure that he would have agreed. But he collapsed and died of a stroke in

17

a steam bath on St. Mark's Place. We had been at odds for several months. Still, when they finally collected his clothes and sorted through them, the only telephone number they could find was my mother's, and so, in a roundabout way, he dumped his body right on my doorstep. Saul always did enjoy macabre practical jokes.

From the time I started using drugs, when I was twelve, I have never worn a short-sleeve shirt out of doors because I wanted to hide the tracks on my arms. To this day the backs of my hands are still swollen and while I gave up using drugs years ago I still wear long-sleeved shirts from force of habit. Old habits, unlike old friends, die a slow death. So here I stand sweltering in the heat of July while I try to evade my own panic. I do not want to go to the funeral home. I do not want to see the cheap wooden box and the thing inside it that never was Saul and that Saul himself could never become. No man's death belongs to him. Death belongs only to those who are able to experience it, so Saul's death belongs to me. He is reduced now to whatever I have become. My eulogy for him is my eulogy for the shabbiness of my own life, since he has bequeathed me nothing from which I might invent an elegy for him, nothing with which I might grace his absence and transform it into something of significance. I have nothing to offer him now but a few counterfeit tears and the sort of dime-store sentimentality he always deplored. "Mmmph . . . Sinbad, your maudlin streak is your perpetual undoing. A man need only scheme in order to survive."

I disagreed and told him so. The conflict remains unresolved. It may be that sentimentality excludes affection; nevertheless it serves to soften the blows inflicted on us by what is given. We scheme, not to survive, but to love, so that we may betray ourselves into choosing survival. We survive through our ceremonial compulsions to tear open our own wounds and at the end of all striving there waits the enchantment of Narcissus's image rippling on the face of the bottomless waters.

In that building, just a few steps from Central Park, my mother once lived. I lived there too, in a manner of speaking, once upon a time. I did not plan to come here today, but I have returned unthinkingly and unerringly to my beginnings, with no more choice in the matter than a doomed salmon fighting its way upstream to its own dissolution.

There are few cars to be seen, fewer pedestrians. Perhaps today is some sort of holiday. On the walk bordering the park a nurse wheels a young child in a stroller. An old man sits on a bench feeding pigeons. The pigeons flutter and flock about his shoulders and skitter away in a rush of wings. A black man leans against a bus stop sign. There is no bus in sight.

On this miserable and muggy morning I know the park is peaceful. Leaves rustle in a humid wind blowing across the lake. The Ramble, its twisting narrow paths lined with shade trees. A certain spot, a rock set at the end of a craggy spit of land that juts into the lake just at the point where the rowboats turn toward the footbridge. A spot where many times I sat hugging my knees, impatient for life to reveal itself to me.

When I first set out to explore the dirt trail that led from bridge to rock I was no more than seven. It was a perilous adventure then, one beset by threats of nameless dangers. What? Perhaps I feared the water rats. Perhaps there were strangers lurking in the trees, behind bushes. But when I found my rock I knew I had found safe haven where nothing could harm me, where I, not dreaming but alive, knew that some primitive spell was lifted, where dangers vanished, where I wove my own web of enchantment unobserved.

The boy on the rock is eleven years old. He is a familiar stranger, but no less a stranger for being familiar. We share the same name. We share snatches of memory. We touch lightly and separate: the man to voyage on and out, the boy to remain forever frozen in sunlight. The boy is safe from the future. He does not know that the summer will end very soon. The boy does not know that he will soon embark on a journey where the sole coin of passage is the surrender to sensations. He knows nothing of dirty needles, of monsters in human form, of pain beyond bearing, in short, nothing of despair. Sinbad and Saul are as yet names unfamiliar to him. And where I, the man, can only interrupt time

19

for an instant, fondle it in memory as I might stroke a wisp of an infant's hair, the boy can indulge himself endlessly in that summer place outside of time, where the man can do him no harm.

The boy has already discovered beauty in his mirror and is pleased by his discovery. The knowledge of his own beauty fills him with a sense of power so intense, so wonderful, that he wishes to reserve both beauty and power for his own contemplation lest either one vanish under the gaze of others. He examines his image with delight while delighting in his solitude, for there is much he must assimilate in his own way, in his own time.

He has black wavy hair. His skin is smooth, the color of amber. A combination of violet eyes with slightly puffed eyelids gives his face an exotic and sensual cast. His eyebrows meet across the bridge of his nose so that he seems to scowl continually, even when he is amused, as if he were concentrating on a solution to some puzzle which as yet he is unable to formulate.

His body is surprisingly well proportioned for his age. Though he is tall, he is well coordinated. His legs are long and firm. They have acquired muscle tone so recently that he still admires them as if they belonged to a stranger.

For as long as he can remember the boy has desired to become invisible. But no effort of will can produce such a potent charm. The power of the rock on the lake is great, but not unlimited, and he is old enough now to scoff at his own impractical daydreams. Instead of wishing for the impossible he expends his energy in setting himself apart as an uninvolved spectator, content to observe and absorb the world ever unfolding in astonishing ways.

He is content to sit on the rock—his private spot—musing, trying to sort out who people are by the way they act. He watches the people boating on the lake they are involved. There are boys splashing each other, diving from the boats into the brackish water. There are lovers holding hands while their boat drifts aimlessly toward the shore. There is a man strumming a guitar and a dark-skinned girl biting her lower lip as she tugs at the oars. There is a man trying to row with one hand and a woman, with a can of beer held between her knees, shouting instructions to him in Spanish.

He wonders how everyone else can be so involved in what they are doing when moods are so unpredictable. He wonders whether people are really happy or sad or whether they just act that way because they think they're supposed to. He wonders why people take their play seriously. He wonders how anything can be taken seriously when people just pretend to be involved, when all they are doing is play-acting. He tries on the feelings of others to see if they fit and finds them uncomfortable. He listens to the complex harmonics of his own feelings like a blind man with a seashell held to his ear.

There were birds skimming over the water and he brought crumbs to feed them—bits of pretzels, potato chips. When there was no more food the birds winged off, fickle lovers departing without regret for fairer pickings. The boy wore only a sleeveless T-shirt, patched jeans, and scuffed sneakers without socks. He changed his T-shirt when he remembered to, for no one reminded him when it needed changing. Besides, he found his own scent, the musk of his underarms, exciting. He sniffed himself and was pleased. Then he looked behind him to make sure that no one was watching him.

When he was restless he would run swiftly through the wild grass of the Great Sheep Meadow, alone, sometimes trailing a kite which he had stuck together.

His mother scolded. He was useless. As long as he was going out why couldn't he take the younger children with him? He evaded. He mumbled excuses. He lied. He needed his solitude, for in it lay the secret of his strength. He loved his little sister and brother. At least he knew that he was supposed to love them, if only he could be sure what love was. He bought a balloon for his sister. He pilfered a Scout knife from the candy store and gave it to his brother. He played with both of them, bathed them, put them to bed. When they were naughty he spanked their bottoms lightly. He did love them. He did love his mother. The alternative was unthinkable. But when he set forth for the park alone he was glad to be free of them all. If only he could be sure what love was. He was certain that he was odd, some sort of freak of nature. Why was he always outside of everything looking in, when it would be so easy to slip inside? All he had to do was play-act, like everybody else. Why did he volunteer to remain outside? He soothed him-self, remembering that he was protected by a spell of his own invention, surprised all the while by the intense surges of feeling that welled chaotically from within, only to scatter and forsake him like the birds on the lake.

I was just, you know, hanging out. I bought a Coke at the hot dog stand and was just standing there, sucking up the last little bit from the bottom where all the ice gets stuck. I didn't even know the guy was standing there until I felt him staring at me. I don't like people staring at me, it makes me nervous, ever since that time by the lake. I was just sitting on the rock and this kid, he was about my own age, like he was in a boat with his boys and they all stripped down to their drawers and dove off the boat into the lake and, you know, were just swimming and fooling around.

Well this one kid, I guess he was scared or didn't know how to swim or something, because he was the only one which just stayed in the boat. So his boys they were all sounding on him and ranking him out and shit, you know. I guess he finally got disgusted and he got undressed too because, you know, they were calling him all kinds of sissies and shit and besides the lake isn't really all that deep anyhow. It's just pretty icky and gooey down at the bottom. But I mean, if the kid didn't know how to swim then he wouldn't of known about the lake not being deep and all so you'd have to say he was a pretty ballsy kid. I mean, if he really didn't know how to swim. So anyhow, this kid, he climbs over the side of the boat and just lets go and slides into the water and all his boys are whistling and hollering and splashing him, you know, like they was just goofing around and I guess, you know, this kid just wanted to goof around with them.

So then what happened was that all of the guys started ducking each other and splashing and shit and this one kid ducks the kid who was the last one in the boat, just like held his head under for a minute and you could see the kid waving his arms trying to get away. And the next thing was the kid stops splashing around and then he was gone. Just like that, he was gone. All his boys stopped fooling around but they didn't know what to do, like who knows what you're supposed to do. Maybe they thought it was all a joke, one minute the kid was there and the next minute, poof—he's not there anymore.

22

Well a man, he was standing on the shore and he musta been watching all this go down because he takes off his shoes and dives in the water with all his clothes on and when he reaches the spot where the kid went down he goes under looking for him. When he comes up the man is holding the kid by his hair which the kid's face is all gooky from the mud and shit. I never seen anybody before just held up by their hair and like none of what's going down seems like it's really happening. They all push and pull the kid into the boat and row over to the spot where I am on the rock and the man swims over too. Me, I don't say nothing because it's none of my business and besides, what could I do anyway? I mean if the kid didn't know how to swim he musta been a real dodo to jump into the water in the first place, right? At least that's the way I look at it. So I just stay there and watch while the man rolls the kid over and starts, you know, giving him whaddaya call it . . . artificial inspiration and shit, but it's no good. The kid is drownt and that's that. Nothin's gonna bring him back.

Well, don't ask me why I did what I did. I didn't even know what I was doing. I climbed down off the rock and kneeled down beside the kid who drownt and kept staring right into his face. I don't know why, but I couldn't help it. I just stayed there staring like there was something important there I had to see which was nothing, because what could I see—the kid was dead and I couldn't bring him back to life, right?

Then one of his boys gives me a hard look and goes, "What the fuck are you looking at?" and tells me get the fuck outta here before you get your ass kicked, which I did, because the kid who said it to me was bigger than me plus he was crying and shit and there as nothing really there to see. Just a dead kid with mud on his face.

Later the ambulance came and the cops too and they put the kid's body in a bag and just zipped it up and put it in the ambulance like a sack of garbage and that was that. The ambulance was gone and so was the kid. The cop stood around writing in his notebook while all the other kids tried to talk all at once and the one that chased me started pointing at me. So then the cop came up and asked me if I saw anything which I told him the kid just jumped in the water and they were all fooling around and then he went under. Just what happened. I was a little scared too because I had this crazy idea that maybe everybody was blaming me because the

23

kid got kilt which was ridiculous, but that's what I was thinking and I said to myself—see, that's for sticking your nose in other people's business, that's what you get for acting all crazy and practically sticking your nose in a dead kid's face. Me, I don't like people staring at me, especially after that. It always makes me think of that kid, the way he drownt and all and the way he looked with the guy holding him up by his hair.

Anyhow, what I started to say is this guy is standing there staring at me and I'm just about to say something when he asks me if I wanna hot dog and I go sure, I don't mind. And something inside of me tells me what he really wants, which is to do it to me and my stomach feels all funny and shit. I mean, I know what the score is. I never did it to a girl yet but I guess I could if I wanted to. I've been jerking off for almost a year and I can even cum a little bit now. I even got some hair starting to grow around my dick. One day I didn't have anything and then boom—all of a sudden it was there. So this guy asks me something, I don't know what and I look up and here I am walking with him, not knowing where we're goin' or nothing. I don't know why I'm walking away with this guy, I mean, like knowing what he wants to go with him for and all. Am I crazy or what? And the craziest thing is that I'm not scared at all, just like anxious to see how it's gonna turn out.

It's like I'm watching myself in a movie, like watching some guy in a Kung Fu flick that you know is only an actor who's getting paid to take apart the whole Chinese army or something. You know it's a fake, but while you're watching you get so hooked up in it that you start thinking well maybe it's real, maybe I could even do all that shit myself, what the actor is doing on the screen. Well, that's what I feel like. It's like I'm watching a movie of myself walking with this guy and knowing whatever else happens it's all made up, that it's not me. I can't explain it right, I guess, about not being scared because none of it seems real. But that's what I feel like, anyhow.

The guy asks me how I like school and shit which I say yeah, it's ok but I play hooky a lot and I don't why I tell him something like that, a perfect stranger. It's none of his business. But after I tell him about me playing hooky I just can't seem to shut up. I tell him also how when I don't go to school I go down to Forty-second street a lot to check out all the movies and also how I come to the park every day now that there's no school. And he asks me what I do when I come to the park which I tell him, nothing much, I just hang out and you know, just fool around. Then he asks me do I like to get high and I go, sure, if you're talking about smoke, which I was smoking even when I was small and living with my grand-mother over on east a hundred and tenth Street and my uncles used to come and visit and they'd all sit around playing conga and smoking up and they'd always pass me some. Even my grandma didn't mind that too much though she always pretended to make a fuss. Around the block everybody smokes, even the little kids right in the schoolyard. The only thing I don't do is let my mother know because she'd beat me black and blue, what with the way she is plus my stepfather being a preacher and all which even in the house all us kids gotta call him Reverend. Even my little brother and sister, which he is their real father, he makes them call him Reverend.

But the thing about it is, this guy is white. I never smoked with a white guy before. I mean kids my own age, sure, but not a man who's old enough to be my father. I mean, he could be a schoolteacher or a cop or something. How would I know? But here we are just walking and rapping and he seems like an all right guy. Like he don't seem weird or anything like that.

We go down this trail where there are a lot of trees all around and then you get to a brook, like, which there are rocks all around and an old wooden bridge which you cross and then the trail ends and there's nothing but bushes. When you get there, to the bushes, you wouldn't know you could walk through unless you know the park real good. You'd think you was at a dead end. This guy must know the park as good as I do because he keeps on going through this one row of bushes like you're supposed to and there's like a little clearing where nobody ever goes.

We sit down and he pulls out a joint which we smoke and there I am with a nice buzz, feeling a-ok and the sun is shining and this guy's ok too. Somehow I know he ain't gonna hurt me or anything. How do I know? I dunno, I just know, that's all. I can tell about grown-ups right away, whether they're ok or not and also I can tell that this guy wants to do it to me and I won't mind it the least bit. What he does is he slides his hand over and puts it on my leg. His hand is hot and sweaty but when it starts moving up my leg it feels good. I don't want him to stop, though maybe I'm a little embarrassed because my dick is hard and I don't know whether that's the way it's supposed to be, like maybe when he feels it he's gonna think that I'm some kinda sex nut or something, which is pretty funny, him being a faggot and all that likes kids so how is he gonna think I'm a sex nut when he's one his own self? Then his hand just touches my dick like it was an accident or something. I know he's gotta be able to feel that my dick is on a bone and he looks at me like he don't know whether I'm gonna jump up and call the cops or whether I'm gonna let him go ahead and do it, which when I don't tell him to stop he unzips my pants and my bone is sticking out right through my drawers. What he does then is he starts jerking me off and it feels a lot better than when I do it myself. First he goes slow and then he goes a little bit faster and I'm high, thinking about how I always wondered when I was small and first started coming to the park about whether somebody was hiding in the bushes or something, waiting to jump out and grab me which makes me laugh because what he's doing feels good and maybe he was the guy who was hiding in the bushes all along and there was never anything to be scared of. Anyhow, when I laugh he looks all aggravated and all like I'm laughing at him which I'm not doing. I just have a nice buzz on and I'm goofing on my own head and he goes, - you want me to stop-, and I go, - no, man, finish what you're doing-. So then he leans over and starts giving me a blow job that even feels better than the jerking off. It feels just like what it must be inside a girl's box and when I start thinking about doing it to a girl while he's blowing me, boom - I cum right away, all in his mouth. But he must like that, the taste of cum, because he keeps on blowing me until my dick feels funny and sore and I push him away.

When we're walking back the inside of my pants feels all gooky because I didn't have nothing to wipe off the spit and cum and I think that as soon as I get home I better throw these drawers away in the garbage so my mother doesn't see them all sticky when she goes to do the wash. The guy, he tells me his name is Mitch and he asks me if I come out here to the park a lot and I go, - sure, I told you before, I'm out here practically every day now-, and he goes, well, maybe he'll see me again some time, which I wouldn't mind seeing him again but not every day because I don't want to do it every day. You can never tell, I might get to like it too much and get all fucked up and maybe become a faggot like him, which of course, I don't tell him that. I mean, I guess there's nothing wrong with him being a faggot if that's what he likes and it don't mean that you're a faggot just because you let a faggot give you a blow job once in a while. I know a lot of big guys that go with faggots too. Plenty of them. So I go, - sure, like I told you I'm out here all the time. I'll probably see you around-, He doesn't say anything after that. He just smiles, gives my shoulder a squeeze and walks out of the park. Me, I stand there like a big dodo until he's out of sight which is when I realize that I forgot to tell him my name and for the life of me, I can't figure out why I want him to know it.

At night the boy lies in his bed exploring his body with his hands. He closes his eyes and projects the image which he imagines the man in the park admired. He tries to capture himself in the eyes of the stranger. The picture intensifies as he becomes increasingly aroused. He is grateful to the man he acknowledges as his secret ally. Through the man it has been revealed to him that he is capable of casting spells upon someone from the real world. He has enchanted himself without knowing it.

The boy attaches no shame to what has been accomplished. What has he done except to be present? He forfeits nothing by permitting himself to be desired. He risks nothing by seeking self-satisfaction at the hands of others. He deludes himself that it is in his power to grant pleasure or to withhold it. He understands little. But he does understand, for the first time in his life, the devotion of his mother to her icons.

The boy lives where he pleases. He is bored in his mother's apartment. He is bored with the Reverend, a sour, desiccated old man. He is bored with meal-time prayers. He is bored with baby-sitting. He is bored with his mother's erratic behavior, with the inevitable cycle of rage, reconciliation, withdrawal, and indiffer-

27

ence. The boy is irritable. The windows of the apartment remain closed. The heat, the smell of incense that clings to his clothes, the ticking of the clock, the whimpering of his little sister in her sleep—all these oppress him. He waits, knowing there is no one to wait for. He dozes and finds himself along with the chirping of insects, the caw-caw of multi-colored birds in a dank, mildewed, decaying jungle where he is ordained to watch for the return of a dead man, waiting until the flesh oozes from his bones and his bones dissolve to mingle with the mud beneath his bare feet.

He awakes. He knows from experience when it is time to leave. His departures are as unquestioned as his arrivals. Both are accepted without comment. While he is at his grandmother's his mother will take no note of his absence. On his return she will not remember that he has ever been away.

It is a relief to escape back to the barrio's benevolent chaos, its storefront salsa blaring over tinny speakers; its garbage spilling over into the streets where children splash in the fire hydrant's spray; its mornings when the sidewalks are transformed into bazaars; its afternoons alive with his own people, people who brazenly refuse to consent to urgency; its dusk when the men gather on the stoops with their guitars, drinking up six packs, arguing, fighting, sometimes stabbing each other over matters of the heart or matters of honor, while the old ones, immersed in their endless domino games, gabble placidly in the shadows.

There is neither park nor trail. There is no lake nor is there a rock jutting out into the lake. There are no trees visible. In the gathering gloom the boy sits on the tenement roof, puffing a poorly rolled stick of Chiba. His legs dangle six stories above the street. Across the river, more than a mile to the west, a magenta sunset dims, then darkens into purple. The boy wishes that he could merge into the dying day, surrendering himself completely to its sorrowful sweetness. In that instant he realizes that nothing is lost in the world.

Below waited dinner. His grandmother always left a pot on the stove so that he could eat when he wished too. At times there was only rice and beans. But more often than not there were delicious-smelling stews of fish or succulent pig ears, fried chicken or spicy sausages. There were avocados and platanos, hot sauce, nutmeg, sofrito, achiote. There was chewy and pungent dried buffalo meat and the inevitable apples, mangoes, or bananas. There was abundance and yet there was solitude. There was ease in the absence of icons, statues, incense, and candles.

The old woman was half Indian. She was white haired. Her nose was hooked. She appeared to be frail. Perhaps this was a deliberate deception. In any case her body was still strong and her mind keen, though every now and then she might fall into a reverie and ramble on in the language of her father, which the boy did not comprehend. The old woman spoke no English, nor had she ever had time to learn how to read or write Spanish. The boy listened. He absorbed the old woman. He slaked his thirst for the world by drinking her words as her ancestors drank blood from cups they fashioned from their enemies' skulls. The old woman's chatter rose and fell as she recounted tales of complicated clan feuds dredged up from a time before the boy was.

The old woman hated her daughter. She reviled the boy's mother, cursed her, summoned God and his saints to witness that justice required the slut be eternally damned. The boy was the old woman's treasure, blood of her blood, flesh of the seed of her dead husband who, with all his vices, was a man, not like the unsexed cabron with whom that harlot fouled her bed.

The boy's blood was pure. He would become a fine man. If only her daughter were dead and the boy safely beyond the reach of her savagery.

"Mami? . . . venganza? Qué venganza, Mamita? Qué tu te refere?" he asked, only because he knew that she wanted him to. Because he knew that she would decline to answer. Some mysteries were too unspeakable for her to impart, even to the boy, unless he commanded her to do so. She dreaded the day when he might require her to tell him the truth.

Yes, he was fine and sturdy. In the occasional angry flash of his eyes she could discern portents of her daughter's downfall. The boy was beautiful. He would grow into a handsome man. He would break the hearts of many girls. He would sire sons. He would work, sing, make love, and carouse. He would curse, weep, rage, and triumph. He would bury her and alone, of all her kin, mourn her death. He would garland her grave with flowers and speak of her to his sons and daughters and then their sons and daughters would honor her grave with the gardenias she loved through all the

29

generations until the blessed dead should rise and she, at last, awaken to be reunited with the boy.

The old woman made no attempt to control the boy. He was moody and headstrong. This delighted her. She was positive that the boy loved her and this delighted her too. The boy slept in the bed with his grandmother, cuddling against the old woman without shame. Often when she awoke the boy was already gone. She sipped black coffee sweetened with honey and set her prayers to protect him. Sometimes she knew that he would not return for weeks and at those times she feared that she was, after all, merely a foolish old woman whose prayers would never be answered. She sighed and spied Death crouching in the corner and she was afraid. But when she thought of the boy, too tender in years to survive alone in the world, she bit back her tears and bade Death leave her be for a while so that she might continue to protect him. For in the pattern of the coffee grounds she discerned that soon, very soon, the boy would leave his mother for good. Then she spat and cursed her daughter from habit and she cherished the boy even more in the mistaken belief that God had graced him with a wise heart.

Saul wanted to be buried. He told me once that he had been baptized while in prison. But he might have been joking. I know of no virtue that he practiced. As for faith, "If you have it, my boy, keep it to yourself. If anyone has to be a chump, let it be God." Hope? "Oh yes, we are saved by hope, for in hope lies total confusion." Charity? "By all means, let us be done with it." Justice? "Blessed is he who approves what he condemns. Even you should have learned that by now."

By the time the conversation turned to interment he was already drunk. He made me promise that I would arrange for his burial in unconsecrated earth. I knew better than to cross him at that particular stage of inebriation, when his smile was so deceptively gentle, so I acceded without argument and promptly forgot the whole affair until two days ago.

So today Saul will be cremated and that will be that. He cannot possibly abuse me for breaking a promise that was given only to placate him. I have no obligation to keep faith with a dead man. The dead have no rights. The ceremonies of death are dictated by the requirements of the living. It is a terrible responsibility, having charge of another man's body. I would prefer to wash my hands of the whole business and sit here on this bench at the entrance to the park so that it will be too late for me to participate in Saul's rite of passage.

Memory is most peculiar. I can clearly remember intricate details of texture, of scent, of nuance of feeling concerning events that took place more than twenty years ago, but I cannot remember what I had for breakfast this morning, or, indeed, if I had breakfast at all.

Five months ago I passed my thirtieth birthday. I began to apprehend that aging was a process involving me . . . me. Even before Saul's death I felt insinuations of my own mortality. I saw my receding hairline in the mirror. I found clumps of hair in my comb. My pants were too tight and I wondered when I started wearing rubbers in the rain. I use vitamin C to ward off colds and vitamin E to ward off impotence. When I massage my scalp with a worthless patent medicine, I remember I have a son. I try to think of something about which I can rebuke him. Perhaps I want to prove to myself that I am capable of inflicting pain on him, no matter how slight the pain or how weak the excuse for inflicting it.

And here is the park where no one dares walk at night. The Goths wait in ambush at the gates. The time of the long knives is at hand. Within the City the revelers carouse and I am here alone, desolate . . . and Saul is dead. My memories hide themselves like fearful shadows lurking in the trees at dusk. I cannot purge what I refuse to relinquish.

I hafta admit I was scared when the cops came to my mother's looking for me. For a minute I thought it was about Mitch. I said Jesus, Mary, and Joseph, don't let her find out about that. I promise I'll stop going out there to look for him. I won't jerk off anymore. I promise I'll stop getting high every day. But it wasn't that. It was about the club and the initiation thing, which was worse. So I hid under the bed but my mother told them that I was hiding there. She didn't hafta do that. She could of said I wasn't there, that I was at my grandmother's. My own mother. Well, after she told them I hadda come out and they took me to the police station and all, but that part comes last.

First I got to tell you about the club. What it is most people would call it a gang which I guess it is also. The club is called the Savage Skulls. They got chapters all over in Bushwick, in the South Bronx, in East Harlem, all over. When you're in the club you get to wear the colors which is a dungaree jacket with a big skull and crossbones on the back and these, like, silver studs all around the collar and the pockets. To get in you gotta be Puerto Rican. No whiteys are allowed and especially no niggers. Everybody knows niggers smell bad which is one reason why I don't like school because they make you sit next to niggers even if you don't want to plus all the teachers are white and they get mad when you talk to your boys in Spanish. But in the Skulls it's all Latin brothers which is one of the reasons why I wanted to join.

Anyhow nobody's gonna say no when they ask you to join because if you don't belong to a club then guys from other clubs'll pick on you and fuck you up and rip you off, whatever, your box, your jacket, which is why almost everybody joins up.

What you gotta do is you gotta be initiated. When they initiate you they do it in the clubhouse which is in the basement of the building across the street. All the guys in the club chip in some-thing, whatever they can afford, say a dollar or two a week, which they use to pay the super. They got it fixed up real bad down there with black lights and posters and a boss stereo and mattresses around the walls and they all sit around in the afternoon and all night drinking beer and smoking herb. Well, anyhow, when you go down there to get initiated you gotta bring a girl with you. It gotta be some girl who's not already some guy's old lady and the girl you bring ain't supposed to know what's gonna happen. But most of them they do know and they go along with it because they wanna hang out and most all of their girl friends are already debs and they don't want the guys to think they're some kind of creep or something.

Well, the only girl I could think of to bring was this girl Maria who is in my class at school. Maria she's tall and skinny, even taller than me. She's got little bitty tits and no ass at all. The thing about it is that she's not all that bad looking, not really. She's kinda brainy

32

in school which is why maybe nobody asked her before and I figured she'd jump at the chance, I mean, not to be my old lady, but to hang out with everybody else. At first when I asked her she looked at me kinda funny like how come a kid who's pretty smart in school hisself like me would wanna get hooked up with the Skulls and all but she didn't say no so I guess she wanted to join too. I wondered if she knew what was gonna happen but I didn't ask her because she didn't say nothin' about it. I guess if she wanted to know then she shoulda asked, right?

Anyhow, we go down to the clubhouse and they lock the door and all the guys make a circle around us. There's no other girls allowed when they're initiating. Just the guy who's being initiated and whoever he brings. There's one bright light on right in the middle of the ceiling. It's the only light on in this whole big basement. Nobody tells you what to do. If you're gonna be in the club you're supposed to know. First you gotta take off all your clothes. You gotta take everything off until you're buck naked which is no big deal because except for Maria it's only a bunch of guys which you all get undressed in school when you go to gym. Me, it don't make me no never-mind which if you got a real small weenie or something all the guys'll laugh and sound on you, but me, I got nothing to worry about, mine's bigger than a lot of theirs. The girl, she's supposed to get undressed too. But Maria starts screwing everything up right from the beginning. Like she just stands there like some big dumb beanpole like she's scared or ashamed or something, just looking down at the ground like something was growing between her toes. So all the guys they start yelling and clapping and whistling but Maria she acts like she don't even hear them which of course she can't help hearing them what with all the noise they're making. And all of a sudden, you know what this big dummy starts doing? She starts bawling. So I go,— well you knew what was gonna happen so why don't you just get it over with?—And she goes,—no I didn't either, I didn't know it was gonna be like this and I'm gonna go home because all of you are nothing but pigs that's what you are—. Well when she says that the guys start yelling and cheering even louder, stomping all over the place and here comes Chino who is the prez and when he starts coming everybody better get out of his way because Chino is one bad dude and he comes right over to Maria and grabs her blouse

33

and rips it right down to her waist—boom, just like that—it's just hanging there in pieces and Maria she got no bra on or nothing which she doesn't have any tits to begin with so she doesn't really need one. And then boy does she ever start bawling for real how she wants to go home this and Mama that. One thing I'll say for her, Maria, she got a good set of pipes on her.

Well Chino, he's sick of it all so what he does is backhand her one right on the mouth and goes,—shut up bitch—, which the blood is dripping out of her mouth. She looked like a mess, an honest to goodness mess. But it was all her fault to begin with even though Chino didn't hit her as hard as he did. I wanna tell him to lay off because I can always find some other girl, I guess, who'd be glad to go through with it without him beating up on this dumb skinny dodo and I woulda said something too, I don't care if Chino is seventeen and bigger than me cause I still know how to pick up a beer bottle and crack it over a guy's knot. But I don't even have a chance to open my mouth before up comes Victor and this other dude. Victor is even meaner than Chino. They say that he split a counselor's skull up in Youth House. Right away Victor gives Maria a shove so that she falls flat on her ass right in the middle of the floor and the other dude starts pulling her dungarees off, which she starts screaming as loud as she can, kicking all over the place. When she tries to kick Victor in the balls, though, he gets mad and practically cold cocks her with a right. It sounded like he tore her head off that's how loud it sounded. Maria she's stopped yelling. She just sorta lays there moaning with her eyes almost closed and the blood pouring out of the side of her mouth. Now the other dude he finishes pulling off her dungarees so she's bare-assed naked right in the middle of the floor and Chino comes up behind me and gives me a little shove to tell me get started. Victor sits on her chest where her tits are supposed to be and the other guy holds her arms and there's no way for me to stop it anyhow so I get on top of her to screw her but I can't get it in. I can't even get a real bone and besides I never actually screwed a girl before, I mean of course I know how to do it and all, that is as soon as I find the hole.

Well, when the guys see this they really crack up. Me, I'm mad as a hornet 'cause I never had any problem getting my dick hard before and Chino's holding his sides laughing and he tells Victor and the other dude to get up offa her for a minute and then he bends down and grabs her by the hair and pulls her up and then he pulls her head right up under my dick and he goes,—suck it, bitch—, Maria she just isn't gonna suck my dick for all the tea in China. She just presses her lips together and shakes her head no and makes these sorta little whining sounds like a puppy does when he's scared. Victor, he comes over and pulls out his figa which is a long knife, from outta his boot and sticks the point right on her neck and he goes,—suck it or I slice your head off right now—. Which, I mean, what can she do? She opens her mouth just a little, just enough so that only the teensiest bit can get inside and the other dude, he sees she's trying to get over so he gives her a swift kick in her cunt which makes her open her mouth fast to holler so now I got all of it inside her mouth. Believe me it don't feel nothing like Mitch. I mean her teeth are sharp and it hurts. It don't feel good at all. She's just scraping it with her teeth and making it sore and besides she sounds like she's gonna throw up all over my dick. But even though it hurts and all it starts to get hard and when it's hard enough Chino pulls her offa me by her hair and tells me,—go ahead fuck her—. So I climb on top of her again and this time I find the hole and go ahead and screw her. Her hole is tight and dry and all that's happening is my dick is getting sorer. I'm humping away but I can't come. No matter what, it just won't come. I don't know why, that's just the way it is. I close my eyes and try to think about something real horny, anything—anything besides the time in the park but I can't think of nothing. My mind's a blank. So what I do is I phony it so the guys won't think that I'm too young to come and I pump up and down a couple of times and make like I'm comin and nobody even knows the difference.

While I'm putting my clothes back on all the other guys are taking turns doing it to her, but that's what always happens and the girl she's supposed to know what's happening and have sense enough not to complain. But not the way they're doing it to her. It's not supposed to happen that way. Chino's on top of her screwing away and Victor is holding her up by the hair making her blow the other dude. After he comes she hasta blow the next guy in line and when Chino's through another guy starts screwing her so she's always got two at once. And then this squirt Peewee he goes,—let's fuck her in the ass—which all the guys go yeah, yeah, let's fuck the bitch in the ass which then Peewee, he pulls out his little pecker and they turn her over and Peewee gets in her ass and while he's doing it another guy is still getting blowed by her.

Me, I don't even wanna watch because it's disgusting. That's all it is is disgusting plus I feel like it's all my fault because I was the one which brung her here in the first place. But finally it's over and Maria's laying there on a mattress all beat up. There she is flat on her back looking up at the ceiling like she's in another world. She got two shiners and probably a couple of teeth knocked out too. For what? Just tell me that, for what?

But now I gotta worry about the second part of the initiation which is that you gotta fight the prez which is Chino. They don't expect you to win or anything because the prez is supposed to be the baddest dude in the club. But you gotta fight him to show you can take it and that you're not a punk.

So everybody forgets about Maria including me and they all get into another circle so they can watch the fight. Chino is a big guy and as strong as an ox and I guess that me since I'm supposed to be half-assed brainy myself, I'll just let him pop me a couple of times and go down and stay there. That will be that and no hard feelings. Here we are out in the middle of the floor. I got my shirt off but Chino, he figures it's all gonna be over right away and he leaves his on. He's smiling and I can see he don't wanna hurt me. He ain't gonna get no rep beating up on an eleven-year-old kid. He's just gonna goof around a little bit so he goes into this phony karate stance, you know, showing off to everybody. He don't know I'm mad as a hornet about Maria and all which they weren't supposed to do it like that, plus I'm the one that brung her here in the first place. So while Chino is showing off, waving and clowning around, I jap him one right upside his head with all I got. So then he looks at me like I'm some kinda nut and I know I'm in trouble 'cause he's mad and I popped him with my best shot and he didn't even shake his head. Me, I start backing up, not running, but just moving away from him. I try to bob and weave but he lands a wild right that nearly tears my head off and there I am down on one knee and don't even know how I got there. Two guys pick me up under the arms and sorta shove me towards Chino who nearly breaks my nose with a hook. He's gonna murder me, no doubt about it. And I say to myself, dummy, if you give him a fair one they'll hafta pick up the pieces with a blotter after he's through with you so what I do is instead of moving back I step in. He's so surprised to see me coming towards him that he forgets for a second to swing, and that's all I need. Wham—I stomp on his foot and lay my head right on his shoulder so that when he swings, all he can hit is the back of my head and break a couple of knuckles while he's doing it and before he can get his foot out from under mine, I bring my knee up hard to kick him right square in the balls.

That was that. Before you could say boo, there's Chino rolling around the floor holding his nuts and hollering his own damn self. Good, I think, good for his monkey ass and besides, nobody ever said when you fight the prez you gotta fight him fair. What was I supposed to do, stand here and get murdered or something?

The guys, I guess they don't believe what happened because it all happened so fast. They just can't believe that I kicked the prez in the balls and won the fight. But I won, and that's all that counts with anybody.

Victor, he comes over to help Chino up, but Chino gives him a dirty look and finally he gets up and brushes himself off. I can see it's hard for him to stand up straight, but he's trying to act cool and I gotta hand it to him for that. He walks over to me, still a little wobbly and sticks out his hand and goes,—yo, my man, you're ok and there ain't no hard feelings because now you're one of the brothers, right guys—. And all the guys go right like they was some kind of fucking parrots. Now they're all over me, slapping me on the back and all and shaking my hand. One dude gives me a can of beer and another one lights up a joint and Chino comes over and he got his own colors in his hands which he puts over my shoulders and goes,—yo, bro, welcome to the Skulls—.

I look around to see what's happened to Maria but she's gone. So there's nothing else to do except hang out. Everybody's drinking beer and lighting up and yakking and a couple of guys are even dancing to the music on the box. Of course they're not dancing together because what guy is gonna dance with another guy? Not the Skulls, they're not, and you better believe it.

Before you know it everybody's fucked up out of their minds and I am too and I'm still wearing Chino's colors. Everybody's just partying and having a good time and nobody says one word about Maria. Finally we all tip and I'm outside on the street by myself. I walk across the street to the park which it is already dark and you gotta be crazy to walk there alone. What I do is look all around to make sure no one's looking and I take off Chino's colors and throw them over the wall into the bushes, which is where they stay and then I get in the wind. Who needs their stupid club anyhow?

I know I must look awful what with the shots that Chino banged me. My nose hurts like hell, too. I know if I go back to my mother's she'll raise holy hell and I won't hear the end of it for a month so I figure why go through that aggravation. Instead, I walk all the way to my grandmother's house which she never says one word about how terrible I look or what happened or nothing. She runs me a hot bath which I soak in for an hour. Then after I dry myself off I go into the kitchen where she got a big plate of chuletas and rice and beans for me and while I'm eating she fusses all over me like it's my birthday or something.

Later I watch TV for a while and figure maybe I should go outside and see who's hanging out around the block and tell them all about the fight and shit and how I whipped the prez's butt, but not the part about Maria. Anyhow, I'm too tired to go downstairs and as a matter of fact I fall asleep right in front of the TV.

I stay over at my grandmother's for a week or so until I figure things are cooled off around my mother's block, about Maria and all and my eye isn't black anymore. And the first night I'm back there is when the cops come and bust me, just like that. My mother, I coulda sworn she was smiling. The Reverend, he just went inside the bedroom and closed the door. He didn't want any part of the whole mess and the kids were crying because they were scared when they seen the cops. So they take me up to the Twenty-fourth Precinct, which is on a Hundredth Street and we go upstairs, just me and the two cops. They made my mother stay downstairs where the desk is at.

There in the squad room is most of the Skulls which I find out that Maria's mother of course raised all kinds of hell about what happened and the cops just swooped up and snatched up all the Skulls figuring it gotta be them even though Maria didn't say nothing because naturally she was scared if she ratted anybody out they'd kill her or something.

What they do is take each guy into a room separately, just one guy plus the two cops. Then they play the good cop–bad cop routine which every kid knows backwards and forwards. That's where one cop slaps you upside your head and then goes out and the other one pretends he wants to help you and tells you he's your friend and if you tell him the whole truth he'll make sure the other guy don't come back and smack you no more. But if you keep your mouth shut like me the first guy comes back and starts giving you another beating. They keep on like that until they're tired of it and let you go and try it on somebody else. Me, I didn't say nothing even though I almost felt like telling them it was mostly my fault, I guess, for bringing her there in the first place, but she shoulda known what was gonna happen. After a while they see they're getting no place with me and give me a kick in the ass and tell me to go on home. When I get downstairs my mother is gone which is ok with me. Outside here comes Chino with a guy who I guess is a cop, who knows? And he goes,—"yo, bro, where ya been? Everything everything?"—And I go,"Yo, Chino, everything's everything—." And he goes,—"Yo, bro," where's your colors?—" And I go,—"yo, Chino, I threw them in the bushes in Central Park—."

And that was the end of that between me and the Skulls. I didn't bother them and they didn't bother me. I just forgot about them and spent the rest of the summer fooling around in the park.

I had never been to the morgue before. There is an attendant at the barred gate to prevent the dead from receiving unauthorized visitors. The visitor is assailed with the formidable scent of formaldehyde and the fear that once across the threshold he will be unable to find his way back to the world. The room itself is not at all forbidding. A decorator's touch is evident in the ecru walls and russet-colored ceiling. It might well be the office of a plant manager, except for certain almost welcome clichés.

For instance, I was surprised to find that there really were oversized drawers, row on row of them. There was a potbellied detective, whose sport jacket was indeed ill fitting, with the inevitable notebook and pencil stub in hand. An attendant opened a drawer. I peered inside and examined the contents. I nodded and the drawer clanged shut. The detective asked me something. I asked him to repeat it.

39

"I suppose you know your friend was a fag."

His tone was unpleasantly insinuating. There was no point in becoming indignant. Policemen, like priests, collect scandals for a living. They absolve only those who are willing to confess to some taint or contamination. I started to walk away from him. I felt his hand on my shoulder and spun around to face him. I never liked strangers to approach me from behind. Probably all he wanted to know was what Saul had been doing in a homosexual bathhouse, although the answer seemed obvious. Whose reputation needed my protection in this place?

"You didn't answer my question."

I would have given him an answer if his hand hadn't lingered on my arm. I knew then that he wasn't the least bit interested in Saul's preferences. It was mine that were under investigation. I shrugged off his hand and shoved him away so that I wouldn't hit him.

"Fuck off, creep," I yelled.

An effeminate attendant clucked disapprovingly.

The detective smiled to let me know that he wouldn't forget my face and slapped his notebook shut. The attendant said something about "disposing." I couldn't focus on what he was saying. I was still furious that the detective had tried to cruise me in the morgue. Someone else mentioned something about "the body." I was completely confused. When Saul collapsed and died it was early in the afternoon. He was quite alone in the steam room at the time. Only he could have enjoyed the irony of it all, that in the end innocence pounced on the opportunity offered and betrayed him.

I walked through the barred gate into the sunlight and wondered how I could ever have wished for death.

I had less than a dollar in my pocket. Crumpled in my hand was a piece of paper on which someone had written a telephone number. I walked the fifteen blocks from the morgue to the hotel, where on and off for many years I have maintained a room, a cubicle really, no larger than a prison cell. I seldom, if ever, sleep there but because my living arrangements have usually been uncertain, it serves as a place where I can receive my bi-monthly Welfare checks. In the cubicle I found an aspirin tin and tapped out the handful of tuinals inside. I swallowed them all without water and lay down on the bed. When I awoke it was dark. Sweat rolled off my forehead onto the pillow. Fuzzy headed, I sat up, and giggled.

I patted my pocket to reassure myself that I hadn't lost the loose change. It was all I had in the world. I had no idea how to go about "making arrangements." I remembered that he was supposed to have a mother in Florida. At least I thought he said Florida. How long ago was it? How could I find her even if he had said Florida, even if she were still alive? I couldn't conceive of Saul having a mother. I couldn't think of anyone who would let me have some money.

To ask my mother was out of the question. Sunshine, Saul's only close friend, never had any money. Why did death have to be so complicated for the living? I went downstairs to the lobby and dialed the number in Newark. I wanted to speak to my son. I wanted his comfort. I wanted him to hold my head in his lap. I wanted to smell the scent of his body. I wanted to cling to him. I wanted to protect him. Perhaps if he had any money he would let me borrow a few dollars. His mother answered the telephone and told me that Salvador had not been home for two days. Before she could ask me for money I hung up.

I started walking uptown. I bought a pint of wine so I wouldn't have to listen to the change jangle in my pocket. At the corner of Forty-second Street and Eighth Avenue I hesitated, trying to figure out where I was going. Then I saw my son, standing with his back toward me, under a movie marquee just a few feet away. I threw away the empty wine bottle and pushed my way through the crowd. I grabbed him by the shoulders and spun him around. I found myself peering into the face of a terrified Gypsy girl who was selling flowers to passers-by. I tried to apologize to her for not being my son, but that didn't sound right so I apologized instead for not having any money. What I meant was that I hadn't any money for flowers.

When I reached Saul's apartment I stared at the door in confusion. There had been so many arguments, so many lock changes. The key in my hand could not possibly fit this lock. But it did. The living room looked as if Saul had just stepped out for a minute. I expected him to walk through the door with a shopping bag full of booze. There was a nearly empty bottle of scotch on the coffee table. On the couch was his floppy old bathrobe. He had

41

forgotten to turn the phonograph off. He had been listening to his favorite, an old Callas recording of *Aida*. I sat down on the couch and finished the scotch. I looked around the room. All of his belongings had become superfluous since last I saw them. They would collect dust and molder away until such time as the dead were resurrected or until someone carted them off. There was nothing in that apartment with which I was not intimately familiar.

Sometimes, when Saul was hugely drunk and hugely sentimental, he threatened to adopt me. The story he told was that his mother was a rich lady. Under the provisions of her will he was disinherited. All would pass to his children, if any. It pleased him to fantasize that he could make me the instrument of his own revenge by becoming my benefactor. Saul was a man who not only enjoyed his practical jokes, but one who insisted on having the last word.

To a certain extent he was serious about the matter of adoption. Once we even consulted a lawyer. The lawyer assured us that if all was as Saul said, and he legally adopted me, I would indeed be his mother's sole heir. We planned luxury trips, fabulous spending sprees, but the technicalities were never worked out. Either he was in jail or I was. Either I was addicted or he was infatuated with someone else. Either I was too angry to be on speaking terms with him or he was too involved working out complex confidence schemes to bother himself with wills. In any case, his mother was now probably long dead. Probably there was never any money to begin with, no bequest. Nothing. What was there was a bank book in one of his jacket pockets. There was a little over three hundred dollars in the account. I could forge his signature in my sleep. He himself had taught me how to do it. All the hints, all these decipherable signs—my mother's telephone number, the lock that matched the key, the easily discovered bank book—might have been left deliberately. He always did find it imperative to impose himself on me when I was least prepared for responsibility. His sense of humor demanded such satisfaction. But if he had prepared a joke, the joke had backfired. Three hundred dollars was not enough for private burial, too much for the public pauper's cemetery on Hart's Island, and just enough to cover the cost of cremation.

"Saul," I whispered, "you're going to get burned."

I could hear him laughing uproariously.

"Sinbad, my boy, there comes a time when one aims for a star and settles for a chorus girl."

I started to laugh with him.

Alcohol on top of tuinals induces a sense of well-being and an overwhelming desire for sleep. I felt that I was reeling. Street signs blurred in a crazy rainbow of traffic lights. I tried not to fall as I dodged a passing car, pirouetted grotesquely, and found myself outside of Tricks.

I paid no admission because the bouncer at the door knew me well. Tricks was mobbed as usual. It was well into the cocktail hour. All the dancers on the tiny stage were males. Most were men, some were boys. There were solo performers who thrashed out at the air and thrust their bodies forward into suggestive postures. Others swayed, embracing partners, crushing pelvis against pelvis. A strobe alternately froze and released the scene. A mirror ball sprayed splotches of light across the dancers. From underneath the glass brick floor lights flickered from blue to violet, then exploded into red. In front of the stage men and older teenagers were packed three deep. I wondered if somewhere in their midst I might find Salvador. Sunshine was seated in his favorite corner far at the end of the bar. I waved at him. He waved back and, smiling, elbowed his way through the press of bodies. He said something I couldn't hear. I yelled in his ear that Saul was dead. He kept smiling. I yelled louder. He stopped smiling.

His hotel was right around the corner. We sat in his room passing a bottle of Dewar's back and forth. Dewar's was Saul's brand. My head felt woozy. We kept trying to make conversation, but I was disoriented and he was very drunk. We were both incoherent. When we got to stumbling over each other's pauses we just shut up and drank the rest of the bottle in silence.

I met Sunshine before I knew Saul and knew Saul because I had known Sunshine. They were close friends. Through the years I sought our Sunshine only when I felt particularly self-destructive or compelled to chastise Saul. Each time we parted company I felt soiled. He is well over sixty now, a squat-brown-skinned man with the face and heart of a toad. Behind the deteriorating flesh is an avaricious child, restless, rootless, good for nothing but good times, who fawns on friends and foes indifferently. We used each

43

other to fill certain specific needs. I have always despised him. After the scotch was gone we both passed out.

I awoke drenched in sweat. Sunshine lay fully clothed beside me on the bed, snoring peacefully. Out of habit I went through his pockets. He had a ten, two singles, and some change. I took it all for old times' sake. In the refrigerator I found a can of beer. Just one can. I took that too. I left him there in his shabby room and closed the door quietly behind me.

The mother watches the sleep of the boy. She is jealous of his apparent serenity. What right has he to peace when peace eludes her? The clock ticks off the seconds. The boy sleeps on his back, his mouth slightly open. One of his arms is crossed over his eyes, the other clutches the pillow to his chest. The mother admires the boy's beauty, knowing that it will be a source of suffering for him soon. She had not brought the boy into the world willingly. God, not she, had given him life. The boy was God's visitation on the woman. She had seen into God's heart and could not forgive what she saw there.

She bears God no grudge. Indeed, she loves Him. God has graced her with a private revelation. It has been revealed to her that God is capable of deliberate cruelty. His malice is infinite. This knowledge makes her love him that much more.

If she cannot forgive God, then God dare not forgive her. Through long hours of prayer she has freed herself from the bonds of repentance. She prays not to God but to God's mother. The mother of God displeased her Son. The plan of salvation requires a mother's endurance and strength, the certainty that through her son the mother can triumph over the world. The clock ticks on.

The statue of the Black Virgin is illuminated by the flickering black candles set on the small shrine beneath her feet. Twisted around the shrine are garlands of decaying flowers, rosaries, offerings of pungent, overripe fruit. The window is shut and crimson drapes are drawn in front of it. No sunlight is permitted to penetrate this room. The mother knows that she has become barren and is pleased. Her mouth tastes of bitter gall. Above her the Son's wounds gape. The heart of the Black Virgin is flintlike. Though it is stone, it can be chipped and worn down. She is the Mother who gives all and receives nothing. The mother relishes her spiritual tribulations, requiring them to bear witness to her living wounds. Her intentions are confused and trail off into nothingness.

The boy dreams. Turning slowly over onto his side he whimpers and hugs his knees to his chest. The pillow falls to the floor. She bends over him, pulling the blanket up to his chin, though it is stifling in the room. She inhales the scent of his maleness and frowns. Is it that, in truth, the mother gives nothing, nothing, and in turn receives all? She thinks of her own mother and dismisses her from her mind—old, superstitious, vengeful, inconsequential in the scheme of things. What scheme of things? As she forgets the question she remembers the answer. Woman is a vessel. Break the vessel and the seed is scattered on the ground. God, after all, expects her to sin. The Son knows that she will sin. Passing from gross error into heresy she smiles. It is His Will that I sin.

She cannot sit still. Others require her attention. She approaches their corner and selects a red candle, examines it, hesitates, and at last lights it. She passes her hand in benediction over the flame. A fly alights on the back of her hand.

She opens her purse, picks out a few pennies, and places them carefully alongside a cigar which lies on a paper plate. She thinks of the two white doves she will purchase tomorrow. She sees herself holding a dove in her hand, cooing to it, soothing it. Her fingers search for the tiny pulse in the fluttering creature's neck. She tests the sharpness of the blade with her thumb. The knife slashes the soft throat. Blood gushes and spurts. Her hand is awash in the blood of the dove. The second bird squawks in terror, straining frantically against the metal band that tethers its legs. Tomorrow.

She rearranges the pennies on the paper plate. Satisifed with the configuration she has achieved she carries the plate to the Black Virgin's shrine, she is content to share the Mother's bitterness, she is content to watch and wait for the sacrifice to come. She fuels the lamp, keeps the flame, wards off intruders. Let the boy sleep, she thinks, he will need his strength. Yes, certainly he will need all the strength he can muster. In her mind she forges a

suffocating bond with the boy, seized as she is with an uncontrollable urge to wound him so that she may bind up his wounds.

I didn't want to do it in the park again. The first time, well, I just
got carried away. I was high and everything and I just didn't know
any better. Then when I started remembering about it I said,
Jesus, supposing a cop would of come by or something, I mean
while he was doing it to me and all. Supposing one of the guys from
around the block hadda come by. I mean, we were right there out
in the open. Anything coulda happened. So what if not too many
people know about that place behind the bushes. I knew about it.
The guy Mitch knew about it, so who knows how many other
people besides us two know about it?

The thing was I was getting tired of sitting on that dumb rock
all the time. I mean, how long can a guy just sit around on his butt
watching the rowboats go by. Jesus, you seen one you seen 'em all.
Then I figured well maybe I'll patch up the old kite and see how
she goes and I even started fixing her up. Then I just threw it all in
the garbage. Here I'm supposed to be the guy which cold-cocked
Chino acting like a little kid who still plays around with kites. So
that was no good neither.

Here I was I didn't know what to do with myself. The guys in
the club, well, I'll say this, that they didn't bother me but still,
they weren't exactly what you would call friendly. Plus I was broke
which my mother she never gives me any money and my grandma,
she'd give it to me if I asked but she got troubles just taking care of
herself, her being on Welfare and all.

What I usta do was break into a candy store once in a while,
you know, just go right up on the roof and swing yourself in the
window from the fire escape or whatever and then just scoop up
whatever they left lying around, like cigarettes and candy and all,
because, of course, they never leave no money around when they
lock up at night and then in the morning what I'd do is sell the
cigarettes to another store someplace else. It was all just little-kid
shit which all the kids do it, but at least I had enough to go to the
movies or buy an ice cream or soda or a joint or two. But after the

cops came to the house I figured I'd better be cool for a while. I
mean, Jesus, with that club shit I hadda nuff trouble to hold me
and I didn't need no more.

So there really wasn't much I could do when you think about
it except goof around the park and wait for school to open which I
knew I was gonna play hooky more than I'd be there anyhow. All I
could do was climb rocks or sit on the bridge where I went with
Mitch and take off my sneakers and stick my feet under this little
waterfall they got there.

Pretty soon I got to realize that I kept seeing the same guys
hanging around all the time. I mean they weren't guys, they were
really faggots. Some of them you didn't have to be no big brain to
figure out, which a guy who's swishing around giggling like a little
girl, I mean, you know he's a faggot, right? But they didn't bother
me so I didn't bother them, which is my motto live and let live I
always say. Which I guess if a guy wants to be a faggot and swish all
around and all, that's his business, as long as he don't bother you,
at least that's the way I look at it. Now Mitch, I'll say one thing for
him, the time I went with him at least he didn't look like a faggot so
if someone had of come by which knew me I coulda said he was my
teacher or my uncle or something and they couldn't of told he was
a faggot because he didn't look like nothing but an ordinary guy.

But there were other guys who usta walk around the bridge
that didn't look like faggots and they would start talking to me, just
asking me dumb questions out of the clear blue sky, but, I mean,
they hadda have some reason just to come up to some strange kid
and start asking him a lot of stupid stuff which you know they
hadda have something else on their minds, like Mitch did.

Like this one nigger he comes up to me and asks me what time
it is and I could see plain as day that he was wearing a watch, so
why would he be asking me what time it is. So I go how come you
wanna know what time it is when you gotta watch and I don't, what
are you some kinda faggot or something which if that's what's
happening you better haul ass before I call a cop. That's what I told
him, I swear I did, and besides I can't stand niggers which is not
only because I can't stand the way they all think they're so slick all
the time and meanwhile they ain't nothing but plain dumb niggers
like the nigger that asked me for the time.

Also there was this Chinese guy. He was real old and came up

47

and just stood on the bridge staring at me, which I hate people staring at me, and he didn't say one single word, but I could tell he wanted to just the same. He just stood there smiling at me until I felt all creepy so I put on my sneakers and tipped.

Another time this other guy kept on following me, I mean, practically all day. Everywhere I went there he was right behind me so finally I got disgusted and I go, hey mister are you following me and he goes, following you? Like he didn't hear me or something which I know damn well he hadda hear me so I go, yeah, you heard me I asked you was you following me so I go, yeah, you heard me I askded you was you following me and he goes, no, why should I be following you and I go, that's what I want to know. And he goes, no, why should I be following you and I go, because you are. So he goes, I'm just out taking a walk, I'm not following you. So I go, well it looks like you are which if you're following me you'd better cut it out right now. So he goes away and I'm sitting there on the bridge with my feet in the water when here he comes again, the same guy but this time he comes right up to me and goes, hi, I see you're still here and I go, yeah, I'm still here and I see you're still following me. And he goes, no, I come here all the time too and then he goes, can I ask you a question? And I go, sure you can ask me a question but I don't hafta answer it if I don't feel like it. And he goes, how would you like to make some money. And I go, doing what? And he goes, well. . . .

That's it. That's all he says is 'well', so I go, well, my left ball. Whatta I gotta do to make this money? And he goes, well, you know . . . have a good time and all. Then I go, whatta you mean by having a good time and all and he goes, well . . . you know. Me, I get fed up with all this crap about 'well' and 'you know' and I say, listen . . you want me to make some money you tell me how, you just tell me so then I know whether I want to do it or not. So he goes, don't you know? And I tell him, yeah . . I know. I know how you want me to make the money but I want you to say it just what exactly I gotta do. Which he stands there with his mouth open and I say to myself, fuck this bullshit and I just tip. Sure I know he wanted to blow me like Mitch did it, but at least with Mitch it wasn't all this bullshit about "you know" and "well" and "you wanna" and all that crap. We just sorta did it and that was that. I gotta admit I wouldn't mind being blowed again because I can't say

I didn't like it, but not by a creep like this guy that was following me around the park all day.

What I'm trying to say is that you can't tell right off about guys just by looking at them, whether they're faggots and all and a lot of them are not only faggots but they're weird like the nigger and the Chink and the guy just now and I'm plain fed up with all these weird guys hanging out staring at me and decide to cut out of the park when who do I see walking down the path towards me but Mitch. Well, as soon as I see him I know I've been bullshitting myself all along and the reason I've been sitting on the bridge for so long is that I wanted Mitch to find me again which is also maybe why I wouldn't let none of those other guys do it because I only wanted to do it with Mitch. Don't ask me why, that's just the way it was.

Well, Mitch sees me and he smiles and starts to wave at me and I'm glad to see him too. There's no sense me bullshitting about it and pretending that I don't remember him so I smile too and I go, hi. And he goes, hi yourself. Which is not much of a conversation but still I can tell he's like he was before and all which I could tell then that he liked me even when we were walking from the hot dog stand I knew he was nice and all and that he wouldn't hurt me.

And he goes, "I was hoping I'd catch up with you again."

And I go, "Yeah, well I told you I'm always around. I been around a lot but I haven't seen you ."

And he goes, "Well, I was looking for you down by the hot dog stand and over by the rock where you said you always go."

"You couldn't of found me there because I stopped going there but I forgot I told you that's where I usually hang out."

"I didn't think I'd find you here, though."

"How come?"

"I just didn't think you'ld come around here."

"Come on, you can tell me how come. You mean because of all the guys around here being faggots, is that why?"

And Mitch, he don't say nothing. He stops dead in his tracks and looks at me kinda funny like, like he's embarrassed or he don't know what to say, or maybe both.

So I go, "Well, I wasn't calling you a faggot when I said that. I didn't mean to hurt your feelings. Anyhow, you don't look like a faggot and besides, I guess whatever you do and you mind your own business, that's your business. At least that's the way I look at it."

Mitch, I can tell by his face that I said the right thing and he knows I didn't mean to insult him or hurt his feelings. He starts to say something, but I wanna finish what I was telling him and all, so I go, "And another thing, if you're thinking maybe I went with anybody around here and let him do it, well you're wrong because I didn't. A lot of guys wanted me to and I didn't. And another thing, which I don't hafta tell you is that you're the only guy I ever let do it to me and that's the truth."

Now Mitch, he's really smiling and he like pats my shoulder like maybe your teacher or somebody would do and he goes, "I'm glad to hear that, I really am."

"Glad to hear what, that I didn't mean to hurt your feelings or about not letting other guys do it?"

"What do you think?"

And he laughs and I laugh too. And I think, it's kinda funny, him being a grown man and all I feel like I can talk to him and forget about him being a grown man like we was friends or something, just say whatever comes into my head and tell him the truth, how I feel about things and all.

"We're just walking and talking like two buddies and I ask him, "You got any more of that smoke?"

"Sure," he says, "I always have a little." And he stops again in the middle of the path like he wants to ask me something but like he's ashamed to and then he goes, "Do you want to go back to that same place to smoke?" which of course I know he don't only mean smoke. "No," I tell him, because I wanna tell him the truth, "I don't wanna go back there."

And Mitch, now he looks all insulted again, like wow, everything I say seems to get him going and I go, "It's not what you think. It's not that at all. You think I don't wanna do it no more, but that's not so. I do. But I'll tell you the truth, I'm scared to do it in the park again because a cop might come by or maybe somebody I know or something."

Mitch, he pats my shoulder again and goes,

"How about coming with me to where I live?"

"Where's that?"

"Downtown?"

"Downtown where? I mean if I'm gonna go there you can trust me that I'm not gonna tell. I didn't tell anybody before, did I? And besides I always like to know where I'm going before I go there."

"I understand. Do you know where Forty-seventh Street is?"

"Yeah, sure I know, that's down by the Square which is where I go to the movies on Forty-second. Is that where you live?"

"Right off Tenth Avenue."

"Down by the river?"

"A block or two away."

"Gee, that's a pretty crummy neighborhood."

"I guess you're right, it is pretty crummy."

I never did tell him it was ok to go, to go to the place where he lives, but I guess we both know that I'm gonna go with him because by now we're on the road that leads out of the park. Mitch, he ain't saying too much, like he's trying to figure things out like maybe he shouldn't trust me and let me know where he lives, but me, I can't shut up. There's a million things I wanna ask him and he'll see, I won't tell.

"Mitch, do you live by yourself? I mean, I guess you're not married or nothing, being a faggot and all."

Jesus Christ, I did it again. Every time I say "faggot" he looks like he wants to find a hole in the ground to crawl into. But for Chrissakes, you gotta call a spade a spade. I mean, he is a faggot, even though he don't look like one. I mean, if that's what he likes then why does he get so upset every time I say the word?

"How come you don't like me saying 'faggot'? Is that why you always go like that, looking all funny, because I call you a faggot? You ain't mad are you?"

"I'm not mad."

"Well, you sure look like you are. Jesus, I mean, you don't look like a faggot, if that's what you're worried about. You're not swishy and all like faggots which you can tell they're faggots. So what's so bad? I mean, it's just a word. I don't mean nothin' by it. It's the only word I know for it. It's no big deal. But wait a minute, how 'bout instead of faggot I say 'queer,' is that better?"

Well, I must said something funny because he really cracks up.

"That's fine, don't worry about it. I know you don't mean any harm."

51

And right there he grabs me and hugs me. He hugs me real hard and pulls me close to him and he's still laughing a little bit. Me, I guess I should be embarrassed standing there getting hugged like I was a little kid right in the middle of the park, plus I really don't know him at all. But I don't really mind it. I know he's trying to show me that everything is ok. And besides, he don't look like a faggot, I mean "queer," so I guess nobody would think anything about what he's doing and when he's through hugging me, he puts his arm around my shoulder and we keep on walking again.

I go, "Come on, you didn't answer my question. You ain't married are you?"

"No, I'm not married anymore."

"Does that mean you was? You really was married once? To a lady and all? Did she know you was a fa—did she know you was a queer?"

"Probably."

"You mean you actually told her?"

"No, I didn't exactly tell her, but women can tell things like that about men. Especially wives."

"You mean a lady can tell by looking at you that you're a queer?"

"No, no. Nobody can look at you and tell anything about how you are inside. But if you're married your wife can tell. There are ways. Little things she notices."

By this time we're out of the park altogether and he goes, "Well, we can catch the subway across the street."

Me, I got a million things I wanna ask him about, like how can ladies tell whether a guy is queer and all about how it feels to be married and be a queer too, a million things, so I go, "Can't we walk?"

"It's a long walk."

"I don't mind. I'm usta walking a lot. But if you're in a rush or something, if you are, we could take the train."

"No." He smiles, "I'm in no hurry."

"Ok, let's walk then, just you and me, ok?"

"Ok."

"Did ya, you know, do it with kids then, when you was married?"

52

Boom. There he goes again with that look. He does it every time.

"I mean, if you don't want me asking you alla these questions, I can shut up. It's just that I wanna know about this stuff, you know?"

"No, I don't mind you asking questions. It's just that there are a lot of things I don't usually talk to . . . . people about."

"You mean to kids . . . that you go with?"

"Because most . . . most of the people I meet aren't interested in talking. Most of them just want to . . . ."

"To do it and not talk about it, right?"

"Yes, that's right, to do it and not talk about it."

"But you don't mind me talking about it?"

"No, I don't mind."

"Well, so answer me then."

"Answer you about what? You ask so many questions that I don't know which one to answer." And he laughs again.

"About the first one I asked you. Do you live alone or what?"

"I live by myself, now. Alone."

"What happened to your wife?"

"She went away."

"She got a divorce?"

"No. She went away. She lives by herself now, too. Just like that."

"And you live by yourself, all alone?"

"That's what I said."

"Don't you ever get lonesome?"

"Lonesome? Why should I get lonesome?"

"I get lonesome and I don't even live by myself. I live with my mother and stepfather sometimes and sometimes I'm lonesome when I'm living with them plus I gotta little brother and sister too."

"No, I can't say I'm lonesome. I like living by myself."

"How 'bout your mother? Don't you ever see your mother?"

"No."

"How come?"

"Because we don't get along and when you don't get along with someone, like your mother, it's better if you don't see them."

"I bet it's because she knows, about you being queer. Is that why you don't see her?"

53

"That's part of it. Do you mind. I'm not angry, really I'm not, but I'd rather not talk about my mother."

"Can I tell you something? I mean, you won't think I'm crazy or nothing?"

"Sure you can. Go ahead."

"Well, I don't really get along with my mother either, so I can understand about how it is with you and all. So ok, we won't talk about mothers. What do you wanna talk about?"

"What do you feel like talking about?"

"Would you be mad if I asked you another question?"

"How do I know whether I'll be mad or not if I don't know what you want to ask?"

"Well, promise you won't be mad."

"I said I wouldn't be mad."

"But you gotta promise. Say you promise."

"I promise."

"Well, just remember you promised. Do you do it all the time with a lot of kids? I mean a real lot? See, you're getting mad, I can tell, and you promised."

"You tricked me," he goes, but he's not mad. He's grinning.

"No, I didn't trick you either. I asked you and you promised and now you gotta tell me."

"No."

"No, you won't tell me?"

"No, I don't run around all the time with a lot of kids. I'm not like that. Really. I don't want you to think I'm like that."

"But you are a queer?"

"Yes."

"Mitch?"

"Yes?"

"When you first saw me down by the hot dog stand, how did you know?"

"How did I know what?"

"How did you know I was gonna go with you? How did you know I was gonna let you do it to me?"

"I didn't know."

"Then how come you picked me? Supposing I hadden of wanted to. Supposing I was a dumb little kid or something and, you know, when you started touching me, I got scared or something and yelled for a cop."

"I can't really explain it, how I didn't think that was going to happen. Didn't you ever feel you knew something about a person, he was gentle and kind and wouldn't hurt you. You can tell just by looking at someone that you don't have to be afraid of him, can't you?"

"I guess so."

"Well?"

"I guess I understand."

"Mitch?"

"Yes."

"Answer me one more question, just one more, please? Mitch? Do I look like a queer?"

"Of course not. Of course you don't look like that."

So the rest of the time we're walking I think about that and there's other things I want to ask him which one of the main ones is how come if I don't look like a queer, then how come he could tell just by looking at me that I'd let him do it because if I looked like to him that I'd let him do it, then I gotta look like a queer, right? But by this time we get to where his apartment is which I knew already was in a real crummy neighborhood. Mitch, he lives in one of those fucked up buildings where they don't even have mailboxes because the junkies rip them off all the time. You walk up the stoop and you gotta have a key to open the outside door because there's no buzzers either.

His apartment is on the ground floor and it ain't too bad. I mean, at least it's clean and all so you could see that he took care of it even if the building is pretty cruddy. What there is, is one room, which even that isn't too big. There's a couch and a big chair and a TV and a dresser and a kitchen table and a couple of little chairs to go with the kitchen table and that's about it.

Mitch, he pulls out the couch into a bed which I wonder if he's tired or something and sits down on the edge of it. Me, I'm just standing there like some kinda dummy because I don't know what to do or where I'm supposed to sit down. Then Mitch lights up a joint and I go over and sit down in the big chair and we sit and smoke up.

"Would you like to hear some music?"

"I don't mind."

What he puts on is some real cornball stuff that sounds like it's somebody's funeral or something. Me, I don't like that kinda sound, but I can't say nothing 'cause it's his house and I guess he can listen to any kinda music he wants to in his own house. So we just sit there and I'm high, but not like the first time in the park. Something's different. Maybe it's that he's not talking much. What I mean is that he's stopped talking completely. He just sits there like a bump on a log, looking kinda sad and cracking his knuckles and I sit there like a dummy too, trying to figure out if I said something wrong or something and what happened all of a sudden to make him so sad. Maybe it's all that cornball music. To tell the truth the smoke made me a little bit high but it also gave me a splitting headache. Finally Mitch goes,

"Well?"

And I go, "Well." Which is not exactly what you could call a very intelligent conversation and then I go, "Well, I mean we finished smoking and all, so, I mean, are you ready to do it now?"

And Mitch goes, "ok," but he still sits there cracking his knuckles and I don't know what I'm supposed to do. I mean, I never went to nobody's house like this. He knows that. I told him so, that I never did it with anybody else, so I go, "Well, how do you wanna do it? You want me to sit here or lie back like last time, or what?"

"Why don't you get undressed, take your clothes off, and get comfortable?"

"Why, why should I do that? Why do I gotta take off all my clothes?"

"It's more comfortable. It's better that way."

"You mean get all undressed, even my sneakers?"

"Sure, why not. You don't have to, but. . . ."

"I don't mind. It just seems kinda funny, that's all."

I feel stupid being all naked in front of him because my dick is on a bone and I don't want him thinking that I'm just a horny kid that does it with everyone which his dick is hard all the time and it's kinda funny that time in the club I wasn't ashamed at all to strip and let all the guys see me and watch me too while I was humping Maria which I don't like to think about that whole time because

56

those guys were dead wrong doing what they did even though she shoulda knew what was gonna happen. But I figure, why should I be embarrassed. I mean, after all, I came here with him and all and I knew what I was coming here for, I think. So I get into the bed with him and lay down and he was right, it is more comfortable this way, and feels better too because there's a few things he does now that he didn't do in the park. And after a while, you know, when he's doing it, he asks me to do something to him which I say to myself shit, no, if I do that then it really is that I'm a queer. But then what he's doing starts feeling real real good and I say to myself, well, why not, he's making me feel so good and all he wants to do is feel good hisself and I guess I wouldn't mind it too much as long as I don't get to feeling sick while I'm doing it. So I go,

"Mitch?"

"Mmmm."

"Promise me one thing?"

"Mmm-hmmm."

"Mitch, promise me you won't ever tell anybody, if I do it, you promise?"

"Mmm-hmm."

"And Mitch, one more thing. Promise you won't hurt me."

After it's over and we both got our clothes on again we smoke another joint, but for some reason all it does is give me a headache so I tell him maybe I oughta be going and he says, ok he'll walk me to the subway which I tell him I ain't no little kid which you gotta take to the subway. I know how to travel by myself and all he gotta do is tell me where the train station is and give me a token so I can get on the train. Mitch, he tells me where the station is which is the same one I got off at when I come downtown to go to the movies. But he don't have a token. What he does is give me a whole five-dollar bill.

"Mitch, I ain't got change of this. If I had change I wouldn't of asked you for a token."

"That's ok. That's yours."

"Mine?"

"Go take yourself to a movie or something. I'm sure you know how to spend it. You earned it, enjoy it."

So that's it. What he's doing is giving me the money to pay me for letting him do it to me and for what I did too. Maybe he doesn't

57

know how that makes me feel. The thing about it is if I throw it in his face that'll hurt his feelings and if I keep it . . .? I don't like it. I don't like it one bit. I really thought he likeded me, I thought even if he is a grown man we could be friends and all. But I guess I was just being dumb. I guess that's the way it happens all the time. He does it with any kid he can find and then gives him money so he won't tell which if he really liked me and could tell about people by looking at them he would of known I'd never tell anybody. Never. But I guess he was bullshitting all along just so he could do what he wanted to. Well, I'm glad I learned how he was. I can be the same way too. So I put the money in my pocket and he goes,

"Will I see you again?"

I feel like telling him to go piss off and find himself another kid to do it to. I'm steaming mad, but I go,

"I don't care."

"When?"

"Tomorrow, if you want. I don't care."

"Ok, tomorrow. Here? About twelve. Is that all right?"

Me, I'm already halfway down the stoop. I figure what the hell, let me walk over to the river and check out the boats and shit and maybe then I'll shoot over to the Automat on Forty-second and get me some franks and beans and then I'll check out a flick. I wanted to tell him how mad I was and that if he wanted to give me money he didn't hafta do it that way, but I guess there's no sense because if he really liked me he woulda known about how mad I'd get.

I know I'll be back tomorrow and the next day too if he wants. Why not? I ain't nothing to him, so he ain't nothing to me. That's just the way it is and to tell the truth, it feels pretty good having a few bucks in my pocket again.

When I was young I recognized that it was simply not in me to be an uncritical disciple treading well-traveled paths. It was my lot to be a voyager, an explorer, and what sort of explorer carries a road map in his pocket? I knew that my journey would be a solitary one which would require the taking of risks. And the everyday world suffocated me. I was willing to chance anything to experience the marvelous. I believed that at journey's end time could be conquered. Then I would finally tear away the last veil and come upon certainty. But that time never arrived. There was never a magical moment when I could see clearly into the heart of things, into the hearts of others, into my own heart, and know that I had finally authenticated myself. Now I have no obligations to myself. I am responsible to him alone.

Sunshine, as I expected, did not show up for the cremation. Neither did anyone else. Inevitably I am his only mourner. Mourning, he said, is healing. Mourning, I add, is but vanity. I reject the mourning and the healing for both are far too self-indulgent. But I accept the vanity and feel no shame in admitting it. He has both filled me and emptied me and he is responsible for nothing.

In the end our torments are chosen for us only by ourselves. The only demand we make on those we claim to love is that they become accomplices to their own ultimate rejection. Each of us is entangled in webs we weave of our own intentions, webs with which we bind ourselves, by accident or design, to our own lives and become our own adversaries.

Once the spell is broken, once the gossamer fabric is unraveled and the morning dewdrops vanish in the dying sun, then neither wish nor touch of fairy wand can stay whatever is to come from coming when it will—in winds, in storms, in cosmic fire, in the outermost depths of starless space. And in the end, too, there will be God, weary perhaps, but still petulant enough to play his pranks upon a world long wearied of his improvisations.

2

Autumn

Hippolytus: *My mother was an Amazon, my wildness which
you think strange, I suckled at her breast.*

Racine, *Phaedre*

THE WORD TODAY IS ECSTASY is what the voice was saying in
the dream.

I'm in a dark place, like a forest, with all trees and shit and the
leaves are dripping wet. In the middle of the forest is this lake. I
know it's deep, real deep, and pitch black too, all the way down to
the bottom where there's nothing but slimy gook. Somebody is
swimming in the lake. Not swimming really, but like treading
water without using their hands. It sounds crazy, but that's what
was happening, they were just sort of floating with the top part of
their body out of the water. He? She? I couldn't tell because their
back was turned to me. They had long black hair down to the waist.
I came closer. I could tell they were naked. I wanted to see who it
was. I was scared of the lake, but I had to see . . .

. . . the word today is ecstasy

I'm awake.

The radio had been on all night. It's just a shitty box I boosted
somewhere but it plays pretty good. I never change the station.
Why should I? Everybody I know listens to the same station all the
time. The voice was the announcer saying that today's word is
ecstasy. They got this same dude on every morning and every
morning he's got a new word for the day which is always corny.

Today the word is ecstasy. The announcer says that ecstasy means a state of great pleasure. I think about the State of New York and the State of New Jersey and I want to bust out laughing thinking about the State of Pleasure. That would really be far out. I can just see all the down and desperate dudes all together in the State of Pleasure, all the hustlers and pimps, all the speed freaks and sex-changes, all the fat chicken hawks and con men, the bums, the weirdos, the winos, the cripples and freaks. I mean, I see all of them, all the desperados just taking off and hightailing it across the border to the State of Pleasure. The announcer says it's twelve minutes past six in the morning.

Fuck the State of Pleasure. I got a bitch of a headache and I stop smiling, fast. I look around. Well, it's a hotel room, that's for sure, but I have no idea which hotel. They all look the same to me, the ones I crash in. The walls are always painted shit green and there's plaster all over the floor and a chair which if you sat in you'd fall flat on your ass. This one don't even have a shitter, just a sink and about three quarters of a mirror I can't see outside because one of us musta pulled down the shade last night and if I didn't hear the radio I wouldn't of known whether it was the middle of the night or what.

A fat guy is in the bed with me. Except that he is wearing polka-dot drawers, he is buck naked. He looks like a fucking beached whale or something, snoring and snorting on his back.

Well, wherever it is I am, it gotta be somewhere around the Square. Where else do they have shit-heap dumps like this?

My head hurts so bad I wonder if I got another migraine coming on. Every fucking nerve in my body says lay there, don't get up or you'll be sorry, but I got too much to take care of today. I half lay there and half sit up hoping that somehow I could figure out when we got here. Did I pick up at the Program yesterday or not? Nope, I can't remember either way. Ok, what day is it? I draw a complete blank, not even a guess. It's ridiculous. I don't even know what month it is. What month is it, I gotta know what month it is. Ok, guess. September, October? My mouth tastes like the bottom of a bird cage.

I nearly collapse when I get up to piss in the sink. There's no hot water, so I run some cold water over my head and splash the back of my neck. The headache is better, a little. At least I can stop squinting and open my eyes. Then I realize I'm sick. Not very sick, but sick. Sick enough to know definitely that I did not go to the Program yesterday. How about the day before? Well, I'm gonna have to think of some excuse to tell them.

The whale is still snorting. He's a real beauty, the whale. Got this thick curly hair all over his chest and stomach and legs. Well, at least he's white. As Saul would say, "Thank God for small favors." When did I meet the whale? His little cock is hanging out of the slit in his drawers. He's a real beauty, the whale is.

What I got to find out is what I'm gonna start the day with. While I pull on my pants I check out the pockets. A couple of loose tuinals. Tuinals? No handkerchief. No dough. An empty meth bottle. No dough. The bottle has my name on it and an October date. Bingo, at least I know what month it is, or do I? When did I pick up the bottle. No dough, no gap. Didn't I get my dough before we got down? Or did the whale beat me? I shake out my socks and a ten-dollar bill falls out of one of them.

When I'm fucked up on pills or smoke or booze, but not fucked up so bad that I don't know I'm fucked up, I get paranoid and hide things. The only thing is that I hide the shit from myself. I'm fucked up enough to know that if I don't hide the shit somewhere I'm gonna get beat for it but I can never remember the next day where I hid it. I'm just lucky I found the dime, otherwise I might still be on my hands and knees peeling up the fucking linoleum to see if I hid any gap underneath.

Well, at least I got enough gap to start the day off with. When I'm dressed I go through the whale's pants. He got a couple of dollars, some change, and a token which of course I take all of it but leave the dude his pants. If I'm scared that they're gonna wake up or something, I tip with their pants too. Not too many dudes wanna go chasing you down the street with no pants and their dicks hanging out. But the whale is out for the count. I don't take his pants, but I open the window and throw his shoes out and that's that. I tip.

There's no elevator so I gotta walk five flights down. A humpback is working behind the desk blowing into a container of coffee. The humpback looks like he hates the world. I tell him my uncle upstairs got the key. He knows I got no uncle and he don't give a fuck. He just keeps blowing on his coffee.

I'm standing on Forty-third Street between Eighth and Seventh and this fleabag which I didn't know from inside is where I crash at least a couple of times a week. It's a trick hotel where hooers and Johns take their tricks. I wonder why I don't remember seeing the humpback before. Two hooers are leaning against the building across the street. One has a silver wig on. The other got an orange one. Both of them are wearing them plastic mini-minis which you can see the crack in their ass and both of them are also as black and ugly as the ace of spades. Nasty black bitches. Me, as the saying goes, I'm Puerto Rican and I'm proud even though I never been to Puerto Rico in my life and the only thing I could be proud about is maybe that I can just make it through another day. At least I'm not an ugly black nigger hooer.

Let me tell you if you don't know already, New York hooers are the nastiest, meanest, and most treacherous around. They'd cut your heart out for a dime, especially the niggers around the Square. They trick all day and they're always broke, every one of them, because they're all strung out. What they don't shoot in their arms they give to their pimps. All nigger pimps look alike to me. They all think they're Superfly and they all got wide hats and long shoes plus they all got big coke noses and big hogs which they drive up and down in all day. It's funny how that shit goes. The pimp beats up on his hooer, the hooer beats her tricks, the tricks go home and beat up on their old ladies, because they got beat, and their old ladies, they beat up on the kids, who are probably tricking themselves.

I can understand about the hooers, though. What the fuck, you ain't out doin' it because you enjoy it. Shit, if you enjoy tricking then you'll never survive because it will wind up with the trick tricking you off which makes you a chump. So naturally, if you know you're never gonna see the trick again, fuck it, you're gonna rip him off, no doubt about it. You ain't gonna go out of your way to hurt him, I mean, but you're gonna rip him off and if he tries to stop you, look out, then somebody may get hurt and better him than me. That's the way I see it. I made that mistake when I first started hanging out. I was small and didn't know no better and I got beat all the time by tricks, all the time. Never had nothin' and was fucked up too, until I learned better. But one thing I never thought of was having a pimp. The only hustler I know gotta pimp is Trizie, but she's a sex-change which I guess don't count.

I figure I might as well head down to the Square because I still got two hours to go until the Program opens. I'm not gonna walk uptown because then I gotta pass the two hooers and they'll say something slick and I'll hafta say something slick back and I'm in no mood right now to get hooked up in that kinda shit. It's too fucking early in the morning.

When I was twelve I was ashamed for anybody to see me walking with a dude,. you know, a trick. I didn't want anybody to know what I was doing. But a lot changes in four years. I don't think there's anybody around the Square that doesn't know that I'm a hustler. So what? All I'm doing is trying to get over just like everybody else. And I'll tell you another thing: I sure as shit don't get chumped off anymore and that's a fact.

Saul says I'm a typical Pisces. A Pisces, he says, is a fish. "Ergo, my boy, your element is water." I don't like water, I tell him. "Mmmph, you like booze. . . . take my word for it, you're a creature of the deep. You're slippery as an eel . . . nobody can pin you down. You're highly emotional and you always fuck up your money." So that's a Pisces, I say. And he goes, yes that's a Pisces, you're a typical Pisces.

It's all bullshit to me. He didn't have to be a fucking fortune teller to figure that one out, about me being slippery and fucking up my money. But Saul, he's never happy unless he's running some kind of game on you, that's just the way he is.

The program, now there's a pain in the ass. They won't give me anything to walk with except on Sundays. Six days a week I gotta get my ass up to pick up there, but I guess it beats being strung out. One time I stole some money from the Reverend and I went to Key West. I hitchhiked all the way down. No problems. I went crabbing in the ocean. In school we learned that Key West is at the end of America. I liked the idea of being at the end of something.

While I was down there I kicked my jones—shit I was just a little kid, practically. When I ran out of dough I started hitchhiking home. In North Carolina it was funny. The cops busted me. I was in a car with a trick blowing me. The cops gave him a beating and put him in jail and they gave me a bus ticket to New York. I cashed in the ticket and hitched to Roanoke, because that's where the guy was going. In Roanoke I copped and got off. A week after I came back to the City I had a hundred-and-eighty-dollar-a-day habit, and that's no shit, a hundred and eighty dollars.

The thing about methadone is that it's legalized dope. They gradually build you up to a certain number of milligrams a day and when you get to a certain point you feel mellow every day and you can cut dope loose. If you shoot dope you won't feel it, so you don't shoot it. But a lot of guys skip a day or two and then get off and they can feel it fine. And when they're broke, they just go back for another bottle of meth. Also if the Welfare knows you're an addict, they won't give you welfare unless you get on a program. So what they're taking is one kind of junkie and making him into another junkie, a legal one though. Nobody knows what that shit will do to you if you drink it for a long time, because it only was invented in Germany under Adolph Hitler which is why it's called Dolophine. A medicine named after a maniac. A lot of people say it eats up the liver. It's a bitch to kick and it gets into all your bones and makes them brittle.

On Eighth Avenue there's a grocery which is open twenty-four hours a day. They ain't supposed to before eight, but the guy lets me cop a quart of cold Colt 45 which I use to wash down the tuinals with.

I chugalug the Colt. Alcohol helps bring the tuinals down fast, but you gotta be careful. If you take too many tuies with too much alcohol you can croak. I o-deed a lot like that. I still need my meth. It's a bitch to be hungry and sick at the same time. Next door is a tiny Greek luncheonette that I go to almost every morning. They give you a tiny little thing of orange juice and two eggs however you want them as long as you want them greasy, and a cuppa coffee worse than what they give you out on the Rock. But it's only ninety-seven cents and it's the only one that's open. I just hope I can keep the fucking eggs down. I pay the guy with one of the singles I geesed from the whale cause if I break the ten I know it'll be gone just like that.

65

To tell the truth I feel like I'm gonna throw up, that's how sick I feel. What I need is a drink, but of course it's still too early for the bars to be open which none of them open until eight. Nothing opens 'til eight in this fucking City.

It's so early that there aren't hardly any people out yet. The wind is blowing and it's as cold as a bitch. Some of the people heading into the subway I guess are going to work. The guys with briefcases and shit. The hustlers are just going home because the after-hours joints are just closing. I wonder what a guy thinks at six o'clock in the morning going to work past a dude who's been out partying all night and is just getting ready to crash. He probably figures, why work? You work you never got nothin' in the bank, anyhow. You hustle, you got nothin' in the bank either. So why work?

Me, I had jobs, plenty of jobs—messenger, stock in the supermarket, delivery. It's all a lot of shit. Whatever you do you gotta eat shit to keep the job. For what? So you can be a slob all your life? Shit, I can be a slob without working.

What I gotta do is kill almost an hour and a half until it's time for the program to open. Maybe I can turn a trick before then. This way I'll have some gap, enough to cop a bag of coke at least. I gotta set of gimmicks stashed in the can behind the shit bowl in some fleabag hotel near Saul's crib. Of course Saul he don't know that, about the gimmicks. If he ever found out he'd kick my ass from now until next Sunday.

I wonder when I spoke to Carmen last? Yesterday? Whenever, I remember she was bothering me about dough which she says she is pregnant and also says that the kid is mine. Well, maybe it is and then again maybe it ain't. I'll wait until I see what it looks like and it better not look like a black nigger. Anyhow, if the kid is mine I hope to Christ it's a boy. Girls are a royal pain in the ass. You always gotta worry about who's fucking them and then when you find out you gotta go fuck them up for fucking her. It's a pain in the ass. Shit, if the kid does look like me maybe I'll call him Saul. That would be a fucking laugh, a baby Puerto Rican named Saul.

I laugh and check out this pretty blonde hooer who's white and can't be no more than fifteen. She looks over her shoulder to check out whether I'm a trick following her or maybe a weirdo who's just laughing to himself. What a laugh. What a laugh! I left my radio back in the hotel room with the fucking whale!

I run all the way back because even though it's a cheap box I don't wanna blow it and hafta geese another. The humpback is still there reading a comic book. I go, did my uncle leave yet? He shakes his head and I run upstairs. There's a garbage can at the end of the hall. I pull out an empty beer bottle and crack it on the radiator. A broken beer bottle is a treacherous weapon, and you better believe it. I got twenty-two stitches from one once and I seen guys had both their eyes gouged out behind beer bottles. One thing is, I ain't gonna take no shit from this dude. I want my radio. And there it is, right on the table where I left it. Just as I go to reach for it the dumb fucker wakes up and goes, "Who? Who are you?" I tell him, "Cool, dude, I just left my box, you know, I just come back for my box . . . it ain't yours, right?" And before he can say something smart like "who" again I slam the door and leave him to figure out what happened and where the fuck his shoes went to. I don't think he even remembered who I was.

By the time I get outside, the street is already starting to get crowded. It's cold as a bitch and the people all look tired like they wished they was any other place in the world except here, having to get jammed into a subway to go to work. The sun is out but I'm freezing my ass off. The hooers are gone. There's nobody out but the working stiffs and an old creep or two, scrounging around with nothing better to do. And of course, there's me, but I'm only out because of the fucking program.

I pass the massage parlor and check out the broads through the window which is what I do every morning. This morning there's a new white cunt besides the same tired old Puerto Rican cunt that's always there. They're both wearing like these Chinese bathrobes, sitting there dangling their legs and sipping coffee out of containers. They don't see me at all.

The streets around the Square are never clean. Sure the garbage trucks come once in a while and flush the shit up one side of the street and down the other, but it don't do any good. There ain't enough garbage cans to begin with and the ones they got most of them get burnt out by the little kids who got nothing better to do at night than get stoned on beer and burn up garbage. Sometimes for fun they go down near the river and torch an abandoned building. Sometimes they pour kerosene over the winos' feet who are sacked out in doorways and set fire to them. They just burn bums up because they're bored. So what? Nobody gives a fuck.

Everything around the Square is burnt out, beat up, shit. Nowhere. The Square is the pits, the asshole end of the world where everything is garbage and nobody gives a fuck about anything anymore except themselves and just making it through the day, burnt out like the buildings, or as Saul says, "It's the isle of the dogs."

There's all kinds of kids from all over, they all got torn T-shirts and no socks, just runaways who nobody wants or gives a fuck about. Some of them are so young their dicks can hardly get hard. You can see them in the morning in the park behind the library, crashing out and probably already somebody has beat them for their beat-up old sneakers while they were sleeping. Kids, just hanging out around the Square, bumming quarters for games with all the other weirdos and rip-off artists and the plain crazies who also are hanging out, dudes who sleep in the all-night movies with the winos and the sickies who like to cut kids up. Yeah, there's a lot of them too and you always got to watch who you go with.

Some of the things you see you don't believe. Not just ordinary sex, but with plastic dildoes and rubber cunts and cocks they make with bumps all over them. They got vacuum machines which you can give yourself a blow job with, there's guys who want to stick little lead balls up their asses and guys who want to get fist-fucked. All kinds of people, just hanging out and you don't know who's ok or sick or an undercover. There's an old broad that walks up and down the street all bent over, carrying a shopping bag, and believe it or not, that "she" is a cop. My boy Benny was busted by him. I warned him that was an undercover but he wouldn't listen. No way that old bag all bent over could be a six-foot cop and a guy too. Of course the pocket book is the slum, what you call the bait. When a dude snatches it, that's it, bro, it's all over. They got a backup cop across the street who makes like he is waiting for a bus all night long and he's the one that makes the collar. So Benny, he gets pinched and still didn't believe it, even when the judge gives him ninety days on the Rock, which he told everybody he didn't mind one fucking bit because it was getting too cold out in the

68

street anyhow. That's Benny, he got his head screwed on backwards. Me, I know where I'm at, and it ain't about doing ninety days on the Rock if I can help it. Just because I'm fucking around on the Square don't make me exactly stupid. I was pretty smart in school, but school is just like the Rock. They even got the same wire screens on the windows and the same dudes you meet in the joint, all fucked up and nuts and the ones who ain't are black niggers who are worse. And the teachers, some poor-assed slobs trying to tell you where it's at and meanwhile they're doing worse than you. Fuck school. Sure I was strung out, so what? I didn't kill nobody or nothing. And I was smart enough that when I kept getting popped I said fuck it. Fuck the Rock and fuck school too. I had hepatitis and nearly croaked, so I said fuck it and got myself on a program. Me, I don't give a flying fiddler's fuck about what somebody tells me I'm "supposed" to do. Everybody's running some kind of game. Like my mother, with all her religious shit and she still don't have a fucking thing but a mortgage and bills and hassles with the phone company and trying to figure out what she's gonna put on that table for the kids to eat because her fucked-up old man, the Reverend, is a weirdo from the word go. No way she can tell me that she's getting over. So what? She gotta house in Queens and a nutty old man and two kids to feed. She thinks I'm fucked up! Shit, she's a fine one to talk when she lives like the Old Woman Who Lived in a Shoe.

Fuck that house shit. For what? So you can have a wife and kids to feed? So you can fuck the same pussy night after night and look at the same four ugly walls and snotty kids with all their bullshit who are always getting sick. For what? So that one day you can go bananas and chop them all up, or you just give it all up and lay around all day watching TV because you know you're trapped and it's not gonna be any different for your kids either because they're gonna be trapped in the same bullshit too and when they get grown and are tired of seeing your ass all the time, then they try to send you away to a home to croak like my mother tried to do with my grandma.

I heard all that shit about dropping out too. Drop out of what? There's nothing to drop out of except your father's dick and your mother's twat. What are you gonna do down here? You gonna clean up the smell of sick dope fiends, you gonna take care of the runaways or little white girls fresh off the farm peddling their asses for jigaboo pimps and the old people who got nothing to do but feed pigeons while they wait to croak. You know what a dropout is? A dropout is a rich whitey. Those are the ones who do all the dropping out. They got everything brand new, new clothes, new houses, new wheels, new boxes, brand-new schools where they ain't got wire screens around the windows and you know what else they got new? They got nice new crisp money, that's what they got. You know I was fourteen fucking years old before I even touched brand-new money, money straight from the bank because you gotta have a bank account to get new money. Who the fuck in the barrio got a bank account? They sure as shit don't give you new money in the check-cashing joints where you go to pop your Welfare digit. And you know something else, I never once in my life ever slept in a bed that nobody slept in before. Never, not once. I'm talking about a bed that nobody else gave you, straight from a store. I'm talking about a bed of my own that I don't have to worry who came all over the mattress or who got crabs or what dumb cunt got her period all over it. See, in the ghetto, it's the real thing and down here too. You're on your own and it's dog eat dog. If you're slow you blow. You do what you gotta do and that's that, period. And you mind your own business.

Fuck all that work bullshit. You bullshit around all your life and what happens? You got nothing to show for it, you go bald, your teeth fall out, you catch cancer or some shit and still you don't want to croak. I know, my grandmother is in her seventies and she doesn't want to croak either. And for what? They give you a gold watch or something and some smart Jew laughs all the way to the bank where he's dropping out on your sweat and shit. Meanwhile they got some fucking Holy Roller preaching at you that if you eat shit now you're going to inherit the earth. Inherit what, when you're six feet under? Who inherits what? Inherit, my ass. The only thing you get is what you take. Nobody's gonna give you nothin' for nothin', take it from me, that's where it's at.

My head is splitting, I think I gotta migraine coming on. I'm trying to decide whether to go down to the Deuce to kill some time or to shoot straight to the Port Authority and see if I can turn a quick trick.

Fuck the Port. I'm here now right at the Deuce, which is what they call the corner of Forty-second and Eighth. Past the news-stand is the hole leading down to the subway. They got a penny arcade there which it is much too early for it to be open. They still got the steel gates up around the pinball machines and fifty-cent photo booths to keep the kids from breaking down all that shit and stealing it. Sometimes when it's early like this you can score with a dude who hasn't been able to find anybody all night and is just ready to pack it in and go home alone but is giving it one last shot. But today there's no one down in the hole but an old Chink sweeping up, no one except for a kid I didn't see at first because he was like standing way in the corner where it's dark and he asks me if I got a cigarette.

This kid looks like he's about twelve. He's white and got blond hair and wears his collar turned up like he's some kind of bad dude gonna Bogard his way around. Just a dirty dopey kid who's been out all night and doesn't know his ass from a hole in the ground because he's just looking to get pinched hanging out down here so early in the morning. The first cop comes down here will spot him right off and ask him why ain't he in school or something and boom, the kid's popped, but what the fuck, I give him a cigarette and have to light it for him too. The little squirt takes one drag and starts coughing his guts out. Some gangster. So I go, "You from Jersey?" The kid, he just stands there like a dummy shaking his head no, so I go, "Well, Jesus fucking Christ, you sure as shit ain't from the City, anybody could tell that just by looking at you."

And he goes, "Whaddyamean?"

I mean, you gotta be from Jersey or someplace if you're dumb enough to hang out down here askin' to get pinched."

"Whaddayamean pinched? I ain't done nothin."

"Because you're a runaway, that's why you're gonna get pinched."

"I am not neither. I ain't no runaway."

"Yeah, if you ain't no runaway then how come you ain't in school?"

"I ain't in school because I'm waitin' for my brother, that's why."

I get tired of this stupid rap so I go, "Cool, man, see you later," and I start to stroll back upstairs.

He goes, "Yo, wait a minute, willya?"

71

"Wait a minute for what? Whatchoo want, man?"

Him, he don't say a thing. Just stands there shuffling his feet like Stepin Fetchit who was another dumb nigger in the movies a long time ago. His sneakers are filthy dirty and got holes in them too.

"Speak on it, my man, I gotta go. I got business to take care of."

Not a word comes outta his face. All he does is stand there looking down between his feet like something was growing there.

But finally he looks up and goes, "You gotta quarter you can spare, man?"

"For what?" I say. "The game machines ain't working yet."

"So I can get a donut or somethin'."

"How 'bout this brother you're waitin for, ain't he gonna buy you breakfast?"

"I ain't waitin' for my brother."

"I bet you ain't even got a brother. Ain't that right? You ain't even got a brother."

"I do so got a brother. His name is Tommy."

"Yeah, well, if you gotta brother where is he and why don't he buy you breakfast?"

"Because he's in jail in Texas someplace, that's why."

So I go, "What did he do, kill somebody?"

And he goes, "Yeah. They got him in jail because he killed somebody."

And all I can think of to say is, "Oh," so I go, "Where you really from?"

And he goes, "Noork."

"Noork? What's Noork?"

"Noork. Noork New Jersey."

"You mean New-Wark."

"That's what I said," he goes. "Noork."

"Oh," I go, "you're from Newark, huh? How old are you?"

He goes, "I'm gonna be sixteen."

"Sixteen, huh. You gonna be sixteen in about four years. That's when you're gonna be sixteen. Why d'ya bullshit like that, anybody can see you ain't no sixteen."

"Well, I'm gonna be thirteen next month."

I go, "Well how come you ran away, Noork?"

72

"Because I felt like it."

"Whatchoo mean you felt like it?"

"I felt like running away, that's all."

I mean this kid is really as dumb as they come. He can't give you a straight answer about nothing, so I go, "Well, I'll give you some advice, Noork. You keep hanging around here and some cop is gonna pinch your monkey ass."

I guess he don't know what to say because he goes back to his routine, watching his feet grow. I don't know why I'm wasting my time with this dodo, but anyhow I ask him, "How long you been out?"

"Out where?"

"Out here, on The Square."

"I ran away Sunday."

"Yeah, well how long ago was that?" Because the thing about it is I really don't know what day is today and the dummy, he starts looking at me like I'm some kinda dangerous nut, backing away and looking like he's getting ready to cry so I go, "Well, I gotta tip. Take care, Noork."

I'm just going up the first stair when he starts in all over again. "Waita minute . . ."

"Jesus fucking Christ, whaddya want now?"

He goes, "You forgot to give me the quarter." He holds out his hand like I'm gonna bite it off or something, so instead of one I give him two quarters so he can buy a coffee along with the donut.

"Watcha gonna do now," I ask him.

He goes, "I'm gonna hang out until maybe a faggot picks me up so I can make some bread."

That's when I really lay into him and tell him that if he got any sense at all he better forget all about faggots and all that shit because down here on the Square them niggers will eat him up alive and spit him out and then what's he gonna do if some big boogie takes him somewheres and gives him about twelve inches of dick right in his ass and then holds him down while all his boogie friends dick him down too. Now he really looks like he's gonna bawl. So help me, the big gangster starts sniffling with snot coming out his nose.

And meanwhile I'm scheming, so I tell him to shut up and stop all that crying shit and let me think and what I'm thinking is that Mitch, who was the first guy I ever went with and who is my friend as well as being a trick, that Mitch would dig the shit out of this kid. Mitch, he loves his young chicken, no doubt about it. I figure he'd be good for twenty at least, no argument either, which of course I would get and give the kid a pound, which would leave me just fine for doin' nothing' except bringing the kid up to Mitch's and staying there with him until they're finished getting down.

So I practically drag him upstairs where he can see the Port building and I tell him, "You see the Port there?"

"Yeah, that's where I got off the bus when I came from Noork."

"Good, now listen, you and me are gonna make some money. You wanna make some money?"

"Sure, I wanna make money."

"Cool, but we ain't gonna make it right now because first I gotta take care of some business and when I'm through I gotta take care of some more business and then when I'm through is when we're gonna make some money. You know the waiting room in the Port?"

"Nope."

"Well, I'm gonna take you there and you wait for me until I get back, ok?"

"Whenner you gonna come back?"

"When I'm through taking care of business, didn't you hear me?"

"Yeah, but you comin back, right?"

"Jesus fucking Christ, I said I'd be back, so I'll be back, right?"

We cross the street and I gotta hold his hand just like he was a little kid. That's how dumb he is, he don't even know how to cross a street in traffic by himself. Meanwhile all the big-time spenders are pouring out of the Port in their suits and ties, rushing to work. This is the rat race that everybody's always talking about and that's just what they are, fucking scared rats racing to work because they're scared that if they're two minutes late their assholes will get fried or something. You gotta practically be Houdini to even get into the Port with all these assholes pushing their way out at the same time. And they're all in such a rush that once they're outside all they can do is stand with their fingers up their assholes trying to get a cab, which is impossible and the fucking traffic is bumper to bumper and the gas smell is giving me a migraine. So I

74

half drag the kid through all this shit and walk him over to where the waiting room is. I bust the dime there and buy him a coffee and a donut and also a comic book, which I'm sure he can't read, being so dumb, but I tell him whatever he does to keep pretending like he's reading the comic book and don't forget to hold it right side up either because the Port cops would never bother a kid in the waiting room reading a comic. The only kids they bother are kids who they can tell are playing hooky and strolling or are runaways. They snag them right away, just like that. But a little kid sitting in the waiting room reading a comic book, never. Don't ask me why, that's just the fucked-up way they do things.

Now once I got him settled in, I figure I'll cruise the mezzanine at the top of the escalator to see if I can turn one quick trick before it's time to go to the program and if nothing's happening then try the men's room which is right across from the Mezannine.

I'm just getting it all worked out, what I'm gonna do and have almost forgotten about the kid and am ready to make my move when he goes, "Hey, what's your name? You forgot to tell me your name."

I go, "What's the difference what my name is? I didn't ask you your name did I?"

"Well," he says, "my name is Chris."

"Well, my name's Sinbad."

"That's a goofy name, Sinbad. What kind of name is that?"

"What the fuck do you care?" I go. "You're a royal pain in the ass, that's what you are. You never been to the movies and seen Sinbad the Sailor from the old times? Well, that's me, Sinbad the Semen, but of course the dummy doesn't get it which is a private joke between Saul and me. Nobody else ever gets the joke and it probably isn't really funny anyhow.

I draw a blank on the mezzanine. The men's room stinks of piss and disinfectant. There's a gray-haired guy standing in front of the last urinal, playing with his dick. Bingo, a score. I stand a couple of urinals away, just in case he's a cop so he can't say I cracked on him and unzip my pants. I don't even pretend to take a piss. I just stand there with my cock hanging out where he can get a good look at it. The thing is that the trick is afraid of his shadow. He looks at my cock, then he looks at me, then he checks everything out over both his shoulders. Jesus fucking Christ, who has time for all this bullshit? I see the guy just making up his mind that I'm ok when in comes another dude with a briefcase who is a commuter who has to take a legitimate piss. So there I am with my dick in my hand, waiting. Finally the briefcase guy shakes his dick and puts it back in and tips and the fucking trick starts his checking-out routine all over again. I'm just ready to give it all up and say fuck it and try the mezzanine one last time when finally, he checks everything out one more time and goes into the shitter and closes the door, but I don't hear him lock it so I stand outside and the door is open a crack which I can see inside. The dude is sitting on the shitter with his pants down around his ankles, beating his meat. So I go in and pull the door shut and make sure it's locked. Right away he makes a grab for my fly and I go, "Whoa, how much?" He don't even look up which he must be pretending that he don't hear me, so I tap him on the shoulder and rub my finger with my thumb which everybody knows means money and he gets this big broad grin from ear to ear, which he points to his ears to let me know that he didn't hear me at all. He's deaf. Another fucking dummy for Chrissakes. What is this, my day for dummies? But the finger and thumb he understands. Everybody understands that. He reaches into his pants pocket, which, as I said, is down around his ankles, and pulls out a pound which he pushes into my hand like he's giving me the crown jewels or something. A fucking pound. He spreads his hands like he's telling me he ain't got any more gap, this is it. So I say fuck it, a pound's a pound and let him blow me for a couple of minutes until my dick finally gets hard which is when I pump back and forth like I was cumming and pull it out and wipe it off fast with some shit paper, zip myself back up and tip. When I close the door he's still sitting there with his dick in his hand, smiling like something really tremendous happened. I bet he thinks I really came.

Most people don't know it but guys can fake cuming just like hooers do. All you got to do is while the dude is blowing you, you bring up a little phlegm, pull your dick out of his mouth fast and grab ahold of it and while you're grabbing it you put the phlegm from your hand onto your dick head. The phlegm looks like cum. I guess it must taste like cum too cause I never had no complaint about it. When I go downstairs I peep into the window of the waiting room. The other dummy is still sitting like I told him, by himself in a corner pretending to read the comic book. I got most of the ten left plus the pound I just turned and as soon as I finish at the Program I'll pick up the kid, shoot over to Mitch's and that'll be that. I can just chill out for the rest of the day.

The Program is just a couple of blocks downtown from the Port. They always open up programs in the worst neighborhoods. Who wants two hundred dope fiends on their doorstep, nodding out, or dealing pills on the sidewalk plus stealing everything that's not nailed down out of the stores that are around. So they open the programs where if people bitch, no one will listen to them anyhow. The Program I go to is between one of those phony going-out-of-business stores where they sell shit to tourists at twice what it would cost if it wasn't on sale and on the other side is a candy store where you can't buy any candy because it's a numbers drop which does very good business off the dudes on the Program. I stand outside waiting for them to unlock the doors at nine. The tuinals have come down on me and I'm not so sick now and besides it won't be long before I get my meth and I'll be straight. One thing I hate is hanging out in front of the Program. People walk by and give you funny looks, like look at the dope fiend. They look at you like you're some kind of gorilla in the zoo or something, which I got to admit that some of the broads on the Program do look like ugly gorillas.

There's nothing more greasy or nasty than a dope fiend broad. Take my word for it. I know plenty of dudes can be strung out and you'd never know it. They got their shit together. The only way you could tell is by the old tracks on their arms or hands. There are guys though that never got off anywhere where anybody could see, like in their legs, or in their necks. I know dudes who before they would hit their arms they'd use the big vein in their dicks. No kidding. There are some guys like that. They don't care if their dick falls off so long as nobody can see tracks. But the broads are different. They got no respect for themselves. You look at a broad you know she's fucked up. And the broads on meth, they're the worst. Meth does weird things to them. Some of them blow up like balloons and swear to Christ that they're pregnant. Their periods stop and everything. Even the doctors can't tell right off. And others it's just the opposite—they lose so much weight they look like scarecrows which if you pushed them all their bones would break. Some of them can't even hardly walk. There, there's a bitch right now, holding up the fucking lampost, she can't even stand straight without falling on her ass, which she would just sit in the gutter until somebody helped pick her up.

While I'm checking out the broad I see two other dudes I know from the Program arguing over a pill. The one who wants to sell it says its a 'lude and the other one ain't sure so they call me over to settle the beef. One look at it and I know that the guy who's selling is trying to beat the other chump. What it is is one of those pills they give you when you got back pains. I know. The doctor wrote me some and they ain't shit. So I look at this garbage and I tell the dude who ain't sure, "Yeah, man, that's a 'lude. Definitely." And he believes me and cops for a pound.

The dude who beat him, I tell him, "Yo, bro', walk me inside so I can get down on a number," which he does. I tell the collector two dollars on a six-nine-oh combination. I always bet sixty-nine, for luck, and I tell my man, "Give him the deuce."

He goes, "What for? It's your number, man."

And I go, "Yeah, that's right, it is my number, but you pay the dude for me 'cause you owe me."

"Owe you what?"

"Owe me for the pound you just beat that guy out of which you wouldn't of if I didn't sanction the shit. The way I see it you owe me a deuce and a half but I'm settling for the deuce. Why, you want me to go back and tell the dude I made a mistake? Then he could put up the deuce. It don't make me no never-mind either way."

So he ups the deuce and walks off talking to himself. Dope fiends are like that. The only way you can get by if you're a dope fiend is to be more treacherous than the other guy. And never let a dope fiend think he got over on you because he'll try to beat you every time he sees you. Once he thinks he got over he'll never stop, never, and you got to wind up icing him. Plus a dope fiend is always paranoid. He's always trying to get over but in the back of his head he always thinks that somebody is really getting over on him. Give him something for nothin', anything, and he won't trust it. He'll figure you got some kind of scam going or something. It's in your bones or something, that's why Carmen and me couldn't make it together. She was my old lady but we went to different programs. So what would happen is I'd bring a bottle of meth back to the crib and stash it, figuring she'd try to beat me for it and she'd do the same for me. But what would happen is we'd both get fucked up on tuinals and forget that we both had stashes or where they were. Then I'd blame her and she'd blame me for beating the stash, which all along was there but which we were so fucked up we forgot about. One time we really got into it and I beat the living piss out of her for drinking my meth, which, of course, she didn't. When I got through beating up on her I got careless and turned my back for a minute and wham, she laid the lamp right over my head. I was bleeding like a stuffed pig and mad enough to fuck a grizzly bear and chased that bitch down the hall and if I caught her it would have been all over because I would of cut her heart out. But the cops come and an ambulance too, which they stitched up my head and just when everything was quiet and we were going to get it on, the whole thing about the stash which started it comes back to me again and I go, "Bitch, why you copped my stash?"

Well that did it. I had enough and made it up to Saul's crib and when I told him about all this grief this bitch was giving me he bust out laughing, nearly broke up.

I go, "What's so fucking funny? I don't see nothing funny about the bitch busting my stash and busting my head."

So Saul is cracking up and he says, "Carmen didn't bust your stash. You drank that bottle here yesterday, don't you remember?"

And I didn't. Didn't remember a fucking thing. I told him I didn't see that it was all so funny though because I had twenty-two stitches in my head which felt like I had a migraine. But finally we both laughed and got high and I stayed over with him for three days until my head felt better.

What it is is that all dope fiends are like that. Half the time they don't know what's happening and the other half they're too paranoid to give a fuck.

Then when you start dropping tuinals behind the meth you don't know whether you're paranoid or whether some wrong shit really went down which makes you paranoid about being paranoid, plus you black out too which is why if I pass by Saul's crib and he sees I'm fucked up on downs he won't even let me in the house. Not that he's trying to be mean but he did put up with a lot of shit from me, and that's the truth. Sometimes he talks just like some half-assed social worker which he says he was, but I can dig it. I may not have finished school but I'm no dummy and that's a fact. I owe him. There's no two ways about it. I don't know how many times he detoxed me when I was strung out, or bailed me out, or went to court and got me sprung behind his rap which is extremely heavy. Anyway he don't want no tuinals in his crib, period.

Well, finally they open the doors and I go upstairs and I don't fucking believe what happens. First the nurse says she will not medicate me until I see my counselor who is an ex–dope fiend and who is still on the Program supposed to be detoxing. I knew the dude when he was nodding and holding up lampposts worse than me and now he got some rinkydink little spot as a counselor at nothing a week and thinks he's some kind of king shit. Right off he gets on my case about why I missed yesterday and I've been missing too much. So I tell him the first thing that comes into my head, that I had to see my P.O. yesterday, the probation officer.

So he goes, "So you went to your P.O. yesterday?"

And I go, "Yeah, that's what I told you. What the fuck do I have to bullshit you for?"

And he goes, "Well, that's very interesting." And I ask him what is very interesting.

"What is very interesting," he says, "is that your P.O. called here yesterday looking for you. What is also interesting is that he said you missed not one but two reports and that he is thinking of locking your ass up, that is what is very interesting. And further," he goes, while my mouth is still hanging open, ". . . and further, as I don't have to tell you, that if it's one thing the doctor does not like is having people busted on the program which makes him look very bad with the Medicaid people and . . ." I can't even get in a word edgewise. ". . . and, while we're on the subject of Medicaid, you still haven't brought in your new card to be xeroxed so that the doctor can get paid and if it's one thing the doctor likes less than people getting busted it's not getting paid, so . . ."

So what the fuck am I supposed to say. I'm sick as a dog. I gotta get my meth. No question about it, as much as I hate fuck-face here I gotta cop out. "Look," I go, "so maybe I fucked up with the P.O. but I'll get that shit straightened out. I'll see him today. No shit, as soon as I get medicated."

"Which means," he says, "that you won't see him today."

I got a sinking feeling in my stomach that the shit is about to hit the fan.

"Sure I'll see him today. I told you, as soon as I get medicated."

"That is what I mean," he goes. "You definitely won't see him today because you definitely, no question about it, are not going to get medicated today, not without the new Medicaid card. That's straight from the doctor, who incidentally is tired of your shit and would much rather terminate your ass but is giving you this one more shot. Dig?"

This motherfucker is like a fucking stone wall. You can't go through him and you can't go around him. No matter what I say he's like a broken record. How can I see the P.O., how can I go down to Welfare and get my new Medicaid card if I'm sick? He's been where I am. He knows I can't be running all around town while I'm sick. Jesus fucking Christ, ain't there nobody else but dummies I gotta meet in this fucked-up day?

The whole fucking world just tumbles on my head at ten minutes past nine in the morning. All these asshole programs are the same. It's all dollars and cents. If the card is late in the mail they couldn't give less than a fuck about you. Jesus Christ, how the fuck can I be responsible for the whole fucking U.S. Post Office. So what's another day? Big fucking deal. They know I'll get around to getting the card. What am I gonna do, sit in the Welfare all fucking day to get a crummy card when I'm sick as a dog and think my gut is gonna fall out, just for what, for a shot of their jungle juice. The trouble is they terminate people all the time, that's the word they use. It sounds like some fucking C.I.A. shit or something. First they build you all the way up to a hundred, a hundred and twenty-five milligrams a day, which ordinarily is enough to kill an elephant, and then boom, no card and your ass is terminated. So long. See you later.

I try once more, "Come on, let me get straight today, just today. I promise you, I swear to God, I'll take care of everything, the P.O., the card, everything. Just let me get medicated so I can take care of business."

But I know it's just not my day. I shoulda known it when I left my radio in the hotel and had to go back and—omigod! That's fucking *it!* I went through all those fucking changes going back and what happens. I left the motherfucking radio right where it was. All that shit for nothing and meanwhile the whale is probably trying to figure out right now how much he can get for it.

Walking down the stairs I try to figure it all out. How everything got all fucked up all of a sudden. Maybe the Medicaid card came to the hotel where my digit comes which I give the guy a fin every two weeks for letting me pick up there since you gotta have an address for Welfare. If it did I'm not in bad shape. If it didn't I definitely gotta cop some meth off the street first thing, just so I can haul ass around town. Talk about being sick. Kicking a methadone jones is ten times worse than kicking dope. You feel like somebody's poking hot needles into your bones. You get cramps. You shit like a goose and it all comes out white. You think you're gonna die. But if I check the hotel out and the card didn't come then I just wasted all that time being sick for nothing. It's too late to go to Welfare. Fuck-face upstairs knows that. You wanna go to Welfare you better be on line by six in the morning, otherwise they don't even let you in the door. You could be a pregnant broad on crutches with one eye and you still gotta be on line by six or you blow. That's the way they run their shit and, like Saul says, "It's their world. We're only passing through."

So let's see, first I gotta cop. Fuck Welfare, that's out for today. Should I check out the hotel first or check out Saul first? I could call Saul, but if he's fucked up he just don't answer the phone so that is a waste of time too. I gotta go up there and have him call the P.O. and straighten that shit out so I don't wind up kicking a Jones on the Rock. One thing I know for sure is that Saul can straighten things out with the P.O. He can con dudes like that right out of their socks. OK, the thing to do is get straight first.

So I check with the dude who bought the beat 'lude and who sometimes has a bottle of meth. You can usually cop outside of a program because a lot of dudes just go and hold the shit in their mouth and spit it out so they can sell it. But the dude says he's not holding and besides he's looking all paranoid at me because he's not sure whether he got beat this morning, but he's pretty sure and nobody else is around, not a soul, not even the broad who was holding up the lamppost. So the only thing to do is stroll down to the Square and hang out until I can cop.

The sun which was out for a little while has gone in and the wind is blowing around corners. Old newspapers and shit are flying all around. A guy's hat goes sailing away and he goes chasing after it into the middle of the street where he nearly gets run over by a cab. Imagine getting kilt over a lousy hat. On the corner of the Deuce is a big shoeshine stand where nobody is gonna sit down in a fucking typhoon and get a shine, but I guess the old nigger keeps it open 'cause he got nothing else to do. There's a couple of hooers on the stroll, just shooting the shit and hanging out until lunch time, which is when they really start turning tricks.

I'm shivering from being cold and sick. My nose is leaking. I must of left my coat somewhere yesterday, wherever I was. I got too much to do. It's just too fucking much all at once. On the Square it's pretty quiet, being past the morning rush hour. A cripple is pushing away the gate in front of one of the movies. There are about eight movies on just one block, the Deuce. All of them are real dumps and they give Kung Fu flicks and science fiction and old gangster pictures and Westerns. The one on the corner is the X-rated where you can watch cunts eating guys or guys eating cunts or cunts eating cunts, whatever.

I usually go to the movies at least every day to chill out and pass the time. Sometimes if you're high you get carried away and really believe that karate shit that there's a real Bruce Lee who can wipe out a whole army of Chinks by himself and catch bullets in his teeth. Me, I don't think they oughta show shit like that, at least not to little kids. They get carried away with that shit and wind up getting hurt or something. But what the fuck, when there's nothing else to do I go to sit in the balcony and get high and munch on some peanut butter cups. All the kids playing hooky try to sneak into a show. What they do is come through the fire doors and mostly get chased out by the ushers. Lately, though, the ushers have stopped chasing the kids because the kids have started chasing the ushers with dog chains and garrison belts. It's no fun anymore.

Besides the movies there's also the peep shows. If you never been to a peep show, what it is is these tiny little booths you can hardly fit into. You put a quarter in the slot and you see a couple of minutes of real horny shit. Some of it is so sick you can't believe that people would do it, not for any money, like a broad getting fucked by a horse or guys shitting all over a hooer. Can you imagine the kinda weirdos who do that. But I guess they wouldn't make them if there wasn't people who wanted to see shit like that. Some dudes hang out in the peep all day long with a pocket full of quarters doing nothing but checking out the flicks. Besides the sick shit you can see straight sex between guys and broads and they have a special section for gay and S & M and also with little kids doing it to each other. Whatever your thing is they got something there for you as long as you keep feeding the quarters into the machines. They always got a guy making change who walks all around telling everybody to find a booth or get out, this ain't a fucking library, and also a guy with a bucket and rag whose job is to go around cleaning up the cum off the floors of the booths. They get a real classy crowd around the Square, no doubt about it.

Under one of the movie signs is the spot where most of the dope deals are made. I don't know why it's this spot. That's just the way it is. Maybe because there's a hamburger joint right next to it and it's open to the street so people come in or go out and hang out, you know, maybe over a cuppa coffee or a thirty-cent hamburger. Anyway, that's where everybody goes to cop. I may be in luck because I see Sheik III rapping with a dude. The Sheik is a good meth connection, usually, if you can get him early like this before he's sold out. Why they call him Sheik III is because there's three Sheiks on the Square, which everybody knows. Sheik I, he's the oldest, about twenty or so. But he's mostly around Bryant Park dealing beat bags and joints to the secretaries and messenger boys on their lunch hour. Sheik II is the youngest one—he's only about fourteen but he's been hanging out almost ever since I can remember. He's a cool little dude, though he never has much to say. He lives someplace up in the Bronx with his mom in one of those real shitty burnt-out blocks like Brook Avenue or something. He's into that karate shit too. All of the young kids are and he walks around, so help me, in a white ghi which is a kind of pajamas you do karate in with a brown belt. A brown belt is supposed to be pretty good, but nobody knows whether Little Sheik is for real or a phony and no one wants to try him to find out. He's a good little hustler. If it's not too cold later he'll be sitting on the jonny pump in front of Playland which is the penny arcade and which is where all the young kids hang out and hustle. So that's Sheik I and Sheik II. Sheik III, he's an albino, I swear to God. He got this white,

white hair and pink eyes, which you better not look at him too hard or he will fuck you up just for nothing, just because he's paranoid.

Nobody knows where he comes from, but like I said, he's usually holding so what I do is try to ease up between the Sheik and the dude he's rapping to who looks like he's just getting ready to cop.

So I go, "Yo, Sheik, I gotta rap to you a minute, right away. It's real important." And I walk him away to where the other dude can't hear.

So the Sheik goes, "What the fuck is so important when I'm taking care of business?"

And I go, "That's what I want to talk to you about which is copping some meth if you got any."

"I got one bottle left, which is 70 milligrams, no cuts, but the dude is gonna cop for twelve."

I go, "Lemme get it and I'll give you whatever I got on me," which comes to fourteen dollars and some change and a token and the other dude is left holding the shit end of the stick. Too bad, when you're slow you blow.

I crack the bottle, which is sealed tight and not cut just like Sheik said and down it right there right in the middle of the fucking Deuce. Fuck it, I'm lucky to cop in the first place. And don't you think I look up and right across the street looking straight at me is a cop. How the fuck did I miss him? Well, I figure, either he's gonna pinch me or not and I see him trying to make up his mind. He's trying to look real bad like Kojak and shit and then he just turns and walks away. I know fucking-A well if I was on his side of the street I'd be pinched but like all cops he's too lazy to cross the fucking street. Still, I figure it's better to keep out of his way for a while. I figure I'll check out the peep and see if I can score, because I just gave the Sheik my last coin.

What you do in the peep is to walk down one roll of booths to the back where there's like a U-turn and then you walk back up the other side. In the U-turn is where the tricks hang out. There's two ways of hustling them. You can pretend that you're looking at the pictures outside the booth that show you what kind of flick it is. They all say something like, "See Flamboyant Filly Fist Fucked" or some way-out shit like that, and then the trick comes up and asks you if you want to see a show and you say yes and then you both ease into a booth without the change guy seeing you and take care of B.I. The other way is to see which door is open a crack with somebody inside. You can't actually see inside because it's too dark but there's a light over each booth that turns red when you put a quarter into the machine, so if you see a red light and the door cracked you know that somebody in there is looking for somebody and you ease on in. If he likes what he sees he tells you to close the door.

Well, I'm looking at the pictures when a big, tall, skinny nigger eases up. Usually I don't go with niggers. But this one got a suit and tie on and looks like he's OK, you know. So he asks me do I want to see the show and I say I don't mind, but the change guy is just rounding the corner and the nigger is already in the booth with the light on so I don't want the change guy to see me ease in. What I got to do is stroll all around the U-turn again and lose the change guy. By the time I get back the nigger got the door closed. I don't know whether he got anybody in there or what so I jiggle the doorknob a couple of times just to see what he does. Finally, after all this shit he opens up and I go in. I ask him how much. It's the same deal all the time. You say how much. They say, "How much you want?" You say ten, they say five, and that's that. That's what you get in the peep, which is why I hustle there only when I absolutely have to. Right away the nigger starts blowing me. Me, I'm sitting checking out the flick where a cunt is getting fucked in the ass while another dude comes on her head and my dick gets hard. Of course I already got the pound in my pocket. You always get your money up front, that's a must.

Meanwhile the dude raises up offa my dick and goes, "You blow me." I tell him fuck no. No way, José, not today. I whip my cock back in my pants and tip. I ain't about to be blowing no fucking black nigger, suit or no suit, not for a pound I ain't. What I shoulda done was crack his skull.

Anyway, at least I got a pound which is better than I was about ten minutes ago and another thing is that I'm not sick anymore. The meth is coming down and I'm feeling cool as a cucumber. All I want to do is smoke some herb and cool out someplace where I don't have to think. The Sheik is gone but I see another dude I know under the movie and I cop a couple of joints off him and say fuck it, I'll go check out Across a Hundred and Tenth Street for about the sixteenth time. When I go in I buy some peanut butter cups, which leaves me with about seven cents in my pocket.

I always sit in the first row of the balcony. The herb is righteous and I gotta nice buzz. I thought I had some tuinals this morning in my pants, but I must be wrong. Anyhow they're not there.

The flick shows how these niggers stick up a numbers bank in Harlem and machine-gun everybody in sight. I mean it's real gory shit and you see them shoot out one of this dude's eyeballs and then how the Mafia chases all of them and catches them one by one. The one nigger first they cut off his balls and then nail him up to a cross. The other dude they drop on his head from about fifty stories up and in the end everybody croaks except this one cop. The part I like best is where the last nigger which they didn't catch yet. He's got a whole fucking arsenal and a suitcase full of money. I'm tripping out on the smoke and I think how boss it would be to have a whole table full of money like that, but not to get wasted like the nigger is going to get in the picture. Enough dough to cover the whole bed—tens, twenties, hundreds—and you pick up the phone and call room service and you tell them send up a bottle of scotch and three of the finest foxes you can find and you give the bellboy a twenty-dollar tip and his eyes are popping out of his skull when he checks out all the gap and let them fine bitches fuck you to death. And I'd get a pretty kid for Saul, too.

They say you can't buy love. Bullshit. Everybody does. All those jokers who say money ain't everything never been out in the streets without a dime in their jeans with no place to go. It's like the end of the world, you're at the bottom with no place to go but down . . . to where the lake is . . . dark . . . someone naked from the waist up . . . (hair?) . . .

I know the face. A forest all wet and cold and smelling of flowers and trees all around and when I get to the lake and look down it's black and I can't see the bottom, feeling like I just want to fall in and sleep for a long, long time.

Sleep.

The lights are on and I wonder where the fuck am I. The movie is over and they're playing that corny music while the people go out. How the fuck long have I been out? I have a splitting headache. When you drink meth you sweat in your sleep.

I'm soaking wet, all under my arms and back and now I gotta go walking out in the cold and catch my death of pneumonia. No fucking coat. No fucking box. No fucking money.

I look up at the clock which is on a billboard on top of the whole fucking shithouse of a Square and it's after one. Three fucking hours on the nod and to top it all off, now it starts to rain. That's it. I mean, that's really fucking it. No way I'm gonna walk down to the hotel and check on the card now, not in all this shit without a coat. Fuck the Medicaid until tomorrow. If I can turn a couple of tricks I can cop some meth in the morning and then take care of B.I. Should I try to score first or should I check Saul out? I don't have the slightest idea what to do. It's like none of it matters the least bit, so I just stand there like a silly fuck who don't have sense enough to get out of the rain, which I must be because I'm soaked to the skin.

Everybody is just standing around under the movie sign trying to keep dry. The whole crew. Two of the Sheiks, the midget, some dudes from the program, Trizie the sex-change, another dude I owe a pound to and it's just my luck I gotta run into him now when I don't have a single dime in my jeans. What a fucking crew. Dope fiend broads, a skinny weirdo who looks like he likes to sniff boys' bicycle seats, a couple of kids with high school names on the back of their jackets who probably come down to cop some beat acid.

The hamburgers smell delicious and Jesus fucking Christ here comes the guy I owe the gap to, easing up, and he goes, "Yo, bro'."

And I go, "Yo bro', what's happening?"

He goes, "You owe me."

"Sure, sure I owe you. I know I owe you. I was looking for you before when I had the gap but you wasn't around."

"Yeah, but I'm around now."

"Yeah, I know, but I hadda take care of some B.I., you know."

"Yeah, well, but you owe me."

That's all the dude can say, "You owe me, you owe me," like some fucking parrot.

So I go, "Yo bro', I gotta turn a trick right now. I mean, I'm late now. So after I turn the trick I'll be back with your dough."

He knows I'm bullshitting. But what's he gonna do? He either goes for the yoke or he don't. If he don't, we throw down right here and probably both get busted. But just in case he decides he wants to throw down I step in real close so I'm almost under his chin. Forget about that rope-a-dope shit you see on television. In a street fight you move in, not out, so you can step on one of the guy's feet and lay your head on his shoulder and all he can do is break his knuckles on the back of your head while you kick him in the balls. That's the way you do it in a street fight.

Well, he sees me moving in and knows I ain't gonna punk out and tells me, "OK, bro', cool—I'll catch you later," and I go, "Yeah, later," and he walks away but I don't turn my back on him. Anyhow, I think I better get off the Deuce altogether for a while, between the cop who wanted to pinch me and this dude who may come back with a couple of his boys any minute.

The rain stops. Ninth, Tenth, Eleventh Avenues. The farther over you go the worse it gets. Beat, dirty streets with broken-down stores and empty lots and burnt-out buildings. You walk looking over both shoulders at the same time in case somebody jumps out and wants to hit you over the head or something. Broken windows, stray dogs who would bite the shit out of you if you go near them. Parking lots where nobody parks. Nothing but discarded junk that the junkies and bag ladies have picked through. Rubbish.

When I was small my mother put me in Catholic school. It didn't last. They threw me out. But I remember this priest, he was probably half a fag the way he used to take me into his study and rap all the time, real close up to me so I could smell his halitosis. He had this real boss study with leather chairs and books all around, religious books, but still, I remember it was a day like this all rainy and gloomy and just like that I asked him about Hell. Was there such a place as Hell? Were you really punished? Did God punish you? I was just a little kid, maybe twelve, but I wanted to know. Did God punish you? How could God punish you and make you suffer if God was supposed to be good? How could he let the Devil punish you if he could stop it? The Sisters used to teach us that the mercy of Christ is boundless. That's just what they said. That's what the priest laid on me—the mercy of Christ is bound-less—but I wanted to know then what kind of God was he to put people to suffer, to put people in burnt-out houses with rats and shit where you freeze your ass off in the winter. What kind of God would let little kids go hungry and cold? I remember he looked right at me, like he was seeing me for the first time, and it all poured out of me. I didn't know what I was saying but it was like "Don't tell me about God's mercy. Don't tell me about that shit when my mother can lock up my grandma in a home so she has to die alone with no one she knows with her. Don't tell me about that shit when the whiteys got everything they want and the only thing left for the spics and the niggers is the crumbs, the shit they don't want." Catechisms. I don't know. I probably didn't put it that way.

When he did say something after a long time his voice was kinda soft, but it was a con job, a straight con job. It was all so easy. I'd understand it all some day if I prayed. But I had stopped praying even then. I didn't have the heart to hurt his feelings so I shut up. The Sisters taught us, "Children, pray for the gift of grace." Grace. But I know what Hell is. Hell is Tenth and Eleventh Avenues. Hell is the Square and the ghetto. Hell is here, right now. Hell is not having any hope, ever—at least that's the way I see it.

Twelfth Avenue is as far as you can go. Then there's the river. I sit on a broken pier that got big holes in it and the pilings are all rotten. There's not a soul around. Nobody but a couple of birds flying in circles over the river. And it stinks of empty oil cans and orange peels and all the garbage bumping against the pilings. I love the sound of the water, plish . . . plash. So I sit on the pier with my legs crossed, looking out across the river which is filthy from all the pollution and shit. Mitch told me he used to go fishing in the river when he was a kid, but all the fish have croaked and you gotta be crazy to even think of swimming. On the other side is Jersey, which I can't see because of the fog and Carmen and a kid growing inside of her that might be mine and might not be mine. I started coming here years ago, when I first met Mitch. I used to sit here and think: I'm invisible because there's no one here to see me. I used to think stuff like that before I started talking like all the down dudes, all that street talk and jive shit. But that's the way you gotta talk when you're out in the streets, otherwise they think you're a punk or something. You gotta put on an act, which is exactly what Saul says I do all the time.

Jesus Christ, I think, I'm sixteen years old and what do I know. What'll I be like when I'm twenty? When I'm thirty? Thirty. No way, I can't see myself thirty. How do I know what I'll be like then when I don't even know what I'm really like now, under-neath?

Heaven. Hell. My mother believes in Santeria and brujas, which are ladies who you would call witches. Not the kind that ride around on broomsticks in fairy stories, but just ladies who have what you call powers. It's no bullshit. One time I ripped a dude off and for nothing, just 'cause I felt like it, I went to a bruja—of course not the one my mother goes to because I know she would tell everything right back to my mother. But this one I went to, the lady, she just looked in my face and told me, "You did something very wrong." Just like that and she knew. Then I got to thinking about it and I wondered did she really know or was it a scam. Every kid does something wrong. So maybe she was only guess-ing, saying it so I would give her some money which she would take the curse off, that's what they do, the brujas. I don't know. How do you know who's a phony and who's for real and if you don't know the difference then who can blame you for being a phony if nobody knows what's phony and what's real? I suppose that's part of Hell too, the not knowing.

The wind is blowing up a storm. I take a piece of newspaper and stuff it under my shirt.

Mitch lives just a couple of blocks away. I should go over there and tell him about the kid, but I don't feel like moving. I'm just too exhausted to move. Sometimes I get like that when there's just nothing worth getting off my ass for.

There has to be something else. Something else besides waking up and getting through the day, going to sleep and starting all over again. But what? Getting high? Getting fucked up? Even that gets to be a pain in the ass after a while. The party got to stop some time. And then what? Suppose I just eased down into the river right now and drowned, it wouldn't make any real difference to anybody. Oh sure, my mother would cry and shit, but then she'd get over it and just go on living. That's why I don't let anybody get too close to me, except sometimes Saul, because if you don't chump yourself off and start caring about somebody else, then, at least, they can never go away and leave you and you can never be hurt by them. That's why I keep my real feelings to myself all the time, so nobody can touch them. Then you're safe—safe from people, safe from yourself, safe from God too, because if

91

you can somehow hide, make yourself so small that even God can't find you, then he can't make you suffer because he doesn't even know you're around.

One time, I think, somebody must have put this old pier here for something, but whatever it was I guess nobody remembers. There must have been ships and boats tying up here with families and kids and balloons and guys selling hot dogs and ice cream. And then what happened? Who knows? People forget. Maybe they don't need a pier here anymore so they leave it to rot and fall apart and break up 'til there's nothing left but a bunch of junk in the river with rats running up and down over everything.

I must of been walking without knowing it because all of a sudden, whoosh, I got dirty water all over my sneakers and pants and nearly get run over by a car. The light turns red and I'm in the middle of the street not knowing whether to go back or across. I look up at the street sign and see I'm way past Mitch's, all the way back on Ninth Avenue. The street here is like a bridge which runs over the railroad tracks, down there where I used to crash out when I was a runaway and strung out too. I'm standing in the middle of it like a big dummy figuring well now since I'm so close should I check the hotel after all or check out the kid and see if he's still there or what? I just can't sort it all out, and to top it off I'm broke and haven't eaten anything since this morning except for a few peanut butter cups, which I'd settle for one now.

There's some kind of hooer across the street. No way to tell whether it's a broad or a sex-change unless you get up real close and check out the hands. That's how you know it's a sex-change, they may not have a dick no more but they still got a man's hands. The bridge here is pretty good for hustling because all the trucks pass by on the way downtown when they come out of the Lincoln Tunnel. And truck drivers are good tricks—they're in a rush, they got dough, and they don't mind spending it.

A big oil rig rolls by, pulls up about ten feet away, and then backs up. I figure he's going for the hooer but instead he stops in front of me and motions for me to get in. I point. Me? He opens the door for me on the traffic side and I hop in and off we go. He pulls right off Ninth and swings all the way back to Twelfth and parks behind an old warehouse where they got a big no-parking sign.

92

There's nobody in sight. Not another car. Nothing. He hasn't said one word. Hasn't even looked at me except when he opened the door. When he got the rig parked, with the engine still idling, he unzips his fly and takes out his dick which already he got a hard-on. He squeezes the head a couple of times like he's getting it ready. I can see all he wants to do is shoot his load quick. Like I said, truck drivers are always in a hurry. So I go down on him and jerk him off while I'm blowing him. A hooer taught me that trick. It makes them come faster. It don't take him two minutes to come, which I got to hold a big load in my mouth until I can get the door open and spit it out. He pulls two tens out and puts them on the seat. As soon as I pick them up he slams the door, puts the rig in gear, and boom, he's gone, just like that, and I'm right back where I came from in the middle of Twelfth Avenue.

The wind comes right off the river and I'm freezing my balls off. That was a nice score, the best one so far today. I figure the first thing to do is see if I can find a bar anywhere where I can go to warm up. I wisht I could remember where I left my coat. Down in the Village there's a ton of bars on Twelfth Avenue, where it becomes West Street, all S & M. But up here you're lucky if you even find one, one of those crummy joints with old Irish ladies and a couple a regulars where everybody drinks boilermakers.

I'm lucky. I find a bar a couple of blocks down. It's warm and steamy inside. They got the radiators on full blast. All these joints are the same—painted dogshit brown, with sawdust on the floors, dark and smelly and last year's Christmas decorations still up.

I order a boilermaker and then I order another one. There's nobody at the bar but me and an old guy in a dirty black overcoat with his head on the bar and a little change next to his hand and a bartender wiping some glasses. It's nice and warm in here. No noise, no one to aggravate you. The booze takes the chill out of my bones. Jesus, I wisht I didn't have to go outside again today. The bartender shakes his head when I ask him where I can get a cab, so I pull my shirt collar up as high as it'll go, tuck my hands under my armpits, and fight the wind all the way back to Ninth, where I finally grab a cab. I tell him to drop me by the hotel where my digit comes and wait, which he does. The guy at the desk says no mail. Fuck the Medicaid. I'll take care of that tomorrow. Now that I got some gap again I'm feeling more like myself, like I'm a bad dude

93

and can handle anything that comes along. It's easy. All you gotta do is know how to hustle.

But wouldn't you know it, when I come out, it's raining again. I'm sick of this shit, so I tell the cabbie to take me to the Bargain Jim's which is one block from the Square where I buy a thin little jacket and an umbrella, the kind that blows apart in the first big wind. By the time I pay the cab and buy the shit I look up at the clock on the billboard and it's after three already. Well, I still got enough gap to buy a nice bag of smoke. I count up my coins. Fuck eating. If I wait until later I can buy a pint of wine now to go with the smoke and get my head really bad.

What I don't feel like doing is going back to the spot under the movie. The dude I owe may still be out, so I decide to cop the smoke from Rob at the Arsenal, which I haven't seen him in a long time anyhow.

The Arsenal is the one and only bathhouse on the Deuce, right in the middle of the block, but unless you knew it you'd walk right by it. There's no sign, no nothing, just a door which you open and walk up the stairs and there's the desk behind a cage, where you pay and they give you a key and a towel. Rob told me that dudes come from all over the world just to check out the Arsenal. It's a whole freak scene. There's a steam bath and little cubicles. In some of the cubicles they have handcuffs welded right into the walls. It's nothing to go down there and see one dude buck naked hanging from the wall by his wrists while another dude is going down on him and both of them are getting fist-fucked by two other dudes. That's the kind of scene it is. It goes on all the time. I worked as a towel boy there for a couple of nights. Rob gave me the gig. But right away I could see it wasn't gonna work out. It was a pain in the ass with all that sick shit and I didn't exactly dig cleaning cum off the floors and I quit.

Rob's a cool dude. He's a young guy, maybe twenty-two or three. He went to college and all and he's a real brain, plus his whole family is hooked up with the Mafia and shit. Rob always got dynamite grass which he only deals keys, except me, he lets me cop a dime or whatever. Anyway, he's the manager, but you never know when he's gonna be there. He's in and out all the time. Right behind the office he got his own little crib, with beaded curtains so you can't look in if you're standing in front of the desk. And he got a chauffeur too. His own fucking chauffeur who picks him up in this old Mercedes whenever he wants him to. Nobody knows where he really lives. He got a coke nose as long as your arm which is why he is always broke, despite the keys and the Mafia and shit. I mean the Mafia got to be in it because if you got a freak bathhouse in the middle of the Deuce you really gotta be into some heavy shit.

I trick with Rob too, but mostly we're like friends. I mean, he lets me cop my little smoke, whatever. He don't exactly give it away but then again did you ever see a Ginney who gives anything away? Sometimes if I got a trick and no place to take him he lets me use one of the cubicles or if I got no place to crash he lets me crash for the night which is when I get down with him. One thing is he's cool that he don't ask no questions and don't want to get into your personal business and shit. So when I come up the stairs I'm glad to see he's on. He's giving a customer some change and motions for me to come around through the door which he has to buzz you in. I can see he ain't busy and it's ok with him if I go in the back and rest my feet and dry off. When he's through with the customer I cop a dime from him and borrow some paper so I can roll it up. But he says to save them and pulls out a coupla huge bombers which we light up and I crack the pint of wine so we can sip and which is sweet and goes great with the herb.

After we smoke the joints he lays out a couple of lines of coke which we blow and zaps me right up. I wisht I had a box now so we could check out some sound. Rob, he don't talk much, so I tell him how I blew the box with the trick this morning and he says, well, I can take his until I cop another one for myself which means definitely that it is a loan and that I gotta bring it back, he ain't saying when, but whenever, that's when I gotta bring it back. Ginney's are like that and they don't forget either.

So we sit on the couch digging our heads and shooting the shit. Just bullshit, like did you see so and so, or did you know so and so got pinched or so and so broke up with so and so.

It's getting dark. I wouldn't mind having a little crib like this, you know, which is mine and nobody else's. When I was small I bounced around between my mother and grandma so much I didn't know which place was home and maybe it was neither of them. Then when I ran away I stayed wherever I could, sometimes in the park, sometimes down by the railroad tracks where no one bothers you. Now when I go to Queens, it's still my mother's crib and of course, the Reverend, and even if you shut the door there's no privacy. Someone is always hollering at someone else, or where did you put this or where did you put that plus the TV going all the time. You can never get any peace and when I'm out hustling I just sleep wherever the last trick decides to go. Well, when you think about it, it's not so bad. What if you get a crib all hooked up and shit and then you get pinched, or someone's looking for you and you gotta take it on the lam? Now you got all that shit you just hooked up you gotta leave behind. So, maybe it's better after all to travel light, because if you gotta split all of a sudden, boom, you're gone and that's that.

I know the herb is righteous because in my mind I'm freaked out on trees. Would you believe it, trees? I used to go to the park all the time. I wonder how long it is since I seen a tree. I fuck around down on the Deuce so much I just don't go to the park anymore. Well, that's not too bad either when you think about it. What can you do in the park besides deal drugs and later for that. That's why I'm on probation.

While my head is into trees I feel Rob's hand on my dick and I know he feels it through my pants getting hard. I tell him, no, man, I gotta tip. I gotta lot of shit to do. I don't want to get down right now. But I guess the herb got him fucked up too because he just keeps on playing with it which feels good, no doubt about it, and I say what the fuck, I like what he's doing and my dick is really hard for the first time today.

So he goes, "Let's take our clothes off."

I think shit, I don't have time to get all lovey-dovey and I tell him, no man, I'll take care of you like this, lean back, but instead he asks can he screw me. I go, "Shit no, man, but maybe later, you know," and then he asks me would I let him for fifty and I say sure, but not now, some other time, I'm just not in the mood.

"Lean back and let me take care of you like this and later for the other thing." It's not the fifty, though I don't usually get screwed, but I let Rob screw me before. What it is mainly is that if I get all undressed and get into bed I know I'll fall out because my head is aching again and I think I'm getting a migraine and I still got an awful lot of B.I. to take care of. Maybe I'll come back tonight and we'll do it then. No, he says, he's leaving later and going to the country and won't be back 'til next week. So he says OK, go ahead, and leans back and I try to give him a real good time while I'm blowing him, you know, playing with the bottom of his dick and balls and all, while I run my tongue around the head. Me, I'm getting horny myself, so I pull my dick out and jerk off while I'm blowing him and right after he cums I cum all over the side of the couch because I'm on my knees and I got a big blob of his cum in my mouth and run to the sink so I can spit it out and rinse my mouth. I can tell he liked it, though, but also I got to split.

He says, "What's the hurry? The driver is gonna come by with the car and you can watch TV until then and when the night man comes in I'll give you a lift and drop you off wherever you want." But it's after four now and I can't wait. I just can't. I got to get up to Saul's right away so he can call the P.O. before five when the office closes. He says, "When are you coming back?"

I go, "Let's see what happens. Some time during the week, bet?" and he goes, "Bet," and then he says, "Wait a minute, take this to walk with," and he lays a pound on me. "Take a cab uptown, it's raining and don't forget your umbrella, you're always leaving it, and, Sinbad," he yells down the stairs after me, "don't forget that box is mine."

"Yeah," I yell back.

"Well just remember and don't let me see it in some hockshop window."

"I'll see you next week," I holler, but don't know if he heard me. I knew he was gonna say something about the box. That's the way Ginneys are.

It's almost dark and the streets are wet and shiny black and the cars squoosh through puddles. All the movie lights are on though it's still afternoon and after the rain it smells pretty good. But as soon as I hit the cold air I really catch a buzz. The cold'll do that to you every time when you're high and you come out of a warm place.

I lean up against a bus stop sign until I can get my head organized. Fuck the cab. I don't need to get stuck in rush-hour traffic. I got enough gap with the pound that Rob laid on me to cop a couple of tuinals and buy a subway token to get up to Saul's, plus I still have all the herb left.

The tuinals I cop in front of Playland and just swallow them like that with no water or nothing. Sheik II is sitting on his jonny pump in his ghi, which he always wears, even when he's hustling.

I say, "What's happening, man?"

And he goes, "Nothin' much, what's happening with you, man?"

And I say, "Nothin' much, but I got some righteous herb and why don't we stroll around the corner and do a joint, you and me."

And he goes, "I don' mind," you know, like he's real cool, and he goes, "What is it, man, Cheeba?"

"I dunno, you know, like Rob's holding it and his shit is always righteous, you know."

"Yeah," he agrees, "Rob's shit is always righteous."

Everybody on the deuce knows that Rob's shit is righteous, that's how good it is, and I go, "What's the difference if he grows it in his backyard so long as it's righteous?"

And Little Sheik laughs up a storm and says, "Yeah, I can dig it, man."

So we go around the corner on Forty-third past the parking lot and sit under the fire escape there, where it's like in the shadows, plus nobody ever comes down Forty-third much anyhow, and light up a joint which right away makes the Little Sheik cough and choke so that I know the shit got to be righteous. And I go, "So what's happening, man?"

And he goes, "Same old, same old, you know." So I ask him what time he got down to the Deuce.

"I just come out," he says. "I wasn't gonna come because it was raining, but then it stopped so I came." Which is about as much as I ever heard Little Sheik say at one time together. Little Sheik, he's a cool dude but he don't have too much to say.

And I go, "So you just came down, man."

And he says, "Yeah, I just came down."

I go, "You score yet today, man?"

"Nah," he says, "I didn't score yet, but there's plenty of tricks in Playland."

"Well," I say, 'cause I hate to think of Little Sheik getting pinched, "you better watch out for them tricks in Playland because they got a lot of undercovers in there."

And he goes, "Nah, I can always tell which is the trick and which is the po-leese."

"Sometimes it's hard to tell."

"Yeah," he agrees. "Sometimes it's hard to tell, but I know which is which."

We finish smoking the joint, which Little Sheik pops the roach into his mouth and swallows it and I tell him, "Well, man, let's split because I gotta take care of some B.I."

And he goes, "Yeah, me too."

We walk back around the corner to the Square. And I tell him, "Later," and he goes, "Later, man" and strolls on down the block towards Playland and I yell, "Take care, Little Sheik," because I really hate to think of him getting pinched, but he don't hear me, or if he does he just keeps on getting up. All them little kids are like that. They all think they're real cool and real down, which Little Sheik is, but when push comes to shove they don't want to hear anything and they wind up getting pinched, even though nothing much happens to them. Like the Children's Court judge will tell them to go home and stay out of trouble and the next day there they are back in front of Playland again, just like nothing happened. Still, it's a pain in the balls getting pinched.

Now I really got to rush to get to Saul's so he can make that call to the P.O. before five. If Saul's not home I'm really up shit creek. So back down into the hole I go again, where I met the kid this morning. The kid, Jesus fucking Christ, he can't still be waiting for me in the Port. I forgot all about him. Nah, no way he's still at the Port. He musta got tired and split, unless he got pinched which he probably did.

But I got no time now to worry about him and two expresses go by, then a third, and still no local. What the fuck is going on, they ain't running no locals no more? When it finally does come I'm so fucked up and nervous about the P.O. and all, and I'm sure I'm gonna catch a migraine, that by the time I get off at Ninety-sixth and Central Park and walk upstairs, I realize that I left the fucking umbrella on the train. And I just bought the fucking thing too.

It's night. Everybody's on their way home. Where I get off is just a block from my mother's old house and Saul is two blocks more, over by Broadway. He lives in one of those old brownstones, two flights up. He got a boss crib with a loft bed and red shag carpets and brown shutters on the windows. Also he got a fireplace and a freaky black leather couch and a bar and one of those mirror balls that go round and round like they got in the clubs which all his trade digs the shit out of the crib.

I never seen a guy with so much trade. I swear to God, sometimes it's like he got wall-to-wall kids. One laying up in the bed, or maybe even two, one crashed out on the couch, maybe two others checking out the color TV. You can walk in there practically anytime and find kids laying around in their drawers all over the place. Sometimes they hang out for days at a time until Saul gets tired of the whole shebang and "cleans up the house," which is what he says when he throws everybody out. Me he never throws out, only if I'm fucked up on tuinals.

I'll say this for him, though, all the time we were together, I mean, whenever I was living there, he gave me the respect and never brought trade in unless he knew I wasn't gonna be there. Like if I called him and told him I was goin' to Queens or something, which he says, "It's only a courtesy to call." Then he'd bring trade up.

I swear he gets all the prettiest motherfuckers too. Some of his trade I wouldn't mind getting down with myself. I don't know how he keeps juggling all those kids around, but he does. Right now he got at least four of them which each thinks that they are his only ace, or steady, or lover, or what have you. Saul, he don't give a fiddler's fuck if they're all in the crib at the same time. As a matter of fact he digs having them all around together. They all got keys to the crib but they never rip him off, never.

I've seen him with my own eyes getting down with all four of them, but one at a time in the bedroom and not one of them complains or says anything about it. The one he wants to stay with him in the bed that night is the one he brings in last. Each one of them he cons and tells him, "You're my real ace, but the other guys are my friends too. They're old friends and I don't want to hurt their feelings. So be cool, try to be a little understanding." Understanding, my left ball. I can't believe that they aren't at each other's throats all the time. I think that the only reason he gets away with it is that he really likes them all, I mean, he really does and he really don't want to hurt nobody's feelings and they dig it, you know. I mean, who ever gave a fuck about their feelings before, you know? One of the aces is this gorgeous, yeah, that's what I said, gorgeous, Latin brother who looks just like an Indian. I mean he got long hair almost down to his ass and wears a red headband like he's Cochise or something and he is one pretty motherfucker. His name is Savage and believe me, they don't call him Savage for nothing. He's one mean, treacherous dude. With my own eyes I seen him slice this dude one time from his gut to his neck, just like that, for nothing, 'cause the dude happened to bump into him or something and didn't bother to say excuse me.

But Saul, he worships Saul. He'd bite the throat out of any motherfucker who even got near Saul. One day we're just sitting around getting high and shit and rapping and Saul's on the phone or some shit and this dude Savage goes, "Hey, Sinbad, you ever get down with Saul?"

Now what makes this ridiculous is that Savage, he knows that I lived with Saul, I mean, lived with him, not just crashed there. What the fuck does he think we were doing in the bed every night, telling fairy tales or something? What it turns out to be is that Saul has laid some kind of rap on him that he is my compadre, my godfather, and never never would he get down with me. And fucking Savage, who knows every street game that was ever invented and has invented a few by hisself, he goes for this shit. It's unbelievable. That's the only word for it.

"Yeah, yeah," he goes, "I know he's your compadre and all, but you know, I was just checking it out." Fucking Savage is actually embarrassed, but not too embarrassed to slice me up one way and down the other if he ever thought I was getting it on with Saul. Well, Saul's like that. He just grows on you. I don't know if deep down the aces believe all this crap or what. Maybe they're scared of him because he's been upstate in the real joint or maybe it's just that the easiest dude to hustle is a hustler. Who knows?

He don't give them any gap either. Not after the first time. After the first time if he's interested he gives them his phone number, which he is always changing, and if they call him again, they're hooked. Saul got them running in and out smoked up, tripping out, feeding them a line of shit and screwing their assholes off and fucking with their heads so they don't know which way is up and before they know it they're bringing him gap instead of vice versa.

What really clinches it is when Saul lays a key on them. Most of these dudes never had a house key of their own in their life unless they geesed it from a trick. Their own mothers wouldn't lay a key on them because they'd steal their mommas blind without batting an eyelash. So when Saul lays the key to the crib on them it's like the biggest thing that ever happened to them and they don't dare rip him off because it would be like ripping their own selves off. Of course when Saul gets tired of the whole scene and cleans house he just changes the lock and that's that.

Me, I gotta admit that when I was living there and of course had my own key even when he changed the locks, I ripped him off once in a while. I mean I was strung out and, you know, just little shit which I always tried to get back from the pawnshop anyhow, and sometimes some gap and of course he'd kick the living piss out of me and I'd tip for a coupla days and always come back and it would be ok. One time he beat up on me so bad that I wound up in the hospital, but I had it coming because I'll say this for him, when I really needed him he was there. Whether it was bail or coming to court, or the police station or hospital or whatever, he was always there. Even when we finally broke up and I gave him back the key, I could still crash there as long as I'm not fucked up on pills.

A couple of months ago when Carmen got thrown out of her house he let us both crash out in the bedroom while he slept on the living room couch until she could get everything straightened out and go back to Jersey. He never said a thing about it. Not a word about how long, or anything. Just gave us the bed and bought groceries and took the phone off the hook and if any trade came to the door he wouldn't let them in, you know, out of respect for Carmen and all so she wouldn't know. That's the way he is. He can be treacherous as a snake, but if you're his ace, he'll go right down the line for you.

When I get to the door, it's like a habit. I reach in my pocket for the key which of course I don't have since I tipped—well actually he threw me out. Still and all it was better that way, what with me fucking around down at the Deuce and the tuinals and shit and I just wanted to be on my own for a while, you know, to see if I could take care of myself. So I ring and hear nothing but King Fu.

King Fu is a monster shepherd which I stole from the pet shop near my grandma's a couple of years ago and gave to Saul for a birthday present, which, being strung out then, I couldn't afford to buy him. Saul calls him Mister Fu because he says anything that big you damn well better call Mister. The only time he ever barks is when he smells me since I was the one that fed him and walked him when he was small and even now I walk him a lot. Fu is really nothing but a big dope who wants to be everybody's friend and loves being petted. But nobody knows this but me and Saul. Anybody else who comes to the crib Saul always warns them about how vicious Fu is, so maybe that's why they don't rip him off.

Sometimes when I walk Fu alone in the park at night, shit, I know that nobody, but nobody is gonna bother me or try to mug me, not with Fu walking right by me like a fucking lion, no leash or anything. All I gotta do is tell him to heel and he walks right with me except you gotta watch out for collies. Anybody who knows anything about dogs knows that shepherds hate collies. Well, one night me and Fu are strolling through the park and here comes this lady walking her collie who also is not on a leash. Fu, he don't say nothing, he just makes a leap. I swear to God, it musta been ten feet or more, and snatches this collie by the throat and boom, he just flips him over like it was nothing and breaks the collie's spine, just like fucking Bruce Lee or something. Well, the lady, she starts hollering about her five-hundred-dollar dog this and her poor baby that and all that happy horseshit and I go shit, lady, that should teach you to keep your dog on a leash from now on. Me, I feel proud like a motherfucker when I walk King Fu, which I hear him barking but nobody answers the doorbell. Saul, he better be there because I don't even have a token to get back downtown, even forgetting about the P.O. and all, so I ring and ring and finally the door opens and it's Saul and Fu is jumping all over me and licking me and Saul, he goes, "Well, if it's not Sinbad the Semen," which is our own private joke and I go, "Your mother's name is Semen," and he goes, "Your mother sucks big nigger dicks."

And then I'm inside and we hug each other like we haven't seen each other in ages which it couldn't really be more than a couple of days and Saul says, "Mmm . . . indeed, the Lord of Hustlers, himself."

And I go, "Hey, man, gettin' any since last time?" which is also a sorta private joke.

So we hug some more and he finally closes the door. The crib is nice and warm and the lights are on and a Barry White side is on the box. It's just a bad crib and right now I wouldn't wanna be anyplace else in the world.

Right away Saul puts out a brand-new bottle of Dewar's White Label scotch on the table. But no glasses. Saul and me, we never drink out of glasses, at least not booze. Saul says we're "bottle babies," which is pretty funny too if you think about it. Well, there's always a plastic pitcher of water, just for a chaser, you know. So we zip the booze and Saul opens the reefer box like he's getting ready to roll, but I tell him, "Hey, man, don't roll up your stash. Try some of this. It's righteous herb."

"Ah, excellent youth, filled with the fruits of righteousness. And where, may I ask, did you cop?"

"It's Rob's shit. Check it out."

See, everybody knows that Rob's shit is dyno-mite. I lay a joint on Saul and light up another myself and put the bag on the table so we can roll some more even though one joint apiece of this shit will get us nice and fucked up. I lay back on the pillows on the old black leather couch and kick off my sneakers. I take a coupla deep tokes and start to relax. It's great to be home.

"Rob? Mmmph . . . time and again I have warned you as if you were own beloved son, he's a stool pigeon."

"Oh, Jesus fucking Christ, let's not start that now, please. All I wanna do is chill out and enjoy myself. Is that too much to ask? I hadda bitch of a day and I feel like I'm gonna catch a migraine."

"Migraine, my asshole. Unfailingly, whenever you attempt to justify the absurd you threaten a migraine."

"Please, Saul, honest, just rub the back of my neck and maybe I won't catch one."

Which Saul can rub the back of your neck so good that it puts you to sleep while he's doing it. As a matter of fact that's not a bad idea at all, so I close my eyes and enjoy the neck rub wishing we could just stay like this without saying nothing but I know once he gets started on somebody's case nothin's gonna stop him. Well, we might as well get the argument over, so I go, "Didya ever stop to think that maybe you're jealous. Maybe you're jealous of Rob or something?"

"Jealous? Of Rob? Madness! What the fuck does that asshole have that could conceivably provoke jealousy in anyone?"

"Well, you know, because I get down with him once in a while . . . you know it don't mean anything."

"Please, please, my boy, don't confuse the issues. We are speaking of Robert's perfidy now. We will discuss your promiscuity anon."

He takes a gigantic swig of Dewar's and passes me the bottle without wiping the top off. One thing you gotta be able to do if you want to hang out with Saul is you gotta be able to guzzle booze. I usta call him sponge gut but that got him sore, so I stopped. I love to watch him tilt back his head when he's drinking. His glasses slip right down his nose, which always gets him aggravated. Saul, he's not exactly what you'd call vain, anyhow, always sitting around in his old floppy kimono which he wouldn't throw away even when I boosted a brand-new velvet bathrobe for him from Macy's. And he's not exactly what you'd call pretty either, what with his gut hanging out and he almost always needs a shave, plus that corny crew cut of his. But what the fuck. I dig the shit out of the guy, or at least I would if he wouldn't keep getting on my case all the time.

"Listen," he says when he finally puts down the bottle and wipes off his mouth with the back of his hand. "Listen, I don't put a stool-pigeon label on anyone unless I know what I'm talking about. Jealous? Do you know what happens to you upstate in that mighty river fortress if you put a bum wire out on a guy, if you falsely intimate that he is a stool pigeon? Since you ask, my boy, let me tell you. You wind up with your throat cut. That's what happens. Jealous? Sinbad, verily I declare unto you that friend Rob is nothing but trouble with a capital *T*."

"Ok, let's get it on. You just won't let me relax for two minutes, will you?" I take a swig out of the bottle myself. It sure looks like I'm gonna need one. I know I'm starting to get bombed already and I just hope I don't say the wrong thing to really set him off. Saul, he got a terrible temper. "So answer me just one question

105

then, as long as you won't get offa the subject, how could he be a stool pigeon when everybody says he's with the Mafia or something? You gonna tell me the Mafia lets stool pigeons in?"

"Sinbad, Sinbad, thou credulous voyager. Ah, the golden innocence of youth . . ."

"Saul!"

". . . out of whose mouths flow words of absolute bullshit! Do you hear me, you clown, *bullshit!*" His face is so close to mine that his breath nearly knocks me out and he's sweating bullets like he does whenever he gets excited about something, which is almost everything. "Hasn't it dawned on you that he *must* be a stool pigeon to get away with all his happy horseshit?"

"What horseshit?"

"Oh, nothing, not a thing. Just an S and M bathhouse smack dab in the middle of Forty-second Street. Nothing much—keys of smoke and coke, by the way, right out in the open in the very hottest part of our infernal metropolis. Nothing, just plain ordinary everyday horseshit."

"Well you don't have to be so car-sastic about it."

"Sarcastic."

"That's what I said, didn't I?"

"Sinbad, my boy, you are not drunk. No indeed. You are polluted."

"So big shit. So what, so are you and you're fucking up my head. I mean, Jesus Christ, do we always have to fight about something? And another thing, gimme a drink because I swear to fucking God you're giving me a fucking migraine."

"Peace, my comely comrade, veteran of many bottles shared..."

"Battles, dummy."

"Exactly as you say . . . ." and he starts to giggle which makes me bust out laughing because we're both high as kites and fucked up on the booze and he staggers over and sits down next to me on the couch and then he starts hugging me and getting all mushy and shit which is a helluva lot better than arguing. Finally I push him off of me.

"Saul. Come on, Saul. Cut it out. No, I'm serious. Answer me one question, please. Please?"

"One, just one, o excellent and artful dodger."

106

"Ok, name me one guy who he ever ratted on. Just name me one guy."

"Who?"

"Who Rob ratted on. Cut it out, Saul, you promised."

"Sinbad, me lad, yer not going to be satisfied until you're the death of yer ould compadre, plaguin' me and houndin' me to an early grave. Ok, asshole. I was upstate with a goombah of this guy's uncle . . . ." That's what's amazing about Saul. One minute he's piss-assed drunk and the next minute, boom, he sounds like he didn't have a drink all day. ". . . upstate with a goombah of this guy's uncle. The name's not important, but he's a Ginney and if you follow the crime news, you'd know the name right off. Now this guy told me, number one, his uncle, who is connected people and very good people himself and who is connected to certain other connected parties in Brooklyn and Jersey, doesn't even talk to him. As a matter of fact your revered connection and erstwhile bed partner was told that if he ever sets foot in Brooklyn he shall be the recipient of a bullet in the back of his skull. Use your head. What the fuck do you think he's doing with that faggot bodyguard and that old beat-up tank he drives around in, besides being too much of a punk to carry his own piece? That's number one. Did you ever see him walk anywhere? No. Definitely no. Too dangerous. Why, why, you ask. I'll tell you why. Because the old man in Brooklyn and some of the Jersey crew would be more than happy to put a cap in his head, that's why, and the only thing keeping him alive today is that he's the other guy's nephew. Now do you understand?"

"Well, not really, I still don't see . . ."

"Did he tell you he got pinched?"

"Pinched? Whadda you mean pinched?"

"I mean pinched, busted, popped, flying high in April shot down in May. Pinched."

"You mean he got pinched?"

"What am I talking, Polish? No, I imagine he neglected to advise you of that while you were busy giving him head."

"For Chrissakes, what the fuck are you talking about? I didn't give him no head. Never." Which of course is a whopper and Saul must know it. It's amazing, I mean, it's amazing, he must have the fucking C.I.A. on me or something. Some of the shit he knows about me is impossible. That's one of the reasons I couldn't stand living with him. I couldn't get over on him worth a shit. He waves his hand like it's not even worth arguing about, like he's positive.

"You did and he did. You sucked his cock and he got pinched."

"I didn't and so what if he got pinched. Everybody gets pinched."

"Your cynicism is well placed, despite its slightly Calvinist flavor. But while, as you say, everybody gets pinched, everybody does not, definitely does not get pinched with two and a half keys of coke and wind up back on the street within twenty-four hours with no bail whatsoever, free as a bird."

"Maybe they dropped the beef. Maybe that's what happened."

"Maybe my asshole dropped. The only thing dropped was a dime by your heartthrob, Sir Robert the Raunchy. No, we are not speaking of local precinct nonsense, bullshit street sales which, as well you know from bitter experience, can be unpleasant enough but nevertheless can be smoothed over by the type of adroit manipulation in which your humble servant takes pride. It takes a bit more than the old flim-flam about, 'Your Honor, this poor unfortunate boy before you . . .,' a wee bit more than that. No, definitely not dropped, not two keys and change. Rather should we say put to bed, put to rest on the back burner, but not for too long. Bet your sweet ass on that, my boy, and your anal orifice will remain virgin for life. It's the feds we're talking about and not the FBI either, who are Mickey Mouse and have lived off that gangbuster shit for years. The D.E.A. on the other hand is well known, and deservedly so, for its efficiency. The Lords of Narcdom, true blue bulls to the last. And they do not give up. Fortunately for you the level of your previous operations was of insufficient magnitude to warrant their dogged attentions. But rest assured they are both unflappable and unfixable. Their modus operandi is a model of simplicity. For example, they pinch Joe Blow. Now they tell Joe, 'Joe, give us your connection or you blow . . . blow about forty years in Atlanta.' The same persuasion is used in the case of Joe's connection until finally they arrive at The Man, who hardly ever knows what hit him or what went wrong. Somewhere in the vast daisy chain you will find your jovial john, Rob, gaily—no pun intended—setting somebody up for the kill."

"But how do you know it was the feds that pinched him?"

"I know the D.E.A. pinched him because I was told, personally advised, by a motherfucking FBI, that's how I know. I'm sure you recall old Barry G. If not, let me refresh your memory. And speaking of refreshment, bring me that other bottle of Dewar's from the bar. I have an immortal thirst and many more immoral lessons to teach you. Mmmm, bless you. Here's to the better days which are long overdue. You do remember Barry, who so kindly helped me out of the counterfeit case and who also through the unmerited prestige of the bureau managed, at my behest, to get you a conditional discharge on a certain sale to a certain undercover which you most certainly made. Well, old Barry, who still owes me one or two, gave me a call to warn me . . . what was I saying . . . mmmm . . . yes, to warn me to keep as far the fuck away from your scurvy sponsor as possible because he, Rob—to be sure you understand the antecedent of the pronoun—is definitely, absolutely, and completely wrong. Wrong, wrong, wrong! Can you dig *that*, buster?"

"Ok, ok. Say he's wrong, what the fuck does that got to do with me?"

"What it has to do with you, you silly fuck, is that this is a small world and the pismire around the Square is even smaller, so small in fact that people may start pointing fingers directly at you when they learn that not only are you sucking the prick of a punk, but the prick of a stoolie punk which makes you, in the jailhouse vernacular, a punk's punk."

Now it's my turn to holler. He's got to be guessing, unless he got a fucking one-way mirror hid in the Arsenal.

"Will you stop saying I'm sucking his dick! Is that all you can say, that I'm sucking his goddamn dick?"

"Jesus fucking Christ," he explodes, and jumps up, nearly knocking over the Dewar's which I have to catch to stop it from spilling all over the shag. "Jesus fucking Christ, if your sole reason for visiting is to give me a hand job, do me a favor, do us both a big favor and stay the fuck away."

"You want me to go, is that it? You got trade coming over or something and you wanna get rid of me? Well if you want me to go just say so, period."

"Listen, do whatever the fuck you want to do. Suck his dick, his balls, his asshole, his cunt, his mother's cunt, suck any fucking thing you want to, but in the name of all that's unholy don't come on all wounded innocence with me when you most certainly are sucking that . . . whatever he is . . . to death, case closed!"

"No goddamn it, the fucking case is not closed," I scream, and we're both up on our feet in each other's faces, all rowdy-assed drunk and poor Fu jumping around trying to get us to stop. ". . . the fucking case is not closed. Why is it closed? Because you say it's closed. Well, fuck you! Fuck you twice!"

Which is not the most intelligent thing I ever said but there's just no way I can say what I want to, which I don't even know what I really want to say. Plus there's no way I can argue with him with all those phony-assed big words he uses. So what do I do? I stand there like a big dummy and bawl my fool head off. Here I am like some big fucking beanpole with water all running out of my eyes like a little kid and poor Fu is whining and scratching us both with his paws to please make us stop all this bullshit. And right in the middle of Fu barking and me bawling the telephone rings which Saul picks it up and starts hollering.

"Nobody's home, so fuck off! . . . . oh, Angel? Yes, dear boy . . . mmm . . . no, not now, I'm busy. I said *no*, goddamn it." And he slams down the phone which I'm glad now he's mad at Angel, whoever Angel is and just maybe he'll stop this bullshit and get off my case.

"Are you through picking on me?" I sniffle.

"Mmmm, I need a drink, and from the looks of you, you could use one too. And for God's sake use my handkerchief . . . here . . . blow. I simply cannot bear to see a hardened hustler cry."

Well, that's the way it is with us. One minute we're like cats and dogs and the next minute everything's all lovey-dovey. Don't ask me why. That's just the way it is, which is why when I was living with him we were always at each other's throats or getting down, one or the other all the time. The thing about it is, all that shit about Rob being a stoolie and shit, well maybe it was the truth and maybe it wasn't. The thing is with Saul you never know. It could be the truth, all of it, and then again it could be all bullshit

110

he just made up so he could find out if I was really getting down with Rob or not. Saul's like that. He'll put himself and you through all kinds of changes and fuck with everybody's head just so he could find out something which probably if he asked you straight up, like about Rob and me, I mighta told him the truth in the first place, which no way would I do now and go through all that shit all over again. Meanwhile I gotta feel like the world's biggest idiot bawling and all like a fucked-up little kid and all because he couldn't ask me straight out.

"Well", he goes, "At least we put on a good show for the neighbors".

"Yeah, well I hope you had fun because I didn't and why you always gotta get on my case like that?"

"Because I love you."

"Don't say that. Don't fuck around like that."

"You disbelieve me?"

"Stop it, right now! I told you, don't fuck around like that."

He looks at me kinda sad, like he's trying to think of the right thing to say, or like maybe he forgot what it was and he like puts his hand under my chin, real soft like, and lifts my chin up so we're looking right at each other and says, "Sinbad, I'm not fucking around."

And I go, "Saul, hey look, man, I can't talk all smart and fancy like you but don't interrupt me with some smart-ass remark, just let me say something, ok?"

He takes his hand away and just sits there, not looking at me anymore, just staring out into space. I feel all funny in my gut because all the time I've known him I never seen him this way. It's like everything's switched around topsy-turvy. Now I'm like a grown man and he's the kid, all fidgety and nervous like I just caught him with his dick in his hand.

The thing is, I don't know what to say, but somebody's gonna have to say something and since he looks like he's gonna let me get in a word edgewise for a change, I might as well let it all hang out so I go, "Yo, Saul, let me say something. Dig. You don't want me, I mean, really want me living with you again and shit, like it was before. For what? Listen, man, you done a lot of good for me, stuck by me all the way, helped me kick when I was strung out, got me out of jail, shit that my mother wouldn't even dream of doing

111

for me. Sometimes, sometimes it was like I was your own son or something, even when we were getting down all the time, which I don't say I didn't like, because I did. But it's different now. It's changed. I ain't that dumb little kid you picked up practically out of the gutter all sick and fucked up. Saul, you helped me in a million ways and you still do and I owe you. I swear, you tell me to I'd go kill anybody you say. I mean it, you know I mean it. But what it is, is that you're the way you are and I am what I am. I ain't sayin' that things couldn't change. Everything changes, I know that. But you, you got your four aces—come on, don't laugh—it's true. You got your four aces which think you're God Almighty and that your shit don't stink either and maybe you're serious with them too and then again maybe you're not. I'm not saying it's any of my business. It's not. But you know that someday you'll get tired of them and you'll change the locks and then they'll be another and another in and out all the time, and the phone calls, Angel this and José that and this one and that one and the next one. You dig what I'm sayin', that's the way you are. You remember when we were living together, we were getting down all the time, I'm not in the mood, I wanna be left alone tonite. Did I ever say that to you? Never, not once. Did you ever ask me, just once, 'Sinbad, you wanna get down tonight, you feel like doin' it?' Not once. You went ahead. I'm not saying that if I said no, you wouldn't of stopped because I know you would of. But look at it my way. It's always in my head, I owe him, I owe him and I don't wanna hurt his feelings. And how about me? You gave me everything. I mean, you took care of me and shit and took me to fancy places too and restaurants and shit and introduced me to people too that you weren't ashamed of me. Don't think I didn't see it just 'cause I was a dopy strung-out kid. I know I'm more to you than a piece of trade you pick up in the street and I know you really got feelings for me, but look at me. Saul, please, I'm talking to you. Look at me. You know what I do all day. I don't have to tell you. What, you think I'm proud of it? But I'm just trying to get over, you know, just trying to get by until whatever . . . until I dunno . . . until I don't have to be doin' what I'm doin' right now which I don't have the slightest idea when it's all gonna change. Getting up every day. Going to the Program. Hanging out. And you know the rest. You know what I was and I'm still doin' the same old same old. I dunno. Maybe it's just that I'm all fucked up and got my head screwed on backwards. What would happen? Suppose I moved back in here. You think it would work out? What about your trade? What about me? You wanna keep me? Saul, if I'm gonna trick I don't want it to be with you. I don't want you wakin' up in the morning and saying well, Sinbad is trickin' with me because I'm keepin' him and the crib is boss and he got clothes and don't haveta worry about nothin'. You think I want you to wake up and think that? You think I wanna wake up and wonder if you're thinkin' that? You think every time we got down I wanna think well, shit, I owe him, even if I don't feel like it. If I'm gonna get down with someone which I don't feel like it, then I want it to be a trick, not you, Saul. It's not so bad. It don't mean nothin'. Not really. To me it's just getting over, but to you it's a big deal just like we were fighting tonight over what? Over whether I gave Rob a blow job or not. Big fucking deal! But to you it is. That's just the point. You wanna have your cake and eat it too. You wanna have feelings for me but you wanna trick with me and you wanna get on my case about the least little shit about hustling which don't bother me at all. Why, you think I got feelings for guys I go with? I know you don't like to hear about it, but let me just tell you what happened today, ok, and then I won't bring it up no more. I went with this dude, Saul, he didn't even look at me, not once. That's it. Whatta you think, I could have feelings for him? It's just my way, that's all. Right now it's what I hafta do and, Saul, it's what I wanna do. Saul, I have feelings for you, you know it. But not all the time. I can't handle it day in day out worrying if I say this will you get mad or if I do this will you get mad, or if I don't do this will you get mad. Not all the time. I dig the shit out of coming to see you and maybe crashing and maybe not and maybe staying for a day or two or three or a week, whatever, but when I feel like tipping I wanna be able to tip without thinking, is he mad? Without you thinking, is he gonna be ok? You dig? It's hard enough just worrying about myself, just getting through each crappy day without all the time worrying what someone else is thinking or worrying about you. So please, if you really feel for me don't make it harder than it is. I gotta nuff to worry about just worrying about me. Don't make me worry about you too. I can't do it. I just can't. Ok?"

Which is definitely the longest rap I ever laid on anybody in my life and I hope I didn't sound like a complete dummy which I'm not too sure what I said myself, so it musta come out all fucked up. Me, I'm talked out and Saul, he don't say nothin'. He just sits there playing with the ashes in the ashtray and then he looks up like he's gonna lay some real heavy rap on me.

And he goes, "Sinbad, my boy, your flowery discourse leaves one question unanswered."

"What, Saul, what question?"

"Sinbad, who the fuck spilled half the booze on my shag?"

Well, that's Saul for you. He can rap his ass off like some college professor or something and just when you think he's gonna get down with something really heavy, boom, he comes right off the wall with some fugazy shit and that's that, period. Maybe what it is, at least now, is that I hurt his feelings which I didn't wanna do, but I got all confused in what I was saying and blew his mind. To keep the peace I guess I should apologize, but I don't know what to apologize for so I go. "Yo, man, I'm sorry. It musta been me that spilled it. I'll get a rag and clean it up." Which is what I do, and nearly fall on my ass because my head is spinning from all the booze.

No way I can keep up with Saul when it comes to booze. I mean, I can do my share of drinking, but not steady, all night long like he can. Plus he don't have all that shit I got in my system, meth, plus tuinals and all the herb I did before I even got here which I don't even remember how long ago it was. So what I do is go into the bathroom and throw my shirt in the hamper and run cold water all over my head and neck and splash it on my face and then dry myself off and put some of his cologne on which I like the name, Aqua di Silva. Saul says it's Eyetalian but I know he's bullshitting because it's really Spanish and means "Water of the Woods." I dig that name. It reminds me of something but I can't figure out what and besides it smells ok too. So here I am tripping out in the can on Saul's cologne but my head at least is a little more together which I figure it better be because with Saul you never know whether it's gonna be nice and peaceful or whether its gonna be World War III.

When I go back it looks like maybe the fireworks are over. He got all the ashtrays empty and the dead soldiers in the garbage and is sitting there with, I swear, another bottle of Dewar's that he

114

musta just cracked, rolling reefer and looking just as happy as a pig in shit and hands me a joint and we light up.

I go, "Saul, you know, I think I'm forgetting something but I can't remember what it is."

"Mmm . . . perhaps if you just lie down for a while, something will come to you in the end."

"Come on, man, I'm serious. Help me figure it out."

"Well, the only way to figure it out is . . ."

But I never do find out what the only way is because, boom, there goes the fucking phone again. I want to tell him don't answer it and I go, "Saul . . ." but by then it's too late, he's already got it. "It's your money, start talking. Of course it's me, dunderhead. Who were you expecting, Alexander the Sixth . . . no, not that one . . . yeah . . . what are you out of your mind? . . . of course not, maybe fifty . . . how the fuck do I know without seeing it? . . . your word? . . . your word is as good as my checks . . . well I didn't really think you *meant* it . . . well, bring it up . . . how the fuck do I know, take a cab . . . yeah, Sinbad's here . . . just ring the bell and I'll come down and pay for the cab . . . yeah . . . Jesus fucking Christ, hang up already, will you. . . ."

"Who was that?"

"Mmmph . . . you're not the social secretary type."

"Smart-ass, who was that you told him Sinbad was here?"

"Name me the dumbest spic in the City."

"Flacco."

That's who it gotta be. Flacco, he's one of the four aces, at least for this month. In Spanish Flacco means "skinny." And besides being skinny Flacco is just about the dumbest spic you'd ever want to meet. He doesn't have a brain in his head and even though he's older than me by more than a year he don't know how to read and write, not even his own name. But one thing about him he's cool with Saul and him and me are allright which I see him down on the Deuce every once in a while. And another thing about him is that he's a good thief. I mean, he's too dumb to be scared and with those long giraffe legs of his he can really get in the wind if he gotta. A lot of guys think he got balls, but he ain't got no balls. It's just that he's dumb and don't know enough to be scared. So I ask Saul what the deal is with the cab and all and he says Flacco just stole a stereo somewhere. Not a normal stereo which you boost and just walk out with in a shopping bag or something. This stereo is supposed to be one of them monsters, you know, a huge cabinet and all, what do they call them? Consoles.

So Flacco geesed this fucking console somewheres that he says he can't hardly carry and is looking to down it with Saul.

"Hey, but Saul, you got two stereos already, one in here and one in the bedroom. Whatta you gonna do with another one?"

"Sinbad, dear heart, if he accepts fifty then the motherfucker must be worth four hundred at least."

"But whatta you gonna do with it?"

"Who the fuck knows what I'm going to do with it. You know I simply cannot resist a bargain."

"Is he gonna hang out?"

"Probably not. Otherwise why should the cadaverous clown be lugging it up here at this time of night? He must be very anxious to dispose of his swag quickly, which means, of course, he's in a rush to cop."

"Coke?"

"Probably, but who gives a fuck?"

"I give a fuck, that's who gives a fuck. Maybe I could beat him."

"Forget it. You're staying, he's going. I'll do the beating. He'll take thirty and lump it. If he doesn't want it, he can just take his console the fuck back where he got it. I can just see him now lugging a console down Central Park at this hour. Wouldn't get two blocks before he was pinched."

"Saul, he got fifty in his mind it's gonna stick there like glue."

"Fuck him. Thirty or nothing."

"That's not a nice way to talk about one of your aces."

"Aces, my ass. Flacco and I are . . ."

". . . just good friends."

And we both bust out laughing until my side hurts.

Saul goes, "Three-shay!"

"Three-shay, what's three-shay?"

"That's one better than touché."

And we crack up all over again, him spluttering and me half choking to death so he gets up and has to pound me on my back. He gotta admit one thing, there's nothing wrong with Rob's herb,

116

not a fucking thing which is why we are laughing like two loony tunes and of course being pretty drunk too.

"Sinbad," he goes, when I can breathe again, "you know what thirty-four and a half is?"

"Nope."

"Dummy, that's half of sixty-nine, you blow me, get it?"

And that does it. I just break up and nearly fall off the couch on my ass. Saul, he drags me back up and hands me the bottle and says kill it, which I do, with no water chaser.

"Well, that takes care of Miss Dewar's. What do we work on next? Take your choice, my boy, will it be gin, gin on the rocks, or gin and Coke? Don't ask for orange juice, there's not a drop in the house."

"Gin and Coke. It tastes like medicine straight."

"Mmm, temperance will be your downfall, my boy. Gin for the gentleman and gin and Coke for the small child, coming up."

The only reason I'm drinking is to keep him company. I mean, I had it long ago, but what the fuck, you only live once except I got an idea what my head's gonna feel like in the morning, which I would prefer not to think about and fuck up the party.

"Saul," I go. "Do me a favor."

"Certainly not. You know I don't get cornholed."

"Come on, no kidding, tell me about your grandmother again."

"What is it with you, you got a thing about my grandmother or something? Sinbad, are you turning queer for old ladies?"

"Come on, tell me. I like to hear about her. Besides we ain't got nothin' to do."

The thing is I really do like to hear him tell about his grandmother and besides when he starts rapping about her I can see that he's serious, you know, not sad serious, but like real serious and I dig it when he's that way.

"Well, as you know, my grandmother, may she rest, was a full-blooded Gypsy."

"What's a Gypsy?"

"You know fucking well. A Gypsy is a spic from Hungary."

"For real?"

"No, not for real. A Gypsy is, cómo se dice, a Gitano."

"Like from Spain?"

"Like from Spain, only these Gypsies were from Hungary."

"Where's Hungary?"

"Didn't you ever learn anything in school besides how to shoot dope?"

"Yeah, sure, but they didn't teach us about no Hungary."

"Go get the atlas, the book with the maps."

Which I do and he shows me Hungary again, which he must of showed me a million times, but I like to see it when he shows it to me.

"Now, where were we? Oh yeah, my grandmother. Never wore shoes until the day she died. A remarkable lady. She married my grandfather who was pure Hungarian and, naturally, they had to emigrate because a union like that was impossible. No respectable Hungarian would accept it. They had to leave and so they came to the States."

"What was wrong with marrying a Gypsy?"

"I told you, to the Hungarians the Gypsies were like spics. They were strangers, they spoke a funny language, they didn't like to work, they stole, and they had too many kids. Imagine your grandmother marrying a Wasp bank president. It was something like that, only worse. My grandfather was a nasty old bastard if ever there was one but Grandma Louisa must have seen something in him . . . mmm . . . yes, whatever it was. And *his* father, Mr. Great-grandfather, served as an officer with Garibaldi."

"Now you're getting me all fucked up again. Whatta the Ginneys have to do with your grandmother?"

"Not too much, really . . . mmm. So where was I? Don't sit there with the gin between your legs. Pass the bottle so I can put it to some use. Ah, yes, my grandmother. Never wore shoes until the day she died and then when they had her laid out, there she was with a pair of brand-new shoes. My father's doing, and his father, the nasty old bastard. At the time, of course, I laid it all on my mother, the spider lady. I couldn't have been more than six, but I was positive of it. She hated my grandmother, couldn't stand the sight of her, said she stank. What she really resented was that the only one I would mind was my grandmother. Here, fill your glass up. You want to be treated like a man, drink like one. Well, let me tell you, when I saw my grandma laid out with shoes on, *shoes*, I

118

threw a fit. Threw a fit right in the middle of the distinguished assemblage. Cried, kicked my mother, fell down and pounded the floor. An award-winning performance, only I wasn't acting. My father, well he must have had a spark of decency left, went over to the box and took the shoes off of the old lady without saying a word. My grandfather started to open his yap and my father just gave him a look that would frost the balls of a saint and threw the shoes in the garbage. And that was it. They finally planted her properly, though, alas, not in consecrated ground. The old lady died a heathen. Had the gift of sight."

"You mean like brujas?"

"Yes and no. Mainly yes, I suppose."

"You believe in that, brujas and all that, Santeria?"

I'm like flabbergasted. I thought that, well brujas and that kinda stuff, was something that only Puerto Ricans knew about, you know, like something only poor dumb spics who didn't know any better believed in, not that my mother's dumb or me either, but I never before even dreamed that any whitey even knew about that shit—and believe in it too? Saul?

"I believe that there are people with powers, Gypsies, brujas, sorcerers whatever you want to call it. Didn't I ever tell you I studied with a lama from Tibet, not in Tibet naturally . . ."

But I don't want to hear about lamas or Tibet, wherever the fuck that is, I wanna hear about brujas and I go, "But the brujas, my mother still goes to them and she got the candles and incense and the pennies for Chango, it used to scare me when I was small, but one time I ripped this guy off, I went by myself . . ."

"Attend, Sinbad, and stop hogging the booze. I shall spin you a yarn about brujas. You remember Alex?"

"Alex? The dude from Brook Avenue who usta live with you?"

"No, the other Alex, the one who did the Mae West imitation."

"The one in the boy burlesque?"

"Precisely. Cuban, as you know. Strange people. Much more superstitious than you P.R.'s in many ways. Well, shortly before I met you there was a time when I was doing very poorly indeed. Flat out busted. Up tight as a frog's ass and couldn't make a move. Just sat up in a five-flight walk-up somewhere off Twelfth Avenue with empty pockets and an emptier belly. A rat hole, really incredible. Couldn't make a move . . . mmmm . . . no, hemmed in as I was on all sides by the parole authorities, the United States Marshal Service, and worse, a few Italian gentlemen whom I had no wish at all to encounter. Sat up in that chamber of horrors all day long and would have starved too . . . mmmm . . . if it weren't for Alex coming by every so often with some groceries and a pint of wine. One day he showed up, no groceries, no wine, empty-handed. You won't need anything, he tells me. And why won't I need anything? Because Alex has just come from a visit to the bruja and she *saw*. Told him that he, Alex, was visiting a very dangerous place. Described it to a tee. The five flights, the whole layout. Described me too, it seems. She told him not to visit that place anymore. Keep away. He was just coming to warn me. The next day the marshals bust down the door and pinched me. Don't know to this day how they found me."

"You believe it, that it was the bruja? Maybe he wasn't telling the truth, just bullshitting. Maybe he ratted you out hisself."

"Alex? Bullshitting about a bruja? Never. He'd cut out his tongue first."

"So you believed it?"

"Of course."

"No shit?"

"No shit. I knew a guy in the joint upstate, a Ginney from East Harlem. You know, they're all Sidges up there. I used to fuck with him all the time about being painted with a tar brush, tell him, Patsy, Sicily's only forty miles from Africa. Drove him up a wall. Anyhow, Patsy was into sorcery—same story, oils, ointments, candles, the same things you get in the botánica. One time there was this other Ginney, he got a letter from his wife, divorcing him. The guy went berserk, ape shit. Went to Patsy and said he'd give him anything, anything he wanted, only please help him get his wife back. Love, as well you know, is a motherfucker. Well, Patsy went through his thing, whatever it is they do, wouldn't take anything up front either which is remarkable for a Ginney. The very next day, the other guy can't believe it. Here's his wife, right there, came four hundred miles to visit him and tell him how sorry she was. Thought it over and wants to stick by him. Overnight she changed her mind. Of course Patsy winds up with a bundle, but that's not really the point is it?"

"No, I guess not." Which is all I can say because I wanna think about it some more, but not right now, because it is kinda scary so I go, "Saul?"

"You called?"

"Saul, we ain't got no more herb. We smoked it all up."

"No more herb? The stash box, right in front of you."

"You ain't got too much here."

"Did it ever occur to you that you might find yourself some steady employment to help support your various vices?"

"A job?"

"Yes, a job. A simple three-letter word."

"You want me to get a lunch pail?"

"There, I knew you'd catch on."

"So why you don't get a job?"

"Because, fortunately, I do not have a P.O. who is ready to lock my ass up because, to coin a cliché, I have no visible means of support."

And the roof falls in. I sober up so fast it makes my head spin. How the fuck could I be sitting here all this time bullshitting and getting fucked up and forget about the most important thing, what I came up here for in the first place? I jump up like a fucking maniac and check out the clock in the kitchen. I don't believe it, almost midnight, seven fucking hours just bullshitting around getting fucked up and drunk and forgot the most important motherfucking thing. I just like sorta slump down in the chair. Well, that's that. My ass is grass, period. I can see him now, waiting right outside the Program just waiting to lock my monkey ass up. Jesus Christ, I feel like bawling my head off again. How could I be so stupid? The whole fucked-up day, losing the box, getting soaked to the skin, leaving the umbrella, fucking around all day turning tricks and not a dime in my jeans, and still gotta turn at least another trick tonight because I can't go back to the Program and gotta cop street meth tomorrow and who knows for how long until I can get a Medicaid card and get hooked up with another program. I just feel like I wanna jump outta the window right now and end it all or O.D. on some shit and croak, just croak, that's all.

"Saul," I go, "I fucked up. I really fucked up this time."

"Mmmph . . . don't tell me, let me guess. You caught a dose?"

"Stop, I'm serious. I didn't tell you because I knew you'd get on my case, but I blew two reports, at least two, at least I think it was two . . . who the fuck knows? The P.O. he called the Program and told them and shit and they're ready to terminate my ass and I hadda cop on the street today and it's all fucked up. My Medicaid card didn't come so I can't even get on another program and that's the reason why I came up, 'cause I was gonna ask you, you know, to call the P.O. and shit before they closed and now it's too fucking late and I don't know what the fuck to do."

"So, what's the problem?"

"What's the problem? What's the fucking problem? Oh, nothin' at all. Nothin' to you, it ain't your ass gonna get locked up, it ain't you gotta cop God knows what kinda shit on the street. Sure, you ain't gotta problem, but I sure as fuck do!"

"Fantastic. I love it. The only thing is we're not in the market for soap operas this season. Now if you have any pornography . . ."

"I'm leaving. That's it. Fuck you and your corny jokes for good!"

"Oh, for Chrissakes, sit down and stop performing like a trained seal. Here, kill the corner."

"I don't want no more to drink. I'm going, period."

"Sinbad, my boy, sit down before I knock you down. Now drink up whatever solace remains in the bottle. That's it—through the lips, over the gums, look out, stomach, here it comes. There you go. Now don't smile. Whatever you do, don't you dare smile."

Which of course I bust out laughin' in spite of my being mad as a motherfucker. I mean, how can you keep a straight face when somebody tells you don't you dare laugh, really serious like? Naturally you're gonna start laughing. I mean what else can a guy do? Saul he gets me every time with it too, the slick cocksucker.

"Good. That's the spirit—spirit of 'seventy-six—my music will pull you through it! As for P.O. Pumpernickel, well, we'll just take care of him in the ayem."

"Not Pumpernickel, you dodo, Rye. You know his name, Mister Rye."

"Rye, Pumpernickel, abigesund, can't tell one Hebe from another, never could . . . mmmm . . . let me hold on to his card 'til tomorrow."

"Shit, man, I dunno where I put it, I even lost my Program I.D. I swear to Christ I don't know why I keep losing everything."

"Like all sensible pilgrims, you travel light. Now let me see, I once had a telephone directory around someplace . . ."

"But whatcha gonna tell him? How about the two reports and shit I blew and then not calling him today?"

"Ach, mein Gott, vott proh-blems, you doubt zee verd uff the eminent Doktor Herr Zigmunt Vakenfuss?"

"Fuck, man, this is serious."

"Ja, Ja, uff course ziss iss zerious, verry zerious. Come in, little leeb-shen und lay down on zee couch und tell Doktor Vakenfuss ven you virst found out you vass qveer."

Two minutes ago I thought the fucking world was coming to an end and now we're both goofin' and fucking around and shit. Nothing makes any sense anymore.

"Common, fuck you, what you gonna say to him?"

"I? Who am I to confound a servant of the law? Mmm . . . no, my boy, for such a confrontation we will have to call upon your shrink."

"I ain't got no shrink."

"To coin a cliché, you know it and I know it, but Officer Pumpernickel . . ."

"Saul, tell me, please, what you're gonna say."

"Oh, who the fuck knows. My best performances are ad lib, anyhow. Let's see . . . mmmm . . . you're in treatment. Very serious case . . . obvious sociopath. But with possibilities . . . provided that treatment is not interrupted. That's it . . . under no circumstances must your treatment be interrupted. Some shit like that. Rest assured, I'll con him out of his jock."

"Will it work?"

"Will it work? Oh, ye of little faith. Have I not before shown you wonders beyond imagining?"

"You won't forget?"

"Ah, should I forget thee, O Jerusalem . . . your cloud-capped towers . . . the stately barge on which she sat . . . No, that's not how it goes at all . . . mmmm . . . let me see . . ."

"Saul, you're drunk and you ain't gonna remember."

"I am drunk."

"You won't forget, promise?"

"Trust me, brother, and count your fingers going out the door. I shall remember."

But will he?

"Whattabout my program?"

"What about your program?"

"Willya call them too?"

"What do I look like, the guy who straightens out bets? Fuck the Program. You take care of the Program."

"My Medicaid didn't come."

"So go down to Welfare."

"I don't have time."

"Then be sick."

"You know how sick I'll be?"

"Better you than me. What have I to do with your afflictions?"

"You're a bastard."

"I know."

"You won't call the Program?"

"No."

"You wanna be like that, huh?"

"I want you to cut that shit loose, that's what I want."

"I can't."

"You can. Just find someplace else to hang out in the morning."

"You really think I could get a job?"

"Possibly."

"What kind?"

"What's the difference, you wouldn't take it anyhow."

"Yes I would."

"No you wouldn't."

"Yes I would."

"No you wouldn't."

"Yes I would."

"Yes you would."

"No I wouldn't."

"See? Case closed."

"I changed my mind. I wanna move back here with you."

"No."

"Why not?"

"Because."

"Because why?"

"Because, as you said before, it wouldn't work out."

"I changed my mind."

"So did I."

"Please, let's try. Whatta you say?"

But I never find out what he would say because just then it's the fucking doorbell downstairs which must be Flacco who I forgot all about and Saul, he's stumbling out the door, down the stairs, with his kimono flying, to pay the cab and all. I hope to Christ he don't trip and break his ass because he's in no condition to be running around the building which I'm sure he just busted his ass because there's this bumping and thumping which I think is Saul falling down to the basement but the next thing is here's Flacco pushing this tremendous box up the stairs and Saul flapping and all outta breath pulling it up on the other end. Finally they get it inside the door and Flacco, he's standing in the little kitchen where you come in with his arms folded while Saul, he circles round this monster like he's checking it out or something which is funny because anything mechanical drives him up a wall. I swear to God, one day I come in the house and there's Saul on the phone, drunk as a skunk, hollering at the landlord that the electricity went off in the kitchen. How the fuck is he supposed to know why it's only the kitchen, he yells, because it's off, that's why. How the fuck do I know . . . I got a puddle of water all over the floor and no ice cubes, that's how I know and slams down the phone. Well, if that wasn't enough he calls the landlord back and hollers some more. "Mr. Schwartz, I demand you fix the electricity right away or you will hear from my attorneys."

Well after he finally hangs up I go check out the refrigerator and you know what it was? It wasn't plugged in, that's what it was. Saul musta kicked the plug out when he was drunk or something and the dodo didn't even check it out before he put the landlord through all those changes which must be sure he gotta maniac for a tenant. So here's Saul, sweating and flapping and circling the box like he's King Fu checking out a fire hydrant, shaking his head, scratching the finish with his fingernail, shaking his head all over again, and he goes, "Mmmph . . . everything appears to be in order."

I go, "Wait a minute, plug the motherfucker in willya and at least see if it plays for Chrissakes."

That's Saul for you, going through all these changes and

forgets to plug it in. Flacco meanwhile, he's still standing there sayin' nothing', with his arms crossed, gives me a mean look which Saul don't see since Saul is now down on his hands and knees looking under this thing for Chrissakes looking for God knows what. I just give up and plug the thing in and go get a side to see how it plays. Flacco, he looks like he wants to shank me right now for gettin' into his business and all but even though he's a dummy he's smart enough to know that he better not say anything bad out of his face because I could kick the shit out of him anytime he wants to start something. Right now, in fact, if he wants to throw down. But I gotta admit the box plays ok, as a matter of fact it's better than ok, which of course I'm not gonna tell Flacco.

"Mmm," says Saul, stalling for me to bail him out.

So I go, "Yo, Flacco, how much you want, man?"

"Haf a yard whatchoo said, man." Which he ain't even lookin' at me but instead is whining to Saul who goes, "Well . . . mmm . . . what I said is I'd check it out, you heard me, Sinbad, right?"

"Sure, that's what you said. I heard ya. I was sitting right here and I heard ya."

"He say feefty, man, you say feefty, Saul Man, that's some wrong shit, you say feefty."

"Well . . . mmm . . . Flacco, let's all sit down and light up a joint and settle this thing like grown men."

"No, man. No, Saul, you say feefty, feefty, man, that's what you say, feefty."

Well, Saul can't say I didn't warn him. I told him that when this dodo got fifty in his mind that it would take a fucking atom bomb to get it out. On the other hand, like he said, where the fuck else can he go with it this time of night, so I go, "Yo, bro', you know that old piece of shit ain't worth no fifty." Saul, he goes to open his mouth and I shoot him a look to keep quiet. Like he asked for me to bail him out so shut up, which he does.

"But he tole me . . ."

"Flacco, yo, man, you know it ain't worth fifty, whatchoo tryin' to do beat Saul or somethin', man? Is that what you're tryin' to do, bro', 'cause you ain't gonna get over."

"Hey, man, hey, Sinbad, hey, Saul, yo, I don't try to beat nobodies. Yo, he say feefty, man, I swear to God, I swear to my mother may she go blind, man, he tole me . . . yeah, that's cool, that's cool, man, how much you give me, I don' cheat you, man, I swear. How much?"

Bingo! Hook, line, and sinker. Now I gotta play the chump in.

"Bentaysinko, twennyfive, bro', that's all it's worth, bentaysinko."

"Benteesinko! I give you mudder bentessinko, maricón, faggot, twennyfive, I gotta carry it down all them stairs when I geese it?"

"Twennyfive."

"Forty! Forty, man! Forty!"

"Twennyfive."

"Thirdyfive, you tryin' to cheat me."

"Thirdy, an you tryin' to get over, bro'."

"Trenteesinko!"

"Thirdy and a tab."

"You got a tab?"

"Saul does. Thirdy anda of sunshine."

Flacco, he frowns like he's thinking it over or something, but I know he's gonna jump at thirty plus a tab of sunshine which it is almost impossible anymore to get except of course Saul and of course Sunshine, which is why they call him that. So now everybody's smiling and yakking and slapping skin all around and Saul peels off three tens which the box really was worth four hundred at least. But nobody's mad since after all we were only keeping the game polished which is what it's all about anyhow and Flacco he may be a dummy, but he knows he gonna smoke up at least a dime of herb for free plus the tab which is at least eight when you can get it so everybody's happy.

Saul, he's like a kid with a new toy. He jiggles this and pokes that and plays one side and takes it off and puts on another and now we all gotta lug this thing into the living room where there's no place to put it anyhow and after about fifteen minutes of fucking around with it, Saul, he's sweating up a storm, he goes, "Aw, fuck it," and leaves it right out in the middle of the floor where sure as shit he's gonna fall right over it and we all sit down and blow some weed.

The booze is all gone so we just sit and zip the last few cans of Old English from the fridge and Saul comes out of his bathrobe with not one but three tabs of sunshine, which three people can get high off only one tab and we wash the tabs down with the last of the English and that's gone too. Saul checks out of the window and the light's still on in the liquor store across the street, which they have to close at twelve but the guy's probably there counting up the day's receipts. So Saul, he gets on the horn fast. That's one phone number he got no trouble remembering, the liquor store.

And he goes, "Yes, yes, apartment three-G . . . mmmm . . . yes, that's very kind of you, very kind indeed, sir . . . let's see, make that a quart of Dewar's, no better make that two quarts of Johnny Walker Red . . . and a quart of Gordon's . . . gin . . . Gordon's gin . . . yes, yes and please be so good as to tell the lad to stop off at the candy store and get a carton of Pall Malls . . . mmmm . . . yes . . . I believe that will be all, and tell him to bring change of a hundred . . . mmmm . . . yes, a check. Very good." And when he hangs up Saul winks at both of us because we both know what the deal is, even Flacco who is a dummy. Sure as shit when he calls up with only that fancy bullshit and tells him to change a hundred, the check ain't worth the paper it's printed on. Saul, he's really only making a loan from the dude and the dude knows it because Saul, he'll hang paper all over town but he don't shit where he eats.

So we just sit there waiting for the booze to come which Saul says the guy is sending his own kid over because the delivery boy has gone home and also for the acid to come down. When you're smoking you don't know just when it is that it hit you and all of a sudden you don't realize it, you're whacked out of your socks, you get what Saul calls the Fordham Flash.

So I just cool out and remember about Saul and checks. Man, one time we was really down, both of us. The hotel they were getting ready to throw us out of was so bad that I told Saul they should float the whole fucking building right down the river and tie it up at the Rock which is where everybody there belonged including us. Finally we was so uptight that they plugged the door on us and all our shit was inside so I had to turn a trick with the desk clerk so we could just get in and get our shit and get out of the cold. Now Saul, he had one check left. Every time things were bad he'd take it out and look at it and shake his head. No way he could pop that fucking check because he had burnt out the account bad and knew if he popped it it was almost sure he would get pinched.

But what else could we do? We hadda eat, right? Plus it was Sunday so we couldn't even sell blood at the blood bank which they never take mine anyhow because of my tracks. So Saul bitches and moans but when it comes down to the nitty-gritty the only thing to do is try to pop that digit and on a Sunday too. So what does he do? He calls up this delicatessen and orders some kind of Jewish fish and shit. Jewish fish, phughh! I ask him how come he's ordering that shit which though I was starving there's no way you could make me eat that, raw fish, it makes me sick to think about. And Saul goes, the reason he is ordering from the Jew is that Jews are the biggest thieves in the world which makes them the easiest marks.

Well, I guess he was right because when the delivery guy comes Saul gives him this fucked-up check and starts rapping up a storm and the next thing this guy is peeling off bills and we got forty-two dollars and change and some fucked-up Jewish fish after Saul gives him a two-dollar tip.

I thought he was just gonna, shit can it, but he sits down and eats it like he likes it and has the fucking nerve to tell me that I ain't got no class because I don't appreciate the finer things of life. The finer things of life? Some finer things—raw fish! And when he's finished he says let's go get a bottle of booze and lay some gap on the desk clerk so we don't freeze our asses off in the street tonight.

I go, "Yo, man, you may like eating fucked-up fish but how 'bout getting me some McDonald's."

And he says, "Sure, why not, that's a good idea."

After McDonald's at least I wasn't hungry but we wound up in a big argument anyhow after we got back to the hotel because we were flat broke again and I told him before not to give that Hebe a two-dollar tip.

Well, there I am remembering about the checks and all those times we had and, wham, I realize that all the time, I've been tripping. You get like this dry feeling in your throat. That's when you know the hit is together which ten times out of nine today you get beat and they give you speed instead or even, sometimes, strychnine. But when you're really tripping you get like this pulse throbbing in your head like everything's going on and off like a strobe, only much slower so that you see everything real clear for a minute and then it fades and comes back again. It's weird. You feel like you're King of the Mountain. You want to do everything at once—rap, pace, cool out, get into the sound on the box, freak out on your own thoughts, plus you get horny too.

Me, I don't sweat behind acido, but Saul sweats up a storm and Flacco, he just looks all stupid like, like what little mind he's got is completely blown. He's in another world.

The three of us are tripping out of our skulls. Saul, he can't keep still, flapping from one end of the room to the other and waving his hands while he's laying some kind of far-out rap on Flacco. Flacco, of course, has forgot about going to cop or going anywhere at all. He don't understand a word Saul is saying. All he wants to do is to get down with Saul so Saul could screw him. Me. I'm watching the mirror ball go round and round, like tripping out on the lights and shit, wondering if, like, my mind is going around the same way the ball is. It's hard to describe, like I don't know whether it's the lights or me that are flashing. I know it sounds crazy but while it's going on I feel that my mind could do anything, make anything move the way it wanted to, no matter how big it was, even if it was as big as a mountain.

But I can never get into anything in this house, it's like fucking Grand Central Station. If it ain't the fucking phone it's the door-bell. Now it's the guy from the liquor store, only it's not a guy, it's a kid. And if I say so myself this is one pretty motherfucker. I can just imagine what's going through Saul's mind when he sees him. Flacco, if he had any sense at all, which he don't, could see right off that no way anybody's gonna get down with Saul tonight except this kid.

He don't look to me like he's more than sixteen, with blond hair down to his shoulders and like these slanty eyes and dark complexion that some Latinos with Indian blood got. Plus he's wearing a black headband that makes him look even more Indian. He got on a white jump suit and gold chains around his neck and wrists and also has on these black patent leather boots.

Saul, he's practically drooling and quick closes the door behind the kid, nice and cool like so that the kid wouldn't get scared that he was gonna get ripped off. Now when the kid gives him the booze and the cigarettes plus the change from the check, I see him slip a fin inta the kid's hand which he thinks nobody sees.

The kid, he smiles and sees right off what the scene is and what's happening and doesn't look like he's in any rush to leave. Saul, he goes, "Mmm, well, my boy, you seem to be all decked out for a night on the town." The kid is most definitely a hustler because he's already got the fin in his pocket and he says something real brilliant like, "Mmm, hmmm," which doesn't stop Saul at all.

"Well," he says, "this is Flacco here, who is suffering from a touch of sunstroke and so has forgotten his manners and this is my godson Steven, who was just getting ready to *leave, Steven,* weren't you?"

And I go, "Who said anything about leaving?"

Saul gives me a look that could frost your balls and practically pushes the kid down on the couch. His name is Carlos, or that's what he says, and yeah, he was on his way downtown. I don't miss the "was" part, either.

"Carlos . . . mellifluous name indeed. Were you on your way to someplace special or just . . . mmmm . . . planning to hang out?"

"Yeah, well, like I hang out on the East Side. There's one club I go to all the time."

"Which club, may I ask?"

"The Mayfair. You ever been there?"

Which everybody knows is a boy-hustler bar and which everybody calls the Maypole and is strictly twenty bucks a pop and up, action. This Carlos ain't so dumb. As soon as he says "Mayfair" he's letting Saul know just where everything's at pricewise. Saul, he's practically coming in his pants which means, number one, somehow he's gonna pull this kid and the kid's gonna stay over. Number two, I'm gonna have to get my head together so I can tip and find a place to crash tonite. If Flacco wants the couch it's fine with me because this trip is already turning into a downer, plus Saul running his shit to this Carlos a mile a minute without coming up for air.

"Mmm . . . yes . . . ah . . . why not stay and join us for a while . . . mmm, Carlos?"

And before this kid can say yes or no he's got a joint in one hand, a tab in the other while Saul is cracking a bottle of booze. Flacco, he's out of it, staring at the color TV which all that it is giving is a priest signing off. Saul is tripping out on the kid who has checked out the pad and who must be tripping out on dollar signs, and me, I'm the only one got the bummer.

All I want is some fresh air so I can straighten my head out. I really don't feel like hanging out anymore anyhow. It's not that I'm jealous. I don't give a fuck who he screws, that's his business, just like it's my business what I do. That's why it wouldn't work out, living together again and shit. It's just that we rapped ourselves out and partied ourselves out and there's nothin' more to do. To tell the truth I'm bored. I just want to tip. So I go to the bathroom and strip down and throw all the dirty smelly shit into the hamper, including my socks and drawers and stand under the shower for about twenty minutes, which Saul got one of these boss stall showers with the glass all around. When I come out my head is down a little and at least I don't smell funky and also put a little cologne under my balls which I am doing when Flacco comes in.

"Yo bro," I go, "don't you knock?"

"I juss come to take a piss, bro'."

Piss, my ass. He's so fucking horny behind the tab that he's checking out my meat which he would fuck a bush if there was a snake in it right now. So I just like push past him and go into the bedroom where I always keep at least one clean change of everything in Saul's crib. By the time I get dressed here comes Flacco back out which he was probably beating his meat in the can and he goes, "You gonna tip?"

And I go, "Yeah, I gotta turn at least one more trick."

And he goes, "Well, I ain't goin'. Fuck that dude. I'm gonna crash out and fuck that dude."

And I go, "Yeah, you do that bro', don't worry, you're still Saul's ace boon coon. Anybody can see that the dude's just trade."

I mean, what am I gonna say to this dodo. He's so dumb it ain't no fun to turn the screws a little bit. Might as well make him feel good at least. Me, I feel like a washed-out piece of shit. So we both go back to the living room and I can see by this time the kid is tripping and Saul already got haffa new bottle packed away in his gut and they're sitting there all lovey-dovey on the couch. Flacco, he goes to the fridge to check out what he can scoff, and Saul goes, "Oh, are you leaving Steven? When will I see you?" like I'm a piece of trade or something which he can't wait for me to leave but you can't blame Saul, that's just the way he is and nothin's gonna change him and I can't kick 'cause he's always been all right with me and besides what I told Flacco was the truth. Like Saul says, "Sinbad, there's nothing in life more dreary than yesterday's trade."

So I go, "Yeah, Saul, I'm gonna tip. And Saul, don't forget to call that dude tomorrow, please . . ." But he's rapping his ass off to the kid again and doesn't even see me close the door, so he probably didn't hear me either.

It's cold as a bitch. Not a car in sight. Way at the end of Central Park you can see the lights of the swank hotels and a million stars in the sky. I'm freezing my ass off even with my jacket on. It looks like one of those cities you see in the movies where everybody just disappeared or something because of a war or some shit and there's no one left. Just empty streets with newspapers blowing all over and a million stars in the sky. But I said that already.

I wish I could just stop here. I mean, have everything just stop and stay by myself for always, just me alone in the City, cold and dark, with everything just like it is and the red lights changing to green and the green lights changing back to red for cars which nobody drives because there's nobody left to drive them and nobody left to run around all the time beating each other and doing treacherous shit and getting fucked up and fucking other people up and hanging out with nothing to do and no place to go.

Because if there wasn't anybody left then nobody could ever be lonely or sad or scared or cold again and everything would just stop. There's nothing out there but the dark and the cold and the stars and after the stars there's nothing again. There's nothing up there and nothing down here. There's nobody to help you. You're completely on your own. You've got to figure out for yourself why nothing makes any sense, why everything's so fucked up.

I have to hop the subway turnstile because I forgot everything up at Saul's—my umbrella, Rob's box. I even forgot to hit him up for some gap so I could get back downtown. It don't matter though. This time of night there's no transit cop on the platform and all the guy in the token booth can do is holler which you can't hear him anyhow because they got him behind bullet proof glass.

I get off at the Deuce. In the hole, the pinball place is getting ready to close for the night. There's a couple of young kids, runaways, twelve, thirteen years old with nowhere to go. Some-times they try to hustle you for a quarter or something and then crash out down by the tracks or maybe in the subway where it's warm but where they're sure to get pinched. Dopey kids who don't know any better, but some are strung out even at that age and would steal the pennies off a dead man's eyes.

I remember the kid this morning, what was his name? From Jersey someplace. This morning? No, yesterday morning because today is now yesterday and tomorrow is today. I wonder who picked him up first, a cop or a john. I feel kinda bad, because I did promise I was gonna come back for him, just a dopey kid who didn't even know how to cross the street in traffic by himself. Fuck him. Why should I worry about him. He ain't worrying about me, some kid who I don't even know that don't know his ass from his elbow. I bet he's cooling out with a trick right now, sound asleep in a nice warm bed someplace and meanwhile I don't have the slightest idea where I'm gonna crash.

Upstairs on the Deuce it's dead. Everything's closed. Just a couple of old bums and that's it. The clock over the bank says four twenty-two. I stand there on the corner looking up and down the street. The way it looks I may have to hop the train again and crash out in Queens which is a pain in the ass because it's an hour ride and then I gotta wake up the whole house to get in unless I bust in the cellar door and just sack out by the furnace and then I'll just wind up sleeping all day and won't get nothing done. Jesus fucking Christ I hope Saul ain't too drunk to remember to call the P.O.

I don't even see the dude ease up until he's right next to me pretending to look in a dark store window. It's my luck it gotta be a fucking nigger. I can't keep my eyes open I'm so tired and the dude comes on with some kind of rap in a language I never heard before. He's black as the ace of spades but maybe he ain't a nigger at that. Who ever heard of a nigger smart enough to learn a foreign language. I try to lay a little Spanish rap on him, just to see, but he smiles and shakes his head. Another dummy, don't understand a word I'm saying. So I point and shit and rub my thumb and finger together which even a dummy understands, even a dumb nigger who don't know any English and he smiles and nods his head real fast up and down. Good, at least he understands something.

So we start to stroll, west, over towards Twelfth and the river which I start getting paranoid and wondering if this black nigger is gonna try and rip me off or something, which would be a joke because I ain't got a dime in my jeans. I'm so tired I don't give a fuck anymore what happens. I wonder what number came out. All I wanna do is lay down, anywhere, right in the middle of the street and all this nigger wants to do is keep walking me all over west hell, freezing my ass off, until finally I see we're coming to the Howard Johnson's motel on Twelfth which I completely forgot about. At least that's cool because it ain't a dump and it's clean and there's a john in the room. The nigger got a camera hanging from a strap on his shoulder which I will relieve him of tomorrow morning if we ever get the fuck upstairs.

He closes the door and puts the key in his pocket. I'm out on my feet. One thing I hate is sucking a nigger's dick, but I wanna get it over with. We both strip down and get into bed and I give him a quickie, which he cums in about two minutes and I just spit it out on the floor and wipe off my mouth with the back of my hand. I can't stand the smell of niggers. He's out for the count, snoring and snorting on his back. I wonder should I tell the operator to call me at six-thirty, but I figure better not, because the phone might wake him and then I'll blow my shot at geesing the camera. Fuck it, I'll just get a few hours' shut-eye and tomorrow, positively, I promise myself, I'll take care of business.

3

Winter

They had been dead for four centuries. Their farms were destroyed, their churches in ruins, their fields and gardens smothered by weeds. But down below, in the graves, in the depths of the eternally frozen soil, time had stood still . . . There slumbered Ozuur Asbjarnason, who died one winter's day and was laid to rest in unhallowed ground. But when the grave was filled in, a stake stood on his chest. And when spring came round and the ice melted, the stake was pulled out and a priest poured consecrated water through the hole onto his chest.

—Paul Herrman, *Sieben Vorbei Und Acht Verweht*

I NEVER KNEW MY FATHER and that is for the best, for I was always free to invent him without fear of disappointment or disillusion. For me he remains only a blurred photo, somewhat stained and frayed at the edges, a figure of seemingly medium stature arrayed in what must have appeared as an impressive uniform. An officer's cap is set rakishly on his head, which sadly is averted from the camera, so that all I could ever see of his face was a third of an uptwirled mustache and the hint of a broad grin, which might very well be a leer. Thus was he frozen in time, forever changeless, amused perhaps, certainly mythic, unable to rebuke or abandon, elusively anonymous, his features forever just beyond my line of sight. He belongs to me alone, to an unknown past, to a present whimsical and terrifying as the sea which embraces his bones in my earliest imaginings, and to a future in which we both shall be saved from the embarrassment of mutual confrontation. The camera catches his left arm resting familiarly on the shoulder of my mother, a young angular wraith, ill at ease in a white muslin dress whose hem burgeons in the wind while she, self-consciously, tries to hold it down with a chaste bony hand.

When I asked her once why she appeared so uncomfortable she confided with rare good humor that she was freezing her ass off at the time and besides, her menses were about to commence. Wryness was never one of her graces, nor self-deprecation one of her attributes, so I pretended to believe the impossible. Clearly her present memory had been flawed by the passage of time. I well remember her lamentations, more familiar than lullabies, wherein she grieved that the flashgun's report preceded by bare hours the moans that accompanied my conception. The time framework was her own reconstruction; the moans, a personal exegesis. Whatever the case, it could not have been the onset of the curse that was responsible for her pained expression, nor the weather either. It is a fact confirmed by my certificate of baptism that I was born in the month of February under the Sign of the Fish. Simple arithmetic places the date of my mother's conjunction with my father sometime in the previous May, thus vitiating against her claim of inclemency.

I suppose that my curiosity will never be satisfied and that the circumstances surrounding my mother's loss of virginity will forever be shrouded in mystery. On the subject of my coming into this world, as in all matters of import to me, my mother remains to this day maddingly close-mouthed. This much I know, or believe I know (or to appropriate one of Saul's apothegms). "If you're absolutely certain about something, then most certainly you are wrong."): My father was a gypsy of the skies, a flight engineer employed by an airline which maintained three rickety DC-3's to shuttle pilgrims to the Promised Land. This in the halcyon days when the City was still Eldorado, a paradise of gold glittering to impoverished Puerto Ricans, irresistibly tempting and alluring, from whence came the siren's song of pomp and wealth.

I am positive that on embarkation my mother sat herself

primly apart from the chaos around her, telling her rosary, oblivious to the clucking of chickens, the squealing of piglets, the cacophonous chatter, and the sensuous evocations of guitars.

I have no idea what inner voice summoned her forth, a shy, uncomely, passionate girl of seventeen, from the dusty town of Arecibo. "Arecibo, me encantan," she used to say. To her, enchanting Arecibo that stood at the edge of the rain forest against a backdrop of hazy mountains, blue in the sunlight reflected from the distant sea. A voice? A temptation bubbling up from her loins? The spell of a sorcerer fashioned from whirlwinds? Or was she merely her father's daughter, impelled by some atavistic necessity to drink life to the dregs, to soar over the cloud-capped peaks on the currents of her own thirst. Did my grandfather unwillingly seduce my mother away from the suffocating constraints of the convent school to which he had consigned his unwanted girl-child? He had problems enough feeding his wife and his litter of worthless sons. He had no need to provide for a daughter who would inevitably provide him with more mouths to feed. There was only one woman alive to whom he accorded respect and she was my grandmother.

Grandmother was strong-willed and industrious. At fourteen she married my grandfather, who was then in his sixties. From that time forward she lived only for him, working hard, crying hard, laughing hard, and remaining devoted to him while she patiently endured his frequent excursions to the local brothel. She found no fault in his excessive carnality, which she thought to be a harmless vice. Cheerfully she bore him the sons he asked for and fiercely she shared his anger and frustration as each of them proved to be as weak and as shiftless as his predecessor. I remember once my grandfather taking me on his knee to inform me that he had always been "pure." I wondered at this since I knew him to be a savage drunk, both avaricious and stingy. Later I learned that he had not intended to lay claim to the astonishing virtue of chastity but merely had difficulty mastering American vowel sounds and had been flaunting only his poverty.

After he chased the last of his ne'er-do-well sons out of the house it must have dawned on him finally that the only true heir of his blood was his daughter, whom he had long ago abandoned to the ministrations of the Sisters of Our Lady of Guadeloupe. He was

138

never one for making amends and by the time he arrived at regret it was too late to reclaim his daughter's affection. My mother hated the old man and never failed to impress on me the dismal example of his selfishness, his coarseness and lewdness (this at a time when my mother earned her living as a streetwalker). Nevertheless, I would like to think that he was secretly pleased with her unforgiving nature and heartily enjoyed the joke perpetrated on him by a God capable of incarnating the iron will of a man in the frail but sinewy body of his daughter, Helena.

Neither could tolerate the presence of the other for any length of time. He was blasphemous, she was devout. He was fanciful, she was purposeful. He raged and kicked against the pricks, she maintained an outward composure. And yet, two disparate natures found certain unspoken congruencies. Both were convinced of their own infallibility, neither ever knew guilt or was capable of repentance. And so, perhaps through some audacious quirk of divine will, the essence of the father was worked into the daughter through the unsuspecting agency of the Sisters of Our Lady.

My mother hated my grandfather until his death, beyond death, or so she said. I suspect that the only hate in her heart was for herself, and if this is so, much becomes clear—her flight, her determination to be rid of him once and for all, and the haste, the determination with which she sought out sin. It explains how my poor, bitter mother managed somehow to ensnare a worldly-wise flight engineer somewhere between the shanty terminus of Arecibo and La Guardia Airport, to woo and win him and to become infused with his sperm. I picture her as the wily aggressor and my faceless father a willing victim. What his intentions, if any, were toward my mother, once he had sown his seed within her, must remain unknown since all aboard the plane perished in a crash at sea on the voyage home. Did he intend to return? I hope not. I am content to be the lust-child that I am, content for her to see in me the mirror image of my sire, content to bear witness to the catastrophic consequences of his casual fornicating.

When it was discovered that she had succeeded beyond her wildest hopes in revenging herself on her father, that indeed she was pregnant, she sped to a telephone to brag of her disgrace. My grandparents hurried to the City, my grandmother with solicitude, my grandfather with perfervid recriminations. On his arrival at the tenement where Welfare had installed my mother, he declared that he would kill the bastard. Whether he referred to his daughter's transitory lover or to the seed which was quickening in her womb was not then clear. It was not until he studied certain lists in newspapers that he acknowledged defeat. My father had indeed fled this world for all time. His remains had vanished in the vast reaches of the Bermuda Triangle where even Grandfather's unquenchable rage could not pursue them once the sharks had done feeding.

Satisfied at last that my father was forever beyond his reach he turned his attentions to the spawn and commanded my grandmother to "fix things." My mother was equally adamant. She insisted that the seed she bore would not only ripen and flower into life but would shoot out branches so that all the generations of my grandfather could testify to her disgrace. Never in her life had she been more happy. My dutiful grandmother was not at all displeased that she might yet have the opportunity to look upon the faces of her grandchildren. She attempted, unsuccessfully, to placate her husband's rage.

At length she reluctantly consented to become her husband's accomplice in the commission of a mortal sin in furtherance of which she procured from an old sorceress, called a bruja in her tongue, a certain decoction of herbs which she introduced into my mother's morning cup of tea. My grandmother, a nominal pagan but a practicing believer, was convinced of the efficacy of the stuff so she concealed from her spouse the fact that but a mere whisper of a drop was actually consumed by my mother. Thus was she able to fulfill the letter of the law and the spirit of her marriage vows.

Thereafter, my grandfather, a nominal believer but a practicing pagan, was convinced that various unmentionable denizens of the nether world were protecting the fetus and any further interference with their purposes on his part would result in catastrophic consequences to himself. Without further ado he consigned me to the Devil, and made no further attempts on my life.

And so it was that my mother came into labor. I was midwived into the world by my grandmother and two crones of uncertain relationship who despaired of the lives of both mother and child during the arduous delivery. All present were startled when I presented to them first my feet, then my posterior, and finally a sickly, bluish head.

I believe that this was the last time in my life when my mother was actually pleased with me. From then on my unusual conception and manner of birth were forgotten and I was condemned to affront her ever after by my very existence.

My grandmother has told me that even her daughter eventually succumbed to the stirrings of mother love. That is to say that while I was never given to suck at her breast, she allocated a small portion of her Welfare check for my sustenance, which sum she entrusted to my grandmother's discretion on a twice-monthly basis. If, as frequently occurred, the check was delayed, well, that was none of her concern. It was sufficient that she inconvenienced herself by reporting irregularly to the Welfare office. She washed her hands of any further responsibility and left the mundane details of my care to my grandmother.

I am told that matters remained this way until my second year when after interminable argument, my grandmother was finally able to have me transferred to her own Welfare budget and maneuvered me into her keeping.

It cannot be doubted that she indulged my every whim. I became fat, pampered, and spoiled. I was a constant source of comfort in her otherwise cheerless life. Unfortunately our idyll was interrupted by my mother's reappearances from the streets where she grimly sold herself. These visits occasioned a cuddle or two, which were always marred by the odd habit she had of suddenly staring out into space for no apparent reason, as if she were trying to forget something or someone. I came uncannily close to the truth when I sensed that the someone was me.

Arrest, confinement to a state mental hospital, and shock therapy provided the jolt necessary for my mother to reinterest herself in her own salvation. Upon her return from the hospital I was at once removed from my grandmother's lodgings. My mother was determined to restore control over my life as well as her own. It was a dreary time, I like to think, not only for me. The flat was cold and gloomy, devoid of any article of interest to a young boy, though it was replete with a newly acquired collection of various symbols of my mother's religious beliefs. No man, including the

141

landlord, was ever permitted to enter the apartment, that is, until the advent of my stepfather. The Reverend, as he is known to me to this day, was an impoverished woodworker who fancied himself a preacher. Though he did provide the household with a sort of seedy respectability, we politely ignored one another. I had but to retreat within myself. There I was free from my mother's permanent disapproval of anything that gave me pleasure. I was free from her silences, her outbursts of outrage which were directed at me and my faceless father. Enhanced by undernourishment my fantasies flourished. I was a changeling destined to bear the martyrdom of my patron saint until I arrived in manhood at a pinnacle of power from where I could revenge myself on the world at large, mothers in general, and my own in particular.

The old woman sits and waits. There is nothing for her to do except guard the door to the tiny windowless bedroom. She has locked the door and the key rests safely between her breasts. Behind her back, behind the door, lies the boy. It is possible that he is already dead.

The old woman sits with her hands folded in her lap. Her back is ramrod straight, as if her endurance alone could void the judgments visited upon the boy. The old woman has few pleasures left in life. She enjoys sipping a cup of steaming black coffee liberally laced with honey. Perhaps her overwhelming love for the boy is merely the fondness of a foolish old woman for the mingling of the bitter and the sweet.

The light is going out of the world, for the boy is dying. It is possible that he is already dead. Sorrow pierces her bones. Wild dogs howl in the streets and everywhere is desolation. She has covered the face of the clock with a black cloth so that she cannot hear its ticking. If the boy were already dead, surely the earth would have opened and she would have been cast into the abyss.

There is nothing for the old woman to do but remain steadfast in her vigil. Though her lips are pressed tightly together she hears herself cursing God for his exacting iniquity.

The old woman is wise. She is wise in the ways of the City and the demands of its miseries. Cursed be the man who trusts the works of this world, its machines, its crucibles, its cauldrons. Cursed be the sharp cutting tools that mortify the flesh, the bitter medicines, the drugs. Her litany stops. In what alembic is distilled the drug to heal the savage sickness of a soul adrift? From the hands of the healers come but death and dissolution. False hope is mocked by false compassion. The heart of man is perverse beyond all healing. What drugs? Her litany continues. Beside the chipped coffee cup lies a syringe. He is mighty who rejects the world within his bowels and sows contempt to flourish in the dust. The boy is dark-haired and pleasing to her failing sight. The boy is wild and restless, summoning up his own temptations. His imaginings hover like flies over a lake of honeyed corruption. The boy will die or he will live.

The old woman knows that she is vain and selfish. She dismisses the long-dead husband, the half-mad daughter, and the indifferent callow sons. There is only the boy, only the boy who quite possibly is dead. Without the boy surely she will die alone. Better that than wrench him from the grave to be returned to his self-imposed bondage. Better death than scourging. The litany continues.

Behind the door there is no time. No chink of light intrudes on the dark. The boy lies immobile on the bed. There are thoughts. Perhaps his thoughts, perhaps a dreamer dreaming of the boy. The boy experiences a bliss that clutches at oblivion like a vulture seizing a putrescent mole . . .

The boy sees a boy wracked with savage cramps, writhing on another bed, his face awash with cold sweat. He tries to sit up and is overpowered by another excruciating spasm. His eyes bulge. Tears run in rivulets down his cheeks. His nose drips mucus. The muscles of his neck are taut and contracted. He tries to sit again, half succeeds, and is positive that he cannot control his sphincter. Now he sits, doubled over.

On the table beside the bed lies a blackened spoon and an empty syringe. On the floor are crumpled glassine bags, also empty. It must stop. The agony of the spasms is monstrous, searing his intestines. The agony is not to be borne. He retches, bringing up a noxious greenish bile that dribbles between his thighs onto the sheet. For a scant second the pain recedes. When he attempts to rise it flows back with renewed vigor. He knows that his stomach is stuffed with glowing coals. The man. The man?

The man opens the door. Through the window behind the bed the man sees a grimy December daylight. He moves casually to the side of the bed where the boy now lies, his knees drawn up to his throat. From his pocket the man withdraws two glassine bags. One he places on the table well beyond the boy's reach. The other he raises like a host, smiling faintly as he tips the white powder out onto the spoon, slowly, carefully making sure that not one grain is lost.

There is a dirty glass on the table. From the glass the man spills a few drops of water onto the spoon. He holds two lit matches simultaneously beneath the spoon until its handle is warm to the touch and the powder and water commingled. The matches burn down to his fingertips. The man wraps a belt around one arm as tightly as he can. He holds the belt in place with one hand while with the other he draws up liquid from the spoon into the syringe. One might think he was a conjurer performing some simple sleight of hand. With ease he inserts the needle into a particular spot in his pit, the soft juncture between fore and upper arm. He pushes down on the plunger, then raises it up slightly. The liquid in the syringe becomes cloudy red. The man thrusts his chin forward and sighs, then pushes down on the plunger again. The liquid fills the vein. He whimpers with pleasure, prolonging the moment. He withdraws the syringe from his arm only after unwrapping the belt. His nostrils dilate and twitch. He smiles. The boy watches everything, his eyes defiant and pleading.

Very slowly the man empties the contents of the second bag into the spoon. The boy's eyes blaze. The man shakes his head with amused indulgence and places the powder-filled spoon well away from the boy's hand. The boy's arm swings out, reaching for the spoon. He narrowly misses knocking the spoon off the table. The man shakes his head sadly. He removes his trousers. The boy's eyes follow his every movement. The man ignores the boy's eyes. He opens the drawer and pulls out a jar of cold cream. He scoops some of the cream onto his now-erect penis. He looks at the boy. The boy's eyes follow. He winces as a new spasm seizes him. Very gently the man turns the boy onto his stomach. His bare buttocks

144

lie just beneath the man, who begins to straddle him. The boy's head is turned awkwardly on the pillow.

The man fondles his own penis lovingly. Then, without warning, he forces himself into the boy, pumping up and down, thrusting until completely swallowed by the small tight anus. The man grimaces as he continues his grinding deep inside the boy. The boy's face is sopping wet. He bites down on his tongue. Blood trickles from the corner of his mouth onto the pillow. The man clenches his teeth. Bucking and plunging he throws back his head to praise God and groans.

At the moment of abrupt withdrawal the boy loses control of his sphincter. Liquid feces ooze between his buttocks down the backs of his hairless thighs. The man slaps the boy hard on the back of his head. Then he grabs the boy by his hair. Twisting him in midair the man hurls the boy into a surprised sitting position on a corner of the bed. The boy's bare legs dangle over the side. Methodically the man slaps the boy's face—first one side, then the other—swinging his arm like a reaper scything grass. He batters the boy without malice, obviously enjoying his work. When he has done beating the boy he places the powder-filled spoon where the boy can reach it. As he turns to leave he delivers a final vicious backhand square on the boy's mouth. Before the door clicks shut the boy is already reaching for the spoon.

The boy climbs the fire escape effortlessly, hand over hand. He knows the position of each foothold so he is able to climb without making a sound. He reaches the fourth-floor window and squats, peering inside where there is nothing to be seen. Night cloaks him. He sways slightly on his perch, still hunched and peering. He has at last become invisible.

Satisfied by certain subtle signs that the room is unoccupied he begins to work with a screwdriver, prying and chipping. Once inside he needs no light to find his way to the shrine where the candles are melting. Through the closed door he is able to discern a shrill voice announcing that a particular price is right. Another voice. This one familiar. A door slams. He stops in his tracks, sniffing. Perhaps for footsteps. There are none. He continues his business, removing the pennies from the paper plate, putting them in his pocket. His hand fumbles for the purse which he knows must be close by. Finding it, he takes out the wallet. It is too dark for him to count the money. Whatever the night disgorges is sufficient. He removes two icons from the shrine and when he reaches the window he hurls them out into the street. As he climbs out of the window he can sense footsteps. By the time the door opens he is already flying down the fire escape. The curtains flap in the wind.

The boy is about to awake. At this moment he is sleeping beneath a railroad trestle which runs some thirty feet above his head. He is curled in a dark corner where no passer-by could possibly see him. For company there is only the gentle lapping of the oily river, the smoke rising from chimneys, and the gulls whirling and crying and swooping. Between the recess where he sleeps and the river stretches a wasteland: garbage, rusty cans, empty oil drums, decayed fruit rinds, and patches of sickly, pallid grass.

The man has been awake for some minutes. He is conducting an examination of the stubble on his chin and face. At last, deciding to shave, he heaves his bulk over the side of the bed where he waits for the wave of nausea and retching. After a period of considerable discomfort he pours four fingers of bourbon into a toothpaste-stained glass and tosses it down neat. When he has completed his showering he pats his cheeks with an herb-scented cologne. Then he drinks another four fingers of bourbon, this time directly from the bottle. He pauses and gulps twice more from the bottle, experiencing now only the mildest sensation of nausea. He wipes his mouth with the back of his hand, assures himself that his mustache is evenly trimmed, and finishes the rest of the bourbon.

After urinating in the same corner where he has passed the night, the boy emerges into daylight. He rubs his eyes, sniffs at his armpit, and is clearly displeased. The wind blows across the river. The boy shudders. He reckons from the position of the now-risen sun that it is around seven-thirty in the morning. From habit he pats his jacket pocket to assure himself that the syringe has not fallen out during the night. Satisfied, he raises his head, somewhat like a gazelle, and inhales, as if he were able to assess the relative intensity of his nausea and cramps through some mysterious faculty incarnate in his sense of smell. He is acutely aware that little time remains before he will be unable to function purposefully.

The man, however, is not cold, not even in the back seat of the unheated taxi where, swathed in a jacket of suede and sheepskin, he smokes a poorly rolled stick of Panamanian Red. He mops his forehead repeatedly. Occasionally he pauses to polish his eyeglasses on which moisture continually condenses. The man sits back at his ease, enjoying the ride through the desolate park. The trees stand barren. The smell of leather is most comforting.

The boy stands in front of the locked amusement arcade. Shading his eyes with one hand he peers through the glass door. There is nothing to see inside since the arcade will not open for at least another hour. He shivers. A black man approaches the boy. The boy stomps his feet and blows on his cupped hands. After glancing over each of his shoulders in turn the black man whispers in the boy's ear. They engage in a rapid conversation. The boy spreads his palms upward and seems to be asking the black man for a favor of some kind. The black man now spreads his palms upward and shakes his head. He extracts several glassine bags from his pocket and shows them to the boy. He says something emphatically and points to the clock visible above the bank on the corner. The boy nods his head as he too points to the clock. Their conversation completed, the black man departs, leaving the boy to pat his breast pocket. The boy begins to shiver again.

As the man passes under the clock his shoulder is brushed by a gaudily arrayed black man who neglects to excuse himself for his rudeness. The man in the sheepskin jacket is about to make an angry and perhaps challenging remark when he sees the boy. He forgets to curse the black man and increases his pace, congratulating himself on his luck. The wind blows in chilly gusts. The black man has disappeared around the corner, so the man and the boy are virtually alone on the street.

The boy's fine black locks fall below his ears. His skin, even at some distance, seems to the man to be the color of translucent amber. The cheekbones are high and prominent, the long legs well developed. The man approaches the boy who is standing perhaps six inches away, still in profile. The man stares directly at the boy.

147

Porcelain, not amber at all. Porcelain. The man examines the boy's crotch. The boy, who has been aware of the man's presence, turns and meets his gaze directly. His eyes narrow and gleam in a peculiar way which the man finds fascinating. The man smiles and deliberately lets his eyes fall once more to the outline in the area of the boy's groin. The man and the boy enter the hotel together. Behind the desk a humpbacked clerk blows on a container of coffee from which steam rises. The man places several bills on the counter and receives a key from the humpback. He pockets the key and deliberately leaves some small bills and change on the counter. The humpback, who does not raise his eyes from the coffee container, waits until the man and boy disappear up the stairs. Then he reaches for the money, blowing on his coffee all the while.

Once in the room the boy undresses rapidly. The man sits on the only chair, fully clothed except for the suede and sheepskin coat which he has tossed on a corner of the bed. The boy's smooth body is streaked with dirt, as is his neck. There is grit under his fingernails. His skimpy briefs are grimy and soiled. The man watches the boy intently, measuring, evaluating, appraising. There can be no doubt that the man is a connoisseur of sorts. When the boy raises his arms to pull his shirt over his head the man suppresses a gasp. His nostrils flare and he smiles openly, appreciating the elegant lines of finger, arm, waist, and hip. The boy turns to face the seated man, hooking his thumbs under the waistband of his briefs. He steps out of his briefs and stands completely naked, crotch thrust slightly forward. One might think that he flaunts his body or that he is proud that he is not erect. He knows that the man is erect. With a head gesture the boy indicates the bed. The man slowly shakes his head, still smiling, and summons the boy with a crook of his finger. The boy seems almost to stalk, tossing his hair from side to side. The man unzips his fly. The boy kneels, reaches into the man's pants and goes about his business. All the while the man continues to smile. When the boy has finished his work he scans the room for a towel. There is no towel, nor is there a sink. The man says something, indicating the door with his hand. The boy nods, slides his briefs up over his hips and opens the door.

When the boy returns from the bathroom the man has already

departed. The man has disappeared. The boy is stricken, realizing that he is very sick, or perhaps he is stricken at the man's departure. It is impossible to say. Then he realizes that his pants and shirt are gone. On the bed lies the syringe, the needle twisted beyond repair.

Where the boy and the priest meet is inconsequential. Be assured that it cannot be too far from the vicinity of the clock and the amusement arcade. In any case they do meet. It is sometime in winter although it is not possible to pinpoint the precise day, week, or even month. It is late afternoon and the boy is sick.

The thought of lying down with the priest disturbs the boy, who envisions him naked wearing a clerical collar. The priest has a rather distant but decidedly kindly manner of speaking, as if he were bewildered or absent, condescending and eager to be done. Perhaps this diversity of feelings cannot exist at the same time. Perhaps the priest is just uncomfortable in the chilly weather. Perhaps he is merely lecherous.

The priest's wood-paneled study is lined with books. It is warm and cozy. A real log fire burns in the fireplace. The room smells of pipe tobacco. The boy examines the study with great interest. He has never before seen so many books in one place. He asks the priest what is in the books. The priest sighs, as if delayed from an important errand. He explains that the books are about God. Cramps constrict the boy's stomach. What about God, the boy inquires. Does God mind what they are about to undertake? The answer to this question means a great deal to the boy. Perhaps the priest has never heard the question put so bluntly. He reflects, begins to speak, then changes his mind and pauses. God, he declares, knows the frailty of man; He sees into the depths of a man's heart and knows his intentions. If we pray to Him earnestly for forgiveness of sins, He will forgive. He will forgive us our sins if we ask Him to with a contrite heart. But what if someone has no choice, asks the boy. Suppose someone has to sin. The priest feels inadequate to explain that the boy has just suggested an unforgivable sin, the sin against the Holy Ghost. He sighs and motions for the boy to stand beside him. The boy shyly obeys. There is time, the priest explains, for you to understand, but right now . . . His voice trails off. He shrugs his shoulders. The boy knows that his question will remain unanswered. A terrible spasm shakes him. With an effort he manages to control his sphincter.

The priest's touch is dry and unpleasant. His hand skims over the boy's body. He heaves himself on top of the boy and climaxes almost immediately, gasping for breath while he does so. The boy and the man with the clerical collar dress in the darkness of the tiny bedroom. On their return to the study the priest writes out a generous check, blows on the ink and hands the check to the boy with a smile. The boy has never before been given a check. He has no idea what to do with it. For what he needs right now, at once, the check is valueless. He explains this to the priest in a voice tinged with rising panic. The priest is patient. He explains to the boy, shows him the contents of his wallet. Certainly the check is good. Certainly the bank will cash it tomorrow. Certainly. The boy stamps his foot and rips the check in half, hurling the pieces in the priest's face. He must have money now, not tomorrow. Tonight. Now. The priest shrugs and writes out another check for a larger amount. He places the check in the boy's breast pocket. Undoubtedly he feels the syringe when he does so. There is nothing more to be said, nothing more to be done, so the boy leaves. Solemnly the priest makes the sign of the cross behind the departing boy. Then he locks the door and falls on his knees before the image of the crucified Christ. Outside in the wind the boy staggers to the corner, where he leans against a lampost and retches.

It is raining. Not a downpour to be sure, but a bleak, steady drizzle. The boy looks helplessly up and down the street. He has almost given up hope of meeting anyone at this late hour. People with sense have found some warm place to wait out the weather. The boy cannot afford the luxury of waiting.

A passing car sloshes through a puddle of water, soaking the boy's pants up to the knees. He curses, futilely trying to dry himself. The car stops, backs up, and squeals to a halt in front of the boy, once again splashing him. The boy is angry. The door on the driver's side opens. An effeminate man with blond hair and bony hands, his lips and cheeks faintly rouged, leans over a burly squat man with hairy arms and invites the boy inside. The tempo of the rain has increased. The boy opens the back door of the car and slips inside. The car rounds the corner and swerves down an avenue. The occupants of the front seat are drunk—at least drunk. The boy asks where they are going and the effeminate man trills a reply, naming a part of the City with which the boy is unfamiliar. The hairy man drinks from a pint bottle which he then passes to the effeminate man. The boy sits, watching the streets sail by in the rain. The effeminate man places a handkerchief doused with ethyl chloride under the nose of the hairy man, who sniffs and then flushes rapidly. The handkerchief is passed to the boy. The boy shakes his head, declining the offering. The effeminate man giggles and covers his own nose with the handkerchief. He too flushes. The whole procedure is then repeated. By the time the car stops in front of a ramshackle one-family house somewhere in an outlying area of the City, the effeminate man's head is nestled on the hairy man's shoulder. The hairy man ignores the other's gaze of adoration.

The boy lies spread-eagled on the bed. His hands and feet are handcuffed to the bed frame. The boy is nude, as is the effeminate man, who attempts to spray more ethyl chloride onto the handkerchief. The bottle is empty. The effeminate man shrugs. He adjusts the curtains and then raises the volume of the radio until the dial can be turned no further. Casually he bestrides the boy's upper thighs and spits on his own hand, lubricating his penis with the saliva. He thrusts himself inside the boy. Each time he thrusts he withdraws almost completely, then thrusts once more as deeply as possible into the resisting rectum. This procedure continues for at least twenty minutes. The hairy man enters the room. He too is naked. He kneels on the bed, his nose inches from the boy's rectal opening. Almost instantly his flaccid organ hardens. Swiftly the effeminate man exchanges places with the hairy man.

It is the hairy man who now bestrides the boy. From a can beside the bed he scoops some Crisco, which he uses to lubricate his right fist. He inserts one, then two, then three fingers well inside the boy's rectum and then, grimly, his entire fist. The boy, who is gagged as well as handcuffed, screams, but all that can be heard is a high-pitched mewl. He arches his neck and back, attempting to rid himself of the awful, intolerable pain. The handcuffs bite deeper into the boy's wrists and the fist drives deeper into his bowels. He screams, one would fancy, like one possessed and then lapses into unconsciousness. He is unaware that the backs of his thighs and the sheets beneath them are soaked with his own blood. The effeminate man, his face aglow with love, masturbates vigorously while he fellates the hairy one, who continues to work with his fist. Both men climax within seconds of each other. When it is over they carry the still-unconscious boy to the car, assiduously wiping up all traces of blood from the driveway. When the boy awakes he will not be able to find his left sneaker, nor will he realize that his underwear has disappeared.

The car stops in front of a street lamp. It is still drizzling and quite dark in the street when the hairy man rolls the boy from the back seat of the car into the gutter in a district of deserted warehouses and abandoned stores. A bridge can be seen from the car window. The car speeds off, sploshing the boy with some oily filth. The boy, partially conscious, is dimly aware of the rain and of a pain so impossible that he cannot recognize it as his own.

The boy pushes the untouched plate of food away from him. His eyes are glazed. His head sags, droops until chin touches breastbone, then jerks upward again. The old woman has been watching. She asks the boy to get her coat. Ever obedient to her will the boy dreamily opens the closet and feels himself thrust inside. Before he can turn around the lock snaps into place. The old woman then bars the door with a chair, puts on her coat, and leaves the flat.

On the first night he is beset with chills, cramps, and the familiar brutal spasms. He sits hunched on the floor of the closet, knees to his chin, weeping at his betrayal. He pounds on the door until his hands are pricked with splinters, until his knuckles are bloody and raw. He hugs his stomach and voids his bladder. He sits in the dark, wet and crying, rocking back and forth.

During the second day his legs are cramped and virtually useless. The spasms and intestinal cramps are abominable. He retches weakly. He pounds his head on the floor and punches himself in the stomach. He wipes the vomit from his lips with his shirt. He bangs on the door once or twice and then begins to batter at it with his head.

On the second night he is dehydrated. He masturbates, inserting his finger into his anus while he does so. Then the itching begins. He scratches his arms, his legs, his crotch, and his armpits. He scrapes his back against the doorknob like a dog. He masturbates again, screaming as he climaxes. He continues to scream long after he has spent himself.

During the third day he can barely move. He sprawls crookedly in a corner, rubbing his legs to stimulate the circulation of blood. His feet tingle. His sobs are choked in his now-parched throat. A trickle of slime rolls down his pants leg. The spasms are slightly less intense and recur with decreasing frequency. For the first time he sleeps, restlessly, mouth agape, but he sleeps.

On the third night he drowses uneasily. He is freezing and unexpectedly hungry. The cramps have become hunger pangs. The sweat has dried under his armpits. He coughs deeply, hacking up phlegm. He awakes and drapes the shreds of his shirt around his shoulders. The old woman unlocks the door and Lazarus tumbles out unconscious. She drags him by his arms to the bathroom where she has already drawn a hot bath. After she has removed and discarded all his clothes, she sponges the naked body clean with sandalwood soap, humming a tune that lovers used to sing when she was a girl. Tenderly she towels the boy down, rubbing the hairless skin red, careful to dry between his toes and under his testicles.

The boy sits at the kitchen table wrapped in the old woman's bathrobe. Before him is a mound of food: yellow rice, red beans stewed with neckbones, the white meat of a chicken. To the boy the scent of the steam rising from the heaped platter is voluptuous. Greedily he shoves food into his mouth. When he is done he lights a cigarette and blows smoke rings. He stubs out the cigarette, rises, and advances toward the old woman, who sits silently across from him, watching. As the boy strides across the space that separates him from the old woman the bathrobe flaps open, revealing his nakedness. He is not ashamed. He stoops, lifts up her head between his hands, and plants a kiss on her forehead. Playfully, he nips the tip of her nose. The old woman chuckles. The boy beams at her, delighted, and declares, "I love you, Mamita."

I guess you could say I was lucky that I broke my arm, but I swear to God I didn't think so when it happened. First off I was just plain greedy, and that's a fact. I already had so much change in my pockets I thought my pants was gonna fall down. But was that enough? No siree. There was plenty of quarters and halves left in the jar which I was scooping up as fast as I could even though I had no place to put them and most of them wound up on the floor anyhow. The next thing I know here's this lady, from right outta nowhere, standing at the bedroom door, hollering her fool head off like she was getting raped or something. I mean, Jesus Christ, I never beat up on a lady in my life, but the way she's carrying on anyone would think she was getting kilt or something.

So I go, lady, I ain't gonna hurt you, I swear to God I ain't, so if you'll please excuse me and let me get by, I'll just be going now. Like me, all I wanted to do was get the fuck outta there and shoot right up to the connection's and get straight. That's all I wanted to do. But the lady, she just won't shut up her dumb yelling, so what can I do, I give her just a little shove, just a push really, just to get her outta the way so I can get past and boom, I'm out the door and tipping down the stairs three at a time. Well, you never saw anybody stop so fast in your life, because as fast as I'm making it down, here's a cop which musta heard all the hollering, making it up the stairs about three at a time his own self only he got a fucking thirty-eight special waving it around like fucking Dillinger was robbing a bank. Holy shit, I think, this is really it. But I can't stop to worry about it right now because the cop, he's only one flight down from me. He goes, "Halt."

Halt my ass. I turn right around in midair like a fucking acrobat and scoot back up the stairs just as fast as I came down them, maybe faster. The trouble is there's not one place to hide. Not one single place except the lady's house which I just come out of and where she had just about shut up and sees me coming back inside and I don't have to tell you, there she goes again, and I mean she got some setta pipes on her. This time I don't say excuse me because the cop is breathing down my neck, practically. I kiss my ass good-bye and dive headfirst outta the kitchen window. It's lucky for me it was only the third floor but when I land I think sure as shit I broke every bone in my body. I look up from the floor and here's the cop leaning out pointing this cannon at me and I go, no way, José, not today, not for my Puerto Rican ass. I got no time to feel sorry for myself or even to figure how many bones I broke. I just pick my ass off and sorta hop and limp around the corner into an alley. Me, I don't know if the cop is crazy too and maybe he's gonna jump outta the window to chase me, but just in case I tip over every garbage can I pass, like to slow him down.

Of course with my luck it's a dead end, with this gigantic fence in front of me and most likely a bullet in my butt behind me. Oh, well, I go, and I still don't know how I did it, but somehow I manage to get the old juices going and here I am at the top of this fence which it looks awfully far down, but when you ain't got no choice you do what you gotta do and that's that. This time I land right smack on my arm and definitely hear something go crack. Don't ask me how but I'm just able to crawl through a basement window where I lay down in a corner and try to catch my breath and figure out how much of what I broke. One thing I know for sure is that I can't even move my right arm which is already swole up like a balloon and another thing I know is that all them kids I hear yelling from blocks away musta found all the change I dropped while I was tracking.

Change? I check myself out which I find I only got maybe five dollars left from all that shit plus nearly killing myself and the rest must be all over the street like a fucking trail. No question about it, if I don't move my ass I'm a dead duck. So I crawl back through the window and pick up all the loose change I can find between there and the fence. The next thing I do is sorta hop, skip, and jump to the corner which I look around and don't see nothing in sight except for a cab. Well, the cab, he gotta stop, because I stand in front of it to make him stop, I mean, he ain't gonna run me down, at least I hope he ain't gonna run me down. While he's calling me every name in the book I just hand him all the change I just picked up and tell him Roosevelt Hospital because that is the hospital closest by.

I jump in and the cab driver he don't say nothing more about it. I know I gotta look like a mess. My jacket is all torn, I got this big hole in my pants which my knee is all bloody, and my arm is absolutely killing me. I don't even know why he lets me in the cab except cabbies ain't choosy, not as long as they know you can pay, which I did already, and as long as you don't tell them Harlem,

155

East or West, because they ain't goin' anywhere in Harlem no matter what you wanna pay them to.

After he leaves me off in front of the hospital, I feel so dizzy for a minute that I think I'm gonna pass out. I start to head for the emergency room entrance which I go, whoa, hold your horses before you get yourself into something you ain't gonna be able to get out of. First off, if I'm smart enough to know Roosevelt is the closest, then the cop is probably smart enough to figure that out for his own self too. He seen me go outta the window. He gotta figure I busted something. And if somebody busts something like an arm or a leg they go to the hospital, right? Plus they would go to the nearest hospital, right? Which they all got telephones, right? Which means I stand a very good chance of gettin' pinched the minute I walk through the door. Plus if they could call this hospital what's to stop them from calling all the hospitals and telling them to look out for a kid who looks all fucked up and got a busted arm or something. Nothing says they're gonna go through all that shit, but then again nothing says that they ain't which means that not only is Roosevelt hot, but every motherfucking hospital around may be hot as a firecracker. Unless maybe I could find some guy to come with me and say I was his kid and all and got hurt falling off a bike or something. Maybe that just might work. All I gotta figure out is which guy, which guy is gonna take me to the hospital and maybe get his ass in a sling. And before I do any more figuring about anything, first I gotta get straight because I am definitely sick.

The only luck I've had so far is that I got a connection not too far away on Broadway which also I find him at home. But after I cop from him, then I gotta pay him to use his gimmicks because I musta lost mine while I was busy jumping outta windows and then I gotta pay him to hit me because I still can't even move my right arm so by the time I get through I'm flat-out busted, not a dime in my jeans, but at least I'm not sick. That's when I think about Sunshine. First off he lives in a hotel a coupla blocks away and second I might be able to con him into taking me to the hospital if I promise to let him have a real good time and do anything he wants when we're through. Well, you don't get nothin' for nothin' in this world, at least that's how I see it.

So I go up where he lives and knock on the door. Just my luck, he gotta be out because all he got is one room so when you knock on the door, right away Sunshine goes "Who?" and checks through the chain to see who it is. But I don't hear a thing and I figure, well, I gotta think of somebody else and I'm just about gonna tip when the door opens wide and I can't believe my own eyes. It can't be. But it is, it's him, the guy who tipped on me with my pants and all, that time at the fleabag hotel. There he is, big as life. I couldn't forget him if I lived to be a thousand. The same corny crew cut. The same horn-rim glasses, the same big potbelly, even the same sheepskin which I can see from where I am, lying on a chair. It's him all right, and that's all there is to it. There's an old saying which everybody knows which is, "What goes around comes around and now it's my turn." I mean, of course he gotta recognize me too 'cause if I recognize him naturally he's gonna recognize me so I move fast. What I do is sorta duck and twist past him and slam the door shut behind me and quick reach down my leg for where my double-o-seven is strapped, only I come up empty with my dick in my hand. I mean, isn't there anything I didn't lose today? Jesus Christ, I'm glad I didn't lose my head offa my shoulders because that's the only thing I got left which ain't gonna do me no good with this big fucking looney tunes. Here I am, alone in the room, no figa, no place to run and me, a hundred and twenty pounds soaking wet with this guy who's about twice my size and looks strong as an ox plus is as nutty as a fruitcake to boot. I mean you gotta be some kinda maniac to run off with a kid's pants for Chrissakes, even forgetting about the shirt.

While I'm trying to figure out what the hell to do he moves in between me and the door and this window is eleven stories up. I'm mad, I'm scared, I wanna kill this motherfucker, and I'm shitting in my pants practically, all at the same time. Well, I must look kinda funny to him, deciding whether to shit or go blind 'cause what does he do but bust out laughing. If it's one thing I can't stand is to have somebody laughing at me and if it's another thing I can't stand is to have a guy who beat me and stole my pants laughing at me when I should be laughing at him while I'm slicing him up into little pieces. Well, when I get mad I see red and sometimes I don't even know what I'm doing. Whoosh, I fire the lamp at him which he just sidesteps and laughs some more. Clank, I miss with the ashtray.

157

There ain't nothing else on the table so I just turn the whole fucking thing over with my one good hand and try to heave it at him, which makes him bust a gut even more. Now I'm standing there with nothin' more to throw so what I do is try to kick him in the balls. He just gives me a little shove and I go flying ass backwards across the bed and bang my head against the wall where I proceed to try to kick his silly teeth out. He grabs both my legs and sorta yanks and this time my bad arm hits the wall and I think I'm gonna die on the spot it hurts so bad.

"Ow, you dumb motherfucker, that's my bad arm."

Him, he's wiping his eyes with a handkerchief, still laughing and goes, "Mmmph . . . haven't laughed so hard since Grandma fell down the well and broke a leg and we had to shoot her."

(He kilt his grandma? This guy's bananas!)

"I don't care what happened to your grandma, just leave off my bad arm, willya?"

"If I let you sit up will you behave like a gentleman?"

"Gentleman my asshole. Just stop shovin' me."

Me, I lay still so this maniac don't shoot me like he did his own grandma and after a couple of seconds he lets me sit up on the side of the bed. There he is, right in front of me.

"Don't."

"Don't what?"

"Don't even think about what you're thinking."

"What am I thinking," I go, all innocent like. "What am I thinking?" Which is when I make a dive and at the same time take a wild swing at his balls. Wham! He backhands me one right upside my head which I see stars and I know it's just no good. I know when I've had enough—he's just too big for me and that's all there is to it.

"Ok, ok, I give." I put my one good hand in front of my face just in case he got it in his head to really do a number on me. "I give. No more, ok?"

What does this fat creep do? He sticks out his hand like I'm supposed to shake it or something and goes, "Peace?"

Me, I wouldn't shake his dumb ugly paw for nothing. Shake his hand? Not for all the tea in China would I shake his hand. Wham! Another backhand. This guy's a lunatic, I'm telling you.

He's dangerous. They oughtta lock him up and throw the key away. And what does he do? The same fucking thing—sticks out his hand for me to shake and goes, "Peace?" So what can I do, I got no choice. It's shake his hand or get my brains knocked out, so I shake. I mean, what else am I supposed to do? Of course I gotta shake with my left hand which I'm glad I don't get smacked for that too.

"Aha, so peace it is! Well done, my angry young friend."

"Mmmm."

"Louder!"

"I said, 'peace,' you dirty creep motherfucker, you heard me all right."

Now he looks for sure like he's gonna smash me again. "Let us establish some ground rules before we seal our new-found peace with a sign. First, keep a civil tongue in your head, sonny boy, or you won't have a head to keep a civil tongue in, get it?"

"Mmmm."

"And second, when I ask you a question, look at me and answer so I can hear you. Get it?"

"Yeah."

"Yeah, what?"

"Yeah, I get it."

"Much better. Much better indeed. An apt pupil, if I may say so. Fine manly voice, and look at me when I address you, or when you address me. Understood?"

"Yeah."

"Tsk, tsk."

"Yeah, understood."

"Now, what happened to your hand?"

"Nothing'." Whack. Another one lands on my mush from way out in left field. "I thought you said you wouldn't hit me no more."

"No such thing . . . mmmph. We spoke of peace. We arrived at an understanding. Just so there is no misunderstanding, an answer means a truthful answer, so let us try once more. Believe me, my boy, this is hurting you much more than it is me. What happened to your hand?"

"I fell on it."

"How?"

"I jumped out a window."

"Indeed, indeed." I guess he believes me, about the window, I mean, but just in case I go to cover up my head again. "Did you perhaps fall?"

"Mmm . . . mmmm, I mean no, I didn't fall."

"Pushed? No, certainly not. Don't bother with that one. Was someone attempting to apprehend you?"

"Apprehend?"

"Pinch you."

"The cop was chasing me."

"So you just jumped out of the window."

"Yeah, and then I climbed this big fence and I hadda jump again and landed right on my arm. That was twice and now it hurts like a motherfucker."

"Where?"

"Here, right here, and here too, all over."

"Your arm, please." Jesus Christ, I can't even lift it up and I'm gonna let this nut poke all over my arm and shit and fuck it up for good. No way. No. I won't do it. And that's that.

He sorta squats down so his head is about even with mine where I'm sitting on the bed and goes, "You don't trust me? Mmmmph. Listen to me, very carefully. Look around this room. Look well." And I can't help it, my eyes follow where he's pointing all around this crummy old hotel room. "Do you see anyone, anyone else? No, that's all right, don't answer, just listen. No one else here. You. I. You, very possibly, have a serious injury. You, very probably, have good reason why you do not want this attended to in a hospital. And you have no reason to trust me, no reason to have faith in me. Listen, it is because you have no trust in me that you must force yourself to. You tell yourself this stranger has no reason to help me, none, and every bone in your body cries out, be afraid, be afraid. I say to you trust me. Take a chance, just as you leaped blindly from the window. Leap now, and trust me." His voice is like almost putting me to sleep. I'm not so mad anymore, my arm is on fire, and he's right. What else can I do? My head is spinning like I have a fever, I feel dizzy, and I'm scared.

"Will it hurt?"

"Yes."

"Bad?"

"Yes."

"But you can fix it?"

"I don't know. I don't know anymore. You'll have to trust enough for both of us." He almost sounds like he don't want to try his own self to fix it, but that like he gotta try, I don't know.

He got me all mixed up. I don't know what to do, he couldn't make it any worse, that's for sure, I mean, just looking at it. I guess he can tell that I've made up my mind cause he goes, "Raise your arm."

"I can't. I can't even move it." I feel like I'm gonna bawl, but somehow I lift it up, just a little, just like twitch my fingers and the pain is so bad I think I'm gonna throw up.

"Stand up." And he got this funny smile on his face which now I'm up on my feet and he takes my arm, real soft and gentle like and lifts it real slow until he got my hand under his armpit and the rest of my arm is like straight out. He touches it in a couple of spots and it hurts so bad I don't even know where he's touching and he's still smiling and thinking, "Yes, I was correct, a mild case of defenestration."

"De . . . what?" and he like pushes and pulls at something in my arm at the same time, and that's when I pass out cold.

When I wake up the first thing I see is him sitting next to me, wiping off my forehead with a washcloth which he got on it some of Sunshine's cologne which always makes me wanna puke. And the next thing I see is my arm in a sling which he musta made outta tearing up a sheet. I can feel he got some kind of splint on it and it's almost like a miracle. It almost stopped hurting, I mean, sure, it's throbbing and shit, but like I can tell it's much much better. I look down and see he musta taken my sneakers off plus my pants too—my pants!

"Oh, no, no you don't, not two times in a row. Gimme my pants. Gimme my pants right now or I'll holler so loud every cop in the neighborhood'll hear."

Well, I guess that musta sounded pretty funny because he puts down the washcloth and starts to laugh, not the funny kinda smile he had before, but like when he saw me throwing all that shit at him.

"Oh, that would never do, never do indeed. The arm?"

"It hurts like hell," I lie, "and if you try to tip with my pants I'll kill ya the next time I see ya."

"Here, here, dunderhead. If they were any closer they'd jump up and bite you. Right on the chair."

"Well, ok." I'm still not sure he ain't gonna go crazy on me again, even though he did fix my arm and all. "Just don't try nothing funny."

"No indeed," he shakes his head like that's the last thing in the world he'd do, something funny, I mean. "I'm always disappointed when a man can't take a practical joke with good humor."

"That was a joke, what you did to me? That was funny, huh? Well let me tell you, mister, you must have some kinda weird sense of humor, beating me outta my dough and tipping with my pants."

"But you did find them downstairs?"

"Sure I found them, but how do you think I felt before I did? Pretty funny, huh? Big joke!"

"Wasn't it? When I picture how you must have looked when you came back and found not only me, but everything else gone, disappeared . . ." And he cracks up, slapping his knee and laughing his head off, which when I think about it, as stupid as it sounds, I guess I musta looked pretty funny at that and so I bust out laughing too. I'm laughing so hard that I bang my arm against the wall and I'm laughing and near crying at the same time.

"Well," I go, when I get myself back to normal and I sit up 'cause I'm feeling better, "still you wouldn't be laughing if itta happened to you."

"Ah, but that's just the point." And now he's all serious again, boom, just like that. One minute he sounds like a laughing hyena and the next minute he's serious as cancer. "That's just the point, indeed."

"What point?"

"That it couldn't happen to me, nor could it happen to you again either."

"You're darn tootin' it couldn't. I'll never go off and leave my pants again with a strange trick and all and another thing, since then I get my money in my slide up front before I even unbutton my shirt."

"Well, then, at the very least, you should be grateful."

"For what, for you making a fool outta me?"

"For me being such a good teacher. Think about it."

So I think about it. "Yeah, well, that's not why you did it, outta the goodness of your heart and all."

"But you did learn a lesson. Two in fact."

"That's for damn sure and while we're on the subject, you still owe me."

"How much?"

"Mmmm, how about ten?"

"You see?" I do see.

"Well, I ain't as dumb as I was then, and now I get it straight before, about how much and all and don't change the subject."

"Hmmmm. Not only apt, but quick. Mark of an intelligent man, my boy. Learn fast, never fall for the same scam twice in one week, and all that. Permit me, then, a small token . . ." Which he pulls some dough out of his pocket and eases it into the sling, but I ain't goin' for no more okey-doke. I pull it right back out and check it out, just to be sure.

"That's a twenty."

"But is it real?"

"Is it phony? You gimme a phony?"

"Does it look phony?"

"Nope, it looks ok to me."

"Then trust that it's as good as it looks."

"It is phony!"

"No, it's quite real."

"How can you tell?"

"You can't, that's just the point. Remember that, boy, and you'll go far in life. Things are always as they seem, Saul's first law."

"Who's Saul?"

"Who is Saul? I am Saul."

"Well, listen, Saul, could I ask you just one question? Why the fuck did you tip with my pants?"

"Because you challenged me."

"What's that supposed to mean?"

"Assume the mask appropriate. If you're hustling, then act like a hustler should. Don't let a trick know how much you hate

163

him. Don't let him know that he, not you, is the piece of shit. And don't, under any circumstances, flaunt your beautiful body."

"Don't say that, about beautiful and all. I don't like that. I'm not a broad and I ain't a faggot."

"But you are beautiful and tricks resent hustlers who use their beauty to humiliate."

"I don't know what the fuck you're talking about."

"I think you do."

"Is that why you took my pants, 'cause I made you feel like shit?"

"I." He laughs. "Certainly not. It was a challenge. I told you, I am a man who enjoys practical jokes."

"What do I hafta do?"

"Do? For what?"

"For the twenty. What do I hafta do for the twenty?"

"Learn how to take a joke. Learn what you want to be real."

"Stop talking in riddles and tell me what you want. Don't be ashamed. Whatever you want, I'll do it, as long as it ain't some sick shit."

"Whatever I want?"

"Nothing weird. I don't do that shit."

"Well, then, two things."

"Yeah, what two things?"

"First, then, buy yourself a new pair of pants."

"Come on, you know what I'm talking about."

"Silence, whelp! I have one request remaining, which is . . ."

"Which is . . .? Yeah, come on . . ."

"Let us be friends."

"What kinda friends?"

"The only kind of friends there are, the kind who trust each other."

"You mean you don't wanna get down with me, is that what you mean?"

"I mean only what I say. Friends. Some friends do and some friends don't."

"Get down?"

"Get down."

"You mean it's up to me?"

"No. I mean it's up to you and me."

"But if I don't wanna, we don't hafta get down, we can still be friends?"

"We *are* friends."

"You trust me?"

"Of course not, not as far as I could throw you, my boy."

"But you just said . . .?"

"Mmmph. A friend never holds another friend to his word. That is the essence of true friendship."

"You're crazy!" I can't help it, but I, like, giggle. I mean, here I was just a while ago throwing lamps at this guy and trying to kick him in the balls, and the next thing he fixes my fucking arm, gives me a twenty for nothing, and now we're supposed to be friends and me, I can't understand half of what he says. It's crazy, that's what it is.

"Are you a real doctor?"

"Do I look like a doctor?"

"Yeah, well . . . sorta. You could be."

"Then remember Saul's second law, my boy, and you can't go wrong: Things are never what they seem to be."

"Now I know you're crazy, you're crazy as a bedbug. Not two minutes ago you told me that things are always what they seem to be and now you say just the opposite. Which one is right?"

"Both of them."

"But that's impossible."

"Aha, intelligent, just as I surmised. You have arrived without coaching at Saul's third law."

"I give up. You got me. I quit. Just tell me, yes or no, are you a doctor or not? Did you ever work in a hospital or not?"

"Yes and no. No, I am not a doctor, and yes, I worked in a hospital."

"Ok, you just tell me how you worked in a hospital then. What hospital lets you work there and not be a doctor?"

"Ah, my friend, a hellish place where nice distinctions are unwelcome. My craft in medicine was acquired in that great castle upon the Hudson."

"See, now I know you're bullshitting. When I was small our class went on the dayline which goes right up the Hudson and there ain't one single castle there, liar!"

"Ah, to think that I have called thee friend. Not 'a' castle, 'the' castle. The slam. The stir, The joint. The can. Old double S. The big house."

"You, you were locked up?"

"Mmmm. Many times. Many, many times, cast into prison, so that I should pay what was due . . . my debt to myself for getting careless."

"I bet I know what happened. I bet you got pinched for stealing some kid's pants."

"Mmm. And if I were a wagering man I would wager you were about to get the back of me hand."

"I thought you could take a joke."

"I thought you were sensible enough not to believe strangers."

"But we're friends."

"Strange friends, then. Peace?"

"Peace." And, well, I might as well say it, he leans over and like squeezes my shoulder, my good one, until we're real close and then, well, he kisses me, not like no friend ever kissed me, that's for sure, which I don't want anyone to get the wrong idea. I may be a hustler and all but I don't kiss tricks, I mean, I almost never do unless it's something special, you know, the dough and all. That's one thing I don't do and it's been a long time since I let a guy kiss me which I'm not saying that right this minute I don't like it and I figure, oh shit, I guess if he wants to get down, why not. I mean, the twenty and all. And I'm just getting into this kissing shit when, boom, he just stops. Like pushes me away, back where I was and stops, like he's forgotten what we were doing right in the middle. It's crazy. I guess maybe I wasn't doing something right, or something, and maybe he don't wanna tell me, but whatever it is it must be bugging the shit out of him to make him stop just like that.

"You're feeling better?"

"Yeah, sure, I'm feeling better."

"No pain?"

"Not much. It's ok, you fixed it real good. Why? What's the matter? Why are you looking so funny?"

"I'd have that checked out, by a real doctor. I mean. When it's cool. No rush. You can wait a couple of days, but I would keep the splint in place, and the sling, of course. Try not to bump it."

"You sound like you're getting ready to tip or something."

"Mmmm. Yes, well, time and tide, you know. I'm sure that Sunshine won't be displeased to find you here . . . mmm . . . I mean, alone, on his return."

"Why don't you wait for him?"

"Sunshine is an old and dear friend."

"So? So what? So why don't you wait for him then?"

"We have a standing policy which permits us to remain friends. I don't fuck with his trade and he accords me the same courtesy."

"I thought we were friends."

"And thus, alas, we kiss and part . . ."

"But we just started being friends, a couple of minutes ago."

"To quote our mutual friend, 'That was then, this is now.' You are feeling better, you are no longer angry, perhaps you even learned something of value."

I mean, what the hell am I supposed to say? I just can't understand this guy. First he's laughing, then he's sad. First he's making jokes and then he's talking some way-out shit which I can't hardly understand him. First we're friends, and the next minute we ain't friends no more. I just don't get it.

"Are you mad at me or something? Did I do something wrong?"

"Mad? Tsk-Tsk, no, my boy. Only dogs are mad, dogs and Englishmen . . . mmm . . . little joke, over your head I imagine. But to address myself to the intent of your question, no, I'm not angry with you, nor with myself either."

"See, you are mad, you are. If I said something wrong then tell me. You don't hafta be like that."

"Our first quarrel, and our last."

"Why, what are we fighting about?"

"You like Sunshine?"

"Sure, he's ok, I guess."

"Ok, for what?"

"Ok, ok, just ok. What am I supposed to be, for Chrissakes, in love with him or something, because I trick with him?"

"Just ok? And you get down with him. How much does he pay?"

"Why, what's the difference?"

"A pound?"

"Most of the times."

"For what?"

"Well, to get down, you know. What the hell do you think he pays for? He's your friend, right?"

"Can't you say it?"

"Ok, he does anything he wants to, but not weird shit or anything."

"Anything he wants to, for a pound. Lucky man, my friend Sunshine."

He lifts up my hand, the one with the holes in it where I get off, where my tracks are.

I pull it away from him and I go, "That's none of your fucking business. That got nothing to do with anything. You know why I'm tricking. You don't hafta be no genius with fancy words to know what the score is. I went with you, right, to that fleabag hotel where I gave you a blow job and you beat me and ran off with my pants because you were too fucking cheap to pay, that's why. All your fancy bullshit. I know why you ran off, so you could get over, like everybody else, so you can think you're slick getting over on a strung-out kid. So I trick with Sunshine. Big fucking deal. I didn't hear you do no complaining while I was sucking on your dick and getting your rocks off. So what is it, you want me to fall down on my knees like you're God or something just cause you fixed my hand? You want me—what—to fall in love with you for Chrissakes, cause you think you're king shit or something, looking at my hands and shit like I was a nothing, like I was a piece of shit? Well, fuck you, then, who the fuck needs you. Just do what you gotta do and find another kid to chump off. Just leave me the fuck alone."

Saul, he don't say a thing, not one fucking word. Just pulls himself up off the bed and looks at me kinda strange like. I can't exactly explain, but like he don't believe one word I'm saying, or maybe like he knows it's the truth, but only some of the truth, not all of it, and he like waves and starts to open the door. Not one word. He can't be going, not for real. All of a sudden I don't want him to go. I want to tell him how I get mad, about my tracks and shit, because I can't stand being the way I am, strung out and all, doing things, things I can't stand doing, just to get straight so I won't hafta worry about being sick, how it makes me sick to my stomach doing some of the things I hafta do to stop from being sick, how I meant what I said just now, about him and tipping and getting over because that's how it musta been, but that I understand, I mean, now it's different, and everybody's gonna get over if you chump yourself off and how he said he needed me to trust him because he didn't really know anymore, like I didn't understand all of it and yet I knew what he meant. How nobody ever talked to me like he did when he talked me into letting him fix my hand. How I just can't help being the way I am. All of it. I wanted to tell him so much and I knew I was bullshitting. It's crazy. Because what I really want, why I really don't want him to go is because I wanna get down with him. That's right. Me, a hustler, which I ain't even supposed to like getting down and all since it's only for money, to get straight, right? All I know is I got twenty in my kick which I don't hafta worry about getting straight. Because I got more than enough gap for tonight and right now I wanna get down with him. Now. I even gotta hard-on, for Chrissakes, which he gotta see, I mean, me sitting in my drawers and all.

He probably thinks I'm a real fucking dodo and me, I go, "Yo, Saul, wait up a minute. Wouldja, you know, just help me get up and I'll tip with you because Sunshine, he'll probably have connipshuns if he finds me here, you know, alone in his house, you know, like maybe I was robbing it or something."

Saul, he turns around at the door and looks right at me, right through me and goes, "You can walk."

"No, honest I can't. I'm feeling dizzy. Just help me up can'tcha, and I won't bother you no more."

He knows I'm lying. He knows I'm all right, that I can get up just fine. He looks at me like he did the first time, at my body, as if he never seen nothing like it before, which is stupid, but that's how it seems. He looks at my legs, from my ankles which are pretty dirty right on up to my banged-up knee, up my thighs and on up. I know what he wants and that's just fine with me—no bullshit, no nothing, just get it on. And I know that there's no way in the world he's gonna leave. I can make him come back, even if he don't want to, even if he can't stand the thought of getting down with a dirty strung-out kid which lets niggers dick him for five bucks a pop, even if it makes him throw up, even if he hates me for having that kinda power over him, to make him do what I want, just like that time in the fleabag hotel. Just like that time. And I know why he took my pants. I lay down. He knows I'm not going anywhere. I stretch my legs out as far as they'll go and rub my hands all down one leg. I don't say a thing. I don't hafta. This time he'll come to me. I look at him. I push my back up offa the bed so he can get a good look. I look at him which he gotta understand. I see he understands I can make him come to me.

He sits down on the bed. I know he hates me for what I'm doing, just a dumb strung-out junky kid that maybe'll be getting down with his best friend in an hour. But he's gentle. Very gentle. His face is all red and he's breathing like we was already doing something together. He's sweaty and nervous and he starts rubbing my leg, just where I was rubbing it, soft, soft, so soft and nice. I can feel that my tits are hard, just like a broad. I take his hand and put it right on my hard-on. This time he's gonna do it *my* way. I reach up with my good arm and pull him down next to me on the bed and start unbuttoning his pants. "Saul . . . that feels so good . . ."

Of course nothing ever works out the way I plan it. After we're done, and I'm just laying back, feeling real relaxed, I realize that he knew it all the time, knew how to get me horny, knew just what to say and just what to do, knew from the moment I walked into the room and started throwing things. He got over again, the cocksucker, and I start to sniffle just a little bit, like maybe I caught a little cold or something, 'cause what the hell, I can't say I didn't have a ball, 'cause I sure as fuck did, and that's a fact. So we lay there, and Saul, he rubs my back nice, all over my back and legs again, just like he did it, just like I like it and then, I guess, I just fall asleep.

When I wake up he's still there. I got my arms around him, or at least my good arm. The bad one I'm resting on his shoulder, and he's still holding me and somehow we get started, you know, all over again and this time it's even better because it takes us both longer to finish. I wish we could just stay like this, but I look at his watch and I know it's about that time so I sit up, even though I don't want to, and I go, "Yo, Saul? Dig, I gotta go down for a while, you know, to take care of my B.I., but I won't be long. Willya wait?"

"If I do, if I'm here, do you want to get down again?"

"Sure, sure I do."

"And if Sunshine is here?"

"Well go to your crib, ok?"

"For a little while or to stay the night?"

"Sure, the whole night if you want. Sure."

"All night?"

"Sure."

"And tomorrow morning?"

"Sure, tomorrow morning, we could get down again, just like we did."

"All day tomorrow?"

"All day, sure, except I gotta go out an hustle a little and get straight, you know."

"So not all day."

"Sure, all day, just like I said, except just when I gotta go take care of B.I. Listen, I mean, I could stay with you, you know, all the time, you know, for as long as you wanted and we could . . . ."

"No."

"No? Ok. Well, then, like whenever you want, I could come by . . ."

"No."

"But I thought you liked it. I thought, you know, we could be friends."

"You don't even believe yourself."

"Sure I do. Whaddya mean, I don't believe myself? I just told you I would, what I'd do."

"Because you're straight. Because you're not sick. Say it in two hours, four hours, whenever you start to get sick. Whenever you get nice and sick. Then talk about staying. 'Ooooo, Saul, I liked it so much, I wanna be with you.' Talk that shit when you're real, real sick, my man, and then somebody might believe you. But not me and not you either. You got what you want, be satisfied. Be satisfied that you can do what very few people in this world can do. Be satisfied that you can always get over by becoming your own victim. I can't afford you. I can't afford you because I can't afford to spend whatever feelings I have in a cesspool. What happens in a month, a week, tomorrow when you're sick and I say, 'No, no money, it's your habit not mine. It's all yours, I give it to you.' What happens when you're just watching and waiting for me to go to sleep so you can rip me off and run to the cooker? What happens if

171

the ugliest, smelliest, meanest, most degenerate scum in the world says, 'Come, come with me. Leave your Saul, come with me, and I'll take care of your jones. I'll keep you straight whenever you want to get straight, whenever you need to.' You'd go in a minute, bet your sweet ass you would. You'd suck twenty dicks an hour if that would stop you from being sick. You hate every minute of it and hate yourself for it. Nothing but hate. You'd wind up begging and pleading and whining and sniveling and I'd hate you and you'd hate me and we would kill it, kill it all and each other too. It was a pleasant afternoon. We both enjoyed each other. Now go run to the cooker and say, 'Good-bye, Saul.' "

"Just like that?"

"Just like that."

"No." And he backhands me right in my eye. "Go ahead, get your rocks off! You wanna get your rocks off beating up on me, go ahead. You won't be the first."

And he backhands me again, knocking a tooth loose and there's blood all over his hand, from my mouth, my nose, who knows, who cares?

"Go ahead, you can hit harder than that! Pussy! Faggot! What? You think I can help myself? You think I can help being this way, strung out, running around all the time, getting up sick, going to bed sick, thrown outta my house, sleeping in hallways, not knowing where my next meal is coming from? You think I like being all fucked up and strung out?"

Wham. He really belts me one, which I'm almost scared he *is* gonna fuck me up bad.

"What do you think I am, a fucking priest? Tell your troubles to a priest. Go cry on his shoulder."

"I can't help it!"

Wham.

We're both on our feet, carrying on like two crazy people.

"Don't tell me you're God. Don't tell me you're Christ, that you can't help your suffering. Monstrous vanity! How dare you tell me you choose to suffer."

"I don't want to suffer," I howl.

"Then stop. Throw your fucking cross down and let them give it to some other chump. Stop. Just get in the wind."

"Saul, please stop hitting me. I think you hurt something in

172

my nose. I know you care about me. Don't ask me how I know, I just know. Please, Saul, sit down and stop hitting me."

And he stops and we both sit down on the edge of the bed, me feeling how many teeth are loose, and him, just, like playing with his fingers, with his hands in his lap.

"Saul? Tell me why I can't stop. Because I tried. You don't know me, nothing about me. One day I was just a crazy kid chipping and the next day, boom, strung out. I cold-turkied before. Once my grandma even locked me in a closet while I cold-turkied. When she let me out I was clean, and as soon as I hit the streets, strung out again. Just like that. And I was clean so I couldn't of been sick."

"How's your mouth?"

"Pretty bad."

"Wasn't it worth it?"

"Worth what, your beating my brains out 'cause you was pissed off?"

"Worth it for you to hear yourself say that you wanted me to stop hitting you, that you wanted to stop being hurt. Isn't it a nice feeling to be able to climb down off the cross?"

"I don't understand half of what you say. Saul, I'm sick. I'm gonna be sick in a little while. I know I'll hafta go out and it'll start all over again. Why, why? What makes me do it?"

"Rage."

"What?"

"Rage. Somewhere along the line, perhaps earlier than most of us, you've looked around and found nothing but despair. You've looked inside yourself and found nothing but despair and it enrages you. You are enraged at the injustice of it all. Is this all there is? Is this what the world is like? And being a child, you think it has to be better, there has to be somewhere, someplace that's better, where people love each other all the time and everybody lives happily ever after. So you're enraged. Why can't I have it, why can't I have a place like that, the big rock-candy mountain, nothing but sweetness and light? Somewhere along the line you start blaming it all on yourself. It's my fault that everything's fucked up and the other side of the coin is that you say, 'I won't live in a world where everything's fucked up.' So you run to the cooker because there you find oblivion, nothingness, fill up your days pursuing nothing-

173

ness, all because of fairy tales. Listen. Listen and trust what I say. The despair, that's all there is. You live with it, you live and make love and take all the good things in life and you accept it. You throw away the rage and you accept the world, now, on your terms, just as you accepted what we did before on your own terms, enjoyed it, took pleasure, sensed power."

The sound of the words is enough. Some of the things I understand and some I don't. I understand about fairy tales that you fill little kids' heads with bullshit and come to find out that when you're down and out, nobody gives a fuck, all they do is take advantage. Maybe he's right, about fairy tales and about running to the cooker because nothing ever seems to go right. I mean, I think that's what he meant. But it's the sound of his voice. He sounded like he knew, like he knew just how I feel, even though I don't know myself, and I listen and just want to rest for a while, but it's all just talk and I'm starting to get sick.

"Saul, I'm getting sick. What should I do? You want me to try turkey, will you stay with me? I could try, you know."

"Turkey? Won't work with you, Sinbad, too painful. It's just the other side of the cooker. Makes you feel you paid your dues. No, Sinbad, we'll do it the easy way, so easy you won't feel a thing. Detox."

"Mmmm." Even though the chills got me shaking a little bit I lean my head against his shoulder, just so he'll keep talking to me. "Who's Sinbad?"

"A great adventurer, my boy, knight of a thousand and one nights, farvoyager into distant realms, wanderer extraw-dee-nair, slayer of dragons, master of all mysteries . . ."

"So what happened to him, I mean, in the end, after all the adventures and stuff?"

"Oh, I imagine he grew a bit stout, gave it all up, and settled down. Probably had the same troubles as all of us, making ends meet, you know, paying the bills, perhaps a touch of arthritis. Ah, but while it lasted, while it lasted . . ."

"Mmmm. Keep rubbing my neck like that, right there. I'm sick, Saul."

"I forbid you to enjoy it. Commend thy body to my keeping, thy jones unto my artifice, and verily, verily I say unto you, surely this day thou shalt be detoxified."

174

"Stop it," I laugh as the cramps start. "Can't you talk English so I can understand you?" I rest my sling on his leg. "Tell me so I can understand, how do they detox you? Does it hurt?"

"He who I raise to overcome himself, he shall suffer no hurt. A hospital, not far from here. We take a cab. I sign you in. There's a special unit . . ."

"Unit?"

"Section, a separate section for boys your age. You stay for two weeks. Good food. Pool table. No phones, no mail. You stay for two weeks and they give you medicine. The medicine makes it impossible for you to feel sick. Each day they give you the medicine, but a little bit less each day, until finally, you're not sick anymore and then you're clean."

"But what happens if I get all through and get clean and all and then I come out and start all over again?"

"You keep taking the medicine once you're out on the street and, *mirabile dictu*, you are never sick again and, even more miraculous, should you, ah, succumb to temptation, natural curiosity, and get off, you can't even feel the skag, has no effect at all, like shooting water, nothing."

"It's impossible. I don't believe you. There's no medicine in the world like that."

"By all that's unholy, if Saul tells you a mouse can pull a freight train, then you, brother rat, hook 'em up."

"Suppose I get there and I don't like the place?"

"Tough titties. You're stuck. I sign you in, I sign you out."

"Two weeks?"

"Not one day less."

"Suppose I'm sick, even with the medicine. Suppose it don't work on me?"

"Suppose, suppose. Suppose pigs had wings, why then they would fly. Trust me."

"You wouldn't lie to me, I mean, about the medicine and all?"

"I would lie to you about anything and everything. That's the adventure, to plunge into the pool without knowing whether or not it is filled. Trust me, chum, and believe. Whatever happens from here on in, it won't be dull."

"When I come out, in two weeks, and I'm ok, I mean, can I stay with you then?"

"We shall dwell together in unity."

"Does that mean yes?"

"We shall be as one."

"Promise?"

"That, I promise."

"Let me see your fingers. I wanna see if your fingers are crossed."

"Smart lad. Always watch a man's hands, especially when he's got you hooked up. Now watch closely. See? Nothing in this hand, empty, right? Nothing up this sleeve, nothing in this hand either, nothing up the sleeve. Now watch the hands. Abracadabra, shoofly pie, the hand is quicker than the eye. Presto!"

He does something with his fingers and boom, just like that there's a twenty-dollar bill, right in his hand and I swear he didn't have nothing up his sleeve.

"How the fuck did you do that? Show me."

"Magic, sheer magic, my boy. Now check out your slide."

I feel inside my sling and my twenty, it's gone. If I didn't see it with my own two eyes I never would of believed it. How the fuck could he get my twenty without me feeling it? And he didn't even come near me either.

He puts the twenty back in my hand and goes, "Make a fist, hold it tight now, tight, tight. Abracadabra, vanity fair, all you have is empty air. Open sesame!" He squeezes my hand which I open it and the twenty is gone, just like that.

"Where is it? What happened to it? Gimme my money, you Indian giver!"

"Your slide . . ." And sure as shit, my twenty is right back where it was in my sling.

"Show me, Saul, show me. You gotta teach me how you did it."

· "Child's play, any two-bit dip does it all day long. Now put that gap in your sock. Only safe place for money, Sinbad, my boy, right under your feet, on terra firma. Here, I'll help you tie your shoelace. And now . . .?"

"You mean, you wanna go right now, to sign me in and all, right now, this minute?"

"Should I leave you to Sunshine's tender ministrations? No,

my boy, take my hand. Have done with sorrow, cramps, and diarrhea."

"Yo, man, I'll go, I promise. Right now if you want, but check it out, couldn't I maybe, you know, just go real quick and cop, just for the last time, you know, so I won't go there sick and all?"

"Forswear thy cooker and you shall have treasure beyond imagining. Come, follow me and fuck the connection, that street junk ain't nothing but garbage anyhow."

So what the fuck, I might as well go to the hospital. It don't sound half bad, that is, if he's telling the truth about the medicine and all. I gotta be crazy. Here I am about to let a perfect stranger lock me up for two weeks and I know I'm gonna be sick as a dog 'cause nothing ever works out for me. But then again, what do I hafta lose? At least it's a change and just in case it's all bullshit, well, I still got the twenty stashed in my sock. I mean, who knows, it just might come in handy.

From the moment Saul said, "Sit down, Sinbad, I want to talk to you," I knew that something was very wrong. There was an air of solemnity in the room which I sensed as soon as I opened the door. He was sitting by the window in his favorite chair, a Salvation Army recliner. I put down my shopping bag overflowing with the fruits of a few random purchases and some serious shoplifting and awaited disaster.

Saul used to sit by the hour ensconced in his shabby throne, observing the ebb and flow of life passing eleven floors below the window. He sat for hours a day, "watching TV," meditating on the peculiarities of perfect strangers.

"Mmmph. Infinitely more rewarding than TV, my boy, all the melodrama of soap opera in the flesh, on a public channel, as it were. No commercials. Sit, observe, learn about the world around you."

Usually upon my return he would share his insights concerning a couple who lived directly across from us. The woman was a virago, the man a battered husband, the marriage tempestuous, and Saul, an ever-appreciative audience. Or he might advise me of his amazing discovery that the scholarly-looking mole who incessantly scurried to and from the public library burdened with bundles of books, was a fence.

"A fence? Now you're making it up!" Impossible, I insisted. Was no one free from the taint of venality? Were all destined to evil merely because they had the misfortune to be viewed through the wrong end of a spyglass which foreshortened and distorted the most simple and natural phenomena? Was not Saul himself peering at virtue through the haze of his own abhorrence of banality? He was clearly affronted.

"Making it up? Asshole! Pollyanna! Pelasgian! I do not interpret, I catalogue. Haven't I taught you a fucking thing? There,"— indicating with a sweep the broad view of the street—". . . the foibles are all there, as old as Paradise, as endemic as original sin. Nothing is hidden from you, nothing, dear heart: the infinite temptations and the delicious weaknesses of mankind, bless 'em all, I say. Right before your eyes and you can't see it." He shakes his head dolefully while admonishing me with pointed finger. "It's clear, you'll never amount to anything. You simply refuse to remember the essential tenet of moral theology, to wit: always judge a book by its cover. Step right up, my boy. See the wonder of the ages, the mighty Egress, one thin dime. It's all there right there before you too." He sulks.

He has me hooked and he knows it.

"All of which makes our mousy friend a fence, right? Is that what you're saying, because if you are, then you've lost me completely. What am I supposed to see, for Chrissakes, a bookworm?"

"No indeed, not for a moment." I'm gaffed and his interest perks up immediately.

"What you should see is a shady character."

"Explain." He loves it. Who am I do deprive him of his pleasures?

"Item: no gainful means of employment."

I'm hopelessly entangled for the moment in the coils of his cynicism, so I might as well play straight man.

"You met him on the Welfare line?"

"Ah, the child sets my teeth on edge. Who ever heard of a

fence on Welfare? For starters, irregular hours, clod. Irregular hours."

"Maybe he has his own business in his house or something."

"Yet receives no mail. Strange business indeed. Mmmph."

"Disabled?"

"Mail, dunderhead. Mail, dolt. No mail, ergo, no checks, no Welfare, no S.S.I., no Disability, nada. Nada fucking thing."

"Terrible."

"My bilingual pun?"

"No, being without a fucking thing. You should be an expert on that subject right now, and while we're at it, why do I have to do all the shoplifting?"

"Because I pay all the fucking rent and further, our friend is hardly impecunious."

"Which friend? Do we have any left?"

"The fence who is the present subject. Rest assured, your insolence will be rewarded, wise-ass. Item: pressed clothing, frequent marketing, daily excursions to the liquor store, nothing at all to indicate either want or need. You follow me so far or am I doing this too fast for you?"

I nod assent, indicating that I am following, no matter how vaguely his grim dialectic to its inevitably perverse conclusion.

"Review"—toting up rubrics on his fingers like some manic pedagogue. "No work, no mail, no checks, no visible means of support, but an amplitude, an abundance of the goods of this world, hence: scam, game, con, flim-flam. We see a man who has 'graved upon his brow the mark of crime. It's written all over his face."

"Ok, so he doesn't work. Maybe he's a crook. But now explain why he has to be a fence."

"Has to be? Calvinist! The man chooses the sin, the sin does not choose the man. Ye gods, where do you come off trying to hand me this fucking imperative bullshit. Willing selection, that's the ticket. Read your Augustine, for Chrissakes, if you can tear yourself away from your short heist."

"Fuck you too, twice. If we're gonna converse like normal people then you will stop trying to bulldoze me by impressing me. I want to know how the fuck you know he's not a burglar or something."

"Elementary, dear boy," announces Holmes to Watson. "Answer this. Think of a burglar, any burglar. Good, now don't tell me his name. But this particular burglar, do people bang on his door at all hours of the day or night begging him to relieve them of their treasures, their TVs, their cameras, their watches?"

"Ridiculous."

"As was your question. We are agreed, then, neither your particular burglar, nor burglars as a class are given to receiving free-will offerings from those whom they fleece, is that correct? Sensible, lad. Now if you were as attentive to your few paltry duties as I am to my serious observations you'd know that this dude has a constant stream of company bearing all of the above-mentioned items and a ton of other shit too. If we assume that he is not running a discreet hockshop then we are left with the irrefutable conclusion that he . . ."

". . . is a fence!"

"Great googa-mooga. I thought you'd never get it. Now be a good lad and pass me whatever refreshment you have acquired in the course of your peregrinations."

"It's Gallo port and don't say a fucking word, because you're lucky I was able to get that.'

"Complain? My dear, gracious, considerate. . . mm-mph. . . enough. Bring me my port and my pot. I have immoral longings!"

"But Saul . . ."—he was already swilling the unspeakable slop—"why does he carry the books?"

"So he likes to read, big fucking deal. What's the matter, a fence can't read?", indicating my dismissal with a lordly wave. It is obvious that his interest is now centered only on the bottle.

"Saul, one more question before you get pie-eyed on that shit and we wind up in an argument."

"Mmmph. No respect, no respect for the communion between myself and my booze. One, just one, o excellent and artful dodger."

"Saul, what the fuck is an egress?"

And so it went. But for me he would have starved to death. His fortunes were at low ebb. There was a pair of "temporary setbacks," which meant that he had two cases pending in Manhattan Criminal Court, a "spell of forgetfulness," indicating that he

180

had jumped bail on a third charge, making further appearances on the "setbacks" impossible, and "unforgivable harassment," referring to a warrant for his arrest issued by the New York State Division of Parole. In short he was in hiding, incognito, on the lam. It was left upon me to risk the embarrassment, or far worse, the incarceration which seemed the certain reward for my far-too-frequent incursions on the local A & P. Our larder was provisioned with such unlikely items as escargots, boysenberry preserves, gooseberry jam, pickled mussels, hearts of palm, candied chestnuts, mock truffles, and crawfish bisque, since the gourmet department proved to be casually guarded and therefore best situated for my boosting. Our rent was occasionally paid by the Welfare Department, at least on those occasions when I outraced Saul to the hotel desk on "check day." Actually, we were surrogates for the real behind-the-scenes competitors, the landlord and the liquor store. It was touch and go, no doubt about it. So when I found Saul most serious and most sober simultaneously I immediately set about reviewing those foreseeable calamities which might have become reality. I tolled: complaints of crashing lamps and clattering crockery concomitant with our passionate disagreements—highly probable but of minor significance; arrest—impossible for the moment since neither Saul nor I was visibly incarcerated; perhaps imminent arrest—most likely, but a subject subject to stringent taboos as a topic of conversation; eviction—highly probable, file and retain; discovery by Saul of my insignificant but very personal coke stash . . . !

"Saul, about the stash, let me explain . . ."

"Sit down, Steven." Father Flanagan was appalling and besides there was no place to sit other than in his lap and so I stood, feeling for all the world like a prospective penitent who has just discovered that there is nothing he dares to confess.

"Your mother called."

I anticipated. I loomed. Nothing alarming thus far, for, unbelievably, Saul stood in very good stead with my mother. They had met often during the course of my hospitalizations, my detoxifications, my detentions by the police, and on each meeting my mother accorded Saul the greatest respect, gladly deferring all de jure authority to his de facto assumption of command and his certainty that in the end chicanery would triumph over the ways of

181

the just. Of course she knew that Saul was her son's lover, a fact of which she had never been officially advised. My mother, however, needed no counsel in the matter. The evidence of our living arrangements and Saul's indulgence of my follies was reason enough for her to refrain from examining the mouths of Greek gift horses. She was perfectly content with matters as they stood, particularly since her prescience in such matters assured her of my eventual damnation. In Saul's soul she had no interest whatever and so they chatted cheerfully on the phone, constantly reassuring each other that I was basically worthless, worse than useless, fundamentally unsound, and a trial and a tribulation to be grudgingly borne. Saul, in short, conned her out of her socks and she loved every minute of it.

". . . called. Your grandmother died last night."

So there it was. I imagine that he must have told me the necessary details. That she passed away peacefully in her sleep, alone in the nursing home where she had been consigned by my mother for the express purpose now fulfilled. That there would be a funeral at such-and-such time and such-and-such place. That hers was a gentle death.

I found myself seated on the floor, snuggled up against his legs, as I snuggled when I was very young, my head in his lap. I locked out the possibility of thought or feeling, content to savor his familiar scent and warmth.

Something clanged open in my brain and there was a rush that made me giddy. I could not possibly stay in this room. I dashed out the door and up the service-entrance stairs. The roof was beset by a whirlwind of snow fluttering out of the starless black sky, twisting and shimmering in the faint glow of neon from far below. Soot-stained snow was everywhere, drifting in mistlike sprays or clumped into heaps by the gale which billowed my shirt up over my ears. I would soon freeze and didn't give a damn. So, I thought, as an icy blast thrust me against the water tower, bruising my shoulder, so this is how it was meant to be. I could not conceive of irreversible separation from her. Could not conceive of conceiving it. I had never before experienced the death of someone close to me, for no one had ever been close to me except my grandmother. Oh, and of course Saul. I was separated from my safe haven by eternity. Now I had no place to run and hide when I wearied of running and hiding. Now there was no one left in the world but those who would judge me, those who were indifferent to me, those who were hostile to me, those who didn't know of my existence, those who knew but didn't care, those who would use my body as a sculptor uses clay. There was no one to know my faults, no one to suffer my sufferings, no one to raise me up when I was cast down, no one to succor me in temptation, no one whose love encompassed all my stupidities, petty cruelties, self-centered petulance, no one who saw into the depths of my heart and the depths of my despair and saw that I was good and received me as a lamb at her bosom. For Mamita was dead and the world too vast and too cold for living. I found myself standing on a parapet with nothing beneath me but a trickle of toy cars and tiny dolls bent in the storm. A vast veil of whiteness and darkness spun from frost and the void beckoned and moaned, returning to pluck at my sleeve, eager, impatient, sighing for me to step forth into its limitless embrace. I spread my arms, a lover bestowing his benediction on the winds and swayed toward the maelstrom.

"Jump!" he commanded from the gloom behind me. "Jump! Oblivion is it? Well, there it is, so jump and be damned! Splatter yourself down there because the whole fucking universe isn't large enough to contain your presumption. Look at it, all of it. Do you think the world exists for your personal entertainment? Do you think any of it exists without senseless suffering? I'm sick of you, sick of pampering a fool. Jackass, go jump into your oblivion. I'd like to strangle you with my own hands to choke off your bullshit. Look at your tracks. 'Because my body was abused I scorned my own body,' is that it? 'Because I was scourged and assailed I scourge and assail myself,' huh? 'Please sir, because I was abased, just let me cast myself off from the world.' Good riddance to bad rubbish. You want truth? Take one more step and you'll find it. You want reasons? Why? Who owes them to you? What makes you think there are reasons? What exempts you from absurdity? 'How dare *she* abandon *me*?' Monstrous! Unbridled arrogance. You abandon yourself to unforgivable vanity by refusing to laugh at it all. You know what life owes you? A swift wrench out of the womb into a comfortless world, and not a fucking thing else. After that you're on your own, no guarantees, me bucko. But you, you don't have the balls of a crab louse. If you did you'd accept the challenge, make up your own rules as you went along, change the rules of the whole fucking game whenever you wanted to, and laugh at all the silly fuckers who complain. You know what a man is? A man is a creature who shouts from the highest mountain, "Fuck you, God, fuck you and get off my back because I can damn well damn you if I want to." So do yourself a favor. Do me a favor, you whimpering punk, jump. Jump before I freeze my balls off."

I remember taking one step and slipping and for an awful instant I thought I was lost. But then I felt his arms around me, smothering me in a bear-like embrace, and I smiled, thinking, "Now he will kill me." And even as I smiled he dragged me from the parapet onto the slush and pebbled tar of the roof.

Later, in bed, I thanked him, feeling no qualms about my hypocrisy. After we made love I rolled over on my side with my back facing him and fell asleep with no difficulty. I was still very angry.

My grandmother would have enjoyed the funeral. A slew of former neighbors attended, a covey of cousins, a brace of her brothers, and even one of my unknown uncles flew up from San Juan. Astonishingly, my mother arrived and seated herself between Saul and me. Throughout the mass she held my hand, and Saul's, completely self-possessed and dry-eyed. But then too, so was I. Only Saul occasionally dabbed at an eye, but he was allergic to most flowers. The flowers: They were truly stupendous. Row upon row, bank upon bank of her favorite, gardenias. They always reminded her of the rain forest and her own girlhood. There were four words written on the card that accompanied the dazzling display: "To Mamita, from Steve."

When we got back to the hotel I accused Saul of having some hand in the business of the flowers. "Out of the question," he humphed. "Gardenias, very poor taste indeed . . ." When the florist's bill arrived he scribbled "addressee unknown" on the envelope and returned it to the post office. It was only a few days later that we were finally evicted from the hotel.

4

Spring

FOR THE LAST TEN MONTHS I've dreamed one dream, the same dream, every night. There's a hotel room somewhere; it could be any one of a hundred fleabags, what's the difference. He doesn't expect me. When I walk in he's sitting by the window, probably drunk, never thinking I'd find him. As soon as he sees me he knows what I'm doing there. He looks around, maybe for a way out, maybe for something to defend himself with. There's nothing, nothing but him and me. He gets up, walks over to me, smiling, starts to hug me, maybe, starts coming out of his mouth with some bullshit. That's when I smash him. I smash him so hard his nose splits in half and there's blood all over, blood all over his face and his shirt, blood dripping down to the floor. And then, I grab him by the throat and squeeze the life out of him, strangle him, throttle him until his face turns black and he shits on himself and he slides through my hands to the floor, still looking surprised.

That's when I always wake up, at the surprised part, and I wake up smiling, and look at the three metal walls and the bars in front of my six-by-eight personal hell and I know it's one day less, one day closer to the end of the dream, one day closer to him. I

185

always wake up with a hardon and I always jerk off first thing when I wake up. I don't put any shade on it, don't bother to get under the covers to do it, don't care who sees me, a guard or anyone. I don't think of anything while I'm doing it, don't make up any pictures, don't imagine doing anything to anyone or anyone doing anything to me. I beat my meat and make my mind a total blank. Then, when I'm done, I squeeze out the last drops of cum and remember the dream and me squeezing his throat and that's enough to get me through one more day.

There's a window opposite my cell. Far down below the level of the window is the gallery where at night four hundred foul-smelling maniacs gawp at the TV while huge wall speakers blare soul music.

There are a lot of fights, usually over nothing. Just jailhouse nonsense—petty gambling debts, somebody owes somebody a pack of cigarettes, somebody bumped into somebody else, somebody cut in front of the chow line. Sometimes they fight with homemade shanks over fags, or young white dudes who are gonna be fags before they get out. Sometimes somebody gets carted off on a stretcher. Sometimes they carry them to the hospital. Sometimes they dump them in the morgue. Over a pack of cigarettes, over a fag, over some slop served up in a metal tray.

The window is always open, summer and winter. You can close it with a long window pole, the kind they used to have in school. But here the nuts are too lazy to get a pole. Even if there was a pole. Even if it hadn't been broken up long ago for firewood by somebody who wanted to heat coffee in their cell or by someone who needed a club. So the window stays open all year long. Of course I don't have to tell you there are bars on the window too, like maybe somebody's going to shinny up forty feet of tile wall to jump out, right down into a yard with twenty-five-foot walls running around it. And then there's always the river, all around the Island, where the currents are so treacherous that guys who have tried it they find twenty miles away floating face down and bloated in the Narrows.

In the winter it's so cold that these little icicles form out of the snot when it runs out of your nose. You touch the walls and your fingers stick, so that when you pull them away you leave a piece of skin behind. All because they're too lazy to close one fucking window. They give you a thin piece of blanket and one sheet and a towel when they remember to. One roll of shit paper a month, because this isn't upstate, this isn't the big time, this is the Rock and the City is cheap and nobody even knows their lawyer's name, the one that told them to cop out in about ten seconds while rapping to them in the bullpen in the back of the court, so who's gonna complain, and who are they gonna complain to? What they got here are the skids and the bums and the winos and the street junkies and the amateur jostlers and the niggers beating old ladies over the heads for the dollar and change they got in their pocket-books and the Latin brothers who beat up on their old ladies when they catch them fucking somebody else and the weird-looking child molesters and the guys who make obscene phone calls, and the two-bit burglars. Real high-class criminals, that's what they got here and they tell you to be happy you get what you get because the City is busted and they're scraping the bottom of the barrel for all the crazy, mean, stupid bust-out lowlifes stuck out on the Rock.

And then I wake up and see that the snow is melting, just patches left, and there are a few clumps of brown grass and the wind smells different somehow and you don't feel it's suffocating you anymore but it's fresh even though it smells of all the oil and shit in the river and the garbage burning in the City dump on another island close by. It's fresh because you know you're through freezing your ass off and outside they got these peacocks—so help me, a flock of peacocks walking in the yard, a father, mother, little babies, walking and pecking in the yard where the wind blows up the dust and a bored hack sits in a gun tower watching an empty yard and a family of peacocks.

And then there are no more days. Forget about all the movies you seen. No big fat smiling donkey sticks out his hand and wishes you luck. Nobody gives you a suit. Nobody gives you nothing except a single token to take the bus or the subway, whatever you want, and that's that. And I look around the cell for the last time, at least for this time it's the last time. What is there? A couple of packs of cigarettes, stale. I put one in my pocket and just lay the others on the gallery. As soon as I turn my back somebody'll snatch them, because they're all hard up. Stale cigarettes, that's a score. You see guys rolling up that State tobacco they give you in paper bags, with twigs and dirt and pebbles and all in it, rolling it up and begging for it when they ain't got none to roll. Me, I don't ask nobody for nothing and I don't give nothing to nobody who asks. You stay out of trouble that way in the can. No arguments. Nobody owes you, you don't owe nobody. That's it, that's what I got to show for ten months—a pack of cigarettes I'm gonna throw away as soon as I hit the first candy store. They don't make it easy for you.

Nobody's in a rush to let you out. You got to wait for a hack to pick you up at the cell-block gate and walk you down to the bullpen in the receiving room where they lock you in for a couple or three hours, like you're gonna escape or something, I mean, on the day you're going home. So you sit there with a couple of other guys who are going home too, smoking and reading the graffiti on the walls, real intelligent shit like, "Chino-147th St." or "Maruca es Maricón" and pissing in the bowl which don't flush and has been stopped up with shit for a week. And maybe they forget to feed you breakfast which was two slices of stale bread and a cuppa coffee, because after all, you're going home. All the guys are going home except nobody, not one of them, has a home to go to. Most of them run right to Welfare and hook up a room which leaves them about fifteen dollars for the week. Mostly by the next morning they're flat busted and do something stupid, throw a brick at the jailhouse they call it, something desperate and stupid for a couple of lousy bucks and before they know it they're right back on the Rock.

Me, I could go to my mother's for a couple of days, I guess, if I could stand it. Give her something to do like ask me why I'm sitting around the house all day and why I don't go out and get a job. Maybe she means "pull a job" because Saul taught me well, very well: Work is for chumps. Only suckers work. Nobody ever got rich on a salary. "Work is the province of cattle." He taught me well. But I'm not going to my mother's which hasn't been home for seven years and wasn't really home then. And my grandma, I wouldn't have wanted her to see me like this, angry, washed up at nineteen. I wouldn't have wanted her to see what it's all come to. Bitter, and what else? It's funny, when I was small and had a habit a mile wide, I'd run to her all the time to clean me up, put a good meal under my belt, a couple of bucks in my pocket, a hug, a smile, a pat on my ass and don't do it again. I guess she figured she owed me, well not owed me but had to because there was nobody else who gave a fuck and, after all, I was just a little kid who was

188

strung out. I probably figured I had it coming to me and just took it for granted. Little kids are like that. They think the world owes them something. But I'm old enough now to know that she didn't owe me one damn thing. Nobody owes me, nobody except him, and that's a debt I'm going to collect, today.

After ten months in the can I'm clean as a whistle. Oh, I haven't shot dope in years. I mean clean of all that meth garbage. All the mornings waiting outside programs sick, waiting for the time to pass so they'll open up, waiting for a connection on Sunday to cop off of because I sold my bottle on Saturday, waiting in bullpens for hour after hour, busted and sick, sick deep down in my bones, shaking and puking and screaming to have some cop beat me upside my head to shut up my hollering. My body is clean and my mind is clean too. Clean and sharp. Every day for the past ten months I've worked out: pushups in my cell hour after hour, lifting weights in the yard in the dead of winter, stripped naked to the waist and sweating. Boxing in the gym, finding I had a sharp left jab and that I was a sucker for a right counter. I've built up my body so that I'm proud of it. I got definition, a chest, a nice back. I don't look like a pretty kid anymore. I look like a man. I feel like a man, I guess. I'm strong, not a monster, but strong enough. I've put a lot of work into my body.

And one way or another I'm going to settle it all, get it all straightened out between him and me—today, no matter what. Somebody is definitely going to get hurt. Does it really matter who? In the dream it's always him, it's him choking on his own blood, looking not scared, but surprised. And yet dreams are funny. My mother used to say you dream something and the opposite comes true. You dream about dying, it means you're going to live a long time. You dream about strangling so-meone . . . Who knows? He's smart, that's one thing I've got to give him, smart and sharp. He'll know I'm coming. He'll have checked up and found out what day I'm coming out. He won't be surprised. In the dream he's surprised, but dreams mean the opposite, remember. He'll know I'm coming and that I've got to come to him. So he can pick his time, his place, have his shit together and he'll be there with some shit, some trick, some kind of scheme.

Maybe I'm doing exactly what he wants. Hasn't it always been that way with us? Somehow, someway he always gets the last sick joke in, the last laugh. Maybe the joke's still on me. So what else is new. I wouldn't be surprised and I don't care. I just want it over and done with so I can feel again, if it's not too late, if I haven't already forgotten how to. I have as much feeling as a razor does when it slices through flesh. It keeps going through my head, was it an accident meeting him and everything that came after, so that everything was always with him, or for him, or because of him, or without him knowing it, or in spite of him and now . . . against him? Did he know it all from the start? Does he know now? Is he laughing, knowing that I have to look for him, knowing that he could hide in the City forever, knowing already that he's going to let me find him? Will he leave me clues which I have to be smart enough to read, leave me false tracks, lead me up blind alleys and at the end wait there for me, knowing how it will all turn out? Is he in my head? Is he outside making me live out the dream? Does he know which ending the dream is going to have, or is he still deciding which one would be the funniest?

They're in no hurry to let us out. Guards pass by, look inside the bullpen, check out papers, walk away. Sometimes it takes a half a day just for them to find your clothes. Sometimes they just forget about you altogether. But I know I won't be that lucky. They'll remember and they'll unlock the bullpen when they get ready and that will be that, unless maybe he already has other plans. I don't think so. I think it will be today. There's nothing to do but stretch out on a bench, a metal bench just like they got in every bullpen I've ever been in, and wait. And think. About what? Not him. That's what he would want now, for me to plan everything so carefully that it couldn't possible work out. Right now he's trying to eat up my mind. I can hear him: "Take away the captain, Sinbad, and you take away the cunning." I shut him out of my head and, for no reason at all, start thinking about Little Sheik.

I guess it's—what?—three years since I saw him and I nearly don't recognize him when he rolls into the block. He's still short, but now he has shoulders like a mule and a scraggly moustache and beard. He can't be more than seventeen, but you'd never know it by looking at him which is why he's in with the men instead of the adolescents where he's supposed to be. I can't think of anything worse than the adolescent quad. Wherever they go, they go handcuffed, everywhere, including when they march to the mess hall. That's another thing, they march and no talking. You talk, you catch a beating right there in the hall. It's only the adolescents they fuck with like that and in a way you can't blame them because those kids are wild. I know, I've been there myself. Those kids throw down in a minute, anywhere, anytime. If they're not beating up on each other then they're beating up on the hacks, on the brass, on the warden too if they could get their hands on him. You see one of these kids who looks like an angel, a real baby face, and ten times outta nine he got a homicide beef. If it's not homicide it's a real bad assault, rape, attempted murder, all heavy stuff. They make most of the guys look like punks. They don't even know what it means to be afraid. When they get tired of fighting they try to fuck each other. When they get tired of cornholing they slice each other up. You see dried blood all over their quad, on the walls, on the floors. Nobody bothers to mop it up. The hacks, they treat the kids like dogs. They kick the shit out of them, fuck with their food, tear up their mail right in front of them, shake them down every day for shanks or dope or files, or for nothing, just to fuck over them. It's a twenty-four-hour-a-day war, so naturally, a guy who has any sense at all, who just wants to do his own bit will lie about his age and get put in with the adults.

It's not that Little Sheik doesn't have heart. He's got mucho corazón. Never ran away from anything in the old days down on the Square. But he always did keep to himself. Never looked for trouble. I always liked him though we never did rap too tough. He was just another kid running around, hustling, trying to get over, hanging out all afternoon in Playland, but there was something about him. I don't know, the way he used to shrug his shoulders as if he was saying, "Who me? I don't give a fuck. Just don't bother me, just don't get too close to me and everything's cool." I see him and he sees me and for a second we look each other up and down because we both have changed and it's not Playland anymore and there's been a lot of water under the bridge and then we both smile and hug each other, hard and quick, like men are supposed to do. Then I steer him by the elbow over to a corner table away from the racket of the TV and tell the nigger sitting there to get lost. It's a Latino table and niggers aren't supposed to be sitting there in the first place. Let one sit down and pretty soon he's got all his boys looking to push you out.

"So whatchoo got, bro'?" I ask him, because naturally in the joint the first thing and only thing most guys are interested in is their case. That's all they want to talk about: how they got busted—always bad luck, never stupidity; what the charge is; how much time they're facing; how fucked up the Legal Aid lawyer is—they're all working for the D.A.; how the cop lied at the hearing. All bullshit nobody else gives a fuck about. Little Sheik though, he just shrugs, like it's all the last thing on his mind, what he's locked up for.

"Assault."

"Yeah? And what? How does it look? Bad beef?"

"Nada me importa, bro', it just happen. Cono, bro', I'm sure glad I run into you. At least I got someone to rap to insteada these morenos." With one quick look, he like dismisses everybody else in the block, Black, Puerto Rican, they're all niggers to him, which means they're dumb, dangerous animals not worth considering. I couldn't agree with him more.

"Well, cono, little bro', you're looking good. What's happening? Whatchoo been into?" You never ask a guy what his hustle is in the joint. Either they want to tell you or they don't. But he knows what I mean, just like making converation and that I'm not trying to get into his business.

"Same old same old, you know."

"Still hanging out downtown?"

"Nah, you know, algunas veces . . . whenever . . ."

"Tricking?"

"Nah," he blushes, and I think maybe I've gone too far. "Nah, I don' do that no more, you know, sucio, bad for you fuck aroun' like that all the time, fuck up your body, fuck up your mind. You gotta keep your mind clean, no bullshit, that way there ain't nothing you can't do."

"What's that supposed to mean, something like mind over matter?"

"Lemme explain. It's no bullshit. You gotta get inside yourself and clear your mind of everything, so nothing's there, no bullshit, nothing. You gotta concentrate on getting everything out of your head and then your mind becomes strong, just like your body does when you work out."

"And what happens then, you get muscles on your brain?"

"Cono, man, don' make fun. It's not funny. It's the truth."

"Where'd you hear this bullshit? Who's been eating up your mind, little bro'?"

"For real, man." He bangs both hands on the table and half stands up like for a minute he wants to throw down and I can see his face is all red.

"Be suave, little bro', cool it, everyone's looking at you."

"Yeah," he admits and sits back down. "It's just that I don' like no one making fun of me."

"I'm not making fun of you. I just don't dig what you're saying."

"It's Shingon man, this dude in the martial arts school, he was teaching it to me."

"So whaddya hafta do?"

"You sit in the lotus position . . ."

"What?"

". . . with your legs crossed—I show you later. Then you fold your hands in your lap like this, see, no, with your fingers like that . . . that's right. Then you chant."

"You what?"

"You chant, 'nam myo-ho renge kyo,' you keep chanting. Like this, nammyohorengekyonammyohorengekyonammyohor-engekyo . . ." Rushing through it so it wouldn't make any sense even if it made any sense in the first place. To me he sounds exactly like a priest in a hurry, mumbling through mass in Latin.

"But what the fuck does it *mean*?"

"It doesn't mean nothing, bro', that's the whole point. You concentrate and keep on chanting. You do it, you see, you don't think about nothing, you don't worry about nothing. You feel like real peaceful and after a while your mind is completely clear and you feel a rush and you're high on your own mind and then you can do anything you want to, except you don't want to do anything because you know there's nothing you can't do."

"Yo, bro', I'm sorry, man, I ain't making fun of you, but it's way over my head. You can do anything you want to do only there's nothing you want to do and all by mumbling something you don't know what it means, is that what you're saying?"

"I'm saying that you can make it so nobody else can control your mind but you. Nobody else can make you happy or sad, nobody else can make you love or hate because you can make it come from inside of you, instead of outside."

"And then, then what's supposed to happen?"

"Happen? Bro', ain't you listening? Escucha me, hombre, you talk about body building and shit to make yourself strong. Can't you imagine building your mind so that it's so strong, nothin' anybody says or does to you can change it one bit? Nobody can make you feel nothin' except if you decide that's what you want to feel. That's what I mean about nothin' you can't do. You can do anything, because that anything is comin' right from you. Look, supposing you got this date with a fox, right? And you wait and wait on the corner and she don't show. How do you feel?"

"Mad. I feel mad, of course."

"Well, that's what this chanting is all about. Because when you get into it, when you make your mind strong, then you wouldn't be mad. Because you know, it's not *you* making you mad, you don't want to be mad, what for, a broad, maybe you're never gonna see her again anyhow. You're lettin' your mind loose and lettin' the chick make you feel mad, even though she ain't even there. But when you make your mind like tight, and empty, then you don' even think about it. She come, she don' come. Who cares, what's that got to do with *you*? Come on, let me show you. Can't you imagine what it would be like, being boss of your own mind?"

No, I can't. Can't even figure out what he's trying to say. But Little Sheik, I always did like him, so I say what the hell, if he wants me to chant with him, why not. As long as it makes him happy. But when I tell him this, after we've been chanting together and sitting in the lotus position which is the most uncomfortable way a person could ever sit, and doing it a couple of hours a day, he blows up.

"Pendejo! You don' do it to make *me* happy, then it's all wrong. You don' do nothin' for somebody else, then it's not real, it's weak. You do it for yourself."

So we chant. We chant in the yard with snow falling all over us and I know everybody's saying we're cuckoo, at least behind our

194

backs—the word must have got around fast about Sheik being a brown belt.

Then I start doing it alone in my cell, when I'm bored, or feeling down. But I can't get into it. I lose interest. I start stumbling over the words. I feel like a goop sitting there saying the same words over and over, words that have no meaning. One time, my mind, suddenly, like empties and I get like a flash, like my whole body is warm and it scares me for a minute and when I get the rhythm of the chanting back, it's gone. I feel ridiculous and it's impossible to make it so you won't get mad if somebody fucks with you and I think of the dream. What would I have, why would I be surviving right now, if it wasn't for the dream, if it wasn't that I have to get even.

It wasn't until a couple of weeks went by that I find out what Sheik did. He never did tell me himself, but you know, in the joint, you hear things. He and his partner were sticking up a liquor store. Just bullshit nickles and dimes. Liquor stores never have nothing, nothing worth risking your life for. Well, a cop just happened to walk in. He got the drop on them and told them to put their pieces down. Sheik's partner, he did, and raised his hands. The cop, he musta got nervous because he put a cap right in the kid's leg and Sheik turned around and blasted the cop's belly open. He was still holding the shotgun. The cop lived, nobody knows how. Of course they fucked Sheik up real good. Shot him a few times and left him to bleed to death, except an ambulance finally came and he lived.

"And you wasn't mad, when you nearly killed the cop?"
He looks at me, like, who told me? "Nah, bro'. I wasn't mad. Shit, he was just doin' his job and I was doin' mine. I told you, nobody can make you mad, only yourself, only if you want to be mad yourself."

So we kept on chanting. But my heart wasn't in it, even though it did make the time pass and I found I didn't mind doing it for an hour or so a day.

One night we were just sitting at the table, not saying much. Me, I remember, I felt like a cigarette but didn't want to smoke because the smoke bothered Sheik and I remember I was thinking about how I could never be the way he wanted to, with his mind so strong nobody else could reach him, because he's my friend, and even though I'm practically having a nicotine fit, I got to give him the respect and not light up because his feelings *do* matter. And Sheik, he was sort of dreaming, looking at snowflakes. I hear them calling a name over the loudspeaker, a Spanish name. They got this loudspeaker in the front where they call you for mail or visits or whatnot. The next thing I know, here's the padre, the house priest standing there, beet red, and he's hollering at Sheik.

"You, you there. No wonder you're in jail. Didn't you hear me calling you for the last half hour over the loudspeaker. I don't know why I waste my time with you dumb spics. No manners. No respect. And by the way, the hospital called, your mother died. Come to mass on Sunday."

Well, the priest's jaw was busted and he was lucky at that. If the hacks hadn't pulled Sheik off, he would have been a dead priest. After that they took turns giving him a beating and threw him into the hole, segregation. That was the last time I saw him, that night, when someone finally got him mad. I guess maybe he had the right idea all along, to make your mind so strong that you can shut out all the bullshit they throw at you. But, I wonder, if you throw out the crap, don't you throw out all your other feelings, don't you throw out all the good times when it was just me and him, when *he* did take care of me and *he* was good to me and there was no one else who mattered in the world? That night was the last time I saw Sheik and the last time I cried. I cried for myself and what I was and could never go back to and for him, what I thought he was and what he did to me and for what I had to do to him. Him? Of course not Sheik. Why should I cry for Sheik? He's a good little dude, strong as an ox, and I never did get to ask him whether he was really a brown belt. I heard they slapped him with twenty-five big ones and shipped him upstate. Why should I cry for Sheik, who was so wrong? I cried for myself and for what I had done to myself when I let him into my heart and for what I had to do to myself to rip him out. In the morning I forgot all about chanting and went back to beating my mat. The days passed more slowly, but at least I knew exactly where I was going.

It must be about nine when they open the bullpen and call us out one by one. You can't help being scared. Even though you want to be cool and get up real casual and maybe even yawn right in their faces to make sure they know you're cool, still inside your heart is pumping real fast. In a few minutes, a half hour, whatever, you're on your own. For ten months the whole rhythm of your life has been dictated—when to get up, what to eat, don't do this but you gotta do that, the bell rang so shut up and go to sleep. And now it's almost over. Pretty soon it's all up to you again to create your own rhythm. Sink or swim. Nobody gives a damn. You gotta decide for yourself what to do, how long to do it, when to stop, and when it's time to do something else. And for me all the decisions have to be packed tight into one day. This day. Finish it, my heart thumps. Finish it so you can be free. Break the pride of his power so you can redeem your soul from him. Redeem? Soul? Win your freedom to roam with the dead and be done with it all. Get rid of him so you can limp away and salvage whatever's left. I tear open the brown property envelope. The watch is there. The one he had waiting for me that first time, after the first detox, when he was there as he promised he would be, when we went home and I was like a little kid walking in to find this beautiful Christmas tree with lights and tinsel and artificial snow. When I knew I was ok for seven days because I had seven bottles of meth with me and his promises had come true and I hadn't been sick at all. And after he showed me the new clothes, not many, but enough of everything and more than I had ever had, and after I tasted champagne for the first time in my life and found out I liked it, he pulled out this package, all wrapped up in fancy paper and a red bow. There inside was a box and inside that this gold watch, the most beautiful watch I had ever seen and on the back there was writing in small script, "To Sinbad: Until Our Hearts Should Condemn Us, S."

"Yo, Saul, it's beautiful, man, it's beautiful." I kept turning it over and over in my hand.

"Mmmm. Gold is more precious than faith, my boy. Can't eat faith now can we? Don't get rid of it unless you really have to."

And I didn't. I gave it to my mother to put away, because it was too beautiful to wear. Even when times were bad, real bad, when we both were out in the streets, I never asked my mother for it back, not even when Saul ranted and raged at my "silly sentimentality." Only this last time when things were going sour between us, then I could finally wear it because I knew I wouldn't be tempted.

197

There it is, good as new—well, maybe the crystal is a little bit scratched but it's almost like it came out of the box that night. I put it on. The band is too tight. I hold it up to my ear to hear the ticking and I smile, knowing that he has never felt sorry for anyone.

They put you in a regulation green prison van, with the wire mesh screen over the window in back. It's a short ride over the bridge, across the river. The door opens and you get out and the van is chugging back to the Rock trailing smoke and I am standing alone on an empty and silent street, the wind blowing free on my face, smelling the salt-sweet scent of spring and lilacs. In my pocket is a subway token. As I finger it I wonder, should I forget my dream?

For a long time I was convinced that I led a charmed life. Whether we were together or apart, intimate or barely speaking, whether he was drunk or I was fucked up on pills, one thing in life was certain: Every time I got busted he would be there and somehow, someway he would con, scheme, wheedle, and finagle and finally he'd get me out of it. There were times I'd get pinched and call him and he wasn't home. There were times when he didn't have a phone. It didn't matter. I knew, just as sure as the sun would rise tomorrow and I'd be in court, he'd be there too. Never mind it was my fault, stupidity, desperation, sometimes even my wanting to get busted, it didn't matter. Every time they'd shoot me down he'd scoop me right back up and out again, maybe not in a day, maybe not even in a week, but I knew that they could never hold me for long. It was unreal the way he did it every time.

I forget what the argument was about. Maybe we were getting on each other's nerves. I know we weren't living together then. Maybe I was taking up too much of his time, maybe I was mad that I took up too much of my time telling myself I was glad to be on my own doing my own thing and pissed off as hell that it didn't seem to make any difference to him at all. Who knows? All I remember for sure is that I won the screaming match and lost two teeth. Then he threw me down two flights of stairs. I was out in the street, with a couple of lumps on my head and I knew my eye would be all different shades of purple in the morning. I had to do something to get even. This time I was gonna have the last word. It was nothing, just kid shit, but I was mad and when I'm mad I do stupid things. I went around the corner and bought a can of spray paint and snuck up stairs and sprayed a huge sign on his door, "Fuck You Too, Signed The Phantom." By the time I was through I was laughing myself and after all he always said he enjoyed a good practical joke.

By the next morning I figured as soon as I finished up at the Program I'd shoot over to his crib and apologize and wash the shit off the door. We'd have a good laugh and forget it and that would be that. I couldn't believe it then when I'm standing on line waiting for my jungle juice and two bulls come out of nowhere and grab me.

"You're under arrest!"

"What for? What for I'm under arrest for?"

I was so shocked I couldn't even talk straight.

"For malicious mischief, that's what for."

I couldn't believe it. They wouldn't even wait until I got my medication. They handcuffed me, threw me in the squad car, and brought me up to the Twenty-fourth Precinct and booked me. The cocksucker had actually filed a complaint and what was worse, he lied too, said he *saw* me spraying that shit on the wall. Here I am sitting in the bullpen, sick as a dog over what? Over a joke. And here he comes, big as life and twice as ugly, with one of the cops. Positive identification, no less. Well, the cop knows it's bullshit, but they have no choice. A citizen makes a complaint, they had to lock me up. So when he tells them he wants to speak to me alone, I guess they figure, sure, why not, he's going to drop the charges and they let him stay there and rap and just walk away to take care of the other big-time criminals.

"Cocksucker, get me outa here, I'm sick!"

"Your reference to my religious beliefs will get you nowhere."

"Fucker, what religion?"

"Your epithet was incomplete. I am a *devout* cocksucker."

"Jokes he makes! Jokes he makes. You dirty motherfucker can't take a joke. Get me outta here now, I'm *sick*!"

"Here, I brought you a carton of cigarettes. That should hold you until court in the morning."

199

"In the morning? *Get me outta here now!*"

"Impossible, my boy. You'd get out and I'd get in. There's a law against filing false complaints. See you in court, bright and early. Oh, and yes, I almost forgot, this . . ."

Damned if the cocksucker didn't score for a bottle of meth someplace and brought it right into the precinct too.

"I take it all back. Everything I said. You're the sweetest, most considerate, most lecherous . . . I love you."

"Flattery will get you everywhere. But not today, old chum. You'll get this in the morning too. I leave you to your forthcoming intestinal problems. Later, alligator."

"Bastard, bitch, motherfucker, sadist, child molester . . . you always said you could take a joke . . ."

"Oh, I can, I can. Comfort yourself with scripture—'Blessed are they that laugh for they shall weep in the end', or something like that. Sleep tight."

And he left me there, just like that, all night long, and in the morning I'm sick as a dog but by the time I get to court in the morning he's already told the D.A. that he wants to drop the charges. Well, nobody's too happy about going through all this shit, just for his benefit, but they really don't have too much of a choice about it. And the judge, he starts getting on the cop's case. Here I am, black and blue, beat up, my nose leaking, looking like I've been run over by a Mack truck and the judge starts hollering about police brutality. The cop doesn't know what to say.

I mean when they locked me up the beef was so petty they didn't even bother with mug shots and now Saul swears that I certainly was *not* in this shape when he saw me at the station house. The cop looks like he wants to explode but there's nothing he can do but stand there and take it on the chin.

". . . and if this boy is ever brought before me again by anyone in that precinct, be sure, be sure that you have him right, because if you're not sure and you harass him, I'll have all your badges . . ." Etc., etc., etc. We laughed going down the courthouse steps and I drank my meth and we went back to his crib and took care of B.I. For a long time he insisted that he had done me a favor on purpose since, for a couple of months after, I had a license to deal pills in the Twenty-fourth. They were scared to pinch me. I almost believed him too, but when I think back it was the first time I realized that he could be as treacherous with me as he was with everyone else.

The next time I remember clearly wasn't funny at all. I sold a bottle of meth to an undercover narc. Nothing else to it. Simple. Only it's not so simple because at that time a sale of one bottle was a "D" felony which carries seven years. No chance I'd get seven years. But six months? Well, it was a direct sale, direct to a cop. Open-and-shut case. When the Legal Aid came back to the bullpen he said he'd "see" if he could get me six months, maybe, if I copped out right now in night court and didn't give the D.A. a hard time. Otherwise . . . He shrugged.

Me, I saw a bullet, maybe eighteen months in that shrug. I was ready, more than ready, practically down on my knees to take the six months right now, tonite. It was one of those times when he didn't have a phone, but when they brought me out, after midnight, from the bullpen, there he was, rapping away to the Legal Aid. I almost didn't recognize him at first in the suit and tie.

In night court they do one thing for sure and another thing, maybe. The thing they do for sure is to arraign you, which really means they set bail. The other thing they maybe do is let you cop out on the spot and get sentenced then and there, if the D.A. and the judge go along with it.

I'm standing there handcuffed by the door leading from the bullpen to the courtroom and here he comes with the Legal Aid. The Legal Aid looks like he lost his best friend. *He* is beaming.

"Steven, I've just been talking with your employer, Mr. Schwartz . . ."

I look for an employer and I look for a Mr. Schwartz, since I didn't know I had the first one and never met the second one. *He* looks like he's coming in his pants.

"Steven, we have a problem . . ."

"You mean *I* gotta problem." Mr. Schwartz says nothing. His smile says it all.

"Don't get smart. Your employer was nice enough to come down. Now look, we got Fishbein tonight. He's the meanest sonuvabitch sitting. I want to adjourn it for two weeks. Let it cool down. We'll work out a deal with another judge . . ."

201

"Out of the question." The first words "Schwartz" has spoken so far.

"You don't believe me, watch. We're on after this case. Just watch."

They bring out some dope fiend broad charged with prostitution. The Legal Aid asks for parole, the D.A. wants ten thousand bail. Five hundred is what most judges would set.

"Twenty thousand," bellows Fishbein.

"Twenty thousand!" the Legal Aide hollers, "Your Honor, my client is on Welfare."

"Welfare? That doesn't speak well for her at all. Bail is set at thirty thousand. Next case."

They call me next. Before anybody can open their mouth, he steps up. "Your Honor, Simon Schwartz, psychologist, United Community Programs, Inc. If I may, sir, address the court on behalf of the defendant . . ."

"Proceed."

And he proceeds. I mean, does he ever proceed. He tells Fishbein how I just started on this job with this program as a counselor for little kids; how he, Schwartz himself, is counseling me. How important it is for there to be "continuity" in my "treatment" and in my "work" with the young "unfortunate" kids. On and on. How he, Schwartz, personally guarantees my appearance in court at any time. How he has "faith" in my "potentiality for rehabilitation," how I need "guidance," not punishment. Fishbein leans forward on one elbow. He's actually swallowing up this bullshit. He nods; he bangs the gavel.

"Defendant paroled to the custody of Mr. Schwartz. Mark ready for hearing in two weeks. Notify defendant. Next case."

And that's it. That's all there is to it. Outside at one in the morning, there's nobody at all in the street around the courthouse. Silent as a tomb. No night ever smelled sweeter. I still can't believe it happened.

"You're a genius."

"Sinbad, my boy, you're a master of understatement."

"I mean it, the suit, the tie, the card."

He has a drawer full of business cards, all phony, all different names, different companies. He gets over with the business cards, though he's never explained in detail how that scam works.

"Why Schwartz?"

"Fishbein. Fishbein—Schwartz. Checked the court calendar before I came down. Only thing tighter than two Masons is two Hebes. And a Hebe who's a Mason too—child's play."

"Fishbein's a Mason?"

"Everybody who's anything is a Mason. The Pope himself undoubtedly is a Mason. Has to be one to get the job. Ah yes, my hand signal . . . and then didn't you see lard-ass leaning on his elbow? Counter signal—simplicity itself."

"What happens next?"

"The case will be put down for a hearing to determine whether there is enough evidence to hold you for a grand jury."

"And then?"

"If the matter is submitted to a grand jury you will be indicted for a 'D' felony."

"Seven years. You're gonna let them put me away for seven years? When I coulda took the six months?"

"Pish and tush. I said *if* it goes to a grand jury. It will not go to a grand jury because at the scheduled hearing date the district attorney will move to dismiss the case."

"Bullshit. Now you're bullshitting me. Even the Legal Aid said they got an open-and-shut case. Direct sale to an undercover. Why should they throw it out?"

"Why indeed, my boy? Perhaps interests of justice." He has a strange twinkle in his eye.

In the cab heading uptown, he turns around to me and says, "We shall now test the limits of your faith," as he pulls a pair of cheap handcuffs from his pocket, the kind they sell in novelty stores around the Square, and hooks me up. "Believe in me, my boy, and all things are possible."

When we pull up in front of the Midtown North Precinct I'm sure that this is just another one of his weird jokes, that he got me out just so he could put me right back in. But somehow I know that this is my night, nothing can go wrong. Tonight he can move mountains, jump tall buildings in a single bound. Tonight I do believe that with him all things are possible.

There's a beefy sergeant yawning at the booking desk. He pushes me so that I stumble and nearly fall right on my face. The handcuffs are for real. So is the station house. So is the sergeant.

For a second I'm scared and then it passes. I don't know how, but I know he's gonna get over. Before the sergeant can open his mouth he's all over him.

"This beauty was just paroled in my custody."

"Mmmm?"

"I need his property." He gives me a quick frisk and pulls two property receipts out of my pants pocket. The one for the six dollars and change they took off me when they booked me, and the other for the meth, which is stamped in big letters, "Evidence."

The sergeant looks at the receipts, looks at me, looks at the cuffs, and sorta slides his ass off of the chair. "Couplaminutes."

And that's what it is, no more than five minutes. He comes back with two brown property envelopes and pushes them across the desk.

"Sign."

"How can I sign, I'm cuffed?"

"Shaddap. You . . ." He motions to Saul, who scribbles his name on some papers and pushes them back across to the cop. The cop doesn't even look at them again before he goes back to his *Playboy*.

As soon as we're around the corner and out of sight of the precinct, he wipes the sweat off his forehead with a big handkerchief.

"Get these fucking cuffs offa me, will you."

"Mmmm. I am sorely tempted to keep you in restraints for a while. Only way to civilize you is to keep you under lock and key and besides, it might be interesting in bed . . ."

"Don't fuck around like that. I got a thing about that kinda shit."

"The sheer stupidity of it. A miserable bottle of jungle juice and to an undercover no less. Hold out your hands so I can loose you to the world, a lamb amongst the wolves . . ."

"Saul, I hate to say this, but I'm sick . . ." I rub the circulation back into my wrists.

"You won't be for long." He pulls the bottle out of one of the property bags. "You are about to have a rare privilege conferred upon you, simpleton. Here, drink up the evidence, every drop, and when you're through be a good boy and throw it down the sewer."

I do. And I start hugging him and doing a little dance around him, right out in the middle of Eighth Avenue.

"I love you, you're the greatest. I'll make it up to you. I promise I won't spray 'fuck you' on your door anymore."

"The settling of accounts will be deferred no longer than it takes for us to wing our way uptown and get into the sack and then, my boy, I most certainly will extract my pound of flesh."

"Nympho!"

"Biologically impossible. Rather say, 'Satyr,' dear heart."

"My money, the other envelope, my six bucks. Lemme have it. That's all the dough I have in the world."

"Pity. What about my fee, motherfucker? What about the cab fare? Naked you came into the world and destitute you shall return to it. Forget about it. It's just enough for a bottle of booze. And tomorrow, do me a favor. If you feel the urge to sell something, lay off of controlled substances and sell your ass. At least they can't put *that* evidence in a paper bag."

Two weeks later at the hearing, the D.A. starts pawing through his briefcase, whispers to his assistant, shuffles through some papers, and asks the judge to throw the case out. "The people are unable at this time to prove a prima facie case."

"Yo, Saul, what the fuck does that mean?"

"It means, dear heart, that the silly cocksucker has egg all over his face. As always the wheels of justice are exceedingly fucked up. Now let's get out of here, I have a damnable thirst."

Other times. Other pinches. Carmen and I were staggering around the Square at three in the morning fucked up on tuinals. I was so bombed out I kept forgetting that somewhere along the night I had thrown away my shirt. Then I bumped into an old trick who made some remark, I don't remember what it was, nothing really, but I was wasted and he was drunk and I didn't want my covers pulled off in front of Carmen who didn't know a fucking thing about that part of my life. I busted the dude right in his puss; clocked him right there in the middle of Forty-second Street at three ayem. There were cops all over me and in two seconds flat they had me cuffed behind my back, dumped in a squad car, and heading for the precinct with me hollering for my shirt. I twisted my neck and saw the dude standing on the corner dabbing at his mouth with a bloody handkerchief. I don't remember how he got me off that one. Maybe he came to court and swore up and down that he was a passer-by who saw the other guy swing first. In the end I walked. I always walked.

There was the time I called him from the Rock where they had me in the bullpen for thirteen hours waiting for some croaker to show and check me out just so I could get some meth. Me, huddled in a corner, my arms wrapped around myself, trying to stop the shaking, and him finding a private doctor in the middle of the night and paying him a hundred bucks just to drive out to the Rock to give me a couple of Dolophines and in the morning he was there convincing the judge to cut me loose to a detox program that didn't exist.

The time when I was living with Carmen in Newark and told him not to call, never to call there, and I got pinched for a couple of tuinals and it was Jersey where he didn't know anybody and I thought this time he had run out of tricks. But somehow he scraped up the bail from a Ginney shylock, which I know he hated owing Ginneys because, "Ginneys, my boy, you pay fast and in full."

The train races and clatters under the River toward the City. Darkness rushes by. The train sways. When I was small I used to love to stand in the front of the first car, peering out into the blackness ahead while a tiny speck of light grew and grew and filled the whole window and became a station illuminated in crackling blue fluorescence for a few seconds as the train rushed on to the blackness ahead.

I drowse. Somewhere ahead in the blackness I will find him. It's not me, it's the train that's rushing. I can wait, knowing that the waiting is over. I am no longer responsible for what happens. I'm being carried, sped a hundred feet below the mud of the riverbed by what? By a masturbation fantasy. By a childish whim to revoke an illusion. By an adolescent need to cancel out childhood with one swift stroke, with one grotesque embrace. In betraying me he revealed himself to me and in revealing himself to me it was I who stood naked and ashamed, betrayed by my own trust, which he had always promised he would one day betray. If I owe him anything it is to act out my own irrational impulse, my own confused compulsion. When the gate clanged shut behind me this

206

morning I left my hatred to molder in the dust. I no longer know the reason. If there ever was one, a reason. There is none now. To find myself I have to rip out my own heart. And this is the only way. I must be completely merciless to myself, and I know he'd be the first to agree.

"Thirty bucks." The pawnbroker takes the loop out of his eye and shakes his head. "Thirty bucks and I'm doing you a favor for old times' sake, Sinbad."

I know he's telling me the truth. I've done too much business with him in the past for him to start fucking me over now.

"All these years I thought it was something. I really did. I saw the box myself from a real fancy jeweler."

"Come on, a slum. Oldest scam in the book. Fancy box, piece of shit inside."

"Not gold either?"

"Shit no. It ain't a beat. Cost about a 'C' note new, but then the company went outta business. Coulda picked it up for maybe half. Can't get parts no more either. Believe me, we know each other a long time. When I tell you I'm doing you a favor . . . Anybody else, I wouldn't fuck with it at all."

He peels off three tens. "No ticket, Sinbad. I can't sell the fucking thing anyhow. Old times' sake, that's all."

"Not gold?"

"Here, here's the loop. Check it out yourself. Nice engraving, the inscription on the back. Good hand. You don't see work like that around anymore. But if you come across any diamonds, gimme the first crack. Diamonds always move."

"See ya, Moe. Don't take any gold bricks."

"Gold bricks, ha ha, that's a good one. Move 'em like hot cakes if I had 'em. Don't forget about me, you know, if you come up with any diamonds, don't matter how small. I can move 'em. Move 'em like hot cakes . . ."

A bell tinkles as I close the door behind me. Outside it's bright and sunny, not a cloud in the sky. On Eighth Avenue a guy is selling hot wallets from a cardboard box. A hooer stops to look. The wind blows her mini-mini over her thighs. Behind her a dip eyes her shoulder bag. A half-drunk panhandler works the crowd. So does a kid selling loose joints and bags. A pimp peers into the window of a hardware store, adjusting his superfly hat. A tourist in a business suit turns to stare at a six-foot transvestite. Nothing has changed. I get that same funny feeling that I've never been away, that the whole time on the Rock was nothing but a dream.

My first stop is Tricks because that's usually his first stop of the day. "Unless I drink of my wake-up, I shall surely be cast into a pit of torment." How many mornings I heard him say that. Inside it's dark. The D.J. booth is empty. There's nobody on the tiny dance floor. The only customers at the bar are a couple of queens, with nothing to do in the morning, who sit dishing the dirt, sipping tall drinks with limes stuck on top. The guy behind the bar used to dance in the boy burlesque. Now he sashays up and down the work area behind the bar, dripping ice cubes and bitchery. He needs a shave. The juke box is blaring only because everybody expects it to blare. Between records conversation stops. It's as if words only made sense when they can't be heard, as if they were unbearable without musical accompaniment.

One quick glance into the gloom and I know he's not here. But Sunshine is, hunched up against the wall on his corner stool.

"Sunshine, look who's back," trills the bartender. He looks over his shoulder and grins, pretending he's glad to see me.

We hug each other for a second and then he slides back into his seat, a brown-skinned old toad whose only ambition is to keep his dick hard.

"Hello there!" He booms his stock greeting. One day he'll sit up in his coffin and boom "Hello there" at the undertaker.

"What's happening, Sunshine?"

"S.O.S., same old shit. Saul's not here. Cop a squat, when dja get out . . . Candy, two double Dewar's on the rocks, hold the rocks on mine. You just got out?"

"This morning, a couple of hours ago."

Candy returns with the drinks, pinches my cheek and plants a wet kiss on the air six inches from the tip of my nose. "This one's with me, baby."

"Luck!"

We clink glasses all around. Candy drinks only Byrrh and Compari with a twist.

"Luck."

"Luck."

"Luck."

"You're looking marvee-o-so, baby, mooey, mooey macho, ooo, look at those arms. Jail's done wonders for you!"

"You look good enough to eat, Candy."

"You gonna eat me whole, Daddy?"

"No, I'm gonna spit that part out."

We all laugh like we never heard it before, just a thousand times, but everybody always laughs. Sunshine gulps at his drink. He's nervous. Candy pats the backs of both our hands.

"Well, boys, be good and if you can't be good, be safe. I gotta run and take care of the paying customers." And she moves on down the bar. "Ooo, Henry, you look mar-vee-o-so . . ."

Sunshine glances sidewise at me. "Well."

"Well."

"It's been a long time."

"Much too long."

"How long is it, six months?"

"Ten months. Ten months and two days. Much too long."

Candy fills up our glasses and this time takes Sunshine's money.

"You know, when I heard, I would've written, but you know me, can't get myself to sit down and write a letter."

"Yeah, I know you."

"You see Benny out there? He's locked up again."

"Nope, but I ran into Sheik, Little Sheik."

"Little Sheik, the one who ran around in that dirty karate suit all the time? What the fuck did he do?"

"Nothing much. Shot a cop in the gut."

"No shit. How much time did he get?"

"Twenty-five. Did he move?"

"Sheik?" He plays dumb for about ten seconds, then gives it up and gulps down his drink. His left eye twitches.

"Come on, Sunshine, it's my turn to buy." I toss a ten on the bar and hold the glass up so Candy can see it's empty. The booze is going right to my head. I got to slow down, can't afford to get drunk, not yet.

"Put it away, Sinbad, it's my party. After all, we're celebrating."

"Don't worry about it. I'm spending up my inheritance and I gotta do it all in one day. Did he move?"

"Of course."

"Dumb question."

"You wanted to know. Come on, cheer up, you should be happy. I mean, happy to be home, out. Cheer up, it'll all be better in a hundred years."

"I know, I won't have a worry in the world."

Stale punch lines and half-hearted evasions. The booze is going to my head.

"You're a sight for sore eyes. Really did put one some weight didn't you?" He feels my bicep appreciatively. "Why don't you come upstairs with me? I got some dynamite Gold. Come up and get comfortable, change your luck."

"You and him are two of a kind. You both got hard-ons where your consciences should be. You got any beauties?"

"You'll come?"

"You got any beauties?"

"Sure, always got what you need for the knot."

"What're you planning to do, party for two days straight?"

"I got a lotta things to take care of, figure a couple of beauties'll keep me going."

I can hear myself slurring the words.

"Maybe for old times' sake? Change your luck."

"No chance, old man. I need a hot shower and some beauties. Cash on the line. Nothing for nothing. The other way it costs much more in the end."

"In the end . . . ?" He chuckles.

He reaches out for my elbow to help me up.

"Don't."

"Don't get paranoid, it's only your elbow."

"It's not that. I don't want to be touched."

"By me?"

"By anyone. Not now. Not today . . . never. I'm a little bit drunk."

"Well, let's go then, a little walk'll straighten you out."

As we're going out, I realize no one left a tip for Candy. I lurch back inside and throw a couple of singles on the bar. "Thanks, luv, wanna quickie . . . oh no, not *that*, you nasty boy, one for the road."

"Keep it warm for me, Candy. I'll be back later."

"He doesn't come in here any more."

"So you know too. Does the whole damn City know?"

"Baby, one thing you learn working behind the bar is be nice to everybody and stay out of their business—unless of course your business happens to be their pleasure."

"Where is he?"

"Someplace he knows you'll find. Be cool, baby, and if, you know, you need a shoulder to cry on, Mama'll be here until closing time."

Outside, a soft spring wind blows newspapers across Needle Park. The little kids are just getting out for lunch from the Catholic school across from the hotel where Sunshine lives.

"Spent a lot of nights in that hotel, Sunshine. A lot of nights. First time I met him he conned me right out of my pants."

"And cleaned you up."

"Cleaned me up with meth. You call that cleaning up?"

"I've been around a long time but I never saw a needle jump off a table into anyone's arm. That's one thing I haven't seen yet."

It always did take forever for the elevator to come and always the same people are waiting for it. The same little old ladies and nigger pimps and Welfare broads with little kids and hooers smelling of musk oil. A hustler going upstairs to see his steady john. Two queens yakking it up. A very fat lady and her tiny old dachshund. I feel like I've never been away. Where the fuck are they all going to go when this dump finally gets torn down? Where's Sunshine going to go? Where did *He* go?

Outside Sunshine's door I get like this overpowering feeling that somehow I'm being set up for a punchline and when the door opens there he'll be, laughing his fool head off, not surprised at all. Not at all like in the dream.

"Is he inside?"

"What's wrong, Sinbad, you got cold feet or just a hot cock?"

"Neither."

"Or both."

"Forget I asked. Besides, you wouldn't tell me the truth anyhow."

"Of course I would." He frowns as he turns the key in the lock.

"Why should you?"

"It's a pain in the ass any other way. Too much of a hassle. You want to smoke some of this Colombian?"

"Not now. I got to take a shower."

I stand under the water for a long time, steaming up the bathroom. When I can't smell the jailhouse anymore, I get dressed and wrap the towel around my head. The towel smells of Sunshine's cologne. It's a smell I always hated.

Sunshine hands me a cup of black coffee, heavy on the sugar like always, and sits down with his hands folded in front of him, looking for all the world like a guy trying to figure out why the cops haven't put the cuffs on him yet. The shower and the coffee have sobered me up a little.

"How much the beauties going for, Sunshine?"

"Four, four apiece. For you, three."

"Here's eight bucks, give me two."

"Fuck it, you want to be like that . . ." He shrugs and shakes two from a little brown pill container. I chase them down with a gulp of hot coffee.

"Better go slow, Sinbad, you'll be tripping like ten thousand."

"Not me. Speed keeps my head clear, that's all."

The money I gave him sits on top of the dresser, which is cluttered with old TV Guides, a few pieces of silverware, a box of Velveeta cheese, a strainer, a power hitter, and some magazines with naked young boys on their covers. His whole life is laid out for casual visitors to inspect.

"You want to smoke now, it's good. It's dynamite."

Sunshine is uncomfortable unless he has a joint between his fingers. That's why I don't want to smoke. I want to keep him off balance.

"Later. Tell me where he is."

"I don't know."

"I thought you said you wouldn't lie."

"No I didn't. I said I'd tell you the truth."

"Then tell me."

"Either way it's a pain in the ass. Why don't you just take your eight dollars back, I'll give you two more beauties and a bag of smoke, and we'll take care of B.I."

212

"You know, there's always one thing I wanted to tell you, when you were doing it all to me, getting everything you wanted out of a strung-out thirteen-year-old runaway fucked-up kid. You know what that was? Every time you put your slimy hands on me, every time I smelled you, that faggot cologne of yours, every time you used my body, I wanted to puke. You're disgusting. You make my skin crawl."

"That explains, of course, why you always kept coming back for more."

"Where is he?"

"Why should I make it easy for you?" Absently, he reaches for the bambu, then remembers that we're not smoking. His hand falls to his lap and twitches a little. He looks as if he doesn't recognize it.

"Make it easy for yourself."

"It's never easy when people insist on taking things seriously. When you're as old as I am you'll realize that."

"I'm not a little kid anymore. I'm bigger than you are and stronger than you are and faster than you are. I could hurt you."

"But you won't. It's not me you want to hurt. I disgust you too much for you to want to hurt me. We have a lot in common, you and me."

The beauties start to come down. I feel a surge of power that I know is artificial and feel all the more powerful for knowing it.

"You don't even know me. You don't even know who I am."

"I know you're a young boy in a man's body trying to burn bridges that never existed."

"You were always jealous. Jealous that I went with him and jealous that he went with me."

"Oh, Sinbad. You complicate everything just to spite yourself. I was glad you went. I get tired of the same pussy all the time."

"You were glad I went with him?"

"Oh well." He shrugs. "Remember, a strange hand is better than none. You're going a million places at once, and all the wrong places. You're like the kinda guy that's humping away, just getting ready to come, who jumps up all of a sudden and yells, 'Omigod, I left the baby in the bus.'"

"Just tell me where he is."

213

"And I wasn't jealous of him either. You both deserved each other. Both of you think your feelings are so, so important. Both of you spend all of your time spiting yourselves. With him it's ridicule. With you it's seriousness. I knew from the start it would end up like this."

"It's none of your business, him and me."

"Business?"

"Is it money? Is that all we're talking about? Are you putting a price on his head?"

"Of course I'd sell him out. Just like he'd sell me out. That's what friends are all about. They can buy and sell each other twenty times a day and sit down at night and get drunk together and laugh and forget about it. You, you're too busy figuring out what you might have forgotten, what something might have meant, what something's supposed to mean. You're too busy to forget."

"Forget, forget what he did?"

"What did he do? Just what did he do that was so terrible?"

"You know what happened."

"I know the story, which I'm sure by now you've turned into a three-act soap opera."

"There are two sides to every story, you know."

"Nope. There's one side, one story. You don't understand that it's completely unimportant what happened. You'll find out when you're my age, nobody remembers punch lines."

"How much did he tell you?"

"More than he told you. I'm sure of that."

"You think it was the truth?"

"I'm positive it wasn't. That's why we seldom argue."

"Because you think it's so cool to be cool, to pretend to have ice water in your veins," I yell. "You're just weak, that's what it is. You have to be able to hurt someone if you really care for them."

"Then you don't have anything to complain about, do you?"

"About his spite, sure I can complain. All of that business about my tricks this and my tricks that, while he's laying up cooling out, with his trade running in and out like it was Grand Central Station. What was I supposed to do, sit around with my finger up my ass waiting for him to throw me a few crumbs or throw my legs up in the air and fuck me?"

"You had moved out six months before. What was he supposed to do, go into a dying swan act waiting for you to show back from the holy family in Jersey? Dear Carmen the pill-head and of course the baby, the one she didn't bother to give your last name to, the one that came out two shades darker than you, the one he bought the layette for while you were sucking dicks in Forty-second Street movies talking all that bullshit about 'I gotta have my freedom.' Oh yes, the best of all possible worlds, that's what you wanted, meaning your way, huh? Grow up."

"I wanted him to tell me to stop. I wanted him to tell me, don't do it anymore. You give it up and I'll give it up."

"What the fuck did you want, a suicide pact? When did you figure it out that he owed you his life?"

"Then why did he try to run mine? I didn't have to tell him about Mitch. If I hadn't told him the truth none of this would of started. I told him about a guy who'd once been nice to a fucked-up little kid and it turned into the crime of the century. How many times I went there, ready to stay over, ready to stay as long as he wanted. . ."

"Ready to stay as long as *you* wanted. . ."

"Ready to live with him . . ."

"Just you and him and Carmen and little Salvador. A regular daisy chain . . ."

"Ready to do anything for him . . ."

"On *your* terms. . ."

"And he acted like he didn't give a fuck. Nice to see you, Sinbad, my boy, but company calls. See you tomorrow. Take care out there on the cruel, cruel sea. Oh, but when I told him I'd seen Mitch a few times, just for old times' sake, just because he knew what the fuck it meant to be kind, then I hadda be every name in the book."

"You could have kept your big mouth shut."

"I had to tell him. I owed it to him."

"You did *not* owe it to him. You owed him the little white lie, the silence, the evasions—all the things that make friendship between two people possible."

I can tell he's exhausted. It's only a matter of time. We sit silently, each of us knowing the other one is right.

"Sunshine, light up a joint, ok?"

"Are you ready to be reasonable?"

"I'll never be ready to be reasonable. That's asking too much."

"You knew he'd get on your case about Mitch."

"You got that one. But I didn't want to go back. Mitch, he was just like someplace to catch my breath. I felt sorry for him. It was a different experience. I wasn't on pins and needles all the time."

"So you had to run to Saul to help you do him in."

"Pass me that joint. I ran to Saul to plead with him, to tell him Mitch wanted me, wanted me to stay with him."

"And he laughed in your face, I suppose."

"Worse, he told me to go right ahead. Thought it was a good idea. He knew I'd never go through with it."

"You told him that?"

"I had to. 'My boy, to the weak you become as the weak.' He was right. It was too late to go back. 'It's the children who are the corrupters,' he said."

"And then?"

"And then, of course, we made love."

"You had sex."

"He was the only person I could give myself up to completely. The only person who could drain all that shit out of me."

"That is as long as it was you and nobody else."

"There couldn't be enough of him to go around, to go all around, just for anybody and everybody."

"Of course not, you being so special and all. But he couldn't have known about the credit cards unless you told him."

"It just slipped out. I told him Mitch was talking about two weeks in San Juan, him and me, the credit cards slipped out and then he wouldn't let up. 'Really, my boy, two weeks of devotion and sunshine.' What the fuck did he expect, that I'd become a monk? Since when did he think my body was so fucking sacred?"

"I remember we had a good laugh one time when you told him you didn't mind sucking twenty dicks a day if you had to but you didn't want to live with him and be kept."

"He laughed at that, he actually laughed at that!"

"Of course. It must have sounded even more ridiculous coming out of your mouth than when he told it to us."

"Us?"

"Me, a gorgeous number in a white jumpsuit—Carlos something or other—Candy, I forget who else. The whole crowd down at Tricks."

"What I told him was that I cared for him too much to put him in a position where he'd always be wondering if I was hustling him."

"And the clothes and the presents and the bail . . .?"

"That was different and you know it. He had no right saying that to a bunch of people, laughing at me behind my back."

"Why shouldn't he? If he laughed in your face, you'd sulk like a spoiled fucking kid for a month. And knowing him, you had a right to tell him about the credit cards?"

"It slipped out."

"It did *not* slip out. You don't just go around telling someone like him, 'Oh, by the way, I got down with my old—whatever— and you know, he got this big bunch of credit cards.' That's like bringing him a bottle of booze and telling him to save it 'til Christmas."

"I just didn't think about it, that's all. I was tired, we were just laying there in bed. I wasn't going to San Juan. But then he wouldn't let up."

"Because you wanted the cards worse than he did. He knew you'd cop them, only a matter of time and then only a matter of time 'til you got pinched working them. He knew if he didn't work them, you'd sure as shit go directly to jail, do not pass go, right to the slammer, so as usual he saved you from yourself, from your own stubbornness and stupidity. And then you even picked the dumbest possible way. Get down with the guy and beat his wallet while he's in the john."

"Why not? I figured if Mitch knew it was me, what the fuck? He wouldn't have me pinched, just notify the companies and stop the account or something. By that time we would have burned them out anyhow."

"He, not we. The only thing you can burn out is the patience of anybody who tries to help you. And you got over, he got over for you, like a fat rat. And meanwhile you figured your 'devoted' whatever would just sit back and take it on the chin, because you're so 'special' and all."

"I didn't get a dime outta it. He beat me outta every red cent.

Not a dime. Chumped off like he's always chumped me off from the very first day I met him."

"Did you ever stop to think that he was holding back from you so you wouldn't act nigger rich and get yourself all coked up and find some quicker way of getting pinched?"

"It was an accident."

"Sure, you beat the guy and two days later, there you are back down on the Square, the very first place the 'devoted whatever' would think of looking for you."

"Why didn't he bail me out? He had the bread. There must of been plenty. Why didn't he get me a lawyer? Why didn't he send me any dough? Why did he just make a fool out of me, cut me loose completely?"

"Maybe after six years he was just tired of all the bullshit, washed his hands of it and walked away. You took your shot and blew. Take it like a man."

"He could of bailed me out, even if he wanted to cut me loose. He could of bailed me out first."

"Sure, with the parole people looking for him, and the Ginneys, which you didn't know about. Just step right up with the dough and explain where it came from, meanwhile get himself pinched and do a helluvalot more time than you did and maybe get a bullet in his back from the Ginneys too. There was nothing to begin with and believe me there's nothing left."

"Don't hand me that shit. I don't want to hear your excuses for him. There was a way. He always found a way. He let my ass rot up on the Rock while he got over with *my* money. I was the one who stole the credit cards. I was the one who fucked myself up with somebody who never did me any harm at all. He did it because it finally came out of him, that he's treacherous to everybody, that he cons you and snows you and hooks you up so that you don't even *want* to think for yourself and then just throws you away like a piece of shit when he can't use you anymore. Don't try to give me a hand job. I've gotta take it right down the line for my own self-respect. If I don't I'll wind up just like you. I don't care what he meant, what he intended, what he could or couldn't do. It's what he did do and what he didn't do. I'm a man now and if you fuck with a man, then you gotta be ready for the consequences. That's something you'll never understand. What it is to be a man. What it is to give yourself to somebody heart and soul, let them do whatever they want with your body, but more important, let them do what they want with your mind, with your whole life, with everything, and they just throw you away just like that and laugh at you."

"No, I never would understand that, never would want to— the need to make a present to someone of your whole life, a present that they never wanted in the first place."

"Sunshine, where is he?"

"I'll tell you what he told me to tell you, and then get out. I'm not making a dime outta this."

"Where? What did he tell you?"

"He said, 'Tell Sinbad I'm off to the Land of the Lotus Eaters.' "

"That's it?"

"That's it."

"You know where he means?"

"Of course I do. So do you."

"So save us all time and tell me. I'm not in the mood for riddles."

"Then get in the mood. Why should I spoil his fun?"

"He's still laughing at me, the cocksucker."

"Go find him and tell *him* your troubles. I could've been doing something interesting, like having some trade suck my cock. He's in walking distance."

I throw his towel down on the bed and turn to go. The eight dollars still sits on the dresser. An old, sour man slumped in a chair who has no interest in riddles, that's all he is.

"Both of you, you both got your heads screwed on backwards," he grumbles.

I slam the door behind me.

Out in the street the sunlight explodes in my face. I'm speeding. Each sliver of color, each splotch of shadow is so intense, so vivid that I can hardly bear to keep my eyes open. I blink, trying to make the pounding in my temples go away. I open my eyes and am startled by the sudden appearance of a pigeon perched on a garbage pail. Each second seems to last too long. That's what speed does to you. My throat is parched. I'm not walking. I'm striding away from whatever is behind me. I'm stalking whatever lies ahead. I'm a hunter in a strange and dangerous dessert. I am paranoid as all hell. I shouldn't have taken both beauties at once. I stop at the stand on the corner of Broadway and sip an ice-cold papaya drink. Lotus eaters. Probably just a false trail. He knows how mad I can get; he doesn't really want me to find him. But I will. For a minute there Sunshine's cranky logic had me going. He had me hooked up in excuses. How do you excuse completely abandoning someone with no explanation, no word, just like that?

How could he possibly stand there in the bar laughing, telling our secrets to strangers, knowing how serious my concern was, knowing how important it was to me to tell him how I felt? For what? So he could be on center stage for five minutes, so he could have a new joke to tell the boys at the bar, or the girls, or whatever. And the joke was me. I was the joke. When things got dull he could always dig out another Sinbad story. Every moment we had spent together, every confidence I had shared with him, our whole relationship—a third of my life—took on a new and ugly meaning. Of course, my boy, nothing's sacred. Woe to the man who takes himself seriously for he winds up flat on his ass, my boy. My boy. *His* boy. His what? His trick, his piece of trade, his toy. Service with a smile, boss. Yowsa, yowsa. Angrily I knock the cup off the counter, spilling papaya juice all over the front of my shirt. The counterman gives me a dirty look. He sees maniacs all day long.

Come on, show off your tricks. Perform like a trained seal. Bravo. Good boy. Now carry on like a yard dog. Howl. A little louder. That's it, good boy. And everybody laughs and applauds. So that's how it was all the time. I was a little wax doll he could try out his games on before he used them in the real world on real people. I was a puppet convinced that he's dancing without strings. Well, good buddy, we'll see who's gonna do the dancing.

I stop to figure things out in Needle Park, a narrow concrete island smack in the middle of Broadway where the winos cut loose their mutts to crap on the grass and old men sit staring out into space and doze out their afternoons on benches caked with pigeon shit. When the street junk dried up, the dope fiends disappeared

220

and gave it all back; nobody wanted it anymore. Sitting there I try to puzzle it out. He's on the lam. Of course. From me? From somebody else too? Ginneys? If I knew who was after him I might be able to figure out where he'd go to cool out. Let's say I'm the one who's after him. Where would he go—within walking distance? "Things are never what they seem to be." "I would lie to you about anything and everything. Forsake logic, my boy, and leap! Everything is always what it seems to be." I practically jump off the bench and dash into the subway. Of course, Sunshine was right, I knew it all along. One stop on the express—that's walking distance Lotus eaters. The land of pleasure. I get off at the Square because there's only one place he can be—Playland.

I come out of the hole, taking the steps two at a time. I'm positive. I look around. The clock over the bank. The legless nigger rolling along on a little dolly, shaking pennies in a beat-up tin cup. The Holy Roller band blaring off key under the clock and the fat old bag shouting hallelujahs, the fat guy who stares at me, trying to figure out where he knows me from, trying to figure out if I was the one that ripped him off. Speeding, I take in the whole scene in a flash, let it sift through my mind, and I'm positive. I'm positive he's not here. I breathe in the smell of hamburgers frying in grease and car fumes and the sweet smell of weed. I sniff and his scent is missing. I've landed down the first blind alley, even though it's a familiar one and I'm glad I'm here. It's great to be back. It's a beautiful day. A perfect day. Anytime I want I can turn around and start all over again. Start looking for him all over again or just plain start over again. Who says you can never go back?

I'm free as the wind. I can stroll down the Deuce with a couple of bucks in my slide and there's no bars, no wake-up bells, no waiting, no more being locked up, no more being locked up in my rage. I'm Sinbad the Semen again, out in the wide, wide world where every day is a fabulous adventure. I have no plans. Fuck plans. I go where I want, when I want to, and no motherfucker with an asshole pointed towards the ground can do a fucking thing about it. I'm young, dumb, and full of cum. I'm the president of the Four-Ef Club: Find 'em, Feel 'em, Fuck 'em, and Forget 'em. If I want money all I have to do is snap my fingers for a trick. If I want to change the scene I can wave for a cab and be gone in a second. It's all here, mine for the plucking. I'm strong as an ox, faster than a speeding bullet, able to leap tall buildings in a single bound.

"Yo, bro', you gotta square?"

The two kids are hanging out in front of Playland. The older one, maybe about thirteen, already he thinks he's cool in his red tank top, squatting on the jonny pump so everybody can get a good look at his crotch. A real little tough guy with stringy brown hair down around his eyes and a "fuck you" sneer stuck on his puss. The younger one—he can't be more than eleven—leans against the window with his back turned to the cheap magic tricks and dirty postcards. You can see he just started coming out—a little blond kid in shorts that come down to his knees with skinny hairless legs, who doesn't belong here. Not yet. I shake out a cigarette for the tough guy.

"Ya gotta light?"

"Maybe you want me to smoke it for you too."

"Ya spare one for my brudder?"

"He smokes?"

"Sure he smokes, he's been smoking since he wuz eight. Right, Tito?"

Chicken Little nods, seriously considering the choice between the two identical cigarettes sticking out of the pack.

"You looking for someone?" asks the gangster.

I bust out laughing at the age-old hustlers' line.

"What's so funny? Whatsa matter? You like 'em younger, you kin go with my brudder." He hooks his thumb in the direction of Chicken Little, who looks like he's afraid to hear the answer. "But if you want him we both go together. He's too small to go by hisself alone."

"Do I look like a trick, bro'?"

"Well . . ." He considers, while rubbing his chin. ". . . why not? You ain't a cop or nothin', are you?"

Finally the shoe is on the other foot. I don't like the way it fits. I don't like it one bit.

"You must be smokin' blankets or something. I ain't a trick. Can't you tell I'm not a trick, for Chrissakes?" I shake my head in amazement.

"Well how the fuck was we supposed to know? Right, Tito?"

222

He sits back down and hugs his knees. "You sure you ain't a cop?"

"No, I ain't a cop, for Chrissakes, and I sure as shit ain't a motherfucking trick either."

Chicken Little looks disappointed.

"Ya got a quarter so we can play a game?"

"I'll give you a handful of quarters if you tell me whether you seen a guy."

"What guy? You sure you ain't a cop?"

"Yeah, ok, you got me. I lied. I'm really a cop. I'm J. Edgar Grummenschidt—ahride youse guys, drop your socks and grab your cocks, the jig's up!" And I do a crazy little dance, making believe I'm gunning them down with my cocked finger. The gangster laughs appreciatively and slaps skin with me. Chicken Little looks doubtful about everything.

"What guy?" The gangster chuckles. "A trick?"

"Fat guy with a crew cut and horn-rimmed glasses."

"White?" pipes the little guy, who suddenly discovers his voice.

"Yeah, white." I plant one hand on his shoulder and slip a buck into his hand. He stands there with his mouth open, looking stupid.

"Take it easy. I ain't gonna hurt you, little bro'. Didja see him?"

"So what if we did?" The gangster has to butt in.

"Shuddup, I'm talking to your brother. You seen him, little bro'?"

"They call you Sinbad?"

"That's me."

"He give my brudder a buck yesterday. Told him to give Sinbad a message if he comes around askin' for him. You didn't give me nothin' either." He glares at the gangster.

"Whaddid he say to tell Sinbad, huh?"

"I remember. He said if a tall guy named Sinbad asts about me, tell him I said he should stop thinking so hard."

"That's it? You're sure?"

"Sure I'm sure. Stop thinking so hard, that's just what he said."

"Thanks, little bro'. Here, here's some change, go play some games."

"Yo," says the gangster, "how come this dude knew you was

223

gonna show and ast for him?"

"Private joke. It's just a game we play, see? No sweat. Oh, yeah, I did forget one thing. Your brother there, if I ever see him down here hustling again, with or without you, I'm gonna pinch you so fast it'll make your asshole twitch."

"See," I hear him complain as I cross the street, "I told ya he was a cop. I knew it all along."

Stop thinking so hard. The whole day is spoiled for me already. There he is, giving me the old finger, knowing I'd get it all wrong. Stop thinking so hard. I lean up against a store window watching them deal drugs under the movie marquee. A guy with a white shirt flapping over his gut and a camera around his neck eases up and pretends to be interested in something he sees over my left shoulder. Stop thinking so hard. The gangster across the street thought I was a trick. He really did. Then he thought I was a cop. He was sure of that too. Something's different. About me. About the way I look. About the way I act. Ten months ago anybody who saw me on the Deuce knew what I was. There was no question about it. Take Fatty the Shutterbug here. What does he see about me that I don't?

"Are you gonna ask me for the time or a match, which one?"

"Huh?"

"Time is money. I don't waste either in conversation with strangers. Whatever you want, the price starts at twenty and goes up from there. Are we gonna talk business or am I gonna call that cop on the corner and tell him that you just propositioned me?"

"Say, what is this? I don't know what you're talking about. I didn't say one word to you, not one word."

"So now that you've checked out the merchandise you decide you're not buying?"

"Buying? You're crazy, kid, I didn't say a word to you."

"If I'm bothering you, *you* can call the cop, go ahead."

He stands there, afraid to go and afraid to stay. I can smell the fear. My dick is hard for the first time since I hit the streets.

"Go ahead, call the cop. No? ok, give me the twenty you owe me."

"For what?" His voice cracks.

"One, for wasting my time, not saying anything, standing here while maybe someone else would have stopped and I could have made some money. Two, for checking out the merchandise. This is the bargain basement down here. Window shopping is definitely not allowed."

"What do you think this is? You can't shake me down, just like that, in broad daylight."

"Shake you down? Farthest thing from my mind. I'll tell you what, my man, nobody's shaking you down. You now have three choices. One, hand over the twenty like a good boy. Two, you call the cop and tell him a perfect stranger just demanded twenty bucks from you. Maybe he'll believe you, maybe he won't. Maybe you've been around for a little while today and he knows what you are. Plenty of maybes. Gives you plenty of room to deal with. Three, I call the cop, who's seen me before, many times, and when I tell him the perverted thing you wanted to do he will definitely believe me, particularly when you suggested doing it with an eleven-year-old kid."

"Eleven-year-old kid?"

"My brother over there, the one with the shorts, in front of Playland."

I wave at Chicken Little, who smiles and waves back. "See, my little brother, just like I told you." I'll call him over right now if you like.

"Suppose I ain't got twenty." He's sweating bullets.

"No problem. Can't get blood from a stone. Tito," I holler, "come on over for a minute."

The kid nearly gets sideswiped by a bus as he scoots across the street. By the time he dashes up to my side, I got the twenty in my hand and the guy is hailing a cab. Just as easy as that. Of course it's easy. Stop thinking so hard.

"Tito, howja like to make twenty, just you, by yourself?"

He stops smiling and hangs his head.

"That's a lot of dough, but, you know, I ain't supposed to go without my brudder, and besides . . ."

"I said by yourself, not with me, not with anybody else, not even your brother."

"But for what, then?" He tries a little smile again.

"Promise me something."

225

"That's all?"

"Promise me you'll stay the fuck offa this street for one month, one whole month. Willya promise me that?"

"Sure, sure I promise. That's easy."

"You know what happens to people who lie to me, Tito?"

"I wouldn't lie. I'll do just like you said."

"Ok, when I give you the twenty, you get right in the train and go home, ok?"

"Sure, Sinbad, just as soon as I tell my brudder."

"I said now, Tito. I'll tell your brother."

"Sure, Sinbad, stay off the Deuce for a month. Now do I get the twenny?"

"Here. Now split, right into the subway."

"Gee, thanks, Sinbad, you're a cool dude." And he scoots. He thinks he's out of sight and then doubles back across to Playland, where I see him showing the twenty to his brother, who shakes his head and looks over at me and then they're both looking at me and laughing and slapping each other on the back. They're still laughing when a john eases up and starts rapping to them. Oh well, win some, lose some, as the D.A. says, and I did enjoy myself, the look on the shutterbug's face and all, I really did enjoy myself.

I check out the clock over the bank. Plenty of time before my next stop. I have a good idea where I went wrong. I stop off at the bar across from the Port and order a double gin and tonic, two twists of lime, pop a quarter in the juke box, and slide into a corner booth. It was ridiculous just tossing away the twenty like that. It was ridiculous and it feels good. After all, isn't that what it's all about? If I want to throw money away, why not? If I want to do something silly or foolish, why not? I don't owe anybody any explanations anymore. Don't have to worry about looking ridiculous to anybody, because since I walked out of that gate this morning I've been on my own, or I will be on my own. Soon. Very soon. If I have to I can make it with my own brain. I just did. I got over. I didn't have to think about it, I just went ahead and did what I had to do, and my instincts were good. I got over, didn't I? I let him convince me that he had to do the thinking for both of us. But that's the way *he* wanted it, so he could lead me around by the nose. Without me you're lost, my boy, a sheep astray among wolves. "My boy." That was *him* getting over, on me.

226

But I'm not a boy—his boy or anybody's boy—anymore. I'm not the one who's lost. I may not know where I'm going, but I know I'll get there. He's the one, he's the one that's lost. He's the one running and hiding and dropping hints like a cunt dropping handkerchiefs. He's running scared, knowing that the clock is running down and I'm calling the shots. We're playing this game by my rules, not his. If I want to throw away twenty or twenty thousand, he's got nothing to do with it. He has no say about anything any more.

We were living down the hall from Sunshine. Oh sure, he was paying the rent—with money I made flat on my back, or flat on my stomach. But as usual, it was him that was keeping me. He paid the rent. I paid the dues with my body, with my dick and my ass. Of course it was nothing to him, just another "temporary setback" in a permanent series of temporary setbacks. I was out there hustling my ass every day, while he was sopping up booze like it was going out of style and playing Lord of the Manor at Tricks. One day a dude from out of town picks me up. Maybe he was too cheap to check in to a hotel. Maybe there was some reason he couldn't. You don't ask questions like that, not when the rent's more than two weeks overdue. So I took him back to the hotel. Big deal. I put the chain on the door. How long were we going to be, twenty-five minutes, if that? I was turning a trick, so what. I turned them all day long, every day, and never heard any complaints when I laid the cash on him. But this time it had to be a big fucking production number. He kicked down the door, threw the dude out into the hall, yelling and screaming and carrying on that I had committed the mortal sin of getting down in his bed. Not "our" bed, "his" bed. Me, I was just the hired help, except that he wasn't the one doing the hiring.

So the trick is gone. The manager is hollering over the phone that he's had it up to here with all our shit and forget about the back rent, get out—today, now. You know who was to blame? Me. Me, of course. He was "merely defending the sanctity of hearth and home." Then he beat me up. Not like the other times, a couple of good back-hands here, a slap or two there. He beat me up with

227

his fists. He literally pounded me into the ground. He hammered at me and wouldn't stop. I heard my cheekbone shatter. My nose split open like an overripe tomato. One eye was completely shut. Then he started kicking me in the ribs, in the head. Wherever I covered up he'd kick me some other place. You know why he stopped? Because he ran out of steam, huffing and puffing like a steam engine. He took a break to sop up some more booze and thought I'd just lay there, waiting for him to come back and kick me some more. I said, fuck this. I may have been a dopey fucked-up kid, but I wasn't crazy, to lay there and get kicked like a fucking dog. He went for the booze, I went for the door—out like a shot. I sat on the fucking roof for hours, it seemed, no shirt, my teeth chattering. I said to myself, if he comes up here, if he tries to kick me anymore, I'll jump off the roof. He didn't come. It got dark. I walked to the edge of the roof and wondered whether I should jump anyhow, whether I should jump because he didn't even bother to come up and try to kick me anymore. It was a long way down and I was scared. I wanted it to be all over and I knew I wasn't ready, not then, not this way, because I wasn't even worth kicking.

I went downstairs to the ninth floor where I knew this fag lived. I didn't know him, her. Just a scrawny little queen who lived in the building. We said hello in the elevator and that was that. I knocked on her door. No shirt, no shoes. She opened the door, took one look at me and pulled me in, slamming the door behind and double-locking it.

No questions. I asked her if I could crash out in that one tiny miserable room with only the double bed, a rickety wooden chair, and a dresser with her makeup kit on it. She had absolutely nothing to give me, nothing for herself. An old queen in a Welfare hotel with nothing but her own dreams about "better days" that never were, for company. She dripped water on my battered face, carefully, tenderly—yes, tenderly—blotting at the cuts and bruises. My head was on fire. I dozed and started. I shook and cried uncontrollably. She shooshed me and clucked like a sad, withered mother hen. Finally we both slept. It was still gray outside the curtainless window when the banging started on the door. She opened the door. I say "she" because I didn't know her name then and still don't know it now. She opened the door and he pushed her, put his hand on her face and pushed her right on her ass. Behind him stood a big nigger, some guy he knew from the joint. He had a big forty-five. Looking into the barrel, the poor fag on the floor must have thought it was a cannon. I was still in bed, trying to figure out what was happening. I ached all over. He was actually going to shoot her. Somehow I dragged myself off the bed. It was inconceivable, "monstrous vanity" was the way he would say it, to shoot an insignificant and harmless stranger for giving me a place to rest my head. Then I did a stupid thing, not a brave thing. I grabbed at the barrel of the gun and pushed it right into my stomach.

"Shoot me, motherfucker," I told him. "Shoot me. It's me you want. You don't have the balls. You don't have the balls, because you know you'd be doing me a favor."

The fag lay on the floor, holding her head. Her eyes were wide open, but she didn't moan or beg or carry on. She had more corazón than anybody in the room.

"Let's go," he motioned with the barrel.

We went back upstairs, while behind us the big nigger was on his knees on the faggot's chest, punching her in the face. I went into the bathroom and threw up all over the floor. When I was done, he pulled me up to my feet by my hair and wiped the filth off my mouth with the palm of his hand. My one eye was still closed. Then he kissed me on my lips, which were puffed up twice their normal size. I kissed him back. He carried me over to the bed and we made love, violently. I felt him deep inside of me and climaxed in great spasms, moaning for more.

"Too much loving makes men mad," he chuckled. I saw his hands shaking and knew that the whole thing was an act. He knew I wouldn't have let him shoot the fag but he was still terrified at the thought that I might have been too hurt to stop him. I lay there. He kissed my belly and groin. I felt myself getting hard all over again. It had to stop, all of it. Now. I saw the forty-five on the table. He was licking the crease between my thigh and lower abdomen. On impulse I snatched the automatic and in one motion put it to his temple and pulled the trigger. It was after I clicked the trigger a couple of times that I realized the clip was missing. It was nothing

229

but a harmless toy. He rolled on his back and laughed, howled. He had planned the whole thing, from beginning to end. Knew every move I would make right up until the time I pulled the trigger and discovered that I wasn't even shooting blanks.

"Ah, Sinbad, my boy, put your trust in me and laugh forever." He wagged a finger at me. "How can you bear chastisement and still not laugh?"

"You're sick," I said, "and I have to be even sicker."

"At least I beat you openly. Better that than interminable resentment and bickering. Catharsis, that's what it is."

"What's catharsis?"

"Purification through the pain of a loved one."

"My mouth hurts."

"See, I feel better already. Your Good Samaritan, I'm sure that the ounce of Acapulco on her dresser will assuage her wounded pride. Then too, my friend Albert should, by this time, be in the midst of performing a most penetrating act of contrition."

"What about scaring her half to death? What about belting her in the mouth? Was that supposed to be an act?"

"Mere love tap, my boy and . . . mmmm . . . she probably loved every minute of it."

I thought of the queen's eyes staring down the huge barrel. I shuddered.

"You'd do all that . . . for a joke?'

"And much, much more."

"And my pain . . . what about that . . . what about that I'm scared to look in the mirror?"

"Ah, a few days . . . a little rest . . ."

"I don't mean my face . . . what you've done to me inside."

"Then, my boy, whatever was done was done to me too. After all, we are of one flesh and one spirit. You can't live without me. You wouldn't have it any other way. So stop whining for justice. We're way past that point. There's no turning back now. Roll over and I'll prove it to you."

I let him do it to me again and once again I spasmed, shutting out everything else except the memory of his hands shaking when he himself forgot that it was all a joke and let the mask slip off for a moment.

And isn't it that way now? Aren't his hands shaking while he leaves his little messages all around? Isn't it just a bluff, just one more con job to make me believe he has no reason to be afraid?

The ice in the glass has melted down. I stretch out my arms. The bartender glares his disapproval. My hands are steady. Not a shake or a tremor. Is it the speed? No, speed makes you excited, nervous, full of phony energy. The calm is flowing from me. I think of Sheik and his mumbo jumbo about being strong and closing yourself off. This is different, what I'm feeling now. I'm opening myself, turning towards the sun. For how long? How long before some new "chastisement," before the next "catharsis"?

The bartender sets another drink in front of me. I have no head for booze today but the speed keeps me sopping it up. Where did it start, this need I have to invent myself? What about Salvador? What about my son? Will he too grow up to give himself up completely as the only protection against giving up completely? How much will he have to pay for survival? Is survival worth abandoning every impulse to feel sorry for others? Is hollow mockery the only solution after you discover the world? Will Salvador too embrace pain merely because he has willed someone to inflict it on him? What alliances will he find on the fringes of sanity? Will weakness be his only shield, his only weapon?

There's so much I want to tell him, but he's only three and I can't risk his believing me. And him. I have to thank him. No one forced me to accept enchantment. No one forced me back to him again and again. I have to thank him for forcing me to slough off enchantment like a snake sheds its skin.

The crowd flows in and out of the Port. Everybody's going someplace. To work, back home, back home to their wife and kids. Me, I'm alone on the outside looking in. I'm the only one chasing my own tail around, howling at the moon. I have to come up with answers to stupid riddles. I have to think up questions to ask myself just to keep from wondering what the fuck I'm doing standing with my finger up my ass. I've run out of patience. When I light a cigarette my hand shakes ever so slightly and I know I'm running out of time.

I tell the cab driver to stop in front of Fort Dodge. From the outside you can't tell what's inside. The window is plastered up with papier-mâché logs. Once inside you think you've walked onto

231

a movie set. It's corny, but it works. A highly polished bar, once used in an old TV western, extends from one wall to the other. The walls themselves are completely panelled with lacquered artificial two-by-fours, decorated with tomahawks, head dresses, and feathers. The air conditioner is much too powerful and the lighting too dim, except for a spotlight aimed at a small display behind the bar — one "Fort Dodge" T-shirt in gold and black with a logo of a naked Indian bending and shading his eyes with one hand while he gets cornholed by a cowboy wearing only boots. This isn't Tricks, though the two bars are right across the street from each other. At the Fort there's no dance floor. No dancing allowed, period. At night the place is jammed with leather freaks, chicken hawks who look like male models, and under-age hustlers. For the chickens there's a pool table, two pinball machines, and a huge juke box featuring a psychedelic light show. The house rules are strict: no hanging outside, no hustling drinks, no fighting, and anyone caught with a hand in somebody else's pocket is thrown out on his ass and barred for good.

The action never starts until after nine at night, but Sandor opens up at three for the one or two regulars, like Saul, who prefer to drink by themselves. Strangers are discouraged, and if you're not an afternoon steady Sandor might just flat out refuse to serve you. When the spirit or the juke box moves him, Sandor will suddenly pick up his tambourine and liven things up with shakes and rattles. He's the best acid connection between the Deuce and Harlem. He'll buy or sell anything for a price, never handling the stuff himself, but taking a cut from both sides.

For the three o'clock regulars he provides discreet and often indispensable services. He accepts mail for them, jots down phone messages. He cures melancholy with soothing words of encouragement and hangovers with noxious concoctions. He knows all secrets, keeps the really important ones, and tosses the rest out on the bar to be gobbled up like cocktail canapés by the chosen few. "Sandor," Saul declared, "to whom all mysteries are revealed and who reveals himself to no one."

Sandor and Saul never met socially outside of the Fort. But there was something between them. There were whispered phone calls in the middle of the night, hastily arranged appointments in the bar, where the conversation would suddenly end when I walked in. I could never nail anything down. For a while I was jealous of Saul and Sandor. They could share too many tales of too many times together before I was even born.

I kept my ears open. Did he have something on Sandor, or was it the other way around? Was there something sinister about the relationship, something not quite kosher on one side or the other? There was the rumor about an old love affair mixed up with some messy business dealings. There was a wire that Sandor was some kind of federal agent, but then again I heard the same thing about Saul. Candy once told me that Saul and Sandor were related in some way. Sex? I doubted it. Sandor was short, wiry, and fortyish, not at all Saul's type. I tried to picture Sandor at my age, but nothing would come, nothing that Saul would find attractive. The gossip I liked best was that they were old "foxhole buddies," cell partners from upstate in the old days.

Once I asked Saul straight out what their "thing" was. He waved his hand. "Mmmph . . . extensive credit, unlimited connections, infinite discretion, and fresh limes."

"The limes of course . . ."

". . . show the hand of a true craftsman—essential for a decent Bloody Mary."

No sense pushing it from that end. If I asked every day for a year I'd get three hundred and sixty-five different answers, not one of them true.

I got into the habit of stopping off at least a couple of afternoons a week, even when I wasn't living with him. I liked the Fort for the same reason as everybody—the pool table, the fantastic box. I even had a small line of credit. As Saul's lover, or "ex," depending on where I was living at the time, I had privileges that nobody else my age had. I was allowed to hang out in the afternoon with the serious customers. I had the pool table to myself and didn't have to worry about somebody challenging me for it. I could use the phone drop to get messages from Saul or leave messages for him. But heaven help my ass if a trick called. Sandor flashed the word back in about two seconds flat. So there were disadvantages. I could not hustle, period. If somebody bought me a drink or two or three, fine, as long as I told them I wasn't available for anything else. Walking out with anybody was a no-no. But I liked the cool atmosphere. With my bar tab I felt grown up and if I wanted to hustle, Tricks was right across the street. Sandor and I never talked much. Oh, I could cop acid off of him, cry on his shoulder when I wanted something to get back to Saul. Every once in a while I'd be shooting pool and catch him checking me out while he polished the same glass over and over.

One day when I was just plain bored, I racked the cue and slid onto a stool. Nobody else was around.

"Come on, Sandor, I'll let you buy me a drink."

"See the sign—'no hustling.' " He smiled.

"Ok, lend me some dough and I'll buy us both."

He slid a pound over to me, built us a couple of bacardi and cokes, added a shot of overproof rum to my glass, and sat down across the bar from me.

"Sandor, what does he really feel about me?"

"You have very interesting eyes . . . very interesting . . . like wild violets, beautiful, lonely, perhaps a bit decadent."

"What's 'dickadin'? It sounds dirty." The overproof had gone right to my head.

"It means you feel it's necessary to enjoy what other people feel is shameful."

"Mmmm. You make good drinks. I could tell it was something dirty."

"I try to please."

"I bet you do." We both chuckled and sipped at our drinks. "Are you two really related?"

"Is that Candy's latest wire?"

"Are you?"

"If you go back far enough, everybody is. We're all brothers to dragons."

"You're as bad as he is. I can never understand what you're saying."

"You would, if you didn't try so hard."

So when I walk in I'm not really surprised that it's just another dead end. Sandor has his back to me, leaning over the bar, talking to a guy I never saw before. The guy taps his index finger against the side of the bar to make some point. He sees me and says something to Sandor, who turns around, then turns back to the guy and shakes his head, no. The guy says something else. Sandor shakes his head again. I'm still standing just inside the front door

234

when the guy gets up, walks right up to where I am, looks me up and down like I'm a piece of meat on a rack, and starts to go out the door. I sorta push his shoulder and he spins around.

"Yo, bro'," I ask him, "you got an eye problem?"

The guy laughs. Not a fruity laugh, but like a half-assed tough-guy laugh. I don't like to be laughed at. Meanwhile Sandor has come around from behind the bar and gets between us.

"Go back there like a good boy and sit down," he orders.

"This guy got a problem, bro'."

"A number of them. Go sit down and try to remember the house rules."

I walk on down to the other end. The half-assed tough guy is still laughing. He says something to Sandor, pats him on the arm. They shake hands and then the guy leaves. Sandor comes back with a Bacardi and Coke, ducks under the service counter, and eases himself onto a stool next to me.

"You forgot the overproof."

"You don't need it today." His face is close to mine. His breath is warm and smells like cinnamon.

"I shoulda busted that creep."

"House rules."

"I shoulda busted him anyhow."

"You know what I was telling him right now, just before he went out the door? I was telling him not to break your kneecaps."

"Half-assed tough guy. They don't scare me."

"No, real tough guy. Real, real tough guy. When you weren't muscle-bound you had better sense. And better manners too."

"What about his manners, huh?"

"In his business he doesn't need them."

"Like that, huh?"

"Sidge—the worst kind. They're all bent. You've been causing me problems."

I drain my drink. He pulls over the bottle and points to the sprayer attached to the bar. "The green button is Coke. Pour your own booze."

"Helluva welcome. You'd think I was carrying the plague or something." I lay a ten on top of the bar.

"Put your money away. It's no good today."

"What do you mean about I've been causing you problems?"

235

"For a while they were almost as interested in you as they are in him."

"Me? Should I be flattered?"

"First scared and then sensible."

"Tell me about the scared."

"For a couple of months they were positive you were in it with him. When he stayed away from you completely, they were positive. Thought he was protecting you."

"In what? I don't know what the fuck you're talking about."

"There's a lot you don't know. You don't know that they were so sure they put a contract out on you. Him, they couldn't find. But you were, shall we say, a captive audience. When they checked and found out you were only a dumb kid, they left the contract on, just for g.p. They're like that."

"For Chrissakes, a contract? For what? What the hell are you talking about?"

I guess he knows I don't trust my hands, because he pours out four fingers for me.

"Forget the details. The less you know the better. The credit cards were only the tip of the iceberg. Now they're mad at the guy who fucked them on the contract."

"Who?"

"Oh, I thought you knew. I guess they didn't know you were close friends."

"Who, for Chrissakes?"

"The guy that saved your life, Sheik."

How can you expect treachery from a guy you hardly know? He had a million chances.

"But they *were* right. Sheik, he's just a guy I knew from down at the Deuce a long time back. We weren't even friends, not until the Rock. And even there we just used to rap and shoot the shit." And chant.

"He got his kneecaps busted upstate."

Me, walking around all day like king shit, thinking I'm the great white hunter and all the time it was somebody else doing the hunting.

"Are you gonna tell me what it's all about or are you just gonna keep on talking in riddles?"

"You're better off sometimes with the riddles. Anyhow, you're cool now, so find yourself a rich old john with a heart condition and settle down someplace where it's warm. Forget about him."

"Sure, that's really almighty fucking it. I mean that takes the cake. First I got a contract out on me which I don't know a fucking thing about for doing something which I don't know a fucking thing about and then I don't have a contract anymore which I also don't know about because somebody I don't know found out I never did nothing in the first place. Just great. Pinch me and wake me up."

"Just be sensible." He pats my knee. "If everything wasn't cool they wouldn't have been here waiting for you."

"That's supposed to make sense?"

"Sure it does. You show up here for one reason only—you don't know where he is either and if you don't know, then you're clean. They were just double-checking. That's the way they are. They don't trust anybody, especially not themselves."

"About the money . . . Was there a lot involved?"

"Not much. But they're cheaper than Hebes. Got the first dollar they ever made and want the last one that everybody else makes."

"Ok, so now I'm cool. Tell them I said thanks. What did you mean about 'number two'—being sensible?"

"Be sensible and don't ask me the question you came here to ask me, because he called me, he called me and told me to answer it."

"You know where he is?"

"Nope. If I did, I'd have to tell the management."

"The guys with the bad manners? But if he gave you a message for me, then you should be able to figure it out."

"I didn't try. Didn't want to. You still have eyes the color of wild violets, you know. Pass me the bottle. I get thirsty when I look at you."

"Here, you want me to pour? You mean it's another one of his riddles that doesn't make any sense?"

"Undoubtedly he thinks it will make sense to you, that you'll be able to piece it all together."

"Sunshine knows where he is," I blurt out, surprised that I enjoy the betrayal.

"Be sure they asked him. Be sure he told them and be sure they didn't believe him. They don't believe in anything unless they get it the hard way. Ginneys are very religious, you know." He pats my knee and smiles. "If you go after him, you're only putting yourself under the gun again, starting them thinking again. They're not very good at thinking. That's why they keep guys like me around."

So he didn't cut me loose, he was using me all the time. By keeping far away he confused them with a false scent, made them figure that we had something planned.

"He figures if I'm under the gun he can somehow keep me there?"

"Better you than him. He knows there's a good chance that it might work. And besides, you know what a laugh he's getting out of it."

"Just suppose I managed to find him without them knowing about it."

"So much the better. He'll be able to con you into getting him out, stashing him someplace until he's cooled off. He has faith in your gullibility. Besides, if they let the leash that loose it means that they're losing interest. That's important for him to know. It's only a matter of time. There really wasn't that much dough involved."

"If they waste me, he can still cut and run. If they leave me alone he doesn't have to run. But suppose I waste him?"

"One out of three, that's house odds. Not a bad play at all. He'll take that chance. You never know what's on his mind. Maybe he wants to see whether you're willing to risk your life for him. Maybe he wants to see how much he means to you. Either way, love or hate, it means putting your life on the line. He's forcing you to sacrifice yourself for him."

"He had an expression for that, for forcing someone to make a present of his whole life. You remember it?"

" 'Monstrous vanity,' something pompous like that. Do you still want to know what he told me to tell you?"

"I feel sorry for him. I really feel sorry for him."

"Which means?"

"Don't give me the message. Can I buy you a drink?"

238

"My pleasure, my pleasure." He gives my arm a squeeze and pats me on the back. "Gimme that dough and stop hustling drinks in my joint."

He takes the ten, puts it in the register, and comes back with nine singles and a dollar in change.

"You know, Sinbad, if I was in his shoes I'd do the same thing he's doing now. Why not? He's just trying to get over. If he was in my position he wouldn't think twice about giving me up, if I was stupid enough to give myself away. There's nothing personal about treachery. Usually it's just a matter of common sense. And then there's you to consider. With him out of the picture . . ."

"Yeah . . .?"

"Oh, come on, you're no child anymore. It's not as if it meant anything to you."

"You see a 'for rent' sign on my chest?"

"If it's just a matter of pride you could always give it away."

"I'm not the willing victim type, not anymore I'm not."

"You wouldn't be cockteasing, would you?"

" 'Bye, Sandor. I think I'll do my drinking across the street. There's too much noise in here."

I get up, leaving the singles on the bar. He pushes them toward me.

"You know, I think I envy him."

"He'd laugh right in your face if he heard you say that."

"Don't be in such a rush. Let's talk some business. Downstairs. There's something I want to show you."

"I'll tell you one thing up front, management or no management, I get paid to listen. If I don't like what I hear, I get paid anyhow. Twenty bucks for a half hour of listening—only. And one more thing. You're smarter but I'm stronger. That evens things out, except that I've got an edge."

"And that is?"

"I have nothing to lose."

I know what's downstairs. The same fake wood paneling, a men's room, some steampipes overhead, and a door at the end of a narrow hallway. He unlocks the door and steps aside so I can go in first.

"After you, Sandor."

239

"You don't trust me?"

"Would I be here if I did?"

The office could be somebody's apartment. Everything is brand new and looks like it's never been used. There's a red shag rug on the floor and a matching cover on the platform bed. There's a big modern desk, all curves and no corners. On the desk is an oversized antique telephone. Against a mirrored wall is a black leather couch, a recliner and a glass-top coffee table. The walls are white stucco.

"Color TV, remote control here, also a dimmer for the lights, eight-track stereo. Over there is the bathroom and over here is a serving pantry. The refrigerator is full. It's fully furnished. Even dishes, glasses, silverware, everything. In the closet you'll find sheets and towels and the safe. The safe is mine. Everything else is yours to use . . . if you want to start out fresh. If you agree."

"Agree to do what?"

"Some leg work. Bacardi and coke?"

"Dewar's. On the rocks."

I stretch out on the recliner, waiting. He comes back with the drinks, a notebook under one arm, and sits on the hassock. His hand rests close to my leg, so close that I can feel its heat.

"These are names . . " He flips through the pages of the notebook, making sure that I can't actually read what's on them. ". . . names of people with expensive tastes. You'd be surprised how long it took to put this together."

"I've seen trick books before."

"Not one like this."

I shrug. "Big deal, cocks instead of cunts. What's so special?"

"The names. Their limits."

"Limits?"

"No more than twelve years old."

"Chicken hawks," I scoff, "they make the world go round."

He pats my calf and smiles an unpleasant smile. "I told you, we're talking about limits. Our clients have no sporting instincts. They're not hunters, like us." His hand molds itself around my calf. "Children, that's all they are. They want to be indulged, pampered. The strangest and most insistent fantasies pop into their heads. When it all becomes too much they pick up the telephone . . ."

" . . . to make an obscene phone call?"

"For room service, which is inevitably expensive. You don't realize just how expensive it can get. But children have no sense of the value of money. And they can be very arrogant. Very cruel, if you will."

I brush his hand off my leg, wondering if he has written his own name in the book.

"And children are easily bored too." His face is flushed.

"I suppose that's where imagination comes in."

"Imagination? . . . no," he frowns, " . . .it's limits we're talking about. Without limits nothing is possible because nothing is impossible. Limits are everything."

"Still, runaways are a dime a dozen and then there's always Playland . . . "

"Not for our clients. They're apt to have snoopy neighbors and suspicious doormen. Oh no, our clients are imaginative only in retrospect. They're among the very few who have any innocence left at all. They can't believe that the angelic-looking little ones can be corrupted."

"What about the 'little ones,' as you call them?"

"Oh, them . . . " He brushes away the question with an annoyed wave. "They can't wait to learn about corruption."

"What do you want me to do, Sandor?"

"You, you're enough of a child to be credible and enough of a man to use the credulity of children to your advantage. It'll be easy for you. Think of yourself as a kind of priest. Everybody wants to feel that his secrets are somehow important or, at the very least, shameful. Convince them that only you can operate simultaneously in the realms of the possible and the impossible. They'll appreciate you, I guarantee it. Playland is a gold mine. I want you to work it for me."

"For you?"

"For them, then. Let's not quibble. In the long run it really doesn't matter, does it? Not as long as you get over."

"And after I deliver a corrupt child to a childlike trick, what happens that's so special, that justifies all this . . . effort?"

"Oh, stop. Please stop. Your sarcasm is completely irrelevant. Can you imagine an obstetrician asking a question like that? All you have to do is provide merchandise. We handle everything else. You'll start small. Five bills a week. But if you apply yourself there's plenty of room for advancement." That same shit-eating smile.

"And there's no rule book? Anything can happen to them?"

"Oh, you are a fool. Anything can happen to anybody at any time. Why do you insist on these fucking moral justifications of the obvious. Don't tell me that after more than six years with our mutual friend you're squeamish. You survived. And while you were busy surviving was anybody scrupulous about your . . . what's the word . . . condition? I'm not even telling you to lie. Believe me, in time the merchandise will come flocking to you. You'll be like the weed connection in the schoolyard. Just don't fill in the details, that's all. Without fantasies what is there? Sinbad, you have to be aware that there comes a point when things have gone too far and then no one can back down."

He looks at me like I'm the one trying to convince him.

"What you're saying is that because they're kids, they shouldn't have a choice?"

"What I'm saying is that telling the truth just makes things worse for people. It confuses them."

"Why me? Why did you pick me, Sandor?"

"Isn't that the kind of question you used to ask him? Nobody can answer a question like that. For Chrissakes, right now there is no choice, not for you, not for me. I'm in a bind for reasons which are none of your concern. And you're fresh out of the can. Call it a certain boyish charm that you still retain. People either underestimate you or overestimate you. That's a great asset in the world of business. Let's say I like the idea of being your boss."

"I want two bills up front."

"Good." He pats my knee.

He leaves the closet door open while he squats and twists the dial of the safe, impatiently stuffing falling papers back inside. It's easy to figure out why he's rushing. The guy has no cool at all. None. He comes back and sits down. He has two hundreds in one hand. His other hand rests on my calf.

"Who's minding the store upstairs?"

"Haven't been gone all that long. If anybody comes in, they can wait."

"When do you want me to start?"

"Oh, tomorrow's fine . . day after . . . whenever you get yourself organized. Do you want to move in here?"

"Nope. I'll get my own room somewhere."

"I think it would work out better if you stayed here."

"Better for you, you mean."

"It's no big deal for you. I told you, I was jealous of him. Just this once and that's it. It's over. Strictly business from then on. Come on. Who knows, it might change your luck."

His hand moves up along my leg.

"You're giving me a choice?"

"Why not?" He shrugs. "I told you, it doesn't change anything."

I unzip my fly. As soon as he leans over I catch him right in the throat with a backhand chop. He bounces backwards onto the floor, gagging and rolling around. He grabs at his neck with both his hands like he was being strangled by a ghost. I bend over and give him another chop just to make sure he's out of my way. I put the two bills in my pocket and give him a good kick in the ribs. All the color drains out of his face. He's out for the count. He had been in such a hurry that he forgot to slam the safe shut. I pull everything out onto the floor and pick up a white envelope about two inches thick. I pull off the rubber band and see right away that I don't have time to count it. All I know is that I've never held this much money in my hand at one time before. My heart is thumping against my rib cage. There's no one in the bar, but as I'm going out the door I bump right into the Ginney from before who's coming back in. We stare at each other. He frowns. For one terrible second I think he's going to say something. I'm sure that my face is going to give me away. But whatever it was he changes his mind and goes inside. I hear him calling for Sandor.

There's not a cab in sight. How long before the Ginney checks downstairs? It's always the same in this fucking City, whenever you want a cab you can never find one. It's late afternoon and rush hour is starting. A light spring rain is falling. When I get to Broadway I look in two directions at the same time for an empty cab. Far across the park the sky is beginning to turn purple. A cab squeals to a stop about ten feet in front of me and a guy in a business suit starts to climb in. I run over and pull him out. He starts yelling and shaking his umbrella at me. The cab driver hollers too. I jump in and slam

243

the door and push a ten through the slot in the bulletproof partition. The cab driver shuts up.

"Downtown," I mouth like a goldfish. "Downtown . . I'll tell you where."

I look out the back window half expecting that I'll see the Ginney and some of his friends. All I can see is a lot of traffic and the guy still waving the umbrella. I can't hear a word he's saying.

My heart is pounding like I just ran two miles. The Ginney must have found Sandor by now. It was a stupid move. Stupid. Now I really got my ass in a sling. I'm hot as a firecracker and the other stuff, now they'll believe I was in that too. What am I supposed to do, call them? Tell them, nah, I didn't have nothing to do with that, whatever it was, just this one, just break my kneecaps for this one. It's not only fear, it's excitement. I start to take the envelope out of my pocket and see that the cabbie is looking at me in the rearview mirror. I got to get somewhere to count it out. Somewhere where I can lock a door and sit down and think. I wonder if they'll believe me that up to the last minute I wasn't sure what I was going to do. What would he say—something about "nice distinctions"? I wish he was around so I could ask him what the next move is. Anything can happen to anybody at any time. It was Sandor's fault for leaving the safe open. Is that what I should tell them? No, things have come to that point where nobody can back down. It's my money now.

We get stuck on Forty-seventh in traffic. I slide the last of the singles in my pocket through the slot. All I have left is what's in the envelope. I got a lot of mileage out of the watch.

It's still drizzling. Across the street is the McKinley Hotel, a fancy place for tourists. A real hotel, not some fleabag dump. I'm still wearing my going-home clothes from this morning. The desk clerk looks at me like he's scared I'm going to stick him up. I tell him I want the best room in the house. Before he can tell me that there's nothing available I find a twenty in the envelope and lay it on him. He remembers that the bridal suite is free. Not free—fifty-seven bucks a night. I pay him for two nights and sign his name. How many times have I heard *him* say that you can't really enjoy getting over unless you have a macabre sense of humor. The desk clerk rings for a bellboy and I have to explain how I left my bags at the airport. My excuses don't mean a fucking thing to anybody but me. The lobby smells of wood and varnish, cigar smoke and perfume. It's a money smell. The women wear expensive gowns. They look like they all just stepped out of the beauty parlor. The men are jowly and balding and wear diamond pinky rings. I shouldn't be here. This is their world. I'm intruding on it. All that stands between me and the service entrance is one envelope.

The bellboy opens the door and shows me around. The bedroom has wall-to-wall everything, including the biggest bed I've ever seen, with a white canopy, no less. The dressers and chairs are light blue with gold trim. There are mirrors all over. The bathroom is huge. I don't believe the round marble tub. The knobs are gold—gold swans. We go back into the living room and he shows me how to operate the push-button control for the drapes and the TV. Saul would love the bar. He'd love the whole place. He'd know how to act and what to do. I tip the bellboy a couple of dollars. I can tell by the way he smiles that I gave him too much.

I empty out the envelope onto the brown velvet couch and, sitting on the edge, stack the money in piles of hundreds, fifties, and twenties. There's nothing smaller than a twenty in the envelope. When I'm done I count each pile. Then I mix all the piles together and start stacking and counting again. There are eight hundreds, nine fifties, and thirty twenties. I jump up whooping and hollering. It's mine. No way they're going to get it back. It's mine. I turn up the radio full blast. The speakers are terrific. If the neighbors don't like the volume, fuck 'em. It's party time. I got over like a fat rat. Fuck the Ginneys. It's mine now and if they catch me they're going to be in for a big disappointment, but I have to move fast. The quicker I spend it the less they can take back if they find me. When they find me. I stare at the money, trying to attach some meaning to it. When I was a kid that would have been three whole weeks' worth of dope. For Saul that's seven months' rent sitting there. Let me try it another eay. In those three piles there are a hundred and fifty tricks. Think how long it takes to turn a hundred and fifty tricks. How many sick mornings, how much hanging out in the middle of winter, how much pain, how many tears does that money cancel out? How ridiculously easy it is to wipe away everything in the few seconds it took for me to pick up the envelope and put it in my pocket. How simple it is to survive when you stop thinking failure. All you have to do is invent

245

success. Look at it. That's more than Sheik bought with twenty-five years. Much more. And how much is twenty-five years worth to him upstate? Shit, I don't give a fuck what they do to me. I got twenty-five years to spend and I can cram it all into one night if I try hard enough.

I put three or four hundred dollars in my pocket and stick the rest back in the envelope, which I hide under the carpet. Then I head down from the bridal suite to the clothing store in the lobby. How many times I've passed the display window and stopped to look, sure that I could never buy anything in there, feeling an immense gap between me and the shoppers who strolled so casually in and out of the store. What an immense gap between me now and me then, and the difference was bridged by a couple of inches of dirty green paper.

I start with a pair of black leather pants. Then a black velour slipover with a high collar and ruffled cuffs. Black banlon underwear and socks. A classy wallet. An umbrella. A bottle of expensive cologne, the kind he liked. I slip a rough nugget of gold onto my finger to see if it fits.

By this time I have both the salesman and the manager trailing after me. I point to a gold chain with a medal that matches the ring. On it is carved a small boy who smiles as he rides on the back of some kind of fish through waves of gold. Finally I have them wrap up a pair of calf-length boots, patent leather with gold buckles.

Upstairs I peel everything off me and throw the whole pile into the wastebasket. After I take a steaming hot shower, I rub myself all over with cologne. I smell good enough to eat.

When I'm dressed I look in the mirror. The kid who used to stand with his nose pressed against the window downstairs has vanished completely. The guy I'm looking at is young. He looks like success. His eyes are bright and clear and smiling. He's got a good build. He's a guy who can handle himself no matter what happens. A guy who snaps his fingers when he wants something. A guy who doesn't ask what something costs.

Back downstairs I pat my pocket to double-check that the wallet is there. I leave the key at the desk and walk next door to a fancy restaurant, the kind we used to go to when things were really going good for him, and order a porterhouse steak medium well and a bottle of champagne. Nobody notices me. I'm not out of place. I belong here.

I take my time. I have all the time in the world, maybe twenty-four hours if I play it smart. When I'm done eating I grab a cab up to Lincoln Center and walk around the block to one of those new high-rises that looks like a fairy-tale tower of terraces and glass sparkling in the night. I'm in another world. A world of rich people going to concerts. A world of cabs and restaurants, of leather and gold. I'm in the real world at last, where everything is first class for as long as the ride lasts. This morning the doorman would have probably made me go around to the service entrance. Tonite he's polite and calls me "sir" when he asks who I want to see.

Frankie is home. Frankie is always home. Still the same red silk lounging pajamas and the big friendly grin. Behind the grin is one treacherous dude. You don't get a fabulous crib like this one by being a nice guy. In the sunken living room with the fountain and paintings and statues I count out five hundred bucks.

"I need a piece."

"Thirty-eight?"

"Too big. I don't want a fucking cannon. Something big enough to stop a dude but not so small that it's gonna make him die laughing."

"I got a twenty-five automatic. Full clip. Clean. Yard and a half for you."

"Sold. And let me have two o-zees of the best smoke you got, whatever, as long as it's the best. Gimme the rest in coke."

Frankie smiles. "What happened, you hit the number?"

"Nah, I hit the whole fucking Mafia." I laugh. Frankie laughs too. I know that as soon as I'm out the door he'll be on the horn. While he's getting the stuff together I count what's left in the wallet. I hit him up for some bambu and borrow his shoulder bag— black leather, of course—to carry everything in.

"Watch out, Sinbad. It's a cold cruel world out there."

"Yo, bro'. You know what they say—it's their world. I'm only passing through."

"Take good care of yourself and keep the bag, for luck."

"I don't need any luck, bro'. Me, I lead a charmed life."

247

I have no trouble catching a cab in front of Lincoln Center. It's one of those old wide Checkers where I can stretch out my legs and roll up some herb on the way uptown.

A light drizzle is falling again as I enter the Europa. From the time it opened to a fanfare of press items the Europa was the most popular bathhouse in town, maybe in the whole country. You waited on a block-and-a-half-long line to get the once-over from the bouncer. Maybe he let you in and maybe he didn't. That's the way it was, take it or leave it. The streets were jammed with El-Dees, Mark IVs, Mercedeses, XKEs, even Bentleys and Rollses. The piss-elegant queens made their grand entrances; straight-looking guys from TV and movies showed on the set, grinning for the flashbulbs. Rich johns came from all over, the ones with white leather trench coats and thousand-dollar watches, and the older ones in dark business suits and diamonds sparkling on their pinkies. And along with the johns came the hustlers. Not the raggedy greasy ones from the Deuce but the bleached-blond pros from Fifty-third, the bronzed hundred-dollar tricks from Miami, the sleek call boys from New Orleans, and the rhinestone cowboys of Los Angeles. And the rock stars arrived in their peacock feathers and the dudes in their tight jeans showing seven inches of cock to the giggling aunties from Cherry Grove. The Europa was it, the only place to be and be seen. How many nights I leaned out of our window, taking in the crowd, which waited impatiently for admission to this most fabulous palace of pleasure. I begged him to take me.

"Please Saul, please . . . I'll pay. I just don't want to go by myself."

"Patience, ruffian. You know how I hate crowds. Wait for the stars' descent."

"Stars? What the fuck do stars have to do with anything?"

"My boy, you'll soon learn: faggotry thy name is fickleness. No matter what: bar, disco, club, bathhouse—at birth their stars rise high in the night sky to blaze in splendor for a few fleeting months, then fall back to Earth spluttering for an instant, and before you know it the party's over and a new star rises in the east. Wait for the fall. Believe me, you'll enjoy it much more then."

"You ashamed to take me, is that it?"

"Nonsense. Those clowns down there put on their white

gloves before they'll even dream about sucking a prick. People like us should always be on the bottom side of elegance looking up. Who the fuck wants to feel self-conscious in the midst of the flesh pots?"

And he was right. All of a sudden, no lines, no more limousines, no more beautiful people. The new customers seemed a little bit shabby—maybe *shady* is the word: uninteresting people who looked back over their shoulders before they took the plunge. But when we did finally go, it was still a luxury trip, if you didn't look too closely in the corners and as long as the lights were dim. With just a scattering of regulars it was like a private club. Because I was young I was an attraction and I loved every minute of it.

The entrance area is tiny. Chula is behind the cage taking money and giving out towels, only there was no one to give them to except me. Still, he had to pretend that there was something to do besides regret the past, so he stacked and unstacked piles of linen. I have to call his name to get him to look up. The press clippings on the wall are three years old, and the carpet is frayed in places.

"Nene, my God, you look divine, so butch. It's been ages."

"Just got out today, baby, que pasa?"

"Oooo, weren't you the lucky boy, locked up with all that rough trade. It makes my asshole twitch just to think about it."

Chula has to be the most beautiful male I've ever seen. He's—what?—about twenty-six or so, but he still can pass for sixteen in the right light. He's Spanish, real Spanish, from Spain—Madrid, he once told me. When he was a little kid he practiced to become a bull fighter. All the kids did, he said, and that's where he must have developed his amazing grace. Each movement, each gesture looks like it's been rehearsed for hours and yet, at the same time, it's completely casual. When he lights a cigarette you feel you should applaud. He doesn't walk, he glides, he performs, he tosses his long black hair—well, arrogantly. Arrogantly, that's the only word for it, like one of those old Spanish conquerors you see in paintings. His skin is olive gold, his face is hairless. When he's excited his eyes burn right through you and he snorts like a horse. As beautiful as he is he still has a man's body: hard and muscular in the right places, especially his calves. Around his wrists and ankles he wears golden bangles. "My gypsy blood," he sighs.

For a few weeks I thought I was in love with him. I was furious with Saul when he refused to try to argue me out of leaving him to be with Chula forever. I had to turn three tricks to get the money to get Chula into bed and then I was disappointed. He did everything expertly, exactly as if he had rehearsed it all a thousand times. He was all flare and no warmth, all flash and no substance. Up close I saw the lines at the corners of his mouth and could tell that he'd been around the horn too many times, that his perpetual cheerfulness could not mask what was actually impatience and boredom. Chula has to be admired from a distance, and then only by an audience. But we stayed friendly, if not exactly friends, and tonight I'm glad to see him because there's nothing at all I want from him.

He wags a finger at me. "I see you've been a naughty boy."

My stomach falls somewhere down around my kneecaps. I pat the bag just to make sure the automatic is safe.

"I mean the fab costume and all. Oooooo, let me see the crown jewels. Mmmm . . real gold?"

"Your voice and God's ears. I wish it was, but don't tell anyone, willya?"

"Your ex has been around . . ."

"Let's not talk about him, huh?"

"As bad as that?"

"What's worse than yesterday's love affair? Anybody else been asking for me?"

"Not a soul."

"When they do, tell me first, before you answer any questions."

I duke a twenty on him, knowing that they'll get around to checking here before long. Maybe I can buy an edge, an extra ten minutes, that is, if they haven't been here already or if they don't duke him more when they get here. All I can count on is Chula's unpredictability. Of course it won't be long before I run out of edges and then it's just a matter of who washes their hands of me first. They'll be knocking each other down to get to the head of the line.

"How long you planning to stay, Nene?"

"Don't know yet. Let's wait and see what happens. But tonite I want the best cube you got and make sure there's a locker for the goodies." I pat the bag again and wink to let him know that as soon as he gets off I'll turn him on. I take the key and towel and give him a little clenched-fist salute. He blows me a kiss and pirouettes back to his laundry.

Above the stairs leading down is an artificial sky studded with electric stars. Then you round a corner and the sky and stars are gone. It takes a few blinks to accustom your eyes to the darkness. Lights of all colors flash over the dance floor, multiplying themselves in the mirrored walls, floors, and ceiling. The d.j. booth is empty. The sound thumps from the juke box, a sad and savage wailing that's followed me around all day long. A lonesome little queen who can't be more than seventeen whirls under the inevitable mirror ball with a phantom lover. She writhes as she stretches out her arms, reaching for her thousand reflected images, which seem to smile their approval. To the left a fantastic waterfall cascades from plastic rocks, gushing through a papier-mâché ravine filled with red and purple plants into the clear emerald depths of the pool some twelve feet below. The whole scene glows eerily in the spectral wash of turquoise floodlights. A wonderful grotto, strange and startling, exotic and cheap.

Around the pool is a mosaic tile walk and on the walk white and green wrought-iron furniture and some beach chairs. In one of them a hairy fat man dozes under an ultraviolet lamp, a towel wrapped around his crotch. He looks vaguely familiar but I can't place him. I think of a beached whale and smile.

On the far side of the grotto is a pool table standing almost in blackness. Light is directed at the table from a swinging green lampshade suspended a foot over the table. Two guys, a year or two younger than me, wearing fringed suede jackets, Levi's, and cowboy boots, are shooting a quarter a game. The same quarters will pass back and forth all night long except for occasional interruptions when one of them goes in back with a trick. When he's through the game will pick up where it left off. The taller of the two chews on a toothpick while figuring out the angles. I stand there for a few seconds, watching the game. The shorter one who's kind of cute, with a pug nose and dirty blond cowlick, gives me the once-over, trying to decide whether I'm a hustler myself or a young trick. I let him think about it for a while and take a seat at the snack bar.

251

With the snack bar and the cocktail lounge next door, the pool, the sauna, the steam room, the disco, and a nice, warm bed back in one of the cubes you could stay down here partying forever—at least until you ran out of money. I remember when the two of us camped out for more than a month and emerged, suntanned—me wearing a cotton shirt and shorts—into a raging blizzard. It blew our minds. We had completely forgotten that there were still seasons.

An old hustling buddy is working behind the snack bar. Zeno is a pretty boy with curly black hair, a solemn expression, soulful eyes, and a slim, hard body. He could get over on his nationality alone, if he had to. Zeno's Greek. He was also a cabin boy and, yes, he told me, everything you ever heard about Greek cabin boys is true. He jumped ship at fifteen, discovered the Square, and hustled happily ever after. The problem is that Immigration can snatch him up and deport him at any time. So he lives as well as works down here and surfaces as infrequently as possible.

"Greek, you old fuck, how's it hanging?"

"My God, look at you!" He throws down the bar mop and hugs my neck. "Sinbad, come home from the wars."

"And rarin' to go. What the fuck happened to this joint? It's as quiet as a fucking tomb."

"Well, you know, it picks up a little, later on—but not much. You look great. Really great. Who the fuck did you rob?"

"If I told you I hit the number would you believe me?"

"Nope."

"How 'bout a mysterious lover?"

"Oh, speaking of your lover . . ."

"Don't. I'm footloose and fancy free and loaded with goodies. Let's go inside and get drunk. Then we can go back to my cube and turn on."

"Whatchoo got?"

"Name it and claim it."

"My God, I can't just walk off now. They'll fire my ass."

"Bullshit. Who you gonna wait on—the two pool sharks over there? Come on, anyone wants anything you can see them from the bar."

He looks around at empty stools and sighs. "Ah, shit, or as

252

your ex would say, 'Come let us sit before the bar and tell sad stories of the death of queens.' This joint is going to pot anyhow."

We have the bar to ourselves, except for DeSantis—everybody calls him Suits-and-Boots—a grim old man who'd rather be caught dead than in the white clamdiggers worn by all the other hired help. He has a different three-piece suit and matching boots for each day of the week. Saul swore oaths by DeSantis's stingers and many was the night that I poured him to bed at four ayem after he'd opened the joint at eight the morning before. "It's the bar stools, my boy, most comfortable fit in town. DeSantis's doing— he's a crafty devil." It was a lounge after his own heart—dim, plush, expensive, with black-and-gold-flecked smoked-glass mirrors on every side, "spawned by a fag with a soul of pure kitsch."

"Build us a pitcher of stingers, you dirty old man," I bellow.

DeSantis looks doubtful. The cost of building will be in the neighborhood of twenty bucks.

"Your old man owes me."

"Fuck my old man. He ain't my old man and I'm tired of telling everybody I don't want to talk about him. You got problems, tell your accountant." And I slam a fifty down on the bar. I can't decide whether he's trying to smile or whether he's sucking on a lemon, but he pours and swizzles and comes up with a jug of 'amber fire, my boy.' "

"Fucker, get out of my head. Can't I even croak in peace?"

"It's like that, huh," says the Greek.

"Shut up, Greek. It's my party and if I want to talk to myself it's my business. Here, gimme your glass."

"You in some kind of trouble?"

DeSantis is polishing glasses with his back toward us, listening to every word. The stingers go down smooth as silk. I've missed stingers. They're sneaky and they make me horny as hell.

"My middle name—trouble." I pass him a joint.

"You still stuck on him?"

"I'm not stuck." I toss a joint to DeSantis, who catches it with one hand behind his back, like a juggler. "He's stuck, Greek, like fucking flypaper. He's all over me, inside and out, and he just won't go 'way."

"What you need is a change of luck."

253

"Is that a proposition?"

"Nah, a suggestion." He hooks his thumb in the direction of the two gangsters shooting pool.

"You like that? I'm buying. Either one or both, however you want it, old buddy."

"You really did hit the number, didn't you?"

The pitcher is already half empty and Frankie's smoke is dynamite.

"Nope. You were right the first time."

DeSantis is all ears.

"As long as money's no object—they're both cute."

"Fuck you, DeSantis, you don't even look like Kojak. Come on, Greek, grab the pitcher and we'll change the scene. And you, you impotent old fuck, if anybody wants my buddy the Greek here, for the next half hour, tell 'em to knock on my door. You don't knock and I'll blow your fucking Ginney brains out, understand?"

I fumble in the bag for the piece and wave it in the general direction of his back.

"Come on, Sinbad, put that shit away and be cool. Don't pay him no mind, DeSantis, he just come home today."

"I ain't got a home and I hate fucking Ginneys" I pout as he leads me out by the elbow, holding the pitcher in his other hand. Either he handles stingers better than me or the ten months on the Rock fucked up my head for booze completely. The Greek checks out my key to find out what cube I'm in. The asshole with the toothpick is staring at me. I don't like people who stare at me.

"Yo, bro'." I point. "Yeah, you with the toothpick, commere a minute."

"Sinbad, don't start nothing."

"Git the fuck offa my arm, Greek. Who's starting anything? You, Toothpick, I told you to get over here."

Toothpick is figuring whether to throw down with the cue stick or go into his pocket for his shank. He decides on the cue stick and motions for his buddy to follow.

"You got a problem?" The buddy eases over behind me. One look at the piece and both gangsters would piss in their pants.

"No, I ain't got a problem. My friend the Greek here got a problem. He's blind in one eye and can't see outta the other, right, Greek? He gotta be fucking blind, because he thinks you're cute."

254

"Sinbad!"

"Shut up. I told you it's *my* party."

"What the fuck do you mean cute? Who's cute?"

"You're cute, leastwise according to my buddy the Greek. Me, I think you're just plain ugly."

"I think I'm gonna bust your jaw." He swings back the cue stick like a baseball bat.

"I don't think you are." And I flash a twenty under his nose.

He lets the cue stick drop nice and easy.

"Why dintcha say so?" He smiles. The blond kid eases around where I can see him, grinning from ear to ear.

"Money talks and bullshit walks, so walk. We're all going back to my cube."

The cube is about the size and shape of a cell. On the floor there's a wide mattress made up with sheets. Next to it is a metal gym locker. The only other furniture is a rickety wooden chair. Greek and me squat on the mattress-bed, with the pitcher on the floor between us. The blond kid is scrunched on a corner of the bed because Toothpick grabs the chair first. A dim red bulb provides the only light. I hand the Greek a joint and tell him to light up. Then I tap some coke out onto a matchbook cover. When I'm through blasting off I tap some more out and pass the matchbook around. Greek snorts and is instantly pleased to meet himself in outer space. Toothpick grunts, blocking off one nostril with his finger so he can get a heavy blow. The blond kid sways back and forth, humming to himself. Nobody has anything to say. I take the Greek's head between my hands and lean forward to give him a shotgun.

"You want one," I ask Toothpick.

"Nah, that's ok." He doesn't want our mouths to touch.

"Yes you do." I crinkle the twenty under his nose. He shrugs and squats in front of me with his lips parted. I grab him by the ears and pull his head forward, forcing his mouth against mine. Then I blow a lungful of smoke down his throat. While he's still choking, my tongue probes inside his mouth. He pushes me away and wipes off his lips with the back of his hand. The Greek shakes his head. The blond giggles. I grab Toothpick by the hair, yanking him forward again. I kiss him, hard. A little blood trickles down his chin.

255

"I told you, bro', it's my party. I'm the one supposed to enjoy hisself, me and my buddy the Greek. You're just the hired help. Any time you wanna quit, there's the door."

I push him back on the floor and toss the twenty in his lap. "Wipe your mouth off with that. You'll be amazed how much better you feel."

The blond kid puts his head down so Toothpick won't see him laughing. Just for that I lay another joint on him. Toothpick sticks the twenty in his pocket and gives the blond a dirty look. I swig out of the pitcher and pass it to the Greek.

"Look at 'em, Greek. Would you believe a guy was trying to tell me today that there's no such thing as having a choice. That it's completely irrevelant."

"Irrelevant."

"That's what I said. And I don't need some fucking Greek to teach me how to talk English."

I punch him in the arm and lay another line of blow on him. I feel like I can see through walls. That I can see deep inside anyone, see everything—their secrets, their greed, the things they're ashamed of, the little places they themselves don't want to discover. Greek is an open book. Right now this room and what's going on in it is the whole world. The minute he leaves it ends, for him. I love him for it.

"How 'bout it, Toothpick? Do you believe in limits, the ones that you can't conceive of?" He looks at me blankly, trying to pick up some clue.

"Whyn't you let it go, Sinbad?"

"Greek, you old hound dog, I love you." I try to kiss him but he slides away. "Don't worry, old buddy, I let go this afternoon and I'm still floating away. Let me enjoy my party my way. You two, strip down, I wanna see what I'm buying."

The blond kid looks at Toothpick, who shrugs. They both stand up and start peeling off their jackets and Levi's. The blond kid is wearing briefs. His legs are white and smooth. Toothpick's boxer shorts are way too big on him. You can see he has less meat than the blond. His legs are well developed and hairy, like a jogger's. The Greek takes a deep breath.

"The drawers too."

Toothpick drops his shorts and lays down behind us on the

bed, waiting for somebody to blow him. The blond looks embarrassed as he steps out of his skivvies.

"Get the fuck offa my bed," I yell at Toothpick. "Who the fuck told you you could lay down on my bed?"

"Well what the fuck do you want to do? Come on, whatever it is, get it over with."

"You want to know what to do? ok, I'll tell you . . . my friend there, the Greek. Get down on your knees and suck him off."

"Bull—shit, I will!" Toothpick jumps to his feet. "Bullshit. I don't play that shit. That's what you want, get yourself somebody else."

The Greek is upset. "Sinbad, you know you don't do things that way. Give it some time, relax. We're supposed to be having a good time, remember?"

"*I'm* supposed to be having a good time, remember? You, old buddy, you got the same choice anybody else does. You want him or you don't. It don't mean a fucking thing to me either way."

"I didn't say I didn't want him, did I?" He smiles as he unzips his fly and pulls out his dick. The Greek has a hardon.

"Come on, Lennie, we're tipping." Toothpick picks up his drawers but the blond kid doesn't move. He sees the other twenty I'm holding.

"One more for you, Toothpick, if you tell me I didn't hear you right."

He stands there, confused, looking at his drawers like he just got caught shoplifting them.

"Well, did I hear you right?" He shakes his head. "Speak up, bro'."

"Ok, fuck it. I'll do it. But you shoulda said something before."

He gets down on his knees in front of the Greek. You can see he's not used to cocksucking. He takes the Greek's dick in his hand and looks it over doubtfully. Then he closes his eyes and eases the head into his mouth. He gags and pulls back. His eyes are tearing. Nobody says a word. The blond watches with growing interest while he strokes his own hard-on. Toothpick looks up at me like he thinks I'm going to tell him it was all a joke.

"Go ahead, Toothpick. Suck his dick and cut out the horseshit."

He looks from side to side as if somebody else should make

257

the decision. Closing his eyes, he swallows hard and goes back down on the Greek. The Greek jams his whole dick in and leans back on the pillow. His eyes are closed too. He starts to whimper. Toothpick chokes and retches but his lips keep slurping up and down.

"Your turn, Blondie. It's buddy-fucking time. Now you get down there and fuck your old buddy while he's sucking my old buddy off."

You can see the blond kid likes the idea. Toothpick pretends not to hear. It's all an impossible joke. I slap some of his drool onto Blondie's dick. Blondie squats and manages to push it into Toothpick's ass. Toothpick's groans excite the Greek. His ass raises up off the mattress as he shoots his load into Toothpick's mouth. While Toothpick is spitting out the cum, Blondie grabs hold of his hips, getting it as deep inside his buddy as he can and grunts while he's coming. He couldn't have been humping Toothpick for more than two minutes.

Everybody except me is breathing hard. I toss Toothpick's drawers to the Greek to use as a shot rag. When he's done he hands them to Blondie. Blondie wipes himself off, never looking at Toothpick. The cube stinks of the cologne I doused myself with. I duke the twenty on Toothpick.

"Here, go buy yourself a new pair of drawers,"

The Greek kills the jug while the pool sharks get dressed.

After I lock the door, I hear them arguing in the hall. Gradually the noise fades away.

While the Greek puts the finishing touches to his hair, I stick another blow under his nose.

"What's wrong, Sinbad?"

"Wrong? I thought you had a ball. I thought that's what you wanted."

"That wasn't sex and you know it."

"But you dug it."

"Don't remind me. I might decide that I don't like you very much."

"I didn't ask you to like me, good buddy, just invited you to join the party. What was it?"

"What was what?"

258

"What was all that if it wasn't sex?"

He turns his palms upward. "I don't know if there's a word for it. The way you've been since you walked in, like a wild man, waving the piece, yelling, the shit with DeSantis . . ."

"He was eavesdropping, the cocksucker."

"So what? He does it all the time and you know it. It never bothered you before. You're ripping yourself apart over something just like my uncle did. Listen, maybe you can understand me. My uncle, he had this orchard, a grove, way out in the country. Olive trees. They have white blossoms and they smell good. The old guy loved those trees like they were his children. Well, the place had been in the family for years, before the Turks, way back. Nobody could remember how long. Wars, nothing, nothing changed the place. Like I said, it was way out in the country. And there he was, the old guy and his olive trees. That's all he wanted. Then the Colonels came in. These weren't Tedeschi, foreigners, they were Greeks, our own kind, the worst kind. All Greeks have a streak of cruelty in them. With the Colonels it was more than a streak. Well, to make a long story short, somebody came up from Athens in a black car. He had a paper that said the old guy owed so-and-so much—for back taxes. Taxes? The place had been in the family for hundreds and hundreds of years. What taxes? And besides, the old guy couldn't read. There was nothing to do. Everybody was afraid, his neighbors, it could happen to them, maybe. So they hoped that the paper was right, you see? That it was happening to somebody else instead of them. Well, with the colonels it wasn't like the Germans. Nobody wanted to get involved. They gave the old guy a couple of weeks to pack up his shit. Not that he had that much, but he couldn't just pack up the olive trees, could he? The last night the house was already empty. Who knows what he was thinking? Maybe, why me, why me and not somebody else? And then, see, if you understood Greek, there's a word—*agon*. It means like suffering agony because you want to, because it's the only way you can get even when everything gets all fucked up and it's not your fault. All you can do is yell at God, "Hey, you, you can't do a thing to me because I'm gonna do it myself." I'm not explaining it too good, am I? What he did, my uncle, was burn all the olive trees down and then he burned down the empty house around him."

259

"Greek, Greek, my buddy." I try to take him in my arms. "Greek, old buddy, I'm drunk and I'm fucked up so tell me, what the fuck do the olive trees have to do with me?"

He puffs on a joint while he gets his thoughts together.

"There must be something very beautiful to you that you can't bear to be separated from. Something you love so much that you'd rather burn yourself up than lose it, before you'd let somebody else touch it."

"And what happens if whatever it is you thought was so beautiful and so wonderful turns out to be a piece of worthless shit? Then what?"

"Maybe that's why people like my uncle do what they do, before it ever can get to that."

"And maybe they do it because they're afraid that they'll find out the truth, that they've chumped themselves off for a fake. Maybe they'd rather burn themselves up before they face facts."

"Facts!"

"It's not a dirty word."

"You remember when we were down on the Square together, me just off the boat and still wet behind the ears, a greenhorn ship's punk. How you used to go with me whenever I went with a trick so the guy wouldn't take advantage of me, because I didn't know what was the right way to do anything. You remember? I do. Who told you you had to do that? In those days you couldn't have did what you did here tonite. We were both out in the streets hustling our asses off to survive, but you cared. For no reason at all. Was that chumping yourself off?"

"Worse, Greek. I was chumping you off. All I was doing for you is what I needed someone to do for me. I shoulda let you learn the hard way. Me, right now, if I want to get rid of everything, believe me, I got my reasons. But it's not because I can't let go, like your uncle. I gotta rip everything out of me—weakness, pity, sentiment—so that there's nothing left for somebody else to come along and rip out."

"Sinbad," he says, getting up and brushing himself off, "I've gotta get back to work. I'll say one thing. When you throw a party it sure is different. Wouldn't of missed it for the world."

"Anytime, good buddy, mi casa, su casa."

"I'll take you up on that later when I'm through work.

Meanwhile, do us both a favor and lock up the piece. You want anything to eat?"

"Not now. Maybe later, though."

"Stay away from the hamburgers. I think DeSantis defrosts them under his armpits. Take care of yourself, buddy."

"Palante, bro'."

After he leaves I strip down and hang everything up in the locker, including the goody-bag. I jiggle the handle to make sure that it's locked. The cube key is on an elastic band, which I slip over my ankle. Then I stretch out on top of the mattress, resting my chin on the floor.

I want to think about something, anything, but nothing comes. The scene with the two kids and the Greek—maybe it wasn't sex. So what? I don't owe myself explanations anymore. The coke has me leveled off on an icy plateau, somewhere where the air is thin and fire no longer gives heat. Somewhere beyond choices, because I'm alone and I've left the world far below. I've left them all and by the time they catch up to me the joke will be on them. I won't be able to feel anything at all. I get up and wrap the towel around my waist and pad barefoot through the corridor. At the snack bar the Greek is camping it up with a customer. The pool sharks are hooked up in their endless game.

I strip off the towel and plunge naked into the pool—down, down, not into cold but into warmth. My fingertips touch bottom. Arching my back I kick out and glide slowly upward. I have complete control over my body. I am cradled in an ocean of ease and well-being. For a moment my lungs forget to demand air. I am content to drift in timelessness, forever freed from dreams, despair, and dread. And then I burst cleanly through the surface, spewing and gulping, my body poised in midair, aching for return to the oblivion of the deep.

The impulse to dive again is almost overpowering. I pull myself onto the tile floor and fill my lungs. I force myself not to look at the pool, not to hear the water's rapturous invitation.

As soon as I enter the steam room I'm enveloped in blinding fog. Fog thick and hot, rising from floor to ceiling. The heat is a living presence, burning my feet, assaulting my legs, pressing on my chest and temples, stinging my nostrils. Sweat erupts from every pore, rolling off my body, sluicing down my face into my

261

mouth. I take two steps forward and can no longer see the door behind. I am something slippery and sinuous, sloshing through infernal mists. All sense of direction has vanished. From unseen recesses issue sounds of lapping and groaning, the slopping of belly upon belly. I grope for walls. I am lost. A hand reaches out. I stumble on in agony. I slip, falling against a seated body. Slithering against each other, we explore each other with hands and lips. We hug, seek each other's tongues, mingle the salt taste of our mouths. I clutch him to me, knowing that if I let him go for a moment I will disappear. He is stronger, much stronger than I am. I gasp for breath but he presses me down, caressing my arms, my thighs, my groin, still forcing me forward and down until the stone rasps against my chest and I am prone and helpless, my head twisted at a painful angle. I want to tell him something and just then he enters me. I feel him thrusting deep inside me and I writhe and moan and come to a blubbering climax. For a moment I am triumphant, knowing that I have broken *his* hold over me at last, knowing that I can now seize pleasure wherever I discover it. He turns me over roughly, kissing my belly and groin, lapping up the fluids of my body. I feel myself swell again and hear him laugh.

"Too much loving makes men mad."

"No," I scream, and beat at the fog with my fists, tearing it away until his face becomes visible for one horrible second.

"You!"

"In the flesh."

And then I am alone and he has vanished. I jump up and make a dash toward where the door should be, banging my head hard against the wall. I find myself stunned and dazed on the floor, wiggling a loose tooth and spitting out blood. The door opens. Someone else comes in and I crawl forward toward the light four feet away.

I pull myself up to my feet. The pool is empty. The waterfall splashes invitingly. Naked and bloody I dash up to the Greek.

"Where did he go? Which way. Tell me!"

"Jesus Christ, Sinbad, what did you do to yourself? You're a fucking mess." He dabs at my bruises with a damp cloth. I push his hand away.

"Where?"

"I tried to tell you he was here, but you didn't want to listen.

262

For Chrissakes, put a towel around you or something. You look like a fucking maniac."

"Where, goddamn you?" I yell as I try to climb over the counter.

"In back, in the cubes. What the fuck is the matter with you? Calm down for a minute and get your shit together."

He hands me a glass of water. I have no idea what to do with it.

"I'm sorry, Greek, I'm sorry."

"I am too." He shakes his head.

I have no time to console him. I feel like I'm suffocating as I turn to race down the corridor. My door is ajar. I must have forgotten to lock it. I fumble for the light switch. Where the fuck is it? In the dark I struggle with the locker, finally matching key with lock. I rip the bag open and pull out the twenty-five. A bright light flicks on overhead. I crouch and spin around to see him seated on the bed, with a towel wrapped around his midsection. His bare legs are stretched out casually in front of him, his face is wrinkled in amusement at the automatic which trembles in my hands, quavering less than a foot from his forehead.

Before I can pull the trigger he tosses my pants to me. Involuntarily I catch them with one hand, while I firm up my grip on the gun butt with the other.

"You'd look a bit more convincing in trousers. It's hard to take a naked man seriously . . . mmm . . . especially one who's armed."

From the time I left the Fort I allowed myself to be carried by a swift soothing current toward a dawn where they waited to rip my guts out. Because I gave myself to them freely, I was beyond their power. All they could do was cause pain, but pain without fear or regret is no pain at all. In fact, it is power.

Now he has reduced me to impotence. He's forced me to drag myself out of the current back into the present, back into the time which it takes for me to finish it with him. He's made me put off my acceptance and by putting it off for the sake of the present, even if just this instant, I must put it off for each instant after. He has condemned me to life and I am once again vulnerable and afraid.

I slip into my pants because I don't know what else to do with them, but I keep my grip on the automatic and never for an instant take my eyes away from his face. My mother was right. Dreams do

263

mean the opposite. He doesn't look the least bit surprised and, I've got to admit, he doesn't look the least bit scared either.

"You're not afraid?"

"Mmmm . . . I'm sure that your fear is sufficient to cover the demands of the situation."

"And I'm sure that you're about to get the shock of your life."

"Gallows humor? Even lower than wryness, my boy. Ah, Sinbad, with all the world so wide why waste what little wit you have? You look simply ridiculous, you know."

"Sinbad's gone. Steven's around now."

"Good. I'm glad that someone has arrived to help me with the baby-sitting chores."

"Hold your hand out. I want to see it shake."

"Oh for Chrissakes, what the fuck do you plan to do, talk me to death?"

"I'll tell you what I've told everybody today—it's my party and I'm calling the shots."

"Puns too? Mmmm . . . at least the rudeness is intentional. Well, then, name your poison. What's it going to be? Dialogue? Monologue? How about improvising a Shakespearean soliloquy—in blank verse, of course?"

"Shut up!"

" . . . perhaps an oration? No, I've got it. Stand there and free-associate for a while, without moving your lips, if you can, and let me catch a couple of zees. I've been waiting for you since early this morning."

He yawns, folds his hands behind his head, and lays down. His eyes blink and close. " . . . and I'm tired."

"If you think you're gonna psych me with that bored routine you're crazy. It won't work."

He opens one eye, glares, and pulls himself back up into a sitting position, his hands grasping his ankles.

"Look Sinbad, Steven, or whoever the fuck is at home right now, am I bothering you? What the fuck is it with you, anyway? You're disappointed that it wasn't some demon lover humping you? Remind me next time to wear my mask to the steam room. Hi, ho, Sinbad, the Lone Stranger rides again. Don't worry, from now on I'll remember you're on a rape trip, or is it Magdelene season? Look, I'm beat. I've had it. I'm knocked out. So go turn your collar around and I'll tell you all about it when I wake up. But for now, just do me a big favor. Go away and entertain yourself with your cap pistol. Find a playmate. Just let me sack out for a while in peace. And really . . ." He stifles a yawn with the back of his hand. " . . . it is a pleasure to see you again."

"That's it? Pleasure to see you, old boy, and all that rot. That's all you've got to say to me after ten months?"

"Suppose I said to you, Sinbad . . ."

"Steven, goddamn it!"

"Suppose I said to you, the last ten months and two days have been the worst time of my life—terrible, awful, and achingly lonely. Suppose I said that I was wretched, that I carried you everywhere, thought of you every day and always with a sense of intense loss. Suppose that in my thoughts I wished you well, constantly. Suppose I said to you, 'Steven, my pain was far worse than yours because you thought your anger to be righteous, while I knew it was misplaced.' Don't you think I knew for the past ten months you were positive that I had wronged you, that you couldn't possibly interpret things differently. You never can involve yourself in your own acts. You always make others take responsibility for them. Certainly I had to know that it would be impossible for you to distinguish between love and betrayal, miss the delight in the fact that inevitably they nourish each other. If I said that to you, would you believe any of it?"

"Yes, I'd believe some of it. I'll tell you exactly what I believe. I believe that part about my not forgetting that after you got over you cut me loose and got in the wind. I believe that, so I believe you when you say you carried me everywhere because you had to know that one day soon you'd look back over your shoulder and there I'd be, with this in my hand. And I believe that instead of running away you let me find you to throw me off, to make me wonder why."

"That's what you believe? But you don't believe that you have this twisted need to convince yourself that if you want things to be one way, they must inevitably work out to be just the opposite?"

"What's that got to do with not involving myself?"

"Everything, you clod . . . Oh, go away and let me sleep. I'm a knave. I've been one all my life. Call me master of lies, call me pre-eminent tempter, monster, serpent, insufferable braggart, cowardly bully, call me sot, sod, despoiler of children, satyr, degenerate hoaxer, call me a fucking nigger in a woodpile if that's what pleases you. They're all compliments. I eat'em up like a bear at the honey pot. But I take full responsibility. No sins of omission for me, my boy—pardon, it's Steven tonite, isn't it?—only mortal sins. But yours is the worst sin of all, the only one that's unforgivable. You not only reject all responsibility, but, infinitely worse, you replace it with cheap claptrap sentimentality which you use as your justification for demanding to be wronged. You've managed somehow to completely corrupt your instincts and so you strew havoc in your wake wherever you go."

"Then I might as well finish it right now. If I have it all wrong, it's your problem."

"That's just the point. . It's not my problem at all."

I raise the automatic and level it inches from his face.

"For once I'm gonna have the guts to follow something through to the end. You can't con me into turning back so that I have to start explaining things to myself all over again."

"Then do it! Surely you don't expect me to feel sorry for you."

"You dared me once before."

"Yes, so I did"—he yawns—"and gave you the singular opportunity to make a choice without taking a chance. But spring training is over. Everything counts now, and that means no do-overs. Alas . . ."—he yawns again—". . . you'll have to excuse me. I simply must catch a few zees . . ."

And incredibly, he's asleep. Not faking, but really asleep, sprawled on his back with his mouth open. He starts to snore.

It's ridiculous. I can't shoot him while he's sleeping. From the start I knew I'd have to face him down. I had to be able to look at him to find some clue. Even in the dream I knew I'd need his help. I can't make this decision by myself. That time his hand shook, was that weakness or just another act? How the hell can anyone figure something like that out? He dared me to find him. Tried to help me. Left messages all over the City. Why? Because he hadn't betrayed me or because he wanted me to think he hadn't? He knows that by acting all innocent he'll convince me that he's guilty, so if he really was guilty he'd act guilty so I'd think he was innocent. It's impossible, impossible to unravel. I found him by accident,

266

stumbled on him in the dark. Or was it an accident? Am I right about him? Yes. Am I wrong? Yes. That's impossible. Yes. How can I break the spell so that I don't have to bleed every time he cuts his finger. I could shoot him. But he's sleeping. I could wait until he wakes up but suppose then he decides to help me to make the wrong choice.

And yet there *is* a solution. Solution! It's sheer genius. If he can wash his hands and throw the responsibility on me, all I have to do is pass it on to somebody else, a stranger—maybe more than one. Let them work it out. I can commend both of our lives to chance. It's so perfect that in all the world only we could have planned it, together. I poke the barrel of the gun into his belly, hard, to make double sure he's not playing possum. He grunts and mumbles something in his sleep that sounds like ". . . poor Gaveston that has no friend but me." I shut the door quietly behind me and tip down the corridor, shoeless and shirtless, with the bag on my shoulder and the piece in my pants pocket.

The D.J. is on the scene and the disco floor is lively. A slim-waisted young man shakes his pelvis at a haughty teenager. My old buddy Trizzie the sex-change spins breathlessly in the arms of a towering black man. Two middle-aged queens venture a dated twist. A totally naked fat man shakes his jelly belly at the mirror. A squat man with a broken nose hops around, pushing poppers under people's noses. He wears huge rhinestone rings on his thumbs.

Two nude hustlers dog-paddle in the pool, watched from the diving board by a chunky Puerto Rican with bulbous silicone tits. The hustlers pay him no attention, but the masseur, who has just come on duty, is fascinated by the polymorph. His hand slowly revolves around the bulge in his crotch.

There are a few customers in the lounge and a couple at the snack bar, but you can see that the joint is dying. The Greek poses with his arms folded across his chest, showing off his basket to anybody who might be interested.

"Well, you look a lot better. That's a nasty bump on your knot, though."

"I'll get over it."

"Want an ice cube? It'll make the swelling go down."

"Nah, it's ok."

I hold the matchbook cover for him.

"Jesus Christ, Sinbad, how much of that shit do you have?"

"If I told you the truth you wouldn't believe me. I don't have the slightest idea."

"Finished playing cowboys and Indians?"

"For a while, Never can tell, though. Anything can happen."

"Well stop being so mysterious and dish me the dirt. Did you two kiss and make up or what?"

"He's sacked out in my cube. Can you believe it?"

"Sure I can believe it. He's been crashing in a beach chair for two nights. Owes the house, owes Suits-and-Boots. They locked up his clothes so he couldn't tip. Took away his key, of course. He's uptight and he's not gonna get over on 'tomorrows' too much longer. Why don't you straighten it out for him?"

"That's just what I'm gona do, straighten everything out for both of us."

"I'm really glad. I'm really glad you got some sense. His pride . . . you know how it is."

"His pride. Greek, old buddy, how come you didn't straighten it out? I mean, since you're the president of the fan club."

"I tried." He blushes. "He told me to mind my own fucking business."

"But you're making it *my* business? Or is this another one of his bright ideas?"

He shakes his head. "I don't understand you. I just don't understand whats happened to you."

"Con respeto, old buddy, nobody asked you to. Me, I'm just hanging out to empty the swag bag here. But if it makes you feel any better, him and me, we'll be leaving together by tomorrow morning. One way or another everything will be straightened out by then, ok? Blondie," I yell, "commere. I wanna rap to you."

Toothpick, distracted, starts to say something smart and shuts his mouth when he sees it's me. Blondie comes over and sits down next to me. Toothpick is standing by the pool table, hands on hips, mad as a hornet.

"It's your shot, goddamn it, Lennie."

"How's it going?"

"Hanging in there, Lennie."

"Blondie's ok, if you wanna call me that. I don't mind." He smiles. He doesn't mind in the least bit what anybody calls him as long as it's backed up with green. Smart kid.

"Greek, here's the deal. I gotta talk to Toothpick for a couple of minutes. Then I got some other shit I got to take care of. Here's a pound. Feed Blondie, keep him happy for a while. His buddy over there is gonna make a little run for me. Gimme about an hour and after that it's party time. Tell old Suits-and-Boots to wake up— what's his trade's name?"

"K.C."

"Tell him to get K.C. off his ass and take over for you. You bring Blondie here and anybody else interesting back to the cube. But remember, give me about an hour, ok?"

"No more sick shit though, Sinbad."

"Cross my heart and hope to die. Just a party, nonstop express. Ok with you, Blondie?"

"Bet."

"One thing, though. Your buddy's not invited. He's just the hired help. If he shows, well, all bets are off. Got it?"

"Hey, bro', he does his thing and I do mine."

"You, Greek? Dynamite party, but when Toothpick shows back from his run, if he decides to crash he ain't included in my promise."

"As long as you tell him, then it's ok with me. I might as well hang out. I ain't gonna make no fucking tips tonight anyhow. How big a party?"

"That's your department. But that dude on the dance floor . . ."

"Which one?"

"The young dude with black hair dancing with the skinny guy, you know him?"

"Sure."

"Count him in."

"Anything else?"

"Yeah, I'm gonna leave DeSantis some cash. You pick up whatever booze we need. See you guys later, about an hour."

I stroll over to the table where Toothpick is trying to figure out how to fuck up an easy bank shot. I pick up the cue ball and toss it over to Blondie at the snack bar.

"What the fuck . . ."

"Game's called, Toothpick. Time to go to work."

His mouth flaps open. He telegraphs a right. I hook under it and my fist bounces off his cheekbone. He falls back against the pool table, breathing hard trying to look mean. It's not that the fight has gone out of him, it just wasn't there in the first place.

"Forget it, Toothpick. You're strictly a street fighter. You can't handle me in a fair one." I grab hold of his shirt, ripping it down to his stomach. "In case you had any doubts about it, I love you too. Now, tough guy, here's your chance to get even and also pick up another twenty without getting cornholed. Interested?"

He glares. "What do I hafta do?"

"You know the Fort, across the street from Tricks?"

"Yeah."

"There's a guy there who's looking to waste me. Believe me, when he finds out where I am, his friends'll be on the way in one second flat. You understand what I'm saying?"

"Yeah."

"Good, because you're gonna tell this guy where I am."

"You're crazy! It's some kinda stupid trick to get me fucked up somehow. You gotta be nuts to do something like that."

I throw a twenty across the pool table.

"Only poor people are crazy. People with money are eccentric. That means I'm paying for your services and not for your mouth. I want you to go, right now, over to the Fort and ask for Sandor. Tell Sandor that Sinbad—that's me—will be down here at . . . let's see what time is it now?"

"Eleven."

"Tell him three. Tell him you're supposed to meet me here at three. Tell him I'm packing . . . this." I pull out the piece and shove it under his nose so he can smell it, just in case he has any doubts. "Also you tell him that you heard on the street he was looking for me. Make up any story. Tell him the truth. I chumped you off and you hate my guts, that's why you're telling him. Remember, three. Then you come back here. At two-fifty-five, that's five minutes to three, I give you this—it's real. It's a 'C' note.

270

You get it as long as his friends aren't here yet. If they come early and they waste me, well, you blow and that's that. So be convincing. Tell them three, make sure they believe it. His friends won't want to hang out waiting anyhow. You got it?"

"Yeah."

"Run it."

"I go to the Fort. Tell Sandor that Sinbad is gonna be here to meet me at three. You chumped me off. I heard he was looking for you, that's why I'm telling him. Tell him you're packing and you'll be here at three, not before."

"And you get the hundred, when . . .?"

"When it's just before three and they haven't showed yet."

"Can you handle it?"

"Yeah."

"Remember, I couldn't give less than a fuck if they get here earlier and waste me. That's the important part. The only one who loses then is you."

"I come right back?"

"Whatever you want. You know what time I pay off."

"I wanna ask you . . ."

"No. My party, remember? Yes or no?"

"It's your funeral."

"That's the spirit. Did anybody ever tell you that you're beautiful when you're angry? Now take your dough and get the fuck outta my sight."

I wait until he disappears up the stairs and then I walk over to the lounge.

"Get the fuck outta my bar, you maniac," hollers DeSantis.

I ignore him and sit down on a stool.

"Give me his tab."

"Whose tab?"

"You know whose tab. The guy whose clothes you locked up. The guy who kept this fucking dump alive for you."

"You think I liked to do that, about his clothes? Look aroundja, it's tight."

"So was your Ginney mother's cunt. Just give me the tab and then go figure out the vig that all the windows and orphans owe you."

271

"He gotta tab upstairs, too."

"Call Chula, but first give me a stinger without the crème de menthe."

"Straight cognac."

"In a highball glass, full to the top."

While he's on the phone, I gulp down the drink like it was ice water. He slides a piece of paper over to me.

"That's it? The whole shit? That's what you're all carrying on about?"

"You talk big when you're nigger rich."

I slide some bills over to him.

"Two things. One, call Chula back and have him send down a receipt and the key to the cube where his clothes are. I want that key delivered to me. Get it? Number two, here's another fifty. When the Greek comes in later give him whatever he wants. It's for me."

"You got it. Look, I'm sorry if . . ."

I backhand him one, not too hard, because after all he is an old man, and besides I don't want to hurt him, I just want to get him sore.

"Tell your Ginzo pals that you got smacked by a wise-ass Spic who thinks he's a tough guy. Tell 'em that. Let's see who got more balls, one Spic or a couple of your greaseball friends."

"You're buying trouble, Sinbad."

"So? I'm buying. Don't worry about it. Anyhow, give me a bottle of brandy to walk with. And DeSantis, that line's had it. Go find yourself a cute nine-year-old to molest. Maybe you can scare *him*."

I leave him polishing his glasses, reminding himself what he would have done to me thirty years ago.

I tiptoe into the cube. He's sleeping like a baby. Not a care in the world. Well, now I've got the whole world off my back too. No more stumbling from riddles to regrets. I've eased back into the current, only now he's there with me, where we both belong. And I pulled it off without even waking him up.

I screw the red bulb back in the fixture, hang up my pants and bag in the locker. Then I lay down next to him on the mattress, squeezing myself between his back and the wall. I reach over and put the bottle of brandy in front of his nose. I snuggle up next to him, with one hand resting on his shoulder and the other holding the automatic.

All his intricate little plots and double-crosses. I've wiped the slate clean for both of us. It doesn't mean a fiddler's fuck anymore whether he was trying to get them off his back by pointing a finger at me, whether he wanted me to save him by setting me up, whether he wanted me to waste him, whether he wanted to mock me because I wouldn't waste him. It doesn't matter. It's enough that I found his weakness. He can be blinded by his own brilliance. His options are all flawed. They're too inconsequential. I alone found the perfect solution, the only way that there's no possibility of weighing and balancing and still coming up short, no possibility of misinterpreting or making a mistake.

I rub my cheek against his shoulder, glad that I can protect us from his deviousness. Until the last he'll think he got over once again. Good. His pride is important to him. Let him have it. Using all that he taught me I've outsmarted him at last. It was the only way. Why grope around foolishly when all you have to do is resign yourself? Since he can't do it, I've done it for him. I've outsmarted them too, the ones who are against us, and made them our tool. And I've outsmarted myself because it's me—I have to stay to watch over both of us. Whatever happens now I welcome, knowing that it all flows from me, but swells over both of us, rushing us helplessly along like olive branches in a spring floodtide. His ridicule, my seriousness. His betrayal, my love. I have fused them, using the fire I stole from him—"the gift of the gods to mankind, Sinbad"—the practical joke. We are two, joined beyond all limits. We are one. I am him. He is me.

I'm too happy. I shake his shoulder and nibble his ear.

"Wake up, Saul, it's Sinbad. I'm back."

"Gadfly!"

"Come on, you big bear, open your eyes and I promise you, you won't be sorry."

He blinks. Blinks again and then his hand darts for the bottle like a snake's tongue. By the time he has struggled into a sitting position the bottle has been opened and he has already taken two great gulps.

273

"Sinbad, comforter of the needy . . . mmm . . . excuse me
. . . one more sip of the water of life . . . mmph . . . that's better,
much much better."

He examines me, trying to figure out what's happened. Then
he sees the automatic.

"I'm sorry, I still have to hold on to it for a little while. I can't
take the chance that you'll run out until I fill you in on a few
things."

"More explanations? I'm going back to sleep."

"No, wait. No explanations. I don't have any."

"That interests me. Instead of going to sleep I think I'll get
drunk. You?"

"Sure. I can't let you go it alone, not tonite."

I take a healthy belt and pass the bottle back to him. The
automatic lies loosely in my hand, the hand he can't grab. I never
take my eyes away from his.

"So, you've given up looking for sleight of hand."

"I did some boxing on the Rock. You learn to anticipate a
punch from the look in the other guy's eyes."

"If you learned that, my boy, then you should have paid them
for your upkeep."

"Well, I did in a way, didn't I? But let's forget about that. Let
me fill you in, that's the only thing that's important. Before I start,
remember one thing. I'm not asking you for your advice. Please,
Saul, understand me. I'm telling you."

The bottle passes back and forth. I watch him very closely.
One false step and I'll lose him.

"Saul, forget about the piece. Five minutes, ten minutes, and
then I'll dump it in the locker. Now listen, there's a solution that
takes care of it all. It's something you didn't think of. Something
you missed. But I found it with your help."

"While I was asleep?"

"Because you were asleep. Listen. The solution cancels out
everything stupid. Help me find the words . . ."

"Moral judgments?"

"I think so."

"More? Selfishness—mine, yours?"

"Yes, the solution takes care of that."

"Despair?"

"That's it. Don't smile at me like I'm the village idiot. I tell you, not promise you, I tell you I've found the solution to that. For both of us."

"And the solution is . . ."

"I can't tell you."

"You mean you won't tell me."

"I said I can't tell you, because I just set the wheels in motion. We'll both know, when the solution arrives."

"Let me see, you've arrived at a solution but you don't know what it is."

"If I knew what it was I'd have to explain it and then it would be no good. I arrived at a solution and we'll know what the solution is when it arrives. You remember, that time in the hotel room when you said, 'Leap now and trust me'? I say to you now, Saul, leap. I'm leaping with you. Trust me that I don't know what's going to happen. This once, you have to give yourself to me blindly, like I gave myself to you. The solution may not arrive, but that too will be a solution. You see, I've allowed for all possibilities. It's foolproof. Will you leap with me?"

"Do I have a choice?"

"I'll answer your question after you answer mine."

"An open-ended solution and foolproof too. You've invented an elegant geometry, that is, if you can really pull it off."

"*We* can pull it off. We *can*, Saul. Will you? Will you? You'll see it through with me tonite, all night? That's all it takes. Look . . ."

I back over to the locker, still studying the expression of his eyes, pull out the bag and throw it over to him. "Look inside. That's all for the party later on, soon. You won't be bored."

"Bribery at gun point?"

"Stop it. You know I had to allow for all possibilities. Stop testing me."

"You make it sound most enticing, my boy, an adventure not to be missed. Well, God protects fools and drunks, which leaves me with a big fucking edge, doesn't it?"

"Give me the bottle and I'll fix that up in a minute. Don't worry there's plenty more on the way. Tell me whether you'll do it."

"I seem to remember a young lad diving headfirst out of a

275

third-story window. Well, a little child shall lead them. Consider it done, then. What are the postulates—ground rules—my boy?"

"No questions . . about the solution. We completely forget about it until whenever . . ."

"Whenever it arrives. Or never arrives? Agreed. Anything else?"

"Whatever goes down, we'll be together. That's the most important part."

He looks at the gun in my hand.

"You trust me?"

"Not as far as I can throw you. To quote an old friend of mine, 'All friendships that are worth anything require mutual mistrust.' "

"Covered everything. Mmmm . . . I always suspected that there might be some depth to you. The ground rules are agreeable."

"Here, light up a joint."

"One question."

"First give me a shotgun." He does. Our mouths meet. My free hand presses against the back of his head.

"Mmm . . quality merchandise. I know I was going to ask you a question. Ah, yes, did I have a choice?"

"Nope. It was my party all the way. Wanna check out the coke?"

"Coke, smoke, pistols, leather trousers, gold ring. Mmmm, don't tell me the old one about hitting the number, first day out of the joint too."

"I hit a number all right. Hit him for about fourteen hundred bucks."

"Nice score. We didn't do that well with the credit cards . . . mmm . . . sorry about that . . . mmmph . . . confusion."

"Don't be. It's not important."

"No? Did he see your face?"

"Yup."

"Recognize you?"

"Yup."

"Bad."

"Don't worry about it. Here, take a blow."

We hold the matchbook for each other, snorting, sniffing, and snorting again. Our eyes meet at the same time. We smile at each other, sharing the high, sharing an affection and bond beyond words. Someone knocks on the door.

"So soon?"

"Nope. I'll be right back."

I open the door a crack and squeeze out into the corridor. Blondie is standing there, wearing a bath towel, holding his clothes in one hand.

"Chula sent me with this."

"Good. Thanks, Blondie."

"Willya hold my clothes for me so I can take a swim before we all come back?"

"Sure. I'll lock 'em up. See ya in a little while."

I put the key on my ankle, close the door behind me, and hand Saul the receipt.

"What was that all about? What's this?"

"One of the company. I didn't want you to see him until they all get here. You've probably seen him around—young, blond, cute, dumb, and horny. A homecoming present from me to you."

"You are, my boy, a miserable shit."

"Saul, what's the matter?"

"This is the matter. Is this your idea of a solution?" He crumples the receipt and throws it into the corner.

"Yes, goddamn it, it's part of it—a small part, but every part is necessary."

"Necessary for me to look like a Welfare case?"

"Necessary to clean up all the bullshit. Come on, it's your money too. I did it and that's that. Besides . . ."—I smile—"there couldn't be any room for error. You can't run too far in a bath towel. I couldn't take any chance that the first time I turned around you'd somehow manage to get your clothes back and tip on me. I bought myself peace of mind, Saul, so I could put the piece away. Locked up, of course."

"My boy, you are living proof of the benefits of incarceration; your words bear witness to the unbelievers who scoff at rehabilitation."

I dump the gun in the locker and throw Blondie's stuff on top of it. Even if I got tempted later on to back out, I couldn't. There

277

just wouldn't be enough time to get to the piece. I sit back down and we smoke some more. I'm content to be with him, turn him on, watch him enjoy himself.

"You shoulda seen old Suits-and-Boots when I backhanded him before. You woulda cracked up. He looked like he was going to shit a pineapple."

"What was that all about?"

"That was about an old bent Ginney with bad manners."

"That means we're both probably barred from here after tonite."

"Ask us if we give a fuck. Do we?"

"Most certainly not!"

"Are we drunk?"

"We are, assuredly, drunk."

"Are we high and fucked up?"

"That we are, my boy."

"And everything's everything?"

"Everything is most definitely everything."

"I hocked the watch you gave me."

"Wasn't worth much anyhow."

"That pissed me off, when I found out. Then I thought, well, it might not have been worth much to the guy in the hockshop, or to me, this morning, but the kid who held on to it for all those years, it was worth a whole lot to him. It was the most fantastic watch in the world and he was proud to own it."

"You admit that everything is what is seems?"

"I do now, but of course, nothing is ever what it seems to be either, right?"

We laugh together until we're interrupted by the pounding on the door, and then the whole party rolls in on us. Instantly the tiny cube is packed with wall-to-wall people. The Greek, still in his clamdiggers, lugs the goodies—ham and cheese, potato chips and pretzels, and right behind him is Blondie, loaded down with bottles of scotch, brandy, gin and amaretto. Saul takes one look at Blondie and rises to play gracious host.

In comes Trizie the Sex-Change in a two-piece silver bikini, a beach bag slung over her shoulder.

"Darlings," she trills. "And now the star of the show, Miss Trizie and her magical bag of music. Da dum!" Providing her own fanfare she pulls this huge stereo radio out. It's already going full blast.

"Music, courtesy of the john in forty-five cube and Miss Trizie's love potion number nine."

"What's that?" I holler.

"Chloral hydrate. It's a knockout!"

Right behind is the skinny guy who was dancing before, only now he's changed into violet hot pants and a Dracula cape tied under his chin.

"Lucky Pierre!" Trizie shrieks.

And last, my own invited guest, the kid who was Dracula's dance partner, shows on the scene. He's striking, that's the only word I can think of, with black glossy hair which looks like it's styled once a week, skin the color of gold, high cheekbones, and wide moist lips. He's young, no more than sixteen, and even though he dresses like a queen, bare-chested and bare-foot, in red velvet leotards, one look at his eyes tells you he's all business, a veteran hustler who's never had to work the Deuce, strictly twenty and up. He walks in with a bag of ice and looks around like he owns the place.

It's obvious that Saul knows him. That's why he's so busy opening a bottle and keeping his head turned toward Blondie, who's watching Pierre, out of the corner of his eye, feeling up Trizie's silicone tits. The Greek watches me and the kid like a referee waiting for the gong to start the first round. I stick out my hand.

"They call me Sinbad."

"Angel."

"What's happening, bro'?"

"Nothing much. Heard a lot about you from your friend."

"The same friend I'm thinking about?"

"Probably. Talks about you a lot."

"For instance?"

"For instance, you're the jealous type. That's what he says."

Before I can think of a comeback, Saul starts pushing everybody out of his way so he can sort things out. Food, booze, ice, and cups get rearranged on the floor between mattress and door. In the middle of the goodies I lay out a bag of joints and half a paper cup full of coke. Me, Saul, and Blondie squat on the edge of the

279

mattress with Angel scrunched behind us. The Greek has cheerfully gorillaed the chair, while Trizie and Lucky Pierre have to make do with the floor. All you can see is assholes and elbows as everybody attacks the coke in the cup with matchbook covers. Then the joints, the booze, the ham start vanishing. Trizie turns the box up so loud that nobody can hear what anyone is saying . . .

" . . . . so I told the ho . . . ."

" . . . . my god, she hollered, I'm sucking a big black dick! . ."

" . . . . . wet birds fly at night . . . . ."

" . . . . mmmph . . law of thermodynamics . . . treat a whore like a lady and a lady . . . . . . like a whore, of course . . . . ."

" . . . and, child, the silicone dropped and her tits were hanging down to her balls . . . ."

" . . . shove the fucking cue stick up your ass . . . ."

"Fly me to the moon . . ."

" . . . . and let me play up in your cunt."

" . . . . her dick was done in Denmark but the tits she had done right down on Delancey Street . . . ."

"He flies through the air with the greatest of ease . . . "

"So, he said, it's my party, you're just the hired help."

" . . . . wet birds DO fly at night? . . . . . ."

" . . . . trade for days, honey . . . . ."

" . . . . . . you know that's my blood you're drinking . . . ."

" . . . . . stop hogging all the coke, bitch . . . . ."

" . . . . . mmmph, and my body, should you choose to eat it . ."

" . . . . . . arf we go to Scotland Yard! . . . . . ."

" . . . . . . please mother, I'd rather do it myself . . . ."

" . . . . let me see your palm, dear boy, my grandmother taught me . . . ."

It's almost as hot in the cube as it was in the steam room. Pierre wraps his cape around Trizie while he gives her a hickey. Trizie is sprawled on the floor. One tit has flopped out of his blouse. He tries to grope the Greek, who has eyes only for Blondie. Blondie ignores him. He gazes adoringly at Saul, whose hand has crept under Blondie's bath towel. Saul fondles him while foretelling somebody else's future. Angel is on his own trip. He sits hugging his knees, aloof, smoking joint after joint. I reach behind Saul and Blondie to offer Angel a blow.

280

" . . . hatchet gets beep aneroid."

"What's that?" I yell.

"I said, 'That shit gets me paranoid.' "

"You like the weed?"

"Dynamite. Paste side peelers cock."

"What? What the fuck did you say?"

He crawls across the mattress to join me.

"I said, 'It tastes like dealers' stock.' "

"It is."

"Thought so."

"Wanna zip?"

"I don't drink."

"Tough keeping up with him if you don't."

"Tough on me in bed. It takes him longer to cum when he's boozed up."

"What does he say about me?"

"We don't talk much when we're getting down."

"You do that often?"

"Often enough."

"Often enough for who?"

He examines his fingernails.

"One thing he did say about you, though."

"What's that?"

"That you ask too many questions."

Saul has pulled Blondie onto his lap and has his tongue deep inside the kid's mouth. The Greek is on his knees in front of Blondie, head buried in his crotch. He is unaware that Trizie has pulled his clamdiggers down around his ankles and is trying to wriggle her nose between the cheeks of his ass. Lucky Pierre fumbles with the back of Trizie's bra while jerking himself off.

"You mind me asking you questions . . about you and him?"

"Yes."

"Is it serious?"

"Business is always serious, isn't it?"

Count Dracula staggers over, kneels, and begins to massage my calf.

"Don't mind the Count," says Angel, "That's his thing, getting something for nothing. Right Count?"

"Maybe that's all you're worth, sweetie pie."

"But you'll never know, will you?"

"Bug off, Count," I tell him. "Can't you see we're rapping?"

"Sharing trade secrets?"

"Bitchy too, Sinbad. Hey, Count, go get yourself a transfusion and leave the grown-ups alone for a while.

Angel shoves him hard. The count slams into the wall and slides to the floor, where he covers his face with his cloak and blubbers.

"So, Sinbad, what is it? You jealous of him getting down with me, or me getting down with him?"

"Now who's curious?"

"I can't even spell it. I'm just letting you know I'm available. Save us both time just in case that's what you have in mind."

Saul gives us both a dirty look and snaps his fingers at Angel. Angel squirms off the mattress and works his way over to Saul. They seem to be arguing about something. Angel smiles. He pushes Saul over to make some room and sits down next to him with his arm draped around his shoulder. Blondie looks crushed.

The Greek tugs at my elbow.

"That fucking Blondie can't keep his eyes offa Saul. He's driving me up a wall. Help me pull him, Sinbad, please."

Trizie begins her striptease number. The Count revives and crawls over to examine her cunt.

"Is it really real?"

"Realer than real, Mary Dugan . . . . everything works and no fishy aftertaste either. Now be a good boy and leave mother's new plumbing alone."

" . . . . so I yelled, you want to put your WHAT in my WHAT . . . .?"

" . . . . mmmph, you will NOT turn a trick with . . . ."

" . . . .you big dummy, of course fairies don't fly . . . ."

I'm sucking up booze like it's going out of style. Saul is lecturing Angel. Angel yawns and continues to massage the back of Saul's neck.

" . . . . lust is ALWAYS appropriate. . . ."

" . . . . before that he was a lady wrestler . . . ."

" . . . . after that she was in boy burlesque . . . ."

" . . . . Finally they both had the operation . . . ."

". . . . she was too butch and so was he . . . ."

". . . . six young boys lined up belly down on the bed . . . ."

". . . . so he grabbed her cunt and came up with a handful of cock."

". . . . so she grabbed his cock and fell into twat up to her elbow . . . ."

". . . . sixteen?. . . . more like thirteen, you mean . . . ."

". . . . and rimmed 'em all, one by one . . . ."

". . . . the cloud capped towers, lo the barge of pleasure . . . ."

". . . . thirteen, more like eleven, you mean . . . .?"

". . . . got clap of the gums . . . ."

". . . . syphylis in the asshole . . . ."

". . . . mmph, bad case of hoof and mouth disease . . . ."

"Blondie, get your ass over here.

"What's up, Sinbad?"

"What's going on?"

"It's about his key. Saul wants Angel to try and get it from you, when you're not looking, so they can, you know . . ."

"What'd Angel have to say?"

"He said, 'Not tonite, I have a headache.' "

I bust out laughing.

"Sinbad, why don't you and me use that key?"

"Why don't you and the Greek use that key?"

"Why don't me and Blondie use somebody's key? Anybody's key."

There's too much confusion. Everybody has their own hidden agenda. I step out into the corridor to catch my breath and bump right into Toothpick. I pull him around the corner and back him up against the wall.

"Well?"

"I did like you told me."

"You found Sandor?"

"Yep."

"Anybody with him? Any friends?"

"Nope."

"Did he believe you?"

"How the fuck should I know?"

"Tell me what he said."

"He ast me why, why I was setting you up. I told him you beat me on somethin' we wuz doin."

"Anything else?"

"Nope."

"No? What did he say when you asked him for bread?"

"Who said that? I didn't ask him for nothin' . . ."

"Want me to beat you to a bloody fucking pulp right here?"

"He gave me a quarter and said he'd owe me the other twenty-nine. What the fuck was that supposed to mean?"

"Get lost, Toothpick, and just pray that I don't see anybody I don't want to see for the next forty-five minutes."

"Whyn't you gimme the 'C' right now?"

"Because that's not the deal, is it?"

"Just forty-five minutes."

"Wrong again. No dough, Toothpick. I'm chumping you off. You're beat, so beat it chump."

He splutters. His mouth works up and down, but nothing comes out. I hope he makes one move, one move for his shank, so I can kick every tooth out of his head.

"Wanna try it? Come on, faggot, give it the old college try."

For one wonderful second I think he's going to let me taunt him into it. He shifts his weight, getting ready to bull his way in, when some spark of sense tells him to back off. All the fight has drained out of him. He can't even look at me until he's halfway down the hall.

"You'll get yours, motherfucker, you'll see. I chumped *you* off, motherfucker. I knew you wuz trying to fuck me somehow. That's why I never went there, never saw the guy. I knew you wuz trying to set me up for somethin' funny. Well, I got *your* twenty, chump, and you ain't gonna get it back. So fuck you, twice."

Of course he betrayed himself with the truth. I might have believed him, except for the quarters. He hasn't got the brains to invent a joke like that. I take a piss break myself. Mainly to give the company time to clear out the cube. I'm standing there with my dick in my hand when this fat guy eases up alongside of me.

"You wanna make a quick ten?"

He holds the bill out to me, checking out my cock and playing with himself through his pants. I snatch the bill from him.

"Sure, thanks."

"Hey, wait a minute. Where ya going?"

"Hey, yourself, whale. For ten dollars you expect more than a peek?"

I laugh all the way down the corridor, trying to figure out where I've seen that guy before.

When I open the door Saul and Angel jump apart. They've been hugging and smooching on the mattress.

"Yo, bro', don't you knock?"

"Not on my own door, I don't."

Angel gets up and smiles, like he gives me that one, but he's got one of his own coming right up.

"Wanna come back to my cube, Saul?"

"He's not up to it tonite."

"And he doesn't have any strings tied to his shoulders, either. Saul?"

"Tell him, Saul."

It's clear that Saul has nothing to say. I know he feels that he's been cheated. That's tough. Tomorrow neither one of us will have to worry about Angel. And Angel, he's not the worrying type at all. I toss him a joint and close the door behind him.

The cube is a mess. Dead soldiers, empty wrappers, cigarette butts and ashes, matchbook covers, roaches, everything scattered all over the place. I push somebody's sandal off of my pillow and brush the crumbs off the sheet.

"Looks exactly like a lady's powder room in Port Said, doesn't it?"

"What's Port whatever it is?"

"Take me too long to explain."

I check out the stash. Joints, four. Coke, none. The company snorted up three hundred bazoomas. But then we won't have to worry about money tomorrow, will we? Will we? I almost start to tell him. Then I realize how unfair it would be to him, to impose my weakness on him.

"What was that you were going to say?"

"He's very attractive, Angel. Very professional too."

"Ah, my boy, wine is a mocker. He that transgresseth by wine
. . ."

"Oh, stop it. Neither one of us is that drunk. Stop acting like a
clown. You think I care what you two were doing?"

"A sticky point, that. No rage, no storm, no savage argument
. . ."

"For what? After all, I didn't think you spent the last ten
months in a monastery."

"Very unlike you, my boy. Very fucking unlike you."

"So you screwed him. Big deal! That was then, this is now. We
took the chance and leaped together. The solution is the only thing
that matters."

"When it arrives."

"When it arrives."

"Or doesn't?"

"I told you, there's nothing to worry about."

"Mmm, you tell me many things. Riddles are so unlike you, my
boy. And resignation? Unheard of. Let's see what kind of trinity we
can invent. Between riddle and resignation . . ."

"How about laying down?"

"No, that doesn't quite fit. There's a piece missing."

"Saul, turn out the light please and let's lay down for a while."

I close my eyes, hear him pad over to the light switch and
thump back down on the bed. I let him put his arms around me as I
snuggle against his chest. My mouth must stink as bad as his.

"Old boozey breath."

"mmm."

I reach down to his crotch and feel him become hard.

"Angel."

Angel, yes, but which one does he mean? We sleep.

There's a room in a fleabag hotel. When I walk in he's sitting
by the window, probably drunk. He's been expecting me.

"You've come to get me out."

"I've come to get us both out, to save us both."

"Bullshit, you've come to save yourself. Look at you, you have
betrayal written all over your face."

"I could have saved myself, but without you, I'm lost."

"Of course, you knew that all along. I planned it that way."

"But I forgot, I forgot why I was going to do it."

"Betray us both?"

"No, damn it, save us both."

He floats over to me, embraces me.

"It's out of my hands, my boy. It's all your responsibility now."

"I want to die to save you."

That's when I grab him by the throat and realize that somehow he has floated away and that I am choking myself.

I gasp for air and fall in front of Toothpick. He wraps his knees around my head and squeezes. The touch of his flesh is hideously exciting. Someone is knocking on the door.

"Run, Saul!"

The knocking continues. "Run, Saul!" I'm awake. The cube is dark. Now? So soon. Fear grips my belly. No, I can't fail us now, not after all this. God, give me strength to endure, strength for both of us, strength to take the whole world, all of our despair, on myself and cast it away. Forever. My heart pounds. I pull open the door . . . *now*.

"Your time is up," says Chula, "it's eight o'clock. If you want to stay, Nene, I'll have to collect for another day."

"Eight o'clock?"

Somewhere along the line I must have put on my pants again. I reach into my pocket and come up with a ten-dollar bill.

"We're gonna tip, Chula. Just let me wake him up and we'll get ourselves together."

"I'm sorry about waking you up like this. DeSantis . . ."

"I know, baby, I understand."

Sweet Chula. I flick on the awful red light bulb. What the fuck happened? What went wrong? How could they *not* have come. It's eight o'clock and it's obvious that they're never going to come. I open the locker and go through the bag. It's empty. We got ten bucks and the few joints lying beside the mattress. We're about to get kicked out of the Europa—into what? Bickering and infidelity, resentment and doubts, questions and more questions, childish riddles and the falsehoods that make each day bearable?

I'm almost as frightened as I was when I heard the knocking. Is this what I condemned us to?

"What did Chula want?"

"It's not important."

And so it begins. So soon. Not even time to catch my breath.

287

Our only defense against each other, against the world is to weave a veil of words which we can use to convince each other that nothing is really as hopeless as it seems. The more idle, the more complicated, the more confusing the words we use, the more we'll be able to confuse each other and lull ourselves into accepting each petty little hurt as part of the natural scheme of things.

"It must be important. You wouldn't be lying if it wasn't vitally important. What the fuck did you do?"

"Saul . . ."

"What the fuck did you do!" He backhands me. I stumble, bumping my head against the locker as I fall on my ass.

"It was the only way to fix things without spending the rest of our lives lying to each other about the last ten months."

He kicks me in the ribs.

"This morning—yesterday morning—when I came out, I was going to waste you. But it all got too complicated. Who was right, who was wrong. Your fault, my fault. Both our faults, or worse, nobody's fault. I couldn't bear that thought, that maybe nobody is to blame for anything. I looked all over. I couldn't find you. I didn't know whether you were taunting me or not. Maybe you just didn't care. You know I can never get things like that straight. You weren't at the Fort. Sandor told me some story about the Ginneys looking for you or looking for me, something about somebody putting out a contract on me and then deciding not to go through with it. None of it made any sense, because all of it could have been true or none of it, or pieces. I told you, I couldn't figure anything out. Then we went downstairs. He told me he was jealous of you, because of me. He offered me a job pimping for him at five bills a week, just so he could have me. All the time I was thinking that you were in trouble because of me, maybe that part was true. He laughed when I said I felt responsible, responsible for anyone that my life touches. Don't you see, I couldn't let anybody hurt you except me. I had to make that choice. He wanted me to believe that it doesn't matter how bad you fuck people up, even people you love, because it's their responsibility that they got involved with you in the first place. It was the same old thing, Saul, the thing I never could live with—that nobody is to blame for anything."

"Go on, tell me exactly what you did."

"Can I get up and sit next to you?"

"Get up, then."

I lean my head on his shoulder and hold his hand in mine.

"The safe was open. He's crazy, Saul. He's a sick dude. I knocked him out and took all the dough that was in the safe. Then I bought the piece and the dope and I came here. I knew you were safe then, because he wouldn't want me after what I did to him, so he wouldn't have any reason to hurt you. I figured, fine, you're safe. You go your way and I'll go mine. And that's when I stumbled into you, just when I had cut us loose from each other. There was nothing we could do. They'd be looking for me and find us. I knew what they'd do. I wanted to save us both, put us both beyond them, so they couldn't hound us forever, so we couldn't hound each other forever. I sent Blondie's buddy over to tell Sandor I was here, figuring his boys would come and . ."

". . . do the job for you. The job you didn't have the guts for. Choices, indeed! So that was the perfect solution, the one that allowed for all possibilities. Mmmph . . . well, if any are ignorant, let us have compassion and scourge them. Of course it was flawed, fatally so. If you weren't so ignorant I could despise you, but as it is, I'm afraid a fool can't be held responsible for his folly. How could you possibly think that you could manipulate the whole world?"

"You do."

"I do not. I only pretend I can. Nobody, alas, believes me but you. I don't even believe myself. Human nature, my boy, is incalculably complex. It's an age-old dilemma. To aspire to omnipotence without first attaining omniscience is monstrous. Now take the Ginneys. You have to understand them. You're not responsible for what happened. True, it was their money. But it was in *his* safe. Sandor's the one that's responsible. He has to pay the price for his carelessness, for thinking with his dick. Nobody can possibly get hurt, unless Sandor tries to collect from you himself, which I doubt. I assume he knows you have a piece."

"He knows."

"Sandor has a talent for venery, not bravery. That kind of money is chicken feed to him. He won't like it, but he'll live with it."

"There was no chance my solution would work?"

"Of course not."

"What now? What are we going to do?"

"We? Mmmph, I am going to my cube to get dressed and then I think I'll pay my old buddy Sunshine a visit for a week or so."

"Then that part was true, about you being uptight, about the money."

"The little chump change from the credit cards was gone in a matter of days. Then the matter of my fancy, my foolish infatuation. Dotage is so very expensive."

"Angel?"

"Ah, Angel. Too much loving makes one mad indeed, doesn't it, my boy?"

"Saul, wait. Don't go. I still have a gold chain. It's not worth much, but at least you can hock it for a few bucks. Call it a going-away present."

"Suit yourself. A little gaudy for a man of my years, but perhaps for a friend, for Angel . . ."

I unlock the locker and slip the automatic into my hand.

"And you're sure that nobody's to blame for anything? Whatever pain, whatever havoc I cause, whatever meanness and spite there is, nobody's to blame?"

"Quite sure."

"Then go to Hell!"

I wheel and squeeze the trigger all in one motion. It takes a second for me to interpret the futile clicks. He reaches under the mattress and pulls out the clip.

"You had it all along."

"You really are a fool. A romantic fool—the most dangerous kind. Do you think I'd leave a man's weapon around where an impetuous child could get his hands on it? I hid the clip the moment I beat you back here from the steam room."

"So everything from then on—just another practical joke."

"To be preferred over bad melodrama, wouldn't you say?"

"Did you enjoy it?"

"It became tedious after a while. Especially your obvious concern about Angel. He's not that good in bed, you know, too professional. And you, enjoying yourself so much playing God, ordaining solutions to nonexistent problems—leaping from basement windows, so to speak."

290

"I meant to waste you—yesterday morning, last night after the steam room, just now."

"Intentions don't mean a fucking thing. All that matters is interpretation, and for that at least one other person must be involved. God, you see, is inferior to man. It's impossible for him to interpret, since he's uniquely alone."

"I can't do it . . . interpret. Even when you spell things out for me I can't do it. I mix my feelings up in everything."

"Which means you're inhuman. The alternative, of course, is unthinkable."

"Are you really going to Sunshine's?"

"Certainly not."

"Did you have to say you were?"

"I thought I owed you the kindness since you find pain so much more tolerable than truth."

"Is that what it's always going to be between us, nothing but pain and pranks?"

"What else makes it all worthwhile? Sinbad, I told you at the start the only way to be satisfied is to suspend judgment. Without laughter one soon becomes morally fastidious, unfit for human company."

"I can't stand being alone."

"Neither can I. That's why we're inseparable. We turn the screw for each other."

"Angel?"

"Nothing deader than yesterday's love affair, my boy. Besides, my financial condition . . . you're the only one I can count on for assistance and . . . mmm . . . support."

"But if you had dough right now . . . ?"

"If! If my grandmother had balls she would have been my grandfather. Why do you insist on talking about intentions when they're so irrelevant?"

"Well."

"Well."

After we both get dressed, we start the long hike upstairs. The lounge and snack bar are closed, the waterfall shut off. The floor of the disco is littered. Only the juke box plays on and on. The night sky and electric stars have disappeared. In their place a two-hundred-watt bulb discloses the shabbiness they hid. Somewhere a vacuum cleaner whines across a carpet. We stand in the foyer, trying to figure things out.

"At least we have the bridal suite for one more day."

"The bridal suite! Imagine that, my boy. And we, the most unlikely honeymooners ever to set foot in the. . . ."

"McKinley."

"That tourist trap?"

"In the words of an old buddy of mine, it beats a blank. Plus I found ten bucks in my pocket this morning. I didn't think we had a cent left."

"Splendid. That's cab fare and a bottle of booze. There isn't perchance, just a bit of smoke left?"

"Four joints."

"Four whole joints and the bridal suite too. Mmm, if only I could recall a suitable line from Canticles."

Outside a light drizzle is falling. There's not a cab in sight. We'll just have to get wet, and that's that. Today we can cool out and enjoy the last few crumbs. No reason why we shouldn't. We need each other. I know it and he knows it. Him, a potbellied old faker and me, a washed-out hustler. We scratch and maul each other for the same reason we cling to each other: to hold off the unknown for one more day, to help each other reject anything we suspect may be genuine. I suppose what Sandor said is true, about truth only confusing people.

Well, tomorrow's gonna be a fucked-up day. I'm going to have to run to Welfare to get a digit and find myself another methadone program. There's no sense kidding myself, now that I'm out I'm going to need a program again. And then? Back down to the Square, I guess. There's nothing else to do for the time being, at least until he gets himself together. It's no big deal, not really. After all, we've got to get over somehow, don't we?

5

The Bruja

And the woman said to him:
Behold, thou knowest all that Saul hath done.

—1 Samuel 28:9

THERE WAS NEVER a particular moment when I awoke to find that the days of my youth had vanished finally and irretrievably, when I discovered with amazement that nothing would ever amaze me again. Metamorphosis is never accomplished self-consciously, and apprehension is only accomplished once experience is filtered through a prism of mourning, so that all I can say is that there came a time when I distinguished a hierarchy of persons costumed as progressive stages of my life.

There was a boy who, seeking solitary beatitude, stumbled upon selfishness instead and accepted a stranger's challenge to eclipse himself.

There was Sinbad, who embraced the summons to leap gladly into despair, possessed with an uncontrollable desire to possess the world. Sinbad, who landed instead in a swamp of gratuitous intentions which defied his awful need to find validity in the experiences which he imposed on himself.

And there, too, the Sinbad, appalled at the prospect of limitless solitude, whose vocation was fidelity to the claims of a single, all-encompassing intimacy from which he derived power through dependence and identity through habit.

There is Steven, the man: absurd survivor of a ghastly practical joke which involved the wrong corpse. Steven, who now helplessly approaches middle age, presuming a reality that gives no grounds for cherishing hope or expecting salvation, since no one remains to be saved. Steven, who is enraged to find that systematic nostalgia has become his sole companion.

I am that Steven, or I think I was when I awoke this morning. I have never been able to exist in isolation for myself and reject the possibility of doing so now. The boy desired only ecstasy and oblivion. The others, all the subsequent me's, relied exclusively on continuous interplay with Saul for vitalization.

Against his scorn I set my intransigence; his infidelities required my endurance; his passions were my temptations and his betrayals, my passions; his mockery compelled dissection of self, while his approval demanded self-justification; his indulgence impelled me toward immolation and his extinction can only be idemnified with spite, spite that redeems him from flesh and fuses me to him completely. I exist on my spite, determined to flaunt my maturity and wisdom, a maturity that demands relinquishing the obsession to be everything and a wisdom that frees me from wanting to be.

I am determined that nothing should change and that I shall change nothing. I have simplified my own life so that it no longer intrudes on me and have given myself over to days spent in searching for landmarks and nights, rejecting all grief. I reside in his apartment, at once intruder and guardian of a shrine. All his belongings remain in their original state of disorder.

My Welfare check is insufficient for all but the most meager sort of substinence so, though irritated that I am forced to involve myself in my own survival, I work as a bouncer several nights a week at the old Fort Dodge. Long ago I made my peace with the management, and in any case, Sandor is no longer there. The last time I saw him he was pushing a mop in a dingy bathhouse on Second Avenue. He had aged considerably and I don't think he recognized me. He looked like a man who hedged bets against himself. I had nothing to say to him and left without telling him about Saul.

I have nothing to do. There is nothing I want to do, except to track myself down, dogging my own footprints like an exhausted hunter circling blindly in a blizzard.

Sometimes I find myself at the foot of Forty-seventh Street, looking out over the filthy river at a spot where once there was a crumbling pier. The gulls still circle overhead. In the shadow of the elevated highway the street is still practically deserted. At water's edge there are only some moldy timbers covered with thick, oily scum.

The wind wafts ashes from the Jersey shore. Once I stood here and wondered how I was going to survive until the next day. I wondered if the struggle was the end itself, whether the struggle was worth enough to validate my intentions. I remember rejecting a universe where suffering was a matter of chance. I demanded unconditional justice. What do I hope to find here, shivering in the dank and smoggy cold? What? A mirror image on the murky gray surface of the river? An obscene counterpart, white-faced, bloated, rank with body gasses, bound by pallid weeds to the rocks below? Is there nothing left but indulgence in some futile gesticulation at my childhood? O brave warrior, indeed, who wars on corrupt children.

Though there are none to be seen, I see the rotting hulks of ancient ships. I have arrived where he promised I would arrive, struggling not with fabulous creatures but with the necessity of paying my bills, rewarded with sciatica instead of treasures, voyaging not from glory but to obliteration, master not of mysteries but of mundane miseries.

For me the time of courage has slipped away, the favor of the gods passed to another. Of this Saul explained nothing. Yet how can nothing be explained? He did not warn me that the measure of the quest lies in its unfruitfulness, as the measure of intent lies in its own unfulfillment. He brewed me an enchanted potion in the fiery crucible of his words, but not a single drop remains within the flagon, for which I can no more resent him than resent myself for awakening from a pleasurable dream.

One by one I stalk my landmarks, finding that most have vanished. The Europa is now a supermarket. The building where Mitch once lived is a vacant lot. Sunshine has been dispossessed and the old hotel itself closed, soon to be reopened as an expensive co-op. The apartment in East Harlem, the whole block on which it stood, has become a burnt-out wasteland of rubble and desolation, abandoned to packs of scavenging dogs. Playland has become a fast-food restaurant, and the hustlers have shuffled off around the corner to lounge in front of a magic store. I recognize none of the new crew under the theater marquee, selling the same old drugs. I assume that most of the old crew is either dead like Saul, in jail like Sheik, or on Welfare like me. Last month I decided to visit my grandmother's grave. But I have never been able to fathom the geography of the outer boroughs and emerged from the subway to find not a cemetery but a roller coaster. I had arrived at Coney Island on a cheerless, windy day. Papers swirled through the dusty concrete alleys. Shutters flapped. On the ramshackle boardwalk I found a bar where I stopped to sip a bottle of beer. The bar was cavernous. The beer was tepid. A country blues singer strummed and wailed to a roomful of empty barstools.

I sat for a while on the bleak and littered beach trying to extract some message of despair from the wash of the waves. An old ragpicker sifted through a garbage pail. On the way back to the train I brushed the sand from my clothes, ignoring the inquisitive grin of a Puerto Rican boy who leaned against a lamppost, crotch thrust slightly forward in the classic hustler's pose. It was almost dark by the time I finally arrived at the wrought-iron gate to the cemetery and found it locked. Perhaps it was just as well, for when I counted up my change there was not enough for even the cheapest bouquet. How could I have thought to come to her without flowers.

I was exhausted when I returned to the apartment to find that the superintendent had left a package for me. In the package was an urn. Inside the urn were ashes. His ashes.

Ah yes, the urn. Until I saw visual proof of his irrevocable absence I believed that he was dead but I did not believe *in* his death. When my father perished, my mother and my grand-mother, knew he was dead. But it was not until my grandfather held the list of those aboard the plane in his hands, read the typed name, that he could rest easy. He could not believe in my father's death until he verified it through his own experience.

Death cannot be internalized through faith, but only through participation. And despite all circumstantial proofs, I maintained fantasies throughout my childhood that somehow he would return. Perhaps an error, a last-minute substitution of flight crew, or a wild one-in-a-million chance that he had survived both the crash and the sea to be miraculously reborn on some unknown Isle of the Blessed. Such were my fantasies, as impossible as they were irrefutable.

I suppose I have been feeding myself such pap about Saul all along, until the urn provided verification that he will never suddenly reappear from nowhere, that his absence is irreversible. I cannot trick myself out of faith anymore than my grandfather could acquire it through the testimony of others. There is no promise of resurrection within the urn, no hope of immortality. He can flourish now only in a hidden kingdom, a kingdom to which only I have access.

The urn. It bids me cease this constant sifting through the ashes of my years, hounding my former selves, destined to be hounded in turn by my future. Doglike I sniff at myself, spinning in ever-diminishing circles until inevitably I must consume myself or disappear. If I were to relinquish my bitterness . . . No. What once is done cannot be revoked. The fall of a single sparrow echoes throughout the universe of time.

And what if time can be abolished, the urn challenges. I need not return to you for you have permitted me to dwell within you. Find me, I am present. Find me and establish a present from out of the ashes, for unless you follow me you must forever lose yourself.

One morning I put the urn in a shopping bag and set out for Columbus Avenue. I find the old storefront botanica, the only shop in sight that has successfully resisted the demolition crews and developers.

It is clear that no one of substance patronizes the shop. The front door has become warped with age. The linoleum floor covering is worn and crumbling. In a far corner twin steam pipes rise from floor to ceiling. Affixed to the grimy whitewashed walls are countless shelves peopled with madonnas; miniature simpering madonnas, sorrowful madonnas, smug madonnas with Child. There are pallid plaster saints whose gilt halos are flaked. There are icons, blue-faced and green-robed. There are lifelike figures posed in puzzling attitudes. One grasps some sort of scissors. This other wields a shepherd's crook. Another smiles on the contents of his empty hand. There is a wooden Indian chief gaudily arrayed in painted robes and feathers. There are Christs aplenty: Christs bearing bloody hearts, Christs exhibiting awful wounds, enraptured Christs, agonized Christs, a Christ who bashfully hides his genitals behind his cupped palm. There are several grim-visaged black entities of uncertain gender. Before each is set a paper plate which holds a certain number of pennies and a single cigar. Of all the spirits of the shelf these are the only ones who do not appear to be in need of dusting.

Other shelves are stocked with various philters, ointments, and unguents arranged according to function. There are balms to requite love pangs and syrups to soothe menstrual cramps; there are salves for the sick of body and snuffs for the sick of soul; there are powders to induce jealousy or infidelity, lethargy or lust; there are decoctions which bind and those which loosen bonds; there are precipitates of wealth and warped roots which guarantee revenge.

There are rows of candles, really large, tubular glasses of congealed wax; white candles and red candles, candles of purple and blue; black candles, rainbow candles, and candles the color of pale emerald fire.

She seats herself at the far end of the table, directly opposite the man. Before her is a goblet hand-carved from a chunk of milky quartz. With one hand she pours water from a crystal ewer into the goblet. With the other she slowly traces the sign of the cross over the descending stream. When the goblet is filled she blesses herself and the man with the same sign.

Using tongs, she extracts a glowing ball of charcoal from a small golden brazier. She touches the ember to a mound of powder in a golden salver and instantly puffs of smoke rise, filling the room with the scent of dead roses. She spreads her palms inches above the salver. Smoke wafts upwards through her fingers. She summons the smoke higher until her face is virtually hidden from the man.

The woman begins to pray, rapidly, diffidently, as if addressing a difficult child.

"Santísimo Justo Juez, hijo de Santa María, que mi cuerpo no se asombre ni mi sangre sea vertida, donde quiera que vaya y venga . . ."

Sweat rolls from her forehead and forearms. Droning on all the while, she rubs the sweat from herself, collecting it in her cupped hands and casting it from her fingertips into the goblet.

". . . que vayan y vengan mis enemigos, salgan con ojos y no me vean, con armas y no me ofendan, justicia y no me prendan . . ."

Her eyes close. Her chin juts forward. She continues to collect the sweat pouring out of her. She collects and sprinkles, rubs and casts the sweat of her body into the sanctified water. The scent of roses and musk is overpowering.

". . . que no sea herido ni preso . . ."

Her facial and neck muscles bulge. Her eyes are squeezed shut.

". . . Ave María, gracias plena, Dominus Tecum, me libre de todo espiritu maligno bautizado y por bautizar. Cristo vence, Cristo reina, Cristo de todos los peligros me defienda . . ."

The man blinks. The candles splutter, flare up, and fade. The woman pounds on the table with both hands.

". . . respondan y hablan por mi . . ."

The man's head lolls on his chest. The woman pounds the table, moaning through clenched teeth.

". . . respondan y hablan por mi . . ."

The man sleeps. His hands twitch in his lap.

". . . respondan y hablan . . ."

It seems to him that somehow, in some way inexplicable and unreal, he observes himself sleeping, observes the woman pounding the table, observes the mist of incense rise toward his nostrils.

". . . *hablan* . . ."

The voice cracks and deepens.

". . . *hablar y abaracar . . . abaracar . . .*"

The voice is gruff and friendly.

". . . *abaracar . . . abaracadabara . . . abracadabra, vanity fair . . . mmmmph . . . all there is, is empty air . . .*"

"You!"

"Indeed."

"Are you really there?"

"Are you?"

"Prove it. Prove you're there."

"Prove you're here."

"How can I?"

"Well, then . . ."

"Without you I don't know who I am."

"Ah, now you're talking sense."

"But you're nothing now."

"That's the way it is, my poor humorless Sinbad. You are something known intimately by nothing. Who promised you anything else? Remember that time on the roof . . ."

"Don't."

"You can shut me up any time you want to."

"Suppose we could do it all over . . ."

"Not a chance. As for myself . . . mmm . . . I should have taken you to the hospital. I should have let the doctor set that fucking arm of yours."

"But you didn't have a choice."

"Of course not."

"And now, is there a choice now?"

"You know where all of those questions lead to, my boy."

"Knowledge."

"Vanity."

"Wisdom."

"Despair."

"Power."

"Pride."

"Interpretations."

"Excuses!"

"It's been awful, not having you around to abuse me."

"Oh, Lord, Haven't you grown out of all that yet?"

"I don't mean suffering. Suffering is too senseless. I'm talking about mattering to someone."

"Sentimental bullshit."

"Help me. Tell me what's going to happen."

"What is it? What is it that you think you must know?"

"Isn't there anything else, besides what's given to you?"

"Certainly. What you give yourself. Accept that and you can forget about whether or not you matter to someone else."

"Hell? Is there a Hell?"

300

"Certainly there's a Hell. Don't you remember, 'This is Hell, nor are we out of it.' "

"That's poetry. I can't understand poetry. Poetry is evasive."

"Evasive only if you fall into the trap of thinking about intentions. Hell is that way, your way, an eminent high-minded way, where you repent every single gift."

"Grace? You mean the gift of grace?"

"Clod! I mean continuity. The illusion of continuity. And by rejecting it you condemn yourself to needless anguish."

"But then . . . salvation . . ."

"Even if there were such a thing, the only way to achieve it would be to repudiate it. Anything else would be monstrous vanity. Besides, how can you be saved from what you give yourself? Can't you get it through your numb skull that you can't justify what no longer exists? It's out of your control, all of it. It's just your damnable curiosity that causes all these problems."

"So it's the same old story. The whole world, everything, is just one big joke. It can't be like that. It can't."

" . . . . . "

"Is it?"

"What isn't a joke?"

"Love?"

"Can you possibly love someone who is not both a god and an enemy?"

"I don't know."

"Then examine your heart."

"Only you are there."

"Me."

"You wouldn't lie. You did love me?"

"I would lie and I did not say that I loved you. You examined your heart and decided what you found there you would call 'love.' Now you answer my question."

"All right. It's not possible—love without adoration and rage."

"And could anything be more absurd? Can you think of a better joke?"

"Tell me what to do. Please. It's not enough, what you left me."

" . . . . "

"Please."

" . . . abaracar . . . hablar y abaracar . . ."

301

The man's head jerks upward. His eyes open. He looks at the woman. Her head rests on the table. She too must have dozed off. Too much fire, too much smoke. The candles have burned down, but the man is not aware of any passage of time. There has been no interruption. Nothing happened. He has not been unconscious. He has heard nothing, seen nothing. The woman merely fell asleep. He wonders if he should awaken her and then decides against such intimacy. He respects her sleep as he would respect his mother's sleep. He picks up the urn and puts it in the shopping bag. He reaches into his pocket and withdraws a small roll of bills. The woman's eyelids flutter as, unnoticed by the man, she observes his calculations. She smiles as he places the entire roll upon a table provided for that purpose. Because of the man's apparent generosity the woman believes that she has satisfied him. She does not know that on the table there are only eight one-dollar bills. Had he not believed the woman to be asleep the man would have left nothing because he is convinced that the woman is a swindler. He owes her nothing since she failed to fulfill their agreement. But to be fully convinced he would have to look into her face to find some clue. He leaves the money, the only money he possesses, so that she will not feel cheated when she awakes.

The second day of January. It is an hour or two before dawn. From the warmth and safety of my blankets I watch the snow swirling about the silent, deserted streets. Soon it will be morning and with morning comes the world, and with the world, the wrench into what it calls reality.

A dreary hike through drifting snow to stand in line outside the Welfare office. The oppressiveness of a day without purpose. The irrational fear of what the next day holds, and the day after. The rational fear that nothing more will be than what is given now. An afternoon of loneliness, confined by answers without questions and questions without focus. Dulled beyond despair. Impoverished. Indifferent. Hungry, beyond the pretense of caring, for a stranger's brusque caress. Spawn of no one. Sire of nothing.

At dusk, nostalgia. Legs shift. Knees jerk. Hand stifles yawn. In the growing gloom a tuneless whistling, an irritated tapping of toes. At last peering through the curtains out onto the world. Seeking no one. Bored and frightened beyond endurance. And at the end King Death shrouds his face, offering eternal disputation with the deaf and silent dead. I roll over on my side, embracing the pillow. I close my eyes, determined still to nullify this day in sleep.

The doorbell is not ringing. I have no visitors. It is not the doorbell. But it is. I yawn and scratch the stubble on my chin and struggle into the old kimino to greet a silly prank played by the neighbor's kids.

I open the door and confront my son, who steps inside the kitchen alcove, shedding snow from his trench coat onto the linoleum floor. He deposits a battered cardboard suitcase in the slush puddle collecting between his feet, sets an Adidas gym bag on the counter and hands me a package wrapped in leftover paper from Christmas past.

"Happy new year, Dad. It's cold as a bitch out there."

"Sal! For Chrissakes, look at the mess you're making."

He flushes and removes his boots. I can think of nothing to say while he goes about redeeming himself. He stoops to light the oven and carries his boots over to where they can dry in the warm draft. After he hangs up his coat, he surveys the scene.

"The floor."

"Oh yeah, sorry."

I cradle the package while he wipes the floor with a dish towel. He straightens up, smiling at me with hands on hips.

"Happy New Year."

I extend my arm, pushing my hand against his shoulder to make certain that we can't embrace. His two hands squeeze mine.

"Happy New Year, Sal."

"Aren't you going to open your present?"

I follow him into the living room and sit down on the couch. Seeing me fumble with the red ribbon he slides over next to me to help. I am not comfortable having him so close to me. His simplest actions seem charged with unpleasant significance. His presence itself is disturbing. His hands work competently with the ribbon. His fingers are slender and tapering and quite unlike mine. He sucks on his lower lip, as he did when he was small. On one pinky he wears a plain silver band; on the other is a school ring. I wonder whether he is still going to school. Soft downy hairs line his forearms. Others are visible on the inch of brown flesh bared between the bottom of his dungarees and the top of his white sweat socks. His body exudes warmth, the fragrance of spice and soap. He is a clean boy, a sensual boy, a very beautiful boy. Very beautiful. Much too beautiful to be my son.

"Champagne."

"I didn't know what to get, you know . . . it's ok, isn't it?"

"Sure it's ok. Haven't had champagne in a dog's age. Why don't you put it in the refrigerator and we'll drink it later on? I mean, you do drink, don't you?"

"Yeah, sure. Beer and shit. But I never had champagne."

"Champagne's an aphrodisiac, you know."

"What's that?"

"It's good for the shnocker."

"You mean it gets you horny?"

"Horny as a hoot owl."

He laughs and gets up to put the bottle away. Instantly I feel less threatened.

"Can I fry myself a couple of eggs," he yells from the kitchen.

"Go ahead. Don't stand the champagne up. Lay it down on its side."

"You want me to make you some eggs too?"

"Too early for me. Go ahead and knock yourself out. There's coffee—instant— in the cabinet. I don't know if there's milk though."

He unzips the Adidas and takes out his box. It must have cost him over two hundred dollars. He flips a switch, filling the room with thumping rock and begins puttering and clattering around, trying to figure out the kitchen.

". . . snowbudda?"

"It's still falling."

He turns around and stares at me.

"What's still falling?"

"The snow. Didn't you just ask me if the snow was still falling?"

"No. I'm looking for the butter."

"There is no butter."

"That's what I asked you."

"Well how the fuck do you expect me to hear you with that thing blaring?"

"I'm sorry." He looks hurt, but turns the volume down. "I'll use this oil here, ok?"

"Go ahead."

The eggs splutter in the pan. The smell of the food turns my stomach. Somehow he's managed the coffee and sits at the table shoveling down the eggs with a piece of stale rye bread. The kitchen is a mess again.

"I think maybe I'll open the champagne."

"Isn't it a little early?"

"You want to try some?"

"Sure. Wait'll I throw these dishes in the sink."

We sit in the living room sipping champagne out of water glasses.

"Mmm, it tickles your nose."

"That's what everybody says the first time. Do you like it?"

"I don't know. It doesn't taste like too much."

"It sneaks up on you."

"Yeah?"

"Makes you giggle too."

"Yeah?"

"Yup."

He puts down the glass and folds his hands in his lap.

"So what'uv been up to, Dad?"

"Nothing much. You going somewhere?"

He frowns slightly.

"What do you mean, going somewhere?"

"The suitcase, the bag. It looks like you're moving."

"I'm getting out of Jersey."

"Oh, you mean you're running away from home?"

"Nope. I'm getting out. I'm not running away. She knows all about it."

" 'She' being your mother, I assume."

"It's time for me to leave, that's all."

"Just like that. I understand you're free as a bird right now. You come and go as you please, do what you want to do. So how bad can it be?"

"I didn't say it's bad. I said that it's time for me to leave. Didn't you ever feel like that when you were a kid? That you just had to do things another way, your own way, without explaining them to anybody. Mom's not so bad. She has her moods. Every once in a while she kicks the shit out of me on G.P., just to convince herself, I guess, that I'm as bad as she thinks I am. That's all she can see in people, is the bad in them. She can't get it into her head that I don't want to bother anybody, don't want to be any trouble to anybody. That's the way I am. She thinks being a mother means protecting you for your own good. But I'm too old for that. I don't need any protecting. I know what's right and what's wrong. If I make a mistake, well, then it's up to me to straighten it out, right? I have to have room to breathe. I feel like I'm suffocating over there."

"And what do you plan to do?"

"I thought maybe, if you didn't mind, I'd camp out here for a while, you know, just until I get myself organized. I start work next week. You know that? I got a job."

"Doing what?"

"Playing the synthesizer. It's definite, the job, I mean. I start next week when the club opens. I'll be making a hundred and thirty-five for three nights and I can crash there too, if I want."

"Is that what you want?"

"Well, I thought, you know, just for a week. It'd be fun, I mean, being with you, getting to know each other again."

"Again? What does your mother think of all this?"

"She doesn't like it. She says the club sounds like a fag joint."

"Is it?"

"I guess so. But that doesn't have anything to do with me, if that's what you're worried about. I don't care what the customers do. That's their business. I'm there to work. To work and nothing else. So whadda you say? Is it ok if I hang out, you know, for a couple of days, just you and me?"

"No."

"That's it, just 'no'?"

"Salvador, save us both a lot of trouble."

He clenches his fists as his eyes mist.

"But I want to know why. Please. Tell me why you don't want me to stay with you."

306

"Salvador . . ."

"Tell me."

"All right, you want me to, I'll tell you. I can't accept you, that's why. Dropping in out of nowhere and trying to dump your life in my lap. Well, I don't want it. I won't have it. It's too late for that. You don't know me and certainly I don't know you. I don't know who you are, Salvador. My God, just a few minutes ago I realized that I didn't even know whether or not you still go to school. I don't know what matters to you, how your mind works. No, stop. I don't want to know. That's what I'm trying to tell you. I can't take that kind of responsibility, Salvador, this sudden intimacy with a stranger. And that's what we are—strangers."

"That doesn't mean it has to be like that. Things could change."

"Can't you get it into your head? You can't smooth over a lifetime of separation in one morning with a bottle of champagne. I don't know you. How could I cope with your secrets, the things you're ashamed of? I'd only get everything all wrong."

"You couldn't do worse than she does. At least you don't try to make things wrong from the start."

"I don't know your mother anymore. Salvador. I gave up knowing her years ago. She's an unhappy woman, a petty woman. But is that really so unbearable?"

"For you it was."

"You see," I almost shout, "you know nothing about me either. Nothing. The suffocation I felt . . ."

"Suffocation?"

"That's not the right word. You know what I mean."

"Yes. She invents things. Drugs. I don't use drugs. Smoke some grass, trip once in a while on mesc. She invents all kinds of terrible things because she wants you to despise me. That's what it's all about."

"And the gun, did she invent that?"

"So, she told you about the gun."

"Of course she told me when she found a gun in a drawer. Your drawer."

"The gun . . ."

"I don't want to hear about it. You have no right to explain. It's completely selfish. You think that by confiding in me you can

307

involve yourself in my life? You think I don't see right through you? How dare you trust me when I can't interpret a single thing you say?"

"Because you're my father. Is it really so terrible, wanting to have a father?"

"Then go find one, goddamn it. That's what I did. How can you think of me as your father when you know I wouldn't sacrifice a thing for you? You think I owe you anything, well you're wrong. Or maybe you think you owe me something? Bullshit! I'm not making any excuses. If you want to leave home, if you want to leap, then leap. I'm not stopping you. I give you my blessing, for what's it worth."

His fingertips touch my sleeve.

"It was worthwhile, I mean, my coming here and all."

"It was stupid."

"No, no it wasn't. You gave me your blessing."

"What blessing? Oh for Chrissakes, that was a figure of speech. You can't take that seriously."

"I can. I do. You don't say something like that, give someone your blessing if you don't really mean it. You'll see, you'll find out that you can trust me. Something like that, a blessing. You can never tell how far it goes. Maybe that was your way from the start, cutting me loose, not calling, so I could take my time and go my own way."

"You're misinterpreting me. You're misinterpreting me completely."

"Is that so important?"

"Understand this, Salvador. If you weren't my son, we might be very good friends. But in the long run I think it's better for both of us to leave things just the way they've been."

"I wish it could be that way. I wish that I could just walk out of here right now and go down to the club and begin from there. But I can't. I need you."

"Nonsense."

"I need you to let me confess something to you. I want to wipe the slate clean."

"I told you once and I'll tell you again—I have nothing for you. If you don't know let me tell you. I'm on Welfare. I work a few nights a week for chump change and juggle a little bit, but it's not enough. So if it's money you want, forget about it. I just don't have it. And if it's not money, well, I won't become involved in your life, and that's final. There is nothing I can do to help you."

"No, no. It's me that want's to help you, if you let me . . . if you let me say what I have to say."

"*You* want to help *me?* What the fuck can you help me with?"

He gazes at the urn, then, gingerly, he lifts it with both his hands, raising it as a priest in a state of mortal sin might raise the chalice of blood.

"Him. I can help you out about all of that, if you let me."

"You're out of your mind. Put that thing down."

"He was your friend."

"Of course. You know that."

"For a long time."

"For a long time."

"He was important to you."

"He was my life."

"And when he died, what happened?"

"What do you mean, what happened? Nothing happened. Nothing at all. Stop it. Put that urn down. You don't know anything about it. It's over and done with. You're just trying to stir things up. You think you can spite me by probing around for a wound. Well, there is none. No wound. Nothing you can say can hurt me."

"Suppose I could?"

"You can't."

"Let me try. What harm could it do?"

"Do it then. Say what you have to say and then leave."

"I came into the City to check out some speakers and I figured I'd stop by, to say hi. I didn't want anything, nothing except to say hello to you, so I came by the hotel where you were living. Mom always manages to keep your address around. I wasn't hounding you or trying to pry into your life. I had your address, I always do. But you weren't there. He told me that you had . . . that you two had . . . that you moved out. But he said you came by a lot and that when he saw you he'd tell you . . . about me coming by. I asked him. I wanted to know whether you ever talked about me, what you said . . ."

"You had no right . . ."

"I told you, I wanted to know . . . all that time, whether it was

309

something I did . . . why you didn't want to see me. No, he said, it had nothing to do with me. It was you, he said. You could never accept having a son, because it meant that you would have to give something and that you had nothing to give. That's what he said, that you had nothing to give."

"Did he explain that, what he meant by that?"

"I asked him. I didn't understand it all, but I remember what he said. He said, 'Your father, my boy, is the world's most sentimental fool. He is driven by the need to give himself up completely to the very worst in others.' I didn't like it, when he said that. Like I said, I didn't understand it all, but something told me that it was wrong, wrong, to say a thing like that. I said to him, 'But you're his friend. You're my father's friend. To be his friend and feel like that about it . . . it's wrong."

"*Betrayal* is the word you're looking for."

"Yes! That's what he said. He said I'd find that out when I got older, that the only way you can show somebody you care for them is by betraying them."

"Of course he'd say something like that."

"He said you demanded it, that's why you got along so good. He gave you exactly what you wanted. And that's when you called. The phone rang and I knew it was you by the way he was talking. I wanted to talk to you, just to tell you I was there, but he hung up the phone. He said you were coming up soon and wanted to surprise you, wanted to see your face when you saw me there. He said, 'I'm an inbetteran . . .'"

"Inveterate."

"That's it. He said, 'I'm an inveterate practical joker, my boy.' I told him, I said, 'I don't see any joke.' I didn't think it was funny, me being there, when maybe you didn't want me to be there."

"And what did he say? Try to remember the words."

"I do remember. He said, 'Put your trust in me, my boy, you'll repent it forever.' I stayed. I waited. I mean, I did want to see you, and besides, he was your friend, so of course I was going to trust him. Oh, I saw him looking at me, the way he was looking at me. I knew what he wanted. I knew he wanted to get down with me. But I was sure I could trust him, and even if I couldn't, well I knew you could trust him, that he didn't mean that stuff about betraying you and all. He sat down next to me and tried to touch me. That's when I told him I didn't want to. I told him that I'm not like that . . . that way, and besides, even if I was, with him, it would be terrible. Terrible for him to do that to you, terrible for me to even think about doing."

"But I imagine, because you're telling me, that you did something more than think . . ."

"He said I had no choice. From the moment I walked through the door I had no choice. He said that I was very beautiful and that we were going to get down in bed and that I had no choice, because if I didn't do what he wanted, every single thing that he wanted, he'd tell you that we had, anyhow. Just by my being there, you'd believe the worst, about me and about him. I told him no, that you'd know the truth, that I only came up to see you. I told him I'd tell you myself what he tried to make me do."

"Why didn't you just get up and walk out? You had that much of a choice, didn't you?"

"I started to. That's when he said, 'My boy, good intentions mean nothing to your father. Good works even less than nothing.' I didn't understand that either and I got up to go. That's when he said that if I walked out the door he'd tell you, as soon as you came, that we'd done it, everything, and that you'd believe him because you'd want to, but if I stayed and did everything exactly the way he told me, then he'd never tell you, because you'd never believe the truth. Nothing I ever heard seemed so bad, so . . evil. I told him that. I told him I couldn't believe he'd do all that just to force somebody to get down who didn't want to. It was like rape. He laughed when I said that. He said I was just making excuses because I was afraid to try it, afraid I'd enjoy it, that he was helping me. 'Accept the challenge, Salvador, take the leap. See if you can overcome what's best in yourself,' that's what he said."

"And of course the fact that he was my friend, the fact that no one had asked you to come there in the first place, that never entered into all this soul-searching of yours, right? It was very tempting to think of . . . doing it with him, wasn't it?"

His whole body starts to shake. No tears, just the shakes, as if he were infernally cold. I make no move to help him. I have no reason to offer him solace. Let him finish what he has begun.

"I wasn't trying to hurt you. You have to understand that. You knew him, the way he could twist things. It was because I loved

311

you that I had to go through it, do whatever he wanted, to save you from finding out. I had to get down with him so you'd never suspect that I did. He told me exactly what to do and how to do it. He watched every move I made while I was getting undressed. He was sitting in the chair, smiling, not moving a muscle. He didn't do anything himself, not that time, He made me do it all. It was the first time. I'd never gotten down with a guy before. I knew I couldn't go through with it, that it would disgust me so much that I'd throw up."

"But, somehow you managed."

"Because it didn't disgust me. That's what made it so much worse. That's what made me feel so ashamed. The things I did, the things he did to me later. None of it disgusted me. I couldn't get enough of it. No matter how many times we did it, I just couldn't get enough. And I'm not that way, you have to believe me. I never did it with anyone, any other guy. I don't want to, ever again. I don't think about guys that way. It was him, something he did to me that made me not care that he was a guy. And then he tried to make me feel better about it, about you. He told me that it had been over for a long time, between you and him, about getting down, I mean. He said that all you two had in common was common temptation.

"How many times?"

"I can't remember, there were so many. I called him, every day. Went to him whenever he told me I could, any time he said it was ok. That's when I went out and bought the gun."

"You were going to kill him?"

"Him? Of course not. How could I kill him? I needed him. I thought I loved him. It was for you, the gun. Because all along I knew it was wrong. No, not wrong enjoying it, but wrong what I was doing to you, no matter how much he said that you can't wrong somebody who doesn't realize he's being wronged. I couldn't stop it with him, so I had to be stopped. I had to stop myself. I had to make sure that I could never be tempted to start it up again. It was the only thing to do . . . take myself out of the picture. But it was for you, not for me."

"But you didn't go through with it."

"He saved me from that. He saved my life."

"How?"

"He died the day I was going to do it."

"So instead, this grand confession scene. You thought it would wipe out everything for you, make you feel clean."

"I wanted you to know so that . . ."

". . . I'd be hurt. So that I'd hate his memory. Is that it? Well, I'm sorry then that you put yourself through these changes. I knew him very well, Salvador, much better than I know myself. Your intentions mean nothing at all. Nothing is changed. Nothing about him and me, at least, because I made my choice before you were born. When I gave him everything, I held nothing back. He held nothing back from me either—no betrayal, no insult—he held back nothing. I bargained for it all."

"But it doesn't change anything for you, knowing how he really was?"

"Oh, for Chrissakes, don't be ridiculous. The whole part about the gun, I find it monstrous. It's nothing but vanity of the most inflated kind, though I know you can't see it like that. Using your life to force your own notions down other people's throats. I'm sure that he would have put it much better, something like, 'Mmmm, that boy of yours is a most dangerous fanatic.'"

And there sits Salvador, apparently at ease, shriven and a fool content in his foolishness. But I can see why Saul must have cherished him—so beautiful and so vulnerable to outrage. I can really believe, well, almost believe, that he somehow thought to purge me and to forge a parental bond between us. Well, it would take a good deal more than this melodramatic claptrap to turn me into a father or him into a son.

A father projects himself upon his son as successor or rival, knowing that the son is destined either to succeed him or eclipse him. A son accepts or rejects his preconceived role and either succumbs or claims control of his own life. Since I have ceased expecting or hoping, since I have learned to accept what is given, I have no wish or need to impose conditions on whatever lies beyond, through the agency of my son. And as for Salvador, it's true he has no choice in the matter. Without the father there can be no son. He can be neither obedient nor rebellious, since I relinquished all authority without ever assuming it. Now there's a joke that Saul would have thought worthy of his own invention.

It is just possible, though, that he fails to see the obvious bond that has been created, a bond of perverse brotherhood that has made us lovers by proxy. I'm sure if he perceives it at all it is in some kind of terms relating to sacrifice, missing the irony of the situation completely. I can no more be compromised by his innocence than he can use my bitterness to absolve himself. And yet, there is always the problem of the rent.

"You did say you'd be making a hundred and thirty."

"A hundred and thirty-five."

"You understand, if I do let you crash here, it's not permanent. You'll have to carry your own weight. With the rent, I mean."

"You mean it, you really mean it? I can stay?"

"No, you cannot stay. But you can crash for a while. A little while."

"Dad . . . Sinbad, let me make a quick run downtown to the club. I'll get an advance, I mean, you know, for the rent."

"Well, then."

"Well, then."

As he closes the door behind him, my son, I feel no guilt. Who else should I betray if not he whom I despise and cherish. Anyhow, he'll soon be gone for good and for me there will come the time when there is no more Time, no more days, no more hours, no more minutes. Saul. Will he be waiting to greet me, to mock my humanity with uproarious laughter? Will he whisper his dare? Will he hold out his hand and bid me to leap into uncertainty just one more time?

I am certain of nothing, nothing but this: It is God who crucifies man on a cross of doubt, discontent, and despair; it is God in his jealousy who beclouds the intentions of man; it is God who makes me stumble through this wilderness of deceit.

And yet I am certain, too, that it has always been within my power to redeem myself, to reject God's false promises and spite. If only it were worth the effort, I might still take a stab at it. If only there were some guarantee. But I know in my heart that only God can guarantee anything, and at my age I'm not about to start asking him for favors.

This book was produced for the publisher by
Ray Freiman & Company
Stamford, Connecticut 06903